Pickpockets and Zulus

Published by Keldaviain Publishing

A CIP catalogue record for this book is available from The British Library.

ISBN 978-0-9928599-8-5

Book 1

Chapter 1

For Sergeant Alex McNamara acclimatizing to the Punjabi summer was proving difficult. Having arrived with the latest draft of soldiers from England only eight months previously he had found himself stationed with his regiment, the Twenty-Fourth Foot, at Rawalpindi. The ship from home had arrived at the very end of the sepoy mutiny and he had missed the fighting. However, the authorities were in a constant state of anxiety over the remaining native regiments. Many were disarmed to discourage mutiny and others disbanded completely, the recruits sent home until further notice. At Jhelum, the Fourteenth Native Infantry was in imminent danger of mutiny according to its officers and now the regiment was on its way from Lahore to Jhelum and marching through the night.

'Did you hear that Alex?'

'Hear what,' said Alex marching in company with his section,

'A bird singing.'

'Bloody hell a bird singing; are you some kind of naturalist?'

'Naw, it means the sun will be up soon and we can see where we are going.'

'That's just great, and in a couple of hours we will be roasting. I haven't become acclimatized yet, the heat is too much sometimes. Do you remember the soldier dying of heat exhaustion on the march from the docks after we arrived?'

'Aye it does happen, still it's a lot easier than marching in the dark and we will be in Jhelum soon and we can put our feet up.'

'You're bloody mad Chalkie, when does this man's army ever let you put your feet up?'

'Just saying, thought it might cheer you up, break the boredom like.'

Alex McNamara turned his head to look at Chalky White, his face just visible in the fading moonlight. Both were Sergeants, lifers, in the army for twenty-one years and just about half way through their service on a second posting to the sub-continent. For the previous four years, stationed on home soil, Alex had trained recruits and in those less stressful times he had met and married Maud and together they had a son, Georgie. He thought about them now, Maud his pretty, clever girl, a seamstress with a rare talent when it came to making clothes. She had even unpicked the seams on his ill-fitting uniform to help turn him out as smart as some of the officers. Then there was Georgie, his pride and joy, a bouncing, healthy boy whom he would not set eyes on for another three or four years. Images of his loved ones flitted before his eyes until Chalky started talking and their memory faded once again into the recesses of his mind.

'They reckon we might have a fight on our hands at Jhelum. Colour Sergeant Jones told me we are to disarm some native soldiers and he reckons that they won't take kindly that. What d'you reckon Alex.'

'I heard something. I don't know but let's hope they do as they are told. If they don't then we will have to make them.'

'I wonder if the colonel will let us stop for breakfast. I am starting to feel peckish.'

Alex grinned at his friend, his features more pronounced as the first orangey light began to arrive from the east, the first rays of the sun spreading through cracks in the landscape and he hoped the day would not be a scorcher. He heard the birds, louder now, above the crunch of army boots slogging it out along the dusty road and ahead the jangles of horses tack. Other than that, there was nothing to break the monotony of the march until a voice ahead called out that they were approaching the cantonments. Alex strained his eyes and there, perhaps half a mile hence he caught sight of tents in the military camp.

The soldiers were aware that the march was just about over, a murmur rising as the men exchanged a few words until the sound of gunfire ended all conversation. At the head of the column, a bugle sounded, officers appeared on horseback issuing orders and the soldiers began to form a line of battle.

Pickpockets and Zulus

Ahead of Alex and his platoon, visible across the vast parade ground British officers were beating a hasty retreat from what appeared to be perhaps a thousand sepoy troops. Outnumbered by almost four to one, the soldiers of the Twenty-Fourth had a fight on their hands. The shrill call of a bugle sounded, the gunners began unlimbering their field guns, turned them towards the mutineers and within minutes the first crash of shot landed amongst the sepoys.

Alex could feel his heartbeat pick up and then a captain appeared on horseback to order the riflemen to prepare to load. Quickly the well-drilled soldiers formed a lose line facing the enemy and Alex took up his position at the side of the platoon, organizing the firing line and drawing a deep breath glanced at the men and satisfied they were ready looked up at the captain. The officer nudged his horse forward along the rear of the line checking the readiness of the other sections and then he barked out the first command, 'load,' then he counted out the numbers as the private soldiers worked their way through a firing routine drummed into them so much that they could do it in their sleep. The cartridges were torn and emptied into the muzzles, the rods followed; ramming home the charge and shot and finally the cap was set in the firing mechanism.

'Front rank at three hundred yards,' the captain said, counting out five and six as the soldiers lifted their guns to their shoulders, 'ready, present.'

The slap of the gunstocks on shoulders rippled down the line. They were ready.

4

'Fire,' he commanded and two hundred and fifty Enfield Pattern rifle-muskets spat fire and death.

The roar of the guns was deafening and as the smoke began to disperse the enemy could be seen running, the wounded stumbling forward as they retreated from the onslaught.

'Advance,' ordered the captain and as one, the line moved steadily towards the mutineers. They were over their initial shock and had halted the retreat, were beginning to fire indiscriminately at the advancing line. The thud of bullets hitting the ground, small eruptions in front of the advancing line were still too far off to cause damage. Then after a hundred yards, a soldier to Alex's right let out a cry and fell to the ground clutching his leg.

'Halt,' commanded the Captain, 'prepare to load.'

The line of advancing troops stopped, the order to load came and after a short pause, a second volley of shot flew towards the mutineers. Several bullets found their mark judging by the cries and as the smoke cleared, the mutineers were once more in full retreat.

'Got 'em on the run now,' commented a soldier near to Alex.

It did seem to be the case but the retreating enemy were heading towards a walled village. That would give them cover but for the men of the Twenty-Fourth there was no such luxury caught in open ground as they were. Alex looked along the line and saw the colonel on his horse waving an arm, directing his subordinates and minutes later, he rode along the line encouraging the men to keep up the fight.

'A flank attack men, the colonel wants us to attack them from the left flank. In skirmishing order follow me,' ordered the company commander.

At a brisk pace, the he led the riflemen across open space to a position out of rifle range of the mutineer's muskets and as the other companies joined formed up alongside them, the whole force began to advance towards the extreme left of the row of village huts and driving the mutineers before them. The well-drilled soldiers were firing independently, each man picking his target before reloading and moving forward.

The tactic was having its effect, return fire became sporadic as the enemy retreated encouraging the red-coated soldiers every more forward. Unable to contain his eagerness, the colonel drew his sword, every bit the gallant warrior, astride on his horse in his brightly coloured uniform. However, he was an obvious target and within minutes, as several bullets found their mark, his horse's legs gave way. The next volley mortally wounded him, clutching at his chest, he tried to stand but the effort was too much, and he sank to his knees beside the dying horse, the stricken animal's legs kicking feebly in the air.

Alex did not see the colonel fall but like most of the men, he bore witness to his removal from the field of battle. It was not a good feeling to see the commander brought down so easily but before he had little time to dwell on the tragedy. The colonel of the rebellious native infantry took over the vacant command and by the sound of his voice; all those within earshot knew he was out to take his revenge on the mutineers.

Pickpockets and Zulus

Alex reloaded his rifle and moved forwards with his platoon, a head appeared at an opening and he took aim. Firing at the head, he watched in fascination as it disappeared from sight and he knew that he had killed his first man. He felt nothing, only a grim satisfaction that he was doing his job, quickly reloading his gun ready for the next part of the advance and moving forward, he saw their new commanding officer speaking with the captain.

The advance slowed as they neared the walled enclave and they received the order to halt. Away to Alex's right the three gun carriages moved into view, the horses staining at their traces as the drivers urged them on. Time was of the essence if they were to position the guns before the enemy could react but the gun most forward was too close to the enemy and in the process of unlimbering, a fusillade hit one of the horses. Next, it was the turn of the men and Alex watched in horror as two collapsed, shot where they stood, then a second horse fell. The remaining members of the gun crew were not slow in reacting, diving behind the dying horses for cover. They had miscalculated the distance from the blockhouse and had paid the price.

Behind them, the remaining guns were in position, out of range of the enemy fire and Alex could see the gunners elevating the barrels. There was a loud roar as the first shot screamed through the air and seconds later the shell hit the blockhouse and exploded. Debris flew high into the air, clouds of smoke and dust obscured the target for several long seconds, and then the second gun fired. Whether it was a well aimed or just plain lucky shot Alex never found out but almost as soon as the gun fired, an explosion erupted from inside the building and half the front wall collapsed.

From troops ready to advance, a cheer rang out, the guns fired again and figures ran from the ruined building in the direction of the river. The enemy was in full retreat, the order to fix bayonets issued and as one, the line of recoated soldiers rose up to charge the remains of the rebel stronghold.

Sweat was running down Alex's forehead, his eyes were blurred but as he wiped it away with his tunic sleeve, he caught sight of Chalkie White running through a gap in the compound wall shouting a personal war cry. Alex saw him lunge forward as his bayonet impaled a hapless native soldier and then two more of them appeared and closed in on him, carrying vicious looking knives. Alex feared for his friend and unable to wait the outcome, he dropped to one knee and took aim. The shot caught the first of the men as he raised his knife high in the air, hitting him full between his shoulders and knocking him flat. Running forward he was no more than a few yards from the second man as he made to stab Chalkie his bloodthirsty roar the only warning of impending doom. Chalkie half turned towards the man as he lunged at him, managing some protection with his raised forearm but it was not enough to prevent the blade slicing through the cloth and into his arm. Gritting his teeth and grunting as if a stuck pig at slaughter, he had enough strength and presence of mind to ram the first of his free hand into his assailants face. A momentary respite, giving Chalkie just enough time to fend off the mutineer for a second or two before he renewed his attack but he was cornered. The soldier had the look of a man facing death and he braced himself for the final thrust.

It never came, not in the way Chalkie expected. Alex was in full attack mode and nothing could stop him, the heat of the battle had heightened his senses, empowered him like nothing he had ever experienced and with a thrust of the bayonet, he impaled the mutinous sepoy, forcing the thrashing body away from his friend and onto a pile of rubble. Repeatedly he thrust the reddened blade into the body until only a dead man's eyes stared at him.

Swinging round he saw Chalkie ashen faced propped against the shattered wall.

'You alright Chalky?'

'Phew, that was close. I'm fine apart from nearly losing my arm. You had better press on with the charge. Come back for me when you've killed the rest of them.'

Alex checked for danger and feeling relatively safe, he propped his rifle against the remains of the wall and ripped the remains of Chalkie's sleeve away from his Jacket.

'Here let me tie this round your wound to at least stem the bleeding.'

Chalkie gave a weak grin and let his head droop.

'Oy, wake up,' commanded Alex beginning to wrap the wound with the blood coloured material. 'Don't be going to sleep you might not wake up.'

Seconds later, with the flow of blood stemmed he glanced down at his handiwork. It wasn't perfect but the bleeding seemed to have stopped.

'I'll be back as soon as I can,' he said wiping his blood soaked hands on the shirt of one of the dead Indians and retrieving his rifle.

Chalkie managed a nod of his head and Alex left him as he clambered over the rubble to follow the sound of gunfire. It was late afternoon, he had not stopped, eaten nor drunk since midnight, and the adrenalin that had sustained him was beginning to fade as the advance finally petered out. They had beaten the enemy, some had escaped over the river but a great many were dead and those that did survive, the soldiers shot wherever they found them.

'Sergeant McNamara,' called Captain McPherson. 'I am afraid Captain Spring has sustained wounds and he is unable to carry on, so for now, I am taking over as company commander. The colonel has ordered a general halt to proceedings, the big guns are low on ammunition and we are to form a defensive line for the night. I have spoken to the lieutenant who is organizing more ammunition for the platoon so as second in command I want you to muster the men ready to take up guard duties. The cavalry will protect the right flank. Carry on sergeant.'

'Sir, permission to speak.'

'What is it sergeant?'

'Sergeant White is wounded sir; I left him in the ruins of the blockhouse. He is in need of some attention sir.'

'Ah…yes, we have several men killed and wounded. I will organise a section to bring in all the wounded. The dead we will attend to tomorrow. Will that be all Sergeant McNamara?'

'Yes sir, save for the fact that the men have not had anything in the way of sustenance since yesterday evening, since before the march to here.'

'Yes sergeant, you are right, I must admit I'm rather hungry myself. I will see what I can do.'

As darkness fell Alex's exhaustion began to take its toll, and knowing that there was a large body of mutineers somewhere out in the darkness did not help. Exchanging few words during the seemingly long night, the men settled down to guard duty relieved occasionally to allow them to snatch an hours' sleep. When the sun did eventually rise, the cavalry received orders to scour the countryside for any of the mutineers still deemed to be a threat.

'Looks like we have them on the run sergeant,' said a bleary eyed corporal.

'Aye, it seems that way. If they had any confidence in taking us on they would have been at us during the night.'

'What do you think the colonel will have us do now?'

'If I was a betting man, which I am, I would say that we will not cross the river and any of them who have crossed will get away but there is still work to do catching those on this side.'

The corporal yawned and shook his head.

Pickpockets and Zulus

'Well at least we might manage some breakfast today; my stomach thinks my throat has been cut.'

Alex almost managed a smile but he had heard the comment too many times and the humour had gone out of it.

'Here comes the lieutenant, look lively he doesn't take too kindly to slackers.'

The corporal frowned and stood to attention as the lieutenant reached them and Sergeant McNamara saluted the officer.

'Morning Sergeant, we had a quiet night thank goodness.'

'Sir.'

'Orders for today are to sweep towards the river to see what we can turn up but from what I hear that bunch will not be causing us much more trouble. Assemble the men ready for the order to advance and you are to kill any of the enemy you find. Carry on Sergeant.'

The day unfolded and to begin with the troops moved towards the river in company strength, the big guns remained in the rear and by the time the sun was high in the sky, they had the river in their sight. The order to fix bayonets came and minutes later, the line of red and white began a steady advance. In the near distance, sporadic gunfire erupted as fugitives broke cover or put up token resistance and then came their cries as the advancing troops over ran their positions and by late afternoon, they had achieved their objective. With bayonets fixed the British soldiers pursued the enemy, killing hundreds of them in the process with minimal loss.

The strain of the events of the previous twenty-four hours showed in the soldiers' tired faces, the faces of men who had fought hard, who had done their duty and now had a chance for some respite. The blood and thunder of the fighting was in the past, they had survived and almost all could think of nothing else but a few hours' sleep and a good dinner, the first proper meal in two days. Nevertheless, their spirits were high and forming up in companies they marched to the sound of the drum towards the military camp inhabited so recently by the vanquished Native Infantry regiment and the following, morning refreshed and reinvigorated the troops mustered for inspection. With ramrod straight backs, their uniforms dusted off they stood to attention, their rifles at their sides. Nearby were the cavalry sitting motionless on their chargers and at their head, sat the colonel and his staff officers.

'Sergeant major, order your men to bring out the prisoners.'

The sergeant major saluted smartly, took several steps forward, and came to attention in front of the ranks. He barked out an order and several soldiers detached themselves, marching away to bring the prisoners from the guardroom. The cavalry had caught them in the sweep towards the river and in their torn and dust-covered clothing; they no longer looked a threat. Most of those captured suffered summary execution where they stood, but for these men a more formal execution awaited them and in the hot Punjabi sun, the wretched procession passed the ranks of red-coated British soldiers.

The lead prisoner, Bhai Jaimal Singh, was no ordinary soldier, he was of the warrior caste, brave and religious and his eyes looked straight ahead hardly hearing the commands of the Regimental Sergeant Major and felt rather than heard the crump of army boots as the ranks came to attention. As a follower of the tolerant creed handed down from the last living Guru, Gobind Singh, and his deep-seated beliefs helped him fight back his fear. Concentrating on the afterlife he quietly prayed, obeying the creed of the Khalsa Sikh. *First consent to death: Give up the desire to live; become the dust of the earth; then come to me. The Khalsa is of the pure great God.* Words and deeds drilled into him from an early age, had prepared him for the ordeal to come as his naked feet carried him towards his destiny.

'Halt, 'tenshun,' said a voice behind him, 'make the prisoners ready.'

The escorting soldiers stopped, released the prisoners bonds before forcibly pulling them towards the waiting field guns securing their wrists and ankles to the wheels so that the smalls of their backs covered the muzzles. From the front of the parade, the commanding officer nudged his horse slowly forward, towards the field guns, stopping a few yards in front of the condemned men.

'You men have mutinied, committed murder in attempting to resist the lawful authority of Her Majesty's forces and it falls upon me to carry out the wishes of the her majesty's high command. May God have mercy upon your souls.'

'Not your God, we have our own God,' said Bhai Jaimal Singh, his eyes piercing those of the colonel.

As the ropes around his wrists and ankles tightened, a silence fell over the parade ground; even the birds stopped singing and only the faint whispered prayers of Bhai Jaimal Singh disturbing that silence. Then it was time and his body noticeably stiffened, the sergeant major issued the fateful command and for those watching, the roar of the guns concentrated their minds. The guns recoiled, vomiting fire and smoke, the white clad bodies convulsed as the violence of the blast ripped through their torsos and scattered their entrails. The restrained limbs whipped sideways, torn from the bodies and there was a discernible intake of breath from those witnessing the executions as lifeless heads arced high above them.

'Gawd, what a way to go whispered the corporal standing next to Alex.

'Yes, not a pretty sight was it.'

'They got what they deserved.'

Alex did not feel much like celebrating. To see men blown away like that was for the ghoulish not really for him. He had killed his fair share of the mutineers during the assault on the village, seen enough blood spilt for the time being and had no wish to prolong the experience.

With the crisis was over Alex finally had time to seek out Sergeant White and found him sitting outside the hospital tent. He looked well enough with a clean dressing to his arm and as soon as he caught sight of Alex, his face lit up.

'I owe you one sergeant.'

'Don't be daft; you would have done the same for me. How are you anyway?

'It's still a bit painful but the surgeon major says I was lucky the blighter didn't sever the main artery. It's quite a cut but I'm told I will heal up with no more than a scar for my troubles.'

'How are you anyway? I see we've despatched the last of the mutineers.'

'Yes, looks as if we are getting some time off as well to recover. I don't know about you but I reckon I could sleep for a week.'

'I can, the surgeon says I should get plenty of rest to give the wound time to heal.'

'I don't know whether you are lucky or unlucky. I'm not sure I would like a cut like that just to get out of duties.'

'I'm not so bad. Apart from the pain, I can manage. What about some grub, I'm starving.'

'Come on then, if you can, we could spend some time in the mess, get some dinner and you can tell me what happened after I left you.'

'Help me on with my jacket and I'll try.'

The surgeon's assistant had cut the damaged sleeve completely off Chalkie's tunic together with its congealed blood leaving it reasonably respectable and once Alex had helped him put his arm in the good sleeve he looked respectable enough. Apart from the odd wince from the pain Chalkie managed well enough and at a steady pace he accompanied Alex to the sergeants' mess and ducking under the tent flap, the two sergeants produced their mess tins for a helping of bully beef stew and a lump of course bread. It was not the best of food but to two hungry soldiers it was welcome.

'Tell me what happened after you left me Alex, did you have to fight anymore mutineers. Do you know how many of our lads we lost?'

'I don't know exactly but I did hear that two of the sergeants were killed, Jones and Kilpatrick I think. They killed Captain Spring and badly wounded the colonel and Lieutenant Streatfeild and maybe twenty other ranks are dead but we gave them a pasting. They shot a lot of them down by the river before they had chance to escape and the last of 'em was blown away this morning.'

'Aye, I heard the guns. Bad doo this mutiny business, still it's over now and perhaps we can get back to some more peaceful soldiering.'

'I hope you're right, we have another four years out here.'

'Georgie, he will be eight or nine when we get back to Blighty won't he?'

'Yes, I hope he remembers me.'

Alex fell silent, the memory of his son fresh in his mind. It would be a long time before he saw him and Maud again but he was a soldier and this was a soldier's lot. He sighed to himself and as he thought of home, a strange feeling seemed to come over him.

'You all right Alex?'

'Yes just a bit of stomach ache I think.

Chapter 2

Sitting on the well-worn steps of the ramshackle structure she called home, Maude clasped her hands about her knees. In the warmth of the afternoon sun, she half closed her eyes, pushing out the misery of her life and thought back to happier times. Alex, his handsome face and proud bearing loomed large in her imagination and she wondered where he was. Almost three years before her husband had left for India with the Twenty Fourth Regiment of Foot and her only connection with him were his letters, those infrequent, precious letters. In her mind's eye she could see him clearly; resplendent in his five-button red serge frock coat, his dark blue trousers, the polished brass buttons. Those buttons had gleamed in the sunlight as he had marched past that last time with his white Foreign Service helmet tipped jauntily on his head.

He had managed a nod and a wink as he marched past, one last farewell and she remembered how tightly she had gripped Georgie to her as she waved back. It was a time of emotions watching them leave and the moment Alex was out of sight she realised that she might never see him again.

He had been a soldier for almost ten years when they had married and for the first year, they lived in the barrack room, scant privacy afforded only by blankets hanging from the ceiling. When Georgie arrived, they moved into newly built married quarters, comfortable, clean and she had been content until the order came for the Regiment to leave. She had hoped desperately that she might accompany Alex, but tradition demanded a lottery for the wives of ordinary soldiers and she had drawn a short straw.

Resting her head against the wall, the warmth of the sun spread across her face and she wondered was it really three years since she had last seen him. It must be, three years since she and Georgie had moved to this dark, damp rookery. The Regiment had left for India in October when Georgie was five years old and it was then they had to vacate the married quarters and to move back to the East End of London near to her sister Jane and that no good husband of hers, William Tyndal.

During those early days she and Georgie were practically alone, Alex's pay was barely enough to feed them and pay the rent but her sister helped a little. When Billy managed to steal a silk handkerchief or a pocket watch perhaps, Jane would manage to get her hands on some of the proceeds. When she did, she would send her daughter Ellen out to by some cheap meat and vegetables from the market to make a decent meal and share it with Maud and Georgie.

Billy Tyndal was a pickpocket and with his children growing up and joining the business, they made a decent enough living but his downfall was drink. After laying his hands on a few coins, he would return home, hide some and with what little conscience he had, share a few pennies with his wife. Jane knew where the rest would go and would dutifully help her husband on with his heavy coat. She knew he would be gone for hours drinking with his cronies to return home in the dead of night hardly able to stand. She hated him for it but she did not want him to die of pneumonia just yet, at least not until the children had grown up, or she had found someone better.

Maude was thankful to her sister for helping to keep body and soul together but she could not rely on her charity forever. She was working as a seamstress when she met Alex, a job she excelled at and she was determined to find some employment to support her and her son. She began her quest to find work enquiring first at the numerous workshops of French Huguenots scattered around Spitalfields. To begin with, she was optimistic, but the silk weaving trade had suffered from cheap calico imports from India, trade had dropped off and Spitalfields had become poor and run down. The myriads of once clean and respectable streets were squalid, inhabited by sallow looking men and women and the prospects for work were bleak.

Opening her eyes her mind drifted, remembering vividly trudging the back streets, knocking on the doors of small workshops only to find there was no work. It was a soul destroying and depressing task until one day they had chanced upon pair of solid wooden gates opening onto a small cobbled yard. Standing outside in the lane was a Costermonger's horse and cart, the horse waiting patiently for its owner to appear. She had stopped and wondered whether to enter the yard when suddenly, a tall scraggy fellow dressed in a pair of woollen trousers and a filthy cotton shirt had appeared. He was carrying a bag of soot that he heaved onto the cart before disappearing back into the yard. Minutes later, he re-emerged with another sack dripping a stream of fine black dust in his wake. He lifted that sack over the sideboard and into the cart, the sweat from his exertions running down his face and leaving white streaks. He had raised his forearm to wipe away the sweat and left a smudge across the upper half of his face. It was then that he noticed Maude and Georgie watching him and had turned towards them. Maude remembered feeling Georgie's grip tighten, the man had stopped and smiled at the little boy's look of apprehension and then a voice had called out from inside the yard.

'You can come back in two weeks my man; we should have more soot for you then. If you pay me the price you are offering today then you may take it.'

A slight, well-dressed man in late middle age then emerged from behind the gate and the Costermonger had pulled a handful of pennies from his trouser pocket to deposit into an outstretched hand.

'Thank 'ee sir, thank 'ee mister Fremeaux,' the Costermonger had said climbing up to the driver's seat and with a flick of the reigns, coaxed the horse and cart across the hard cobbles and only then did Daniel Fremeaux notice her and Georgie.

'And who might you be?'

'My name is Maude sir and this is my son Georgie. Say hello to the gentleman Georgie.'

Not a sound came forth and she had nudged Georgie gently against his shoulder with the back of her hand.

''Lo,' he said, bringing a smile to Daniel's lips.
Maude remembered liking Daniel straight away; he seemed a kindly enough man and she smiled to herself remembering how she had finally plucked up the courage to blurt out in a rush, 'sir, I am a seamstress and

Pickpockets and Zulus

I am looking for work. My husband is overseas in the Army and the money I receive from his pay is not enough for us to live on. Would you have any work sir?'

'Well, business is not so good these days I'm afraid.'

She had lowered her eyes; a feeling of hopelessness crossing her face, a look Daniel had seen many times.

'London is full of destitute people looking for work but you seem different, you have skills I think.' He had noticed with a practiced eye how expertly patched were their clothes and he did have a vacancy. 'Don't look so despondent, I may have something that will suit you, though I'm afraid that the work does not pay a great deal. Tell me first though. Who made the little boy's clothes?'

'Why, I did sir.'

'Hmm, I thought so. The stitching is very neat and close. I can offer you some work...'

'Oh thank you sir, thank you.'

'Not so fast my dear, let me finish. You might not want the work I can offer,' he teased her, but her eyes told him that she would take anything.

'I need someone with fine skills like yours to re-work the sub-standard garments my girls sometimes produce. Often they forget to stitch a seam properly or it might have pulled away and be in need of some reworking. I can pay you four pennies for each ten garments you repair to my satisfaction. You can do the work from home. I have two other girls working this way and my barrow boy will deliver and collect. Well what do you say?'

For a moment, she had been speechless, dumbstruck.

'Well Maude, what do you say, do we have a deal?' Daniel had repeated, holding out his hand.

Quickly she had returned to her senses, clumsily shaking his hand and saying 'oh yes sir, thank you sir.'

Daniel had smiled and patted Georgie on his head, gave the boy one of the pennies he had received from the costermonger and said, 'here boy, take this and buy yourself some sweets.'

Georgie's shyness had fallen away at the sight of that large, round, copper coin and he had stretched out his grubby hand. Not quite seven years old, he was already aware of the value of money from those evenings watching his Uncle Billy divide his spoils and the reaction of Aunt Jane.

'Say thank you Georgie.'

''Fank you,' Georgie had said, lighting up Daniel's face.

Maude was thankful to Daniel Fremeaux, his kindness had probably saved them from the workhouse and as soon as he had given her the job, she had rushed back to her sister to tell her the news. 'It's good news Maude, maybe you can move away from that hovel you are living in, find somewhere not quite so damp.'

'I would love to, it's not good for Georgie's health and if I am to work from home I will need a bit more space.'

'Tell you what; let's try to find you a better place. I will ask around.'

Jane knew a lot people in the district and she soon heard of a room for rent in one of the less dilapidated rookeries. Straight away the sisters took their children to have a look and it was then that Jane confided in Maude that she had saved some money from her husband's criminal earnings. She said that she hid as much of it away as she could – 'for emergencies' she had said and opened her purse to tip some silver and copper coins into Maude's hand.

'That will help you pay your first week's rent and buy you some food.'

'I will pay you back as soon as I can,' said Maude, tears of gratitude welling up in her eyes.

'You're my sister; you don't have to pay me back. Now children, come along we will need to buy or beg some furniture and a bed for Aunt Maude.'

Since moving into their new home they had managed well enough, the money she earned working for Daniel Fremeaux and the part of Alex's pay allotted her by the paymaster just about saw them through. On occasion, when Billie pulled off a job and shared some of his spoils Jane would help with a few essentials, like Georgie's second hand shoes.

Maude opened her eyes to the sound of Georgie playing across the yard. It was the summer of 1867, hot, dry and warmth of the summer sun penetrated her clothing leaving her feeling content. She thought about the morning sermon, about Father McManus preaching to the congregation, reminding them that they must be strong in the face of adversity. Almost all the people there were poor Catholics, surviving from day-to-day in the unhealthy and overcrowded slums and finding it hard enough to put enough food on their tables. They needed his spiritual guidance as much as anyone and he made it his mission in life to help where he could.

Maude chatted with him most Sundays after the service and she had learned a little about him, of his early life in his native Ireland, a poor farm labourer forced out of work by the devastation of the great potato famine. He had volunteered to serve in the Army of the

Pickpockets and Zulus

Public Poor and for six months spent his days preparing and serving soup to starving people and that experience had made him feel that perhaps his true vocation was to do God's work. From those humble beginnings, he had somehow managed to learn the rudiments of reading and writing, eventually ordaining in the priesthood.

Years later, after the worst of the potato famine, he had left his native Ireland to take up a post in the North of England. To begin with, he had worked in the cotton towns of Lancashire amongst an Irish population working in the mills or labouring on the new iron roads cutting their way across the length and breadth of the country. He had had witnessed their hardship, helped where he could and eventually he had followed the railway south to London.

Today he reminded his flock that their earthly life and labours were but mere preparation for the time when God would call them, to live with Him in paradise. He truly believed in life after death and worked hard to convince the congregation to worship God, try to live by the scriptures and secure their place in Heaven and afterwards he did what he always did; spoke with every parishioner. A 'good morning,' a few kind words and a question or two about their circumstances showed he cared and when it was Maude and Georgie's turn to say goodbye he had taken her free hand in his and asked if she had enjoyed the service.

'It was lovely Father Brian; I did so enjoy the hymns you chose.'

'And little Georgie, was he singing too?'

'Yes, Father he was, he was singing beautifully,' she said gazing down at her son.

Pickpockets and Zulus

'And what of your husband is there any news yet? Will he be home soon d'you think?'

'I don't know Father; it has been six months since his last letter. I do hope that he will be back soon though, Georgie is growing up and he is in need of his father.'

The step was hard and Maude twisted her frame a little, finding a more comfortable position and watched Georgie for a few moments playing a skipping game. Yes, she thought, Alex had been away too long, if it was not for their son she was sure she would have forgotten how he looked but Georgie had his father's features, light sandy hair, those lovely enquiring brown eyes and a strong frame. Alex had told her that she must make sure he had plenty to eat because he had seen the weak looking recruits arrive at the depot, undernourished and he did not want his son to be anything but healthy and strong.

Suddenly a group of older boys wandered into the yard through the arch, disturbing the peace and looking for trouble. Each dressed in the rags of street urchins and not a pair of shoes between them.

'Got any ha'pennies you don't want missus?' said one of the urchins walking up to her.

She tried to ignore him but then a chorus of voices struck up asking for ha'pennies. She felt intimidated and looked round anxiously for support but apart from her and the three children, there was no one.

'No I ain't, now go away and be'ave yourselves.'

The boys laughed. Everywhere they went grownups told them to behave, but they never did. In their young and dysfunctional lives, they had not yet come up against real authority, too young for the police to be too concerned about, not much of a threat to anyone except a lone women or a drunk.

'Come on missus you must 'ave some money,' said one of them.

'Yeah, where's your purse?' goaded another.

The largest of the group stood apart from the others with his hands on his hips surveying the yard. He was tall for his age, probably about twelve years old, but very thin and with the same gaunt look of his companions. A street urchin, abandoned by any family he might have, street wise, surviving on the scraps the streets offered and he saw an opportunity.

'Hey look at that kid,' he said pointing towards Georgie, 'he's got some shoes on, we'll 'ave em.'

The other members of the gang looked at Georgie who was oblivious to their presence, playing out his game with the two little girls. They had found a piece of frayed rope and were trying to skip with it but the girls were unable to jump high enough and kept tripping. Georgie fared better when it was his turn and as the rope swung round and round he jumped, clearing the swinging cord by barely an inch. Then the game came to an abrupt end as the tall boy, the leader of the gang, put a grubby hand on Georgie's shoulder.

'Oi! you! Gimme those shoes,' he said. A pair of shoes would fetch money in a pawnshop, probably enough to feed them all for the day and he was not going to miss the chance. 'Are you deaf? I said gimme those shoes' he repeated pointing to Georgie's feet.

'No,' said Georgie. They were his shoes and he was not going to give them up.

The gang leader did not wait to negotiate, simply lunging straight at Georgie, pushing him backwards, trying to knock him down but Georgie was ready for him and managed to keep his footing as the urchin forced him backwards. The eldest of the two girls playing the skipping game screamed but the boy took little notice, stepping forwards as Georgie stepped backwards.

'Gimme those shoes,' he said once more.

By now, Maude had realised the danger and jumped to her feet, her heart beating madly.

'Get off 'im you,' she shouted, 'leave them alone and clear off out of 'ere before I call the Peelers.'

The boy turned his head arrogantly towards her, she was no bigger than he was, just a woman and did not pose a threat. Maude took several steps towards Georgie and the girls, the boy turned his head towards Maude once more as if to say 'I win', his concentration transferred from Georgie and in that instant Georgie leaped forward, crashing his clenched fist into the side of the boy's head. The force was enough to knock the thug senseless to the ground and stunned by Georgie's sudden action, the other boys did not move. Then one recovered, shouted 'get him!' and the pack surged forward pushing the screaming girls aside to descend upon Georgie.

As well as he could, he put up a fight, swinging his fists, catching one on the chin but they were just too many. Maude ran towards the melee trying to fend them off with the flats of her hands but she did not have the strength to make much impression. Two boys managed to grab a hold of Georgie arms, forcing him to the ground and a third attempted to prise the shoes from his feet when a man's voice boomed out.

'Leave him alone.'

Pickpockets and Zulus

The urchins were too intent on their prize to take any notice until they suddenly felt strong hands gripping their collars and one by one, a man in a soldier's uniform dragged them away from Georgie.

'Clear off you lot. What d'you think you are up too attacking a defenceless boy and these little girls? Go on clear off.'

The boys took little persuading, getting to their feet and careering from the yard leaving their leader prostrate on the ground. Maude looked at the man, the strong sunlight blinding her a little and she held her palm over her brow to shade her eyes.

'Alex is that you?'

'No ma'am, I'm afraid I'm not Alex.'

She moved towards Georgie, helped him to his feet and gained a better sight of the soldier. No he was not Alex, he was taller, had black hair and a moustache, Alex could not grow a moustache like that.

'Oh, the uniform, I thought you were my husband, I am sorry. Thank you for helping us,' she said in a breathless voice.

'You must be missus McNamara?'

'Why yes, how did you know?'

'My name is Albert Roberts and I am a Sergeant in the Twenty Fourth Regiment of Foot. Alex described you to me more than once.'

'Ah, Roberts, I remember the name, but you were just a Private before the Regiment left Chatham.'

'That's right ma'am, they made me up to Sergeant out in India.'

Before he could say anymore, the leader of the gang revived and climbed unsteadily to his feet looking the worse for wear and stumbled towards the archway in silence. As soon as he was out of sight, the soldier turned his attention back to Maude.

'Missus McNamara, I have some news for you, perhaps you should sit down.'

This was Sergeant Roberts's second visit of the day and he had two more to make before he could return to his parent's home in Peckham. He was keeping a promise, a bond of comradeship between soldiers. It was inevitable that some of them would not return home, dying on active service, a fate they accepted with a shrug and it fell to those who survived to inform the fallen soldiers' loved ones.

Maude did not understand at first; staring blankly at the sergeant until a cold feeling gripped her heart, her legs began to feel weak, unable to support her weight and she stumbled. The soldier took her arm to support her and helped her towards the steps.

'Missus McNamara,' he said, an emotional lump forming in his throat. 'Alex, your husband, was a fellow soldier and a good friend to me. It grieves me to have to tell you that he has not returned with the Regiment.'

The Sergeant remained silent for a few moments, allowing the news to filter through and he looked down at the boy, knowing that he would have to grow up without a father.

'Ww... What happened?' stuttered Maude, 'how long ago? I haven't received a letter for more than six months.'

'It would be getting on for a year ago, some tribesmen were giving trouble up near the Afghan border and we were sent to deal with them. We encountered snipers and were involved in some minor skirmishes as we made camp and then a horde of tribesmen attacked us. Alex and his Company moved to a strong point to defend the camp, to buy us time until we could bring the field guns to bear and then, once we had the situation under control, the Cavalry charged. We finally drove them off, captured their leader and stopped any further trouble but Alex's company had suffered heavy losses. I'm afraid your husband was killed missus McNamara, I'm sorry.'

The soldier looked at the ground, refraining from saying anymore and Maude knew that her husband had died a brave man doing the job he loved. Then Sergeant Roberts held out a small brown paper bag for her.

'Here, take this, a few personal possessions your husband gave to me to bring you in case he died. A few of his belongings he wanted you to have.'

With a trembling hand, Maude took the bag and held it to her bosom and the sergeant wished her luck before leaving as suddenly as he had appeared. Walking briskly away he wondered if he done the right thing telling such a story because, as with so many of his comrades, Alex had not died fighting the rebellious tribesmen, instead he had died of the fever.

Chapter 3

On the dusty earthen floor outside their hut, a small boy sat with his mother, his teeth gently nibbling at the fingernails of one hand. He watched attentively as his eldest sister and the older girls of the village began to dance. Back and forth they swayed, stamping their feet in unison their bodies gyrating to ancient rhythms, singing a traditional Zulu song as they danced. They wore little clothing, skirts of elephant grass, coloured beads fashioned from fruit seeds hanging loosely about their necks and bracelets of Ivory and wood on their forearms. To Nkosinathi the sights and sounds were mesmerising and he could not stop his eyes following every move the girls made practicing the special dance.

His sister, Thandeka, had spent days preparing her costume, collecting the stalks of a particular long grass, seeds of dried fruits for her necklace and colourful bird feathers for her head dress. She had spent hours threading strips of dried cow skins with the seeds and today Thandeka and the other girls of the village were showing off their costumes before the trek to the King's royal homestead to perform the Reed Dance, the special dance for the King himself.

Nkosinathi was still quite young and lived in his mother's hut, spending his days tending to the smaller animals, a few goats and newborn calves. Each morning shortly after sunrise, he would stand at the edge of the central Kraal to watch the older boys prodding their sticks at the cattle, herding them out to pasture.

Many of the boys were brothers and half-brothers, children of the headman and it was their job to take care of the wealth of the village. Nkosinathi had sisters too and one, a twelve-year-old girl called Nozipho whose job was to tidy her mother's hut and to keep an eye on her younger brothers. She was diligent and bright, took her duties very seriously and thought nothing of scolding the younger boys if they stepped out of line. It was a girl's destiny to look after the men folk of the village, whereas the boys thought of nothing else but to become warriors.

With a loud whoop, the girls finished their dance and beaming with delight, crossed the open ground towards their mothers. The rehearsal was over and soon they would prepare for the journey to the Royal Kraal to perform the Reed Dance with girls from across the Zulu kingdom. The King and his courtiers would watch closely and from the swaying ranks of the nubile young girls, the King might choose a wife.

The following morning Nkosinathi's mother and sisters left early to work in the fields leaving the three younger children behind. It was the job of Nkosinathi and his younger brother Sibusiso to milk the few goats left in the Kraal, to fill gourds and take them to their mother's hut for the safekeeping of Nozipho.

'Nkosinathi, little brother, thank you for the milk,' said Nozipho as they reached the hut with their gourds. 'Put them there in the shade and I will work with it later.

Now go and feed the goats with grass and then get me some firewood for the cooking fire.'

Nkosinathi looked at his sister with big brown eyes not daring to say a word for she had a sharp tongue and he knew she would scold him if he spoke out of turn. He was a good Zulu boy, obedient and resourceful and he set about the task with vigour. He led Sibusiso to the entrance of the kraal and through its protective wall of thorn bushes towards the fields of tall grass and with only their bare hands the two boys gathered as much as they could carry, returning several times to spread it amongst the goats. The rest of the morning and the early afternoon was spent gathering brushwood, dragging it into the Kraal, piling it outside their hut watched closely by their sister milling corn in a hollowed out stone.

'You have done well boys,' she said as they dropped the last of the wood on the ground. 'I see you have worked hard, go and drink some milk as a reward then come and help me with the corn.'

The two boys grinned at their sister and dashed into the hut, thankful for some respite from their toils. After consuming some of the milk, they had taken from the goats they crawled back through the entrance to the hut to stand and watch Nozipho for a while and then it was time for the herd to return. The brothers heard the cattle approaching, their contented mooing and the shrill calls of the older boys as they entered the kraal and after Nozipho told them they could go, they ran to the corral fence to watch the beasts slowly lumber past, their udders bursting with milk.

Once they had the cattle safely penned, some of the older boys could not resist the urge to show off and standing together a little way off, Nkosinathi and

Sibusiso watched. The boys paired up, held their fighting sticks at the ready and began to circle. Zulu boys carried their fighting sticks everywhere with them, one for attack the other for defence and they spent hours practising the art in preparation for the day when the King would summon them. Nkosinathi's dream was to follow in their footsteps and to one day become a warrior, and to become a Zulu warrior he must be proficient in the art of stick fighting.

Sibusiso was a year younger, smaller in stature and relatively easy to defeat and so, eager to show off his own prowess as a fighter, Nkosinathi challenged his little brother. The two of them stood face to face, holding their small sticks in the customary way and slowly began to circle one another; Nkosinathi to gain some advantage and Sibusiso because that's what his brother was doing and he always copied him. Suddenly Nkosinathi reached out and struck Sibusiso across the top of his head and the younger boy let out a loud shriek. The blow was unexpected, Sibusiso was unable to defend himself and Nkosinathi prepared to repeat the exercise but before he could strike another blow, Nozipho came running to investigate the commotion.

'Hey little brother, what are you doing to Sibusiso?'

Nkosinathi turned his head towards his sister with questioning eyes, he knew in his heart that little Sibusiso had been no match for him and now Nozipho's scolding was making him feel guilty.

'I'm teaching him to fight,' he said sheepishly.

'Well you are not doing a very good job. Come and help me crush the mealie for the bread cakes. Stop fighting, I do not want to get into any trouble because you have hurt Sibusiso, you should fight boys your own size.'

She took hold of the younger boy's hand and led him sobbing back to their hut to help her crush the corn and a deflated Nkosinathi followed.

'Get me some wood for the fire Nkosinathi. Here Sibusiso, let me get you something for that cut to your head.'

She dropped to her knees and crawled through the entrance tunnel into the hut, returning with some crushed tree bark and rubbed it into the wound.

'There, that will help it heal, now go and get the firewood.'

The boys began breaking the brushwood they had collected for the cooking fire, Nozipho threw the twigs onto the embers and when the children's mother and elder sisters returned the fire was burning brightly and their mother began to stoke it up ready to cook their evening meal. Themba's daughters took the mealie flour Nozipho had prepared, mixed it with a little water and salt and began skilfully kneading flat cakes for their evening meal. Themba hummed a traditional song as she worked and then stopped, looked at her youngest son and wondered why he was so quiet? Why was he holding his head?

'What's happened to Sibusiso?' she asked. 'Come here.'

Sheepishly Sibusiso, keeping his sitting position, shuffled across to his mother not daring to look at her.

'What's this?' she said, noticing the bump on his head. 'What have you been doing to have such a lump on your head?'

Pickpockets and Zulus

'Nkosinathi thinks he is a brave warrior and has been fighting with him,' said Nozipho, dragging the big earthenware cooking pot towards the fire.

Themba looked sternly at the youngest of her sons, one forlorn, the other grinning with pleasure at the thought of himself as a warrior. With a swiftness that took them all by surprise, she reached out for the broom Nozipho had been using to sweep the hut and swung it in a low arc. With a loud 'thwack' it made contact with the back of Nkosinathi's legs making him jump in fright and beside him the two older girls looked on in amusement and Nozipho stopped dragging the pot to stand in silence and witness the brave little warrior's reprimanding.

'Zulu warriors do not pick on small helpless boys, next time pick on someone your own size if you want to fight. Real warriors kill lions not rabbits, now go and help Thandeka get ready for the dancing this evening.'

Suppressing his tears Nkosinathi turned away from his mother to follow his eldest sister to a corner of the hut where she began to arrange her costume.

'Here, brave warrior, put my bracelets over there on the calfskin.'

Nkosinathi did as she told him; it was something else to think about and took away the stinging in his legs. Perhaps he was wrong to hurt his little brother like that and he promised himself that from now on he would only fight bigger boys than himself.

Soon the smell of the cooking drifted into the hut and Thandeka said they should join the rest of the family. Nkosinathi's appetite had returned, his legs did not sting so much and he was glad, sitting beside Sibusiso as if nothing had happened. Later in the evening, after their meal, the boys and their sisters joined the whole village as it assembled on the open ground at the centre of the kraal. Again, the girls danced the *Umkhosi Womhlanga*, the Reed Dance, in preparation for the King. It would take place at his iKhanda, the royal kraal of Nodwengu, the place where the marriageable young girls of his kingdom would gather to dance and demonstrate their virginity.

'The King will watch and if it so pleases him then he might choose a new wife. Your sister Thandeka looks beautiful does she not,' said Themba to her youngest daughter. 'In a few years it will be your turn, so watch and learn and be aware my daughter, if the reeds do not stand up straight but wilt, then it is a sign you are not a true virgin and shame will descend upon our household.'

Nozipho looked away from her mother and towards the girls preparing to dance. She was too young to appreciate the significance of the dance but she did want to wear such a costume.

Sitting a few yards away with boys of his own age, Nkosinathi watched the girl's begin to dance, their hips gyrating to the beat of the drums, the beads around her neck swinging back and forth and he looked across at Sibusiso sat with their mother. He was receiving special attention for his suffering and Nkosinathi was glad he had not hurt him too much and then his attention returned to the dance.

The drums started, "cr...rrump" the girl's feet stamped the ground in unison, signalling the start of the dance and for the next hour they swayed back and forth, their sweet feminine voices singing out in unison until eventually the drums became silent and they excitedly broke formation to run towards their mothers.

'My daughter you look beautiful in your dance costume,' said Themba. 'You will catch the King's eye I'm sure and maybe he will want you for his wife.'

Thandeka looked at the ground embarrassed, regaining her composure, and then she turned to her little sister.

'Here, carry these for me Nozipho,' she said, holding out the bundle of reeds.

Nozipho jumped up and eagerly took them from her, proudly following Thandeka and their mother back to the hut and following sheepishly behind came Nkosinathi and Sibusiso, friends once more.

The day of the march to *Nodwengu* approached and one evening, as the women sat round around the embers of the fire, a shadow passed over them and their chatter ceased. It was Mondli, Nkosinathi's father, the headman of the village, the King's Induna and when his deep voice cut through the chatter, he gained the immediate attention of everyone round the fire.

'My second wife Themba, soon we are to go to *Nodwengu* for the festival of the virgins. When next the moon is full, the Sangoma will tell us of the day we must leave and you will prepare my daughter. The King will expect all who dance to be virgins and so to make sure we are not shamed the Sangoma will come and protect Thandeka from evil and keep her pure.'

'Yes my husband' said his second wife lowering her eyes in a sign of submission, 'it will be as you say.'

Mondli nodded his head, satisfied and shrank into the darkness, returning to his own fire and the company of men and then a mysterious chanted verse floated over the womenfolk and they froze. Then a rhythmic tapping came from out of the darkness and quite suddenly, a Sangoma appeared, sickly aromatic smoke drifting from a clay pot in his hand. The strange smelling smoke wafted over them, instilling fear and apprehension because each was aware of Sangoma's power, everyone knew that if he were offended he might destroy them with his spells.

'Where is the virgin?' he said. 'Come to me to be protected from evil.'

Thandeka, terrified and dressed in only a simple kilt began to shiver as the Witch Doctor approached and her mother pushed her to her feet to face him and sitting in the shadows away from the fire, Nkosinathi felt the hairs on the back of his neck began to stand up. The close proximity of the Sangoma making him weak with fear and involuntarily he shrank further into the shadows.

The flickering light of the fire exposed a dark form, eyes mysterious black sockets and on his head, a plume of black ostrich feathers that made him appear taller than any man. Across his shoulders, he wore a cape of buffalo hide and around his waist a kilt of cow's tails that dangled to the floor. In one hand, he carried a human skull, in the other the pot of burning incense that he swung slowly, mesmerizingly, back and forth, its acrid smell drifting into the nostrils of everyone there. Nkosinathi felt sick but he dare not move as he watched Thandeka standing alone and then the Sangoma beckoned her to him. He towered over his sister who had terror written all over her face and then she sank to her knees.

Standing over her slight feminine frame the Sangoma undid his cloak and let it slip to the ground, exposing his semi naked body completely covered in a white powder and mumbled an incomprehensible prayer. He had come to examine Thandeka and unknowingly she had passed the first test. If she had stumbled stepping the few paces towards him the Sangoma would have found an excuse for guilt, marking her as a fallen woman and then he could put her through a torturous ordeal to ward off the evil spirits. As it was, he merely chanted more unintelligible verse, swung the pot of incense around her three times, sprinkled some white powder over her and left as quickly as he had appeared.

For several minutes there was silence save for the occasional crack of a burning twig and then the brave Thandeka slowly rose to her feet, her eyes staring into the darkness beyond the fire and she began to weep.

The sun had barely risen when Mondli led his people on their journey to the royal homestead with his war shield slung over one shoulder, his stabbing spear gripped tightly in his hand. Alongside him his brothers, the warriors of the Kraal, carried their own shields and spears and behind them came the women and girls. At the rear of the caravan, the younger boys and teenagers drove a small herd of cattle, selected as gifts for the King and amongst them marched a proud Nkosinathi.

For two days they journeyed, eventually reaching the banks of the White Umfolozi to camp for the night, crossing at daybreak. Nkosinathi had never seen such a river and stared in wonderment at the expanse of slow moving water covered in the swirling, early morning mist and shivered from the cold. He stood on the riverbank and watched the villagers begin to cross; Mondli led the way, the rest of his extended family following in a strict pecking order. He knew the river

well and had selected a ford where the flow was less
turbulent, where the water was shallow, the riverbed
even and flat, a place where even Nkosinathi could cross
and aided only by a tight grip on an older brother, he
entered the water. Nkosinathi felt the cold-water swirl
round his bare feet and as he waded further in the water
reached up to his waist and the current tugged at him
but he held his brother's grip and soon found himself
breaking free, running gleefully through the shallows
and towards the far bank.

Safely across, Mondli led them towards *Nodwengu's*
and by early afternoon the kraal's cooking fires were
clearly visible. As they neared the Royal homestead,
other small groups similar to their own appeared it was
such an important social event in the Zulu calendar and
everyone wanted to be there. It was a chance to re-
establish friendships, to catch up on the gossip of the
Kingdom and as they approached the Royal Kraal, a
party of warriors emerged from a hollow to confront
them.

'*Sawubona*, I see you, I am Mondli.'

'Sawubona Mondli, we are the King's guard and he
bids you welcome.' They knew of Mondli, he posed no
threat, so they passed by to continue their duties, and
from amongst the cattle Nkosinathi watched them.
Strong men that towered over him, their shields slung
across their backs, spears held ready and he promised
himself there and then that one day he would become a
warrior just like them.

By noon they had crested a low hill from where they
could survey the whole valley below and there stood the
Royal Kraal in all its splendour, six hundred huts
surrounded by a stout stockade of intertwined thorn

branches. Within the hour, Mondli's party reached the walls of *Nodwengu* and made camp, the women began preparing food, the boys sent out to look for firewood whilst Mondli and the older men sat on the grass. Taking small horns from slits in their ear lobes, they poured out minute amounts of snuff onto the backs of their hands to talk and while away the time until the food was prepared.

Even before the new day had dawned, everyone had risen from their sleeping mats to prepare for the festival. Mondli and his eldest sons took hold of the nose ring of the first of the slaughter animals and, followed closely by Nkosinathi and a group of smaller boys, pulled it out onto open ground and Mondli held out the stick he was carrying to point it at Nkosinathi.

'Fetch a bowl Nkosinathi; you can catch the first blood. Today you can take your first step on the path to becoming a warrior.'

Nkosinathi's heart missed a beat, for his father to single him out from the crowd and to bestow upon him such responsibility was indeed an honour. The slaughter animal was to be a gift to the King but the unfortunate animal seemed not to understand, its eyes opening wide and its ears pressing hard against its head as a warrior pulled it by the nose ring. Slowly, inexorably, the beast yielded, unable to resist the pressure on its soft fleshy nose and followed to the place of slaughter. Eventually the rope relaxed and the animal could stop, begin grazing and then, from out of the morning mist, appeared the Sangoma. Ghostlike, streaks of the white powder covered his face and a clutch of monkey skulls hung from a stick in his hand. He approached the small

43

group in slow, deliberate movements and at the same time, Nkosinathi returned from the camp clutching a large earthenware basin. His heart was full of joy at the thought of being involved in the slaughter of the cow until he almost ran into the Sangoma. Fearing he had disturbed the Sangoma's theatricals, he expected to encounter his wrath and stopped dead in his tracks, staring hard at the ground and not quite sure what to do. His father had sent him on an errand and he must obey his wishes but here, blocking his path was the Sangoma, a being that even a brave warrior was afraid of. But today the Sangoma was not looking to ward off evil instead he had come to bless the sacrificial animal and Mondli was in charge of the situation. After all, the Sangoma expected his share of the carcass and was not about to upset the chief and risk going hungry.

'Stop' said Mondli, aware of Nkosinathi's approach, sweeping his spear in an arc in front of his body to assert his authority. 'Look Nkosinathi comes with the blood bowl. Hold still boy whist the holy man blesses the sacrifice.'

At his father's words, Nkosinathi dropped to his knees and held out the bowl with both hands, eyes still fixed on the ground in front of him and slowly the Sangoma turned towards him, glowering at the intrusion. Holding the stick of monkey skulls over the outstretched hands of the boy the Witch Doctor mumbled an unintelligible chant and shaking the stick, he reached forward to touch Nkosinathi's head. The monkey skulls swayed before the boy's eyes and Nkosinathi closed them tight, shaking with fear and gritting his teeth. It was not a pleasant experience but he held himself steady until the Sangoma's attention

44

moved back to the cow still patiently chewing on some grass.

Only the Sangoma's feet were visible to Nkosinathi's lowered eyes and, mesmerised, he watched as they moved away out of his view before daring to look up. His eyes met Mondli's stern gaze and with a twitch of his spear his father commended him to rise to his feet, a further twitch commanded him to follow the Sangoma on his exaggerated, melodramatic path towards the cow.

A calm animal would yield better meat than a frightened one, and so they had left it standing alone for a while and snorting steam into the cool morning air, the animal appeared relaxed, chewing slowly on a mouthful of grass, oblivious to the Sangoma. Mondli pointed his spear, this time towards a son by his first wife whose honour it was to slaughter the animal. The young man, his short stabbing spear held tightly, calmly took his place alongside the ruminating animal and without warning, thrust his blade deep into the animal's chest. The sharp steel pierced the animal's heart, releasing bright red blood and spurting into the bowl in Nkosinathi's hands. The deluge gradually subsided and then blood began to exit from the animal's surprised open mouth and within seconds, it collapsed onto its knees and with a last gasp the stricken beast rolled over onto its side, kicking out in one last desperate act to hang onto life.

Nkosinathi stood back, his bowl brimming and the bright red, sticky liquid splattered across his arms and face, red dots of congealing blood. Nkosinathi's father and the men of the Kraal took the bowl from his blood soaked hands and passed it around, each taking a mouthful and after the Sangoma had his fill of the first blood, they fell upon the hapless animal to skilfully cut away its hide and butcher the carcass. They cut the carcass into manageable joints, mostly as gifts for dispersal amongst the King's household because Mondli knew if he could please the King's extended family, then by association, he would please the King.

From a few feet away Nkosinathi and the younger boys watched with fascination and then Mondli spoke to the eldest of his sons telling them to wrap the joints in leaves and to carry them to the huts of the King's stepmothers. It was tradition that these fat, indolent women received the first of the bounty. To please them was important, very important, for they had the ear of the King and their influence could not be underestimated.

'We have done well my sons. We are amongst the first to give meat to the royal mothers. They will tell the King and we will be known as a generous family' he paused for a while before continuing. 'Dumisani you are nineteen and have lived as a Cadet for the past year and soon you will be called to serve the King. I have heard that a new regiment is to be formed and so you will remain behind when we leave.'

The boy nodded, 'yes father, I am proud to be of service to the King and to honour your name.'

'Good, I know you will. It is a great day when the King calls you into his service.'

Mondli patted his son on his head as a sign of his pleasure and turned his attention to the carcass of the slaughtered cow and gave the order for the youths to carry remains of the meat to their camp to begin roasting it.

46

Pickpockets and Zulus

In their makeshift camp, the girls were making the final changes to their costumes, collecting reeds from the nearby stream and picking out the best for the dance. Near the fire, Mondli and the men of the kraal were busy making ready to roast the meat when a group led by a tall, well-made man of about fifty years of age approached. He was dressed in only a loincloth and as he approached, he raised his hand in greeting.

'*Sawubona*, I see you.'

'*Ngikhona*, I am here' replied Mondli, grinning from ear to ear.

Dumisani standing next to his father was a little puzzled at his reaction, normally a stern and unfeeling man he appeared like a small boy who had just received his first spear.

'Nongalaza, my old friend, it has been many seasons since our paths have crossed.'

'Mondli, you are well? It is a long time since we last met. We had good days together in the iHlaba regiment did we not?'

'Ha Ha' boomed Mondli in his deep voice, recalling the kinship of the 'stabbers' regiment. 'Oh yes, my friend, and you have done well? And these are your sons?' he asked with a wave of his hand.

Nongalaza nodded proudly, reaching to his ear lobe and taking the small polished horn from it.

'Mondli, will you take snuff, let us sit a while and recall the old days,' he said, removing the stopper from the horn.

'These are my eldest sons by my first wife, this is Siphiwe and this is Manelesi his younger brother, their sister is to perform the Reed Dance today and like you I have brought my family.'

Pickpockets and Zulus

The two men sat a while and talked, reminiscing about their time together in the iHlaba regiment, their service to the King and of their lives since the King had released them from military service. The old King had relaxed the rules a little, given the regiment permission to marry earlier than normal and they were delighted. Without the King's permission, they could not marry and with most of the warriors of the iHlaba well into their thirties, it was reason to celebrate.

'I hear your Kraal is up in the old hunting grounds of King Shaka near the Black Mfolozi.'

'Yes, we have plenty of sweet grazing for our cattle and good hunting up in the hills, and you Mondli, Where is your Kraal?'

'I am south of Nodwengu, across the river, two days trek. The country is good for the herd, I have many cattle and like you, I have brought my eldest daughter to catch the eye of the King.'

They talked some more, their sons sitting quietly and respectfully behind them until their fathers stood to their feet, the encounter concluded.

'Goodbye old friend, I am glad we have met,' said Nongalaza. 'We will take snuff again before you return home.'

'We will,' said Mondli.

As Nongalaza and his sons made ready to leave Thandeka stood almost naked behind a screen of animal skins as her younger sister and her mother smeared her body with animal fat to make her skin glow. Themba was not taking any chances, apart from the fragrant oils she had procured a potion to ward off the evil spirits that might spoil her daughter's chance of marriage to

48

the King and unseen, she smeared it across Themba's naked back.

'You will be the most beautiful and desirable girl to pass the King. Make sure you sway your hips as I showed you daughter.'

Thandeka did not reply, apprehensive and shy she simply closed her eyes and nodded, a positive enough response for her mother and then she emerged from behind the screen to admiring glances from the women and girls threading coloured seeds to make bracelets. She looked beautiful and they felt sure that she would catch the King's eye.

The whole encampment was buzzing with excitement by the time the sun had reached its zenith for quite soon the festival would begin. The older women in the camp fussed around the eligible girls, giving them last minute advice, helping them with their costumes and adornments and advising them of the important protocols.

'Thandeka, you must not look at the King or any of his wives and you must show deference to the Princesses for to show anything other than total obedience could mean death to you and maybe all of us, your family.'

Thandeka nodded, aware of the inherent risks of causing the King or his wives displeasure, nevertheless, the buzz of excitement spreading through the camp caught her in its thrall. She soon forgot her mother's words as the inhabitants of the royal household and the visitors from every corner of the Kingdom began to spread round the twenty-acre parade ground at the centre of the village. The older boys had already driven the Royal herd out to pasture and would remain with the cattle until the King had chosen his new wife but for everyone else it was a time of celebration as one hundred thousand people congregated in and around Nodwengu. The women dressed in their finest apparel; soft skins adorning their bodies and necklaces of coloured beads around their necks. They had plastered their hair with red clay to form a knot on the top of their heads that caused them to walk with an upright, elegant gait. Their menfolk wore kilts of cow tails and garters of fine combed animal hair fastened just below the knees and stretching down to their ankles. The married men carried shields and spears, their head rings polished to perfection whilst the *Insizwas*, or unmarried men who were not permitted to wear the head ring, strutted about in peer groups, their tall ostrich feathers headdresses swaying provocatively as they walked into the Kraal and with them came crowds of happy singing Zulus to await their King.

Nkosinathi and his younger brother stayed close to their mother as they entered the Kraal, threading their way between the closely packed beehive huts to find a good place to view proceedings. The grounds sloped gently uphill towards the King's huts from where he could look down and dominate his subjects. Then he appeared and there was a sudden hush as the crowd caught a glimpse of their King in all his finery before averting their eyes. He wore the tallest and most colourful plume of ostrich feathers Nkosinathi had ever seen and he could not help but stare.

'Nkosinathi,' said his mother clipping his ear, 'do not look at the King, your eyes must not meet his or he will have you put to death. It is a sign of evil spirits to look directly at him.'

Pickpockets and Zulus

Shaken, the little boy looked straight at the ground. His family were always taking precautions to prevent the spirits inflicting harm on the Kraal, the InSangoma were always present and many times his father had sent him with gifts of food to a Sangoma in payment for protecting the herd. However, this was something he had not experienced, he was in the presence of the King, the master that one day he would serve and for a time he felt afraid until the King signalled the drums to begin.

Immediately intoxication rhythms spread throughout the kraal; two regiments appeared through the entrance gateway to arrange themselves around the perimeter of the central parade ground. Erect warriors faced each other, proud and fearsome in their regimental regalia. Each man held his distinctive black and white patterned war shield against his chest, a short stabbing spear in his right hand and as the King rose to his feet, the watching crowd became silent. The King's wives stood to one side of him, the Princesses to the other and for a moment, he stood still to survey his subjects. Satisfied, he raised his ceremonial spear high above his head, bringing it down suddenly, swiftly, thumping the ground, the signal for the festivities to begin.

He passed his spear to a warrior of his bodyguard thundered out '*Bayete*' and thousands of feet slammed the ground in one great thunderous salute. Stretching out his arms in a deliberate, exaggerated movement, he brought his hands together in a barely audible smack, but it was enough. Two lines of opposing warriors filled the parade ground began to slowly converge, moving first one foot forward to stamp the ground and then the other, sending out a thunderous 'cr...rump' each time. Excitement grew, the gap between the two rows closed inexorably and when the opposing warriors were within six feet of each other they halted, shields held out and stabbing spears pointing threateningly. Then for a few moments, silence, until the Induna of the older of the two Impis gave the order for their war chant, answered immediately by the opposing regiment's own special chant. Then together the two highly disciplined forces stamped the ground and to the battle cry of *'Bayete,'* 'bring on our enemies,' the lines disengaged, retreating to their starting positions.

The preliminaries over the festivities began with first one regiment, then the other performing their own particular war dances and manoeuvres, demonstrating prowess and discipline only a Zulu army could perform. Indunas sang out orders, the lines of warriors answered in unison, dancing towards the King and his retinue, their powerful black bodies twisting and turning. The rhythmic beating of the drums periodically changed until after four hours, the King stood up to command silence. After he had recognised their absolute obedience, he grasped again his ceremonial spear and swept it towards the entrance at the lower end of the Kraal and from behind him, his chief Induna gave the signal for the start of the dance of the virgins.

It began with the drums beating out a fast repetitive refrain, encouraging the first of the virgin girls to enter the arena led by the chief Princess of the King's house the girl's tongues rapidly ululating as they went, repeating over and over *'woolala woolala woolala.'* The volume increased as more girls entered the Kraal until eventually they broke into song, a song their mothers had been teaching them in preparation for this moment. Five thousand female voices filled the air, and in each

hand, the girls carried tall reeds, holding them in front
of them for the King to see, swaying to the sound of the
drums. They sang over and over '*Com a com a layaa,
ooma ooma a layaa*' and the procession made its way
relentlessly towards the Royal party. The younger males
eagerly awaited their arrival but King Mpande was old
and not much interested in another wife.

Mpande was King in name, but his son, Cetshwayo,
was the power in the land, defeating and killing his
younger brother Mbuyazi in internecine warfare to take
control of the succession. It was Cetshwayo who was in
need of a wife and he watched with interest as the girls
approached, seeking out a strong-bodied woman to bear
his offspring. However, he was not yet crowned King,
and so today he could only watch, glancing occasionally
at his aged father, wondering how long it would before
the old man visited his forbears and then he, Cetshwayo,
could be crowned King and take any of these girls he
wanted.

The dancers reached the top of the gently sloping
ground, singing the King's praises in joyous mood, their
fine bead-work and skirts a blur of colour. They offered
up their reeds for inspection as they swayed past the
throne, demonstrating their virginal purity to the King
but Mpande knew he did not have long to live. The old
King did not need nor desire another wife, he was tired
and all he could do was to sit with a blank, uninterested,
expression on his face.

Thandeka sang out as her rank passed the King, her
heart beating madly as she held up her reed, not daring
to look at the Royal party. She tossed the reed onto the
ever-growing pile in front of the King just as the other
girls had done and passed on by. The old King's eyes

moved a little as he took in her beauty, but she was too slim, he liked fat girls, all his wives were fat and Thandeka caught a brief glimpse of him as she passed. In that brief instant she was glad that such an old man had not chosen her, she did not like what she saw and had no desire to be the wife of such a man.

After two more days of feasting and dancing, it was time to leave and on that last morning, Mondli rose from his mat, his head splitting from all the beer he had drunk. His old friend Nongalaza and some of the other headmen had visited him and they had passed the snuff around, they had drunk beer and talked long into the night and now he was suffering. He screwed his eyes tight to clear his head and clapped his hands.

'Wake up you lazy good for nothings. We have a long journey in front of us. Come on, get ready.'

Nkosinathi was instantly awake and jumped to his feet.

'I am ready my father,' he blurted out taking Mondli by surprise.

'You are a good boy Nkosinathi. Go with your sister Nozipho and fill those gourds with water from the stream ready for the journey.'

Nkosinathi needed no encouragement, he had enjoyed their stay in the Royal homestead and he had helped with the ritual slaughter for the first time. The King's soldiers had impressed him, he wanted more than ever to become one of them, and then Nozipho appeared and interrupted his thoughts.

'Come little brother, we have work to do.'

Together they skipped down to the stream, filled the gourds, and within the hour Mondli's party was breaking camp and Mondli's mind was clearing. As he led his family across the river, one idea dominating his thoughts, the King, he had not taken a wife this year and the slayers, the King had not ordered them to execute anyone. He could see that King Mpande kaSenzangakhona was losing his grip and he could see that Cetshwayo kaMpande would soon be King. Then what?

Chapter 4

Four more Reed Dance ceremonies came and went the most recent no more than a month earlier and this time the King did take a wife. Cetshwayo succeeded his father, took his place on the leopard skin throne, picked out a wife and sent his slayers to execute wrongdoers. The signal was strong, the people knew they had a King who would rule with the strength and cunning of a lion and they quietly shuddered.

Nkosinathi was still too young to understand the change to the Zulu kingdom and sitting cross-legged on a small knoll overlooking the pasture he chewed on a small piece of dried meat. The goats in his care seemed content, grazing steadily on the short stubby grass left behind by the cattle. Most of Mondli's goatherds were brown and white but some were black and white, prized, not only for the meat and milk they produced but also for the pattern of their hides. He imagined his first warrior's shield, made from one of these black and white goatskins, small compared to the war shields of the men, but good enough for him to learn to fight like a warrior.

He tore off a piece of meat from the strip in his hand with his strong white teeth, his clear dark eyes scanning the pasture as he ate. In the distance, he could see his father's cattle, some just black dots stretching almost as far as he could see. His father was a wealthy man, possessing over four hundred head of cattle, able to support four wives and more than twenty children and it was the job of his sons to look after the herd.

Nkosinathi was ten years old; too young to look after the cattle but together with other boys of his age, he looked after the goatherd. It was the start of his journey into manhood and in a few years, when he was old enough he would be trusted with the cattle. As a youngster he had lived in his mother's hut but tradition dictated that when he was ten he would move into the hut with the older boys and it was not long before that Mondli had made a surprise visit to his mother's hut, calling Nkosinathi to come to him.

'Nkosinathi, you are no longer a child, it is time for you to join the other boys. Tomorrow you will go to the boy's hut to begin looking after the goatherd, learn the ways of the land. Find two good fighting sticks and soon you shall have your first shield. Go now, tell your mother, gather your things together', said Mondli with a rare smile.

The head of the village was proud of all of his sons and Nkosinathi was no exception. With so many wives and children, he did not spend much time with the younger boys, mixing instead with his eldest sons and the older men of the extended family, but it gave him pleasure to watch the younger ones take their place in the community. He remembered his own youth, how he had learned to look after the herd for his father and then the arrival of the King's messenger. All Zulu youths yearned for that day, the day when the king commanded them to report to the Royal Kraal and from that day forth their lives were in his hands.

Pickpockets and Zulus

From all across the kingdom young men of the same age would receive the call to congregate outside the Royal iKhanda, wait for the King to inaugurate a new regiment and then kill a black bull from the King's herd with their bare hands. They would feast, slaughter more animals with similarly marked skins and from them make their distinctive black and white regimental shields. Mondli's regiment was the iNdabankhulu and he remembered with pride how the regiment had served the King, destroying enemies and pushing out the nation's frontiers. All this, he told his son, was to be his destiny but first he must serve his father.

Nkosinathi chewed on the dried meat and yawned, more in boredom than from tiredness having squatted in the same place all morning and he was running out of daydreams. He looked around at the goats still happily munching away; at least they were all still there. If any went missing, he would receive a beating from the other boy's and he had no wish for that to happen. In the near distance, he could see Mapita standing amongst the small group of goats in his charge, waving his fighting sticks in mock battle with an imaginary enemy.

Plucking a wide flat leaf of grass, Nkosinathi clamped it firmly between his two thumbs, wrapped his hands together to form a simple acoustic chamber, put his thumbs to his lips, and blew hard. He simultaneously opened and closing the chamber by lifting his fingers and allowing it to emit a high-pitched screech. It had the desired effect, Mapita swung round grinning, it was a call to have some fun and he waved his sticks in the air in acknowledgement. Nkosinathi dropped the blade of grass, reached out for his fighting sticks lying beside him and sprinted across the open ground towards Mapita.

Pickpockets and Zulus

'Hey brave little Nkosinathi, you want to show me how to fight?' goaded Mapita, a year older and standing two or three inches taller.

'I can beat you any time' said Nkosinathi taking the stance taught him by an old man who had seen many battles in his youth. In his old age, the ancient warrior took great pride in teaching the younger boys the proper skills and Nkosinathi had been an attentive student.

Grinning broadly, his white teeth glistening in the bright sunlight, Mapita held out his sticks, one in each hand matching Nkosinathi. 'I will crack your head little one, prepare yourself for some pain.'

Nkosinathi said nothing, simply watching his opponent's eyes, just as the old man had told him, 'Confidence is a great thing' he had said 'but overconfidence can lead to defeat. Many times have I seen Shaka lead an enemy on, making them believe the Zulu army to be weak and easily defeated, exploiting their over confidence. Then we would draw them into a trap and like lightening we would strike.'

The old man's stories of Shaka inspired Nkosinathi even more to become a warrior, to do the Kings bidding and to kill his enemies. Each day he swept the sticks before him as if in battle but today he had a real enemy to fight. Unexpectedly, Mapita reached out with one of his sticks and administered a short sharp blow to the top of Nkosinathi's head protected only by his tightly curled hair. The speed of the move took the boy completely by surprise and before he had fully recovered he felt a sharp pain in his buttocks as Mapita dodged round him and struck out once more.

'Nkosinathi, you are slow, how can I have sport with you if you are so slow?'

Pickpockets and Zulus

Tears of pain and frustration welled up in Nkosinathi's eyes, dismayed at his inability to respond to the attack and Mapita stood laughing, giving just enough time for Nkosinathi to recover his senses before hitting him once more. Taking up a defensive posture, Nkosinathi brought his sticks up in front of him, protecting his head and focusing on his opponent's eyes, mocking eyes.

'Come on brave little warrior, put up a better fight, you are making it too easy for me.'

Defiantly, Nkosinathi shook both sticks at Mapita, his face contorted in pain and anguish. Why did he not see the sticks until he felt their blows? Confused and angry he lunged at the more skilful Mapita, both sticks flailing, only for him to once more feel blows to his arms and back. This time, too late, he felt one of the sticks pass between his legs and with a sharp twist; Mapita threw him to the ground where he lay helpless, defeated.

'Well, I think you are beaten Nkosinathi. You have a lot to learn about fighting. I don't think the old man has shown you much,' mocked Mapita as he reached out and hauled Nkosinathi to his feet.

'You are cut on your head; here rub some grass into it. Look, your goats have scattered, you had better get them back before anyone sees or you will have more cuts and bruises' laughed Mapita.

Alarmed, Nkosinathi saw his goats wandering off in search of better pasture and as he hastily left the battlefield, he shouted defiantly to Mapita. 'Next time I will fight better, I will beat you',

It was beginning to get dark and Nkosinathi wearily returned to his goats herding them towards the Kraal for the night. His head was throbbing from the fight, his upper right arm and shoulder still hurt him but worse than that was the damage to his self-esteem. As he pushed the last of the goats into the pen, two of the boys from his hut came past already aware of his fight with Mapita and could not resist teasing him.

'Brave warrior, we hear you almost beat Mapita in your very first fight. We will sing your praises tonight,' the first boy sniggered.

'You will be the greatest warrior in the nation one day Nkosinathi,' said the second, a mischievous grin spreading across his face.

Nkosinathi's blood boiled but the pain in his body reminded him that it was probably a good idea to keep quiet. 'One day you will eat those words just as the carrion eat dung,' he said under his breath.

Still laughing the two boys left him with his anger and frustration, a fight with Nkosinathi the last thing on their minds, he was no match for the two of them.

'Nkosinathi, you look sad. I have heard about your stick fight today, is this why you look so sad?' said a voice from behind.

Nkosinathi turned to be met by the gaze of the old man, the teacher who had promised him so much and yet here he was defeated, devastated. 'I could not fight back Ndukwana; he was so quick I could not see the sticks moving.'

'You are young and you have only had one real fight Nkosinathi. Do not forget Mapita is older than you are, bigger than you and he has had many fights with the other boys. I know that he has not won all of his fights and he will have looked at you and thought how easy you were to beat. If you had been bigger and more experienced, he would not have been so arrogant. Go and take your food then come and see me at my fire and we will talk,' said Ndukwana waving him away.

Nkosinathi took his place amongst the other boys already sat around the fire, sitting cross-legged to wait for his sister, Nozipho. Minutes later the girl came to him with to a gourd full of mealie, her eyes shining with obvious pleasure at seeing her brother.

'Big sister, what have you made for me today? It looks like mealie,' he teased, it was always mealie. Sometimes there might be a little beef if their father had decided to butcher a cow, or perhaps a small animal such as a rabbit.

Nozipho was unimpressed by his comment; she was growing up and fast developing a strong mother's instinct. Of all her brothers and sisters, Nkosinathi was the closest to her, she looked out for his welfare, and now she raised her eyes slowly to the top of his head, drawing in her breath at the sight of the dried blood caked in his hair.

'Nkosinathi' she whispered, 'what have you done, has a wild animal attacked you?'

'No sister, I had a fight with Mapita and he beat me many times on the head.'

'Eat this while I go and fetch some water to wash the wound. I will ask mother for some herbs and a potion to make you a better fighter.'

Scurrying away between the huts, she returned a short time later with a pad of soft goatskin and some water and before he could stop her, Nozipho had set about cleansing his matted hair of the dried blood watched by some of the boys sitting opposite. None mocked him or his nurse, they had all been through the initiation of stick fighting, each one had felt the pain of

62

an older and stronger boy's ferocity, they too had bled and their sisters had fussed about them. This first time they said nothing but should Nozipho make a habit of nursing her brother each time he was hurt, then they might mock him.

'Mother says I should rub these herbs into the wound to help it heal,' she said applying the compound and causing Nkosinathi to wince under the pressure of her fingers. 'She says that you should keep this pouch of herbs and use them next time you are hurt in a fight. She says that many times you will feel much pain before you are as expert and as strong as the older boys.'

Nozipho left her brother eating, the pain from his wound beginning to ease and his mind tussling with his defeat. He sighed and then remembered the invitation to Ndukwana's fire; perhaps he should go there and learn from the old man. He found Ndukwana huddled round his fire, an animal skin cloak across his shoulders and a stick in his hand that he used to prod the embers.

'Welcome to my house Nkosinathi, come and sit here by me, tell me more of your defeat today. Do not worry boy, you are young and expected to lose your first battles. Shaka lost his first fights but he thought about his defeats, why he was losing and then he returned to defeat his foes just as you will. He began to dream up new ways of fighting and look what he achieved. I was a warrior in my youth, a warrior in the army of the great King Shaka and I have seen many battles, killed many enemies. You my young friend will grow up to be a fine warrior, I can see it in you already.'

Nkosinathi's eyes opened wide, the old man's words cheering him, and the throbbing in his head eased as he listened.

Pickpockets and Zulus

'The father of the nation told us to believe in the strength of our discipline. Strength and discipline will always defeat enemies. It is the duty of every Zulu boy to grow up to serve the King, to become a strong and obedient warrior. You will become a warrior one day and until then you must practice with your sticks. Fight the shadows as I have shown you and begin to believe in your own invincibility. When the time comes to face an enemy, where death can be the only outcome, it will be you that will triumph.'

The old man fell silent, re-living his own past victories, battles from long ago with the people of the forests, with the white men who came to steal their lands. He remembered his fallen comrades and for several minutes sat in silence, watching as the last of his ghosts disappeared into the flames and then, with some difficulty, forced his aged body to a standing position.

'Come Nkosinathi, let me show you some more moves with the sticks. You must go away and practice them and soon you will win your first battle and then you can come and tell me about it.'

Standing a short distance from the fire, fighting sticks in each hand the old man drilled Nkosinathi in a new aspect in the art of stick fighting. First, he attacked and then he retreated, drawing his opponent on to him, next he showed the attentive boy how to parry the onrush of his opponent. Back and forth, they went on for some time until Ndukwana, exhausted had to sit down to regain his breath and the lesson was over.

'Ha, you are too strong for me already,' said Ndukwana, a glint in his eye. 'Go back to the boys hut and remember this lesson for I have no more to teach you tonight. Perhaps we shall meet again to talk once

more of Shaka and his battles. I will tell you about the
Ndwedwe and their chief Zwide kaLanga, how we fought
them near the White Mfolizi. "*Hamba kahle*" 'go well
my young friend.' A tired gnarled old hand reached out
and patted the top of Nkosinathi's wounded head
making him wince but the old man's eyes, faded with
age did not notice.

The greyness of the pre-dawn spread across the village,
the early morning mist swirled between the rows of huts
as the ghostly forms of Nkosinathi and the other boys
clambered into the goat pen. They could recognise each
individual goat by its markings and before herding them
out to pasture for the day, they made sure none had
gone missing during the night. At the far end of the
central enclosure, the older boys were in amongst the
cattle, giving them their first milking of the day, before
they too led their charges out to graze.

Nkosinathi reached out with one of his sticks,
cajoling his goats in the direction of the gateway when
he saw Ndukwana, wrapped in a blanket sitting cross-
legged outside his hut. The old man lifted his hand
slowly in greeting, his gnarled old fingers spread and
bent with arthritis but still he managed a smile
"*Sawubona*".

"*Sawubona*" replied Nkosinathi tapping the lead goat
on its shoulder and saluting with his stick. Ndukwana
watched the goats and cattle pass by, smiled at the boys
shepherding the animals out of the Kraal and wished
that he could be going with them but he was too old and
could not keep up. Most days he spent sitting outside his
hut, alone with his memories. He had never been a rich
man, serving the King until he was almost forty years

old until finally, the King gave the regiment permission to marry and he had returned to his home kraal. He had endured much in his long life, as a young warrior he had fought in Shaka's army against the Ndwedwe taking from them their lands to the north near the Phongolo River. Then the whites, with their strange facial hair had arrived in wagons pulled by many oxen, a sight that had fascinated the Zulus to begin with but when their guns began to spit fire and death the fascination had turned to hatred. King Dingane had massacred the Boer leader and his followers at uMgungundlovu, and later attacked their encampments in the foothills of the uKhahlamba and he, Ndukwana, had been there.

His heart felt heavy as he remembered his sweetheart, Zanele. He had loved her but he was too poor to afford the bride price her father demanded and so, with a heavy heart, he had married the widow of one of his brothers and now, she was dead and her children had left the village. He was alone; his only solace was that the daughters had fetched a good price in cattle when they had married. He had thirty head mixed in with the main herd, and the women of the village looked after him, bringing him food and sending girls to clean his hut but he knew that he was becoming a burden. He had not visited the King's Kraal for several years and he knew it would not be long before they came for him.

It was sooner than the old man realized for later that same day, when the village was quiet, the boys and cattle out on the veldt and the women working in the fields four warriors arrived at the entrance to his hut.

Pickpockets and Zulus

'Ndukwana, we have come from the King he has decreed that we *send you home*. Come with us,' said one.

It was futile to resist, how could an old man like him escape the clutches of these strong young men. As a young warrior, he himself had sent old people home, to be with their ancestors, not one had escaped, and so, looking straight ahead, he resigned himself to his fate and shakily got to his feet. Still the proud Zulu warrior he was unable to resist the soldiers as they took hold of his arms, two of them lifting him so that his feet barely touched the ground, sweeping him out of the compound and towards the river.

He hardly felt the pain in his arms as they dragged him up to a bluff overlooking a wide deep lagoon. On the very edge of the low cliff, they held him firm and one of them took a prepared concoction from a moleskin pouch fastened to his waist, scattering the mixture of herbs and dried entrails onto the surface of the water. Ndukwana gritted his teeth, his old heart pumped blood and adrenalin around his system for the last time as he faced his impending death with the courage and resignation of a true Zulu warrior.

'You have not been seen by the King for a long time Ndukwana. He has decreed that we send you home. He says you have been a loyal and trusted servant and he salutes you.'

For the King to say such words was an honour in itself, it made Ndukwana feel that his life was complete and he was grateful for some recognition. Stiffening his body in anticipation, he faced the inevitable as the leader of the group nodded to the soldiers and Ndukwana's captors lowered him roughly to his knees.

Quickly they moved aside and behind the old man a warrior lifted his polished knobkerrie high above his head and for Ndukwana it seemed that time stood still. In that split second he re-lived his youth, the battles he had fought with the regiment, the parades in front of the king but before any more memories flooded back a swift, powerful blow from the knobkerrie smashed through his thinning skull. Slipping forward, his dead body's own momentum carried it over the edge of the low cliff, sliding down its sheer side and into the murky depths. The water opened its arms to receive him, closing again over his body as it entered the lagoon, sending ripples far across to the opposite shore and drawing the attention of a float of resting Saurians.

The smell of for Ndukwana's blood intoxicated the crocodiles and slowly two large males began to thrash their tails back and forth, sliding from the muddy bank and into the water. Moving imperceptibly just below the water's surface, they crossed the expanse towards Ndukwana's body, face down and half submerged. With his arms outstretched, the old man's body made an easy target for the two reptilians to clamp him in their murderous jaws and spin wildly, tearing the corpse limb from limb. The feeding frenzy lasted no more than a few minutes leaving the water red with blood, all that was left of the old man.

Chapter 5

Holding a piece of chalk loosely between his fingers, Georgie concentrated hard as he meticulously copied the letters of the alphabet onto his slate. Around him the rest of the children were doing the same, until one little girl sitting by the open window let out a howl.

'Gaw blimey, can you smell that!' she exclaimed.

Georgie looked up, his nostrils flaring as the pungent air drifting across the room towards him, the stench of open sewers and rotting vegetation and it began to make him feel that he might vomit. After weeks of heavy rain, the Thames had overflowed at Lambeth and Rotherhithe, a large area of the South Bank was underwater, raw sewage and mud had spread like a spider's web through the low lying streets and the stench had finally reached across the river to Spitalfields.

'To be sure children, 'tis an awful smell coming through the window,' said Father McManus entering the room. 'Missus Kavanagh, would you mind if I closed the widow for a while? I'm sure the children will work better with that smell out of the way.'

'I was just thinking the same. Will there be a plague this year Father?'

'I don't know, we can't rule it out. We are far enough away here in Spitalfields I think, though my colleague;

Father Donnelly, will have his work cut out across the river.'

The priest walked to the window and pulled up the sash, locked it in place and turned towards the children. Twelve boys and girls assembled in Mrs Kavanagh's living room, as they did every Sunday to gain a few hours of rudimentary education, children of poor families, nine or ten years old and forced to work during the week to supplement their parent's meagre incomes.

Mrs Kavanagh's husband was an Irish gang master, a robust barrel chested man who controlled around fifty labourers unloading ships in the port of London and he had been moderately successful. He lived with his wife and three daughters in a large terraced house and luckily for Father McManus, Mrs Kavanagh was a religious woman. She was a committed Catholic and she had brow beaten her husband into allowing Father McManus to hold his Sunday services at their house.

'Children, finish the letter you are writing, wipe your slates clean and bring them to me before you leave,' said Mrs Kavanagh. 'I want you to think about what you have learned today, you can recite the alphabet quietly to yourselves during the week and next Sunday we will have a treat.'

The children looked up eagerly, a treat, what treat could she have in store for them? Their young lives were devoid of treats of any kind and the mere mention of something pleasant was good news indeed.

'Next week we will have reading practice and you can all hold the book in your own hands' Mrs Kavanagh said smiling.

The young faces returned her gaze with disappointed looks. Only Georgie, the oldest, smiling back because he could read a little and he enjoyed the stories. 'Which book would it be?' he wondered, the book of fairy tales was his favourite, but that only came out at Christmas...no it would probably be the one about Jesus.

'Children bring your slates to me and you can go and don't forget to recite the alphabet.'

'No missus they mumbled as one by one the laid their newly wiped slates on the table and wandered out of the room. Georgie was tired from his schoolwork and Maude was deep in thought as they said their goodbyes to Father McManus, Mrs Kavanagh and the other parishioners. Since her husband's death, Maud no longer received a part of his pay and she was finding it hard to support them both on the money she earned as a seamstress. The lack of money had forced them to move from the tenement block to a dingy cellar in one of the cheaper Rookeries. The room was damp at the best of times and lacked sunlight except for one or two hours a day when it shone through the only window protruding no more than a foot or so above the ground but at least she had managed to persuade a street locksmith to take Georgie on as his assistant. The boy spent his days pulling the man's handcart, knocking on doors to proclaim their services and the few pence he earned helped a little but still she found life a struggle.

Georgie had taken to the work, the locksmith and his trade fascinating him and he had grown strong pulling the cart. After drumming up business, Georgie would stand and watch his master sharpening knives, scissors and fashioning keys from the blanks he carried on the barrow. He would watch as the old man gripped small pieces of metal in his vice, sawing and filing them until in no time at all he had copied the key. If a key had been lost then he would use his special keys to expertly open the lock and fashion a new one and if business were slow, the locksmith would let Georgie have a go, teach him a few rudiments of key making and metalworking. They were long hours for a twelve-year-old boy, his mother could ill afford proper schooling and so the only chance Georgie had of learning was the Sunday school in Mrs. Kavanagh's house.

It began to rain and Maude pulled her shawl more tightly around her shoulders. 'Come along Georgie, we don't want to get wet, we will never dry our clothes. We can have some stewed ox cheek and potatoes tonight. I have some firewood so we can have a hot meal. What do you say to that?'

Most days they lived on just bread and dripping or sometimes his mother might boil a few potatoes. The only time he had a proper hot meal was on Sundays or when they visited Aunt Jane and the thought of a hot meal made his mouth water. They made their way past people returning from Sunday worship, street urchins and beggars, on street corners small groups of men chatted, whiling away the few hours of relaxation their toil allowed them and from the public houses came the sound of drunken laughter. In a few hours, it would be dark and then night people would emerge in search of victims but for the moment Maude and Georgie were safe enough. It was still daylight and the streets were emptying because of the rain. They were too poor to rob, they had nothing worth taking and the local rogues would most probably leave them alone.

Rounding the corner into their street Maude caught her breath, a girl she recognized was sitting on the wall outside the rookery, Ellen, her niece.

Pickpockets and Zulus

'Look, Ellen, why is she sitting on our wall? Something must be wrong. Ellen,' Maude called out.

'Oh Aunt Maude, it's the flood,' said the girl jumping down from the wall and running towards them. 'We've been flooded and mother sent me to ask if we can stay with you for a few days until the waters go down.'

'Where is your mother Ellen, where are your brothers?'

'They're at 'ome trying to save our things. The flood started last night in the street and today it came into the 'ouse. The water is up to the chairs,' said the girl, looking forlornly at her aunt.

Ellen was two years older than Georgie, a good-looking girl with striking blue eyes, jet-black hair and a strong personality. She was an expert pickpocket, working the streets with her brothers and wayward father and she was the one who brought in most of the family's income. Her elder brother had carried that burden for the past year or two but Billy was spreading his wings, mixing with other young villains and hardly coming home. Her younger brother, James, was a good boy but he was not in the same class as his sister when it came to lifting purses and silk handkerchiefs. Ellen was the real expert, and it fell to her to provide for the rest of them.

'Where is your father?'

Ellen knew the reason for the question. 'No need to worry Aunt Maude, he isn't at 'ome, said he was going away 'till the flood had gone and the 'ouse was liveable again. He gave mother some money and just left.'

'We must leave, it will be dark in an hour or so and it will not be safe on the streets. Georgie and me have to go to work tomorrow so we 'ad better take a blanket each and stay with your mother tonight. We can 'elp but we must come back early in the morning. You and your mother and little Jimmy can come with us and stay for a few days. Where's Billy, will he want to come as well?'

'No need to worry about our Billy, he can look after himself.'

Maude did not want to worry about Ellen's elder brother Billy; he was too much like his father. At sixteen years old, almost a man, he was treading in his father's footsteps committing petty thefts and house breaking. Billy junior was trouble.

'Right, let's get over to your mother and see what we can do,' said Maude.

Her sister had been there for her when she had fallen on hard times and she would repay that kindness come what may. Hastily she gathered up some blankets, wrapped the half loaf of bread she had for their supper in an old newspaper, gave it to Ellen to carry and Georgie picked up the bundle of blankets.

For the next hour, in the gathering gloom, they made the journey across the bridge to Lambeth, walking through ankle deep water and mud, the stench leaving them close to vomiting. Finally, they turned into Tanner Street, and Maude could see the devastation the flooding had caused, the torrent totally swamping those unfortunates living in the cellars, their meagre belongings littering the pavement. Luckily, her sister's home consisted of two rooms on the ground floor and Maude could see her struggling with a mattress.

'Jane, are you all right?'

'Oh Maude, I am so glad you are here, we're managing' better than this morning. Better, since that no good 'usband of mine decided to bugger off. 'Ere 'elp me with this mattress will you. Pity about the rain it was nearly dry.'

Maude rolled up her sleeves and though slightly built, she was strong and together the two women dragged the mattress back in the only bedroom.

'Oh I am sorry,' said Maude, as she looked round at the muddy line left by the flood. 'At least the water has gone and you have got rid of some of the mud.'

'Isn't all mud, smell that horrible stink,' said Jane screwing her nose up. 'That window's broken as well. Look, that's where the rain got in and soaked the mattress.

'Come on, give me some rags and I'll help you clean this slime off the walls and floor and then at least the smell won't be so bad. Here Georgie take the pail out to the tap in the yard and see if you can get some water to clean this floor,' said Maude.

Georgie picked up the old tin bowl from behind the door and set off in search of some clean water whilst the two women started on the floor. Ellen and her brother picked up some rags and began wiping down the chairs and table in the second room and after two hours of exhausting work they returned some semblance of order to the dwelling.

'I put some wood up here on the shelf with our food. It's still dry so I can make a fire and boil the kettle, make some tea if you like,' said Jane, reaching up.

After a long half hour, the kettle finally boiled and Jane was able to make a pot of tea, Maude cut up the bread she had brought with her and with a chunk of cheese Jane had manage to salvage from the deluge made the best of the situation.

'It's this 'orrible smell I don't like Maude, that's why I sent Ellen to fetch you. We cannot stay here, not until this smell goes anyway. Can we stay with you for a few days? Billy gave me some coppers before he left so we 'ave money for food.'

Maude did not need any convincing, the smell was overpowering and her sister was in need of help, but as she settled down for the night on the damp mattress she wondered how they would all fit into her and Georgie's tiny room. At least Billy Tyndal and his eldest son would not be staying with her she thought as her eyes closed and she slid down the dark slope into a fitful sleep.

Within seconds, it seemed, Maude's eyes were opening again, the first stirrings of dawn were trickling through the cracked windowpane, but it wasn't the grey light of the dawn that had disturbed her. Someone was entering the room, the door creaked and she could hear a muffled sound of feet on the bare wooden floor and then a faint clanking noise reached her ears and she saw a shadow flitting across the room.

'Who's there?' she demanded, fully awake.

'It's alright, it's me Billy' came a voice from the murk.

'What are you doing, what time is it?'

'The knocker upper isn't about yet so it's before six and it gets light around five so work it out for yourself mother,' said the voice with a hint of sarcasm in it.

'I must get up. Oh I'm all damp from that mattress. What are you doing coming in so late?'

'Oh it's you auntie, bin' doin' a bit of work,' said young Billy.

Maude knew better than to ask too many questions. Goodness knows why her sister had fallen for such a wastrel as Billy Tyndal and now it looked as if her eldest son was following his father's example.

'Georgie, wake up' said Maude giving her son a gentle shake.

'It's all right mother, I'm awake.'

Georgie had woken first, feeling rather than hearing his cousin twist the handle of the door. He had been fully alert before the door was even half-open and his young eyes had easily pierced the gloom, recognising cousin Billy as he came through the doorway.

'What's that?' demanded Jane rising from the mattress to confront her son.

Billy looked sheepishly at his mother. 'Done a job last night and got some fine silver.'

'let's have a look then,' said Jane reaching out to open the neck of the sack and peer inside. 'Hey, this looks good stuff,' she said, pulling out a silver candlestick and placing it on the floor, then another and finally a set of silver condiments and a milk jug. 'Where d'you get these from?'

'Went up West last night with Arnold and Freddie Gosling, Arnold 'as a girl in one 'o them big houses on Brompton Road. She let 'im in for a sandwich an' a glass 'o beer an' a bit 'o this an' that I 'spect. The master was out to the theatre 'an whilst he kept 'er occupied, me an' Freddie sneaked in and 'ad a good look round. We 'ad one o the best jobs ever last night, must 'ave cleared twenty pounds each at least. Poor 'gel's in for it when her master finds out. Still she knows nothing so she won't be lyin' when she says so.' Anyway, I only came home to grab some sleep before I get this stuff fenced. What are you and Georgie doin' 'ere Aunt Maude?'

Pickpockets and Zulus

'They came to help clear up. More than you or your father could manage. We are going to stay with your Aunt Maude for a few days until this smell clears a bit an' things dry out. What are you going to do? Maude hasn't enough room for you as well'

'No need to worry about me mother, I will manage all right. I will go and sell this silver an' come back 'ere for a few days, keep an eye on fings. I'll come to Spitalfields tomorrow to see me old mum an' give 'er a few bob to keep 'er going. Might even find dad and bring 'im along' he said with a twinkle in his eye, knowing very well how much Maude disliked his father, even his mother preferred him only in small doses. Nevertheless, Billy Tyndal senior was his dad and he had taught him all he knew about thieving and fencing and without this knowledge; he would be doing a backbreaking job twelve hours a day with hardly a ha'penny to his name. No, to him his father was a man to look up to.

Georgie, Ellen and young Jimmy rose from their make shift beds and gathered together the few belongings they had, Jane and Maude stood the mattress up against the wall and young Billy took his swag into the adjoining room, pulled a chair up to the fireplace with its long dead embers and settled down. With his feet resting on the hearth he was soon snoring heavily and the two women, followed by the children, left him to make the journey back across the river.

'Jane, me and Georgie 'ave to go to work. Can you look after things 'ere for us 'till I get back tonight?'

'Course I will darlin', 'ere, take this,' said Jane placing three half pennies in Maude's hand, 'and here's a penny for you Georgie. You can both get something to eat today, it's a thank you for helping us.'

Pickpockets and Zulus

Georgie and his mother gratefully accepted the money because other than the bread and cheese, they had eaten very little in almost twenty-four hours and both had a hard day's work ahead of them. A vacancy had occurred and for the past three months Maude had worked in Daniel Fremeaux's workshop, a job that paid a little more than working from home and she could ill afford to lose it.

'Sorry I'm late' she said to the overseer as she rushed into the workshop, 'my sister was flooded out and I spent yesterday evening helping her clear up. We didn't dare come back home in the dark.'

The woman, dressed in a starched bodice with a high collar looked sternly at Maude.

'I shall have to dock your wages you know that don't you?'

'Y...yes ma'am' stuttered Maude, averting the woman's gaze.

The woman was Daniel Fremeaux's sister who, for all her sternness, was a good Christian woman. She had watched Maude progress from re-working garments at home to manufacturing them in the workshop, noticed how clever and industrious she was and Daniela was only too aware it was the work of women like Maude that helped her and her brother make their comfortable living.

Most of the women in the workshop lived from hand to mouth in run down and unhealthy dwellings earning what they could when work was available. Seamstresses were ten a penny these days but exceptional ones like Maude were far and few between and they needed workers like Maude to give their garments that something extra that would attract the well to do buyers.

'Go to your sewing machine Maude, you have never been late before so perhaps we will say no more about it.'

'Thank you ma'am,' said Maude with relief as she made her way past the other workers, busy winding the handles of their sewing machines and glancing at her from the corners of their eyes as she passed. Reaching her own workbench, she picked up the Frock Coat she was close to finishing and carefully looked it over. She had only to hand stitch the silk lapels to complete the garment and as she searched in her drawer for the paper pattern, she called to the boy whose job it was to provide the women with their raw materials.

'Michael, fetch me some black silk will you.'

'Right 'oh' he said, shuffling off to the store room.

Maude turned her attention back to the pattern and searched for her small scissors suddenly wincing with discomfort. What was that feeling in her stomach? It must be hunger pangs she thought, goodness she had suffered enough of those during the past few years, but this did feel a little different.

For the next two hours, she fashioned the silk lapels and stitched them on with fine silk thread, so cleverly that it was impossible to see her stitching except in the strongest of sunlight. She cast her eye over the seams and the buttonholes looking for any imperfection and, satisfied, she called out.'

'Miss Fremeaux, the frock coat is finished.'

Daniela Fremeaux came to Maude's bench to inspect the garment Maude had spread out for her, casting her eye along the seams, eyeing the stitching and found no fault with Maude's work. Maude had produced a garment good enough to clothe the most noble of

80

gentlemen, she was an asset to the firm and she was glad she had not scolded her too severely for her lateness.

'That is a very good job Maude, we have orders for two more of these from a gentleman who is a Member of Parliament and because this is such a good job and he is an important client, you can make those as well. I have his measurements in my desk. Wait while I get them for you. Michael, you can take this coat to be wrapped ready for delivery.'

Maude began to clear her bench ready to start her next job. She reached across to pick up some off cuts of cloth when the pain gripped her like a vice, squeezing her lower abdomen until she cried out, distracting the girls working nearby.

'What's wrong Maude?' said one girl, 'not pregnant again are you, didn't know you 'ad a fella.'

'Shut up you stupid thing. Of course I'm not pregnant; it's just hunger pangs.'

The girl grinned, her blackened teeth showing through her pale thin lips, her tousled hair laying limp across her face and covering one eye, but with the other she spotted Daniela and quickly returned to her work.

'Here are the measurements Maude, the tailor is cutting the cloth for you and it should be ready soon.'

'Thank you ma'am,' said Maude, wincing as the pain shot through her once more forcing her to grip the edge of the bench to steady herself.

'What's the matter Maude, you look ill?'

'I'm just 'ungry ma'am, didn't eat much yesterday and slept badly.' She winced again as the pain increased.

'You're not well, go home for the rest of the day you can't work properly in that condition,' said Daniela, suspicious of Maude's symptoms. She had seen them before and did not believe that they were simply hunger pangs and she did not want Maude in the workshop. 'Don't worry about your job Maude; it will still be here when you return. Go home to bed for a while and get yourself well.'

'Thank you ma'am' said Maude, needing little encouragement. The pain was getting worse and she could feel a movement in her lower abdomen. Grabbing at her shawl, she threw it untidily across her shoulders and made her way past the other girls who looked anxiously on and hurried home as fast as she could. Reaching the Rookery she began to wonder herself if it was more than simply hunger pains as she made for the plank of wood with its row holes located over the open sewer.

The pain was excruciating and she must have passed out, because she found herself slumped on the floor and struggling to her feet, she managed, with difficulty, to reach the door to her room, pushing it open to collapse on to the hard wooden floor.

'Maude, what is the matter?' said her sister, shocked at her sudden appearance.

'I...I don't feel well.'

Jane could see that she wasn't well, the paleness of her skin, its coldness and as she helped her sister onto the bed. Maude's eyes rolled in their sockets sending a clear and terrifying message to Jane who had seen the illness before, seen whole families succumb. A killer of rich and poor alike, it was the dropsy.

Quickly Jane helped Maude off with her outer garments, laid her on the bed and lit the primitive wood burning stove to try to boil some water but it was little more than lukewarm when she brought it to bathe her sister's face and neck.

'Jimmy, go and find your sister. Go and tell her to find your father and bring him here as soon as she can. Aunt Maude is ill and we need 'elp. She'll be down Whitechapel towards Mile End and your father is probably in The Prospect.'

Ellen was walking slowly along the pavement in the busier part of Whitechapel Road, searching for a victim, a lone woman out shopping with baskets so full she could hardly carry them. Her ploy was to offer her help in carrying these heavy loads for a farthing or halfpenny reward, chatting to the woman as they walked, putting her at her ease. Her victims were often trusted servants out shopping for their mistress or older women struggling with heavy bags, grateful for some relief and willing to give her a ha'penny. But Ellen was after more than that.

'Ere Missus. Let me carry your basket for you,' she called out to a large middle-aged woman.

The woman, dressed in good clothes carried a wickerwork basket piled high with vegetables her face betraying her exertions, just the sort of person Ellen was looking for.

'Carry your basket for you missus,' said Ellen cheekily.

'How much to carry the basket as far as Duckett Street?'

'As much as you want to give me missus,' replied Ellen.

'All right I will give you a ha'penny if you can carry it that far.'

Ellen held out both arms to take the basket off her but the woman wasn't finished with shopping and beckoned her to follow her into a butcher's shop. Ellen was not surprised that the woman was prepared to pay for help carrying such a burden to Duckett Street, why, it was almost half a mile away but Ellen did not intend to complete the journey.

After buying a pair of hares and some eggs they eventually set off towards Duckett Street, the woman with the hares whilst Ellen carried the vegetable filled basket. How the woman would have managed to carry all this on her own Ellen could not begin to wonder. Perhaps she hired an urchin every time she went shopping. Hmm..., she thought, that's why she was so relaxed about hiring her, she did it regularly and she guessed that the woman might be sharper than she looked. Better be careful, bide her time and wait her chance.

Her chance soon arrived in the form of her younger brother, Jimmy.

'Ellen' he shouted from across the street. She did not hear him at first, the noise of a horse drawn tram trundling by drowning out his cry. James could see his sister had not heard him and came closer bellowing her name once more and this time she looked at him.

'It's Aunt Maude, she is ill, mother says you 'ave to go and find dad and bring 'im 'ome.'

'Oh, what?' Ellen said with some surprise and putting the basket down.

'What are you doing girl?'

'I 'ave to go ma'am, something is up,' she said pointing to Jimmy waving his hands on the far side of the street. The woman turned to look, her attention taken by the franticly waving Jimmy.

Ellen seized the moment, she had noticed the woman kept her purse in her coat pocket and could see it protruding slightly. She made her move, stepped close to the woman and deftly lifted the purse from the pocket, slipping it inside her vest and with her heart beating violently resumed her position beside the basket.

'Sorry ma'am, but I 'ave to go now 'fanks for lettin' me carry your basket. Don't bother wiv the ha'penny,' she said leaving the woman looking bemused.

Experience told her she might only have seconds before the alarm sounded, the woman would realize her purse was gone and who had taken it. Crossing the street in double quick time Ellen dodged horse drawn carts and pedestrians alike and reaching the other side grabbed hold of Jimmy's hand.

'Oi, let go of me', said Jimmy indignantly.

'Shut up stupid, we've to get as far from 'er as quick as we can. I 'ave 'er purse in me vest, come on, run.'

Even before they had turned away, the shrill sound of a police whistle reached Ellen's ears and she knew the chase was on. As soon as she had run off, the woman had instinctively felt for her purse and realised that the urchin girl had taken it and she had called to a nearby policeman for help. The sound of the whistle spurred Ellen on; she dragged the still protesting Jimmy down back alleys and across streets jammed with traffic, dodging between the horses until, out of breath, their legs tight with fatigue they fetched up near the river and slumped against a tree gasping for breath.

'Blimey Ellen, you can run when the Peelers are after you. Wot you been up to?'

'This' she said, pulling the purse from her grimy vest and holding it before her brother's eyes. Jimmy took a swipe at it but his sister knew him only too well and had expected some sort of reaction like that. Both he and Billy junior always tried to take from her anything in her possession they fancied, but she had learned to resist and fighting with them had made her tough.

'Not so fast you, if you be'ave I'll give you something but if you try that again I'll smack you. 'Ere, let's 'ave a look inside.'

She pulled the drawstring of the purse and tipped the contents into her hand, some pennies, halfpennies and silver sixpences, but that was all. Ellen's face dropped, she was disappointed with her haul. She should have known that the more the woman spent the less there was to steal.

'Ere, 'old yer 'and out Jimmy', she said giving him three pennies, 'that'll 'ave to do fer now.'

Jimmy looked at the coins in his hand a grin spreading across his face. Three pence was a lot to him and he wasn't the least bit disappointed.

'Now, tell me, what were you shouting about mother and Aunt Maude?'

'Aunt Maude is very ill and mother finks she might die. She sent me to tell you to find dad, you 'ave to tell 'im to come quick she says.'

'Alright then, 'e'll be down the Prospect I expect or in one 'o them other waterfront pubs I'll bet. I will go down there and ask about. You get off home and help mother an' I'll be back before dark.

Pickpockets and Zulus

They stood up and walked together as far as Whitechapel High Street before parting company, Ellen to peer through the grimy windows of the public houses her father frequented and James to return to the Rookery and had almost reached the entrance when he saw Georgie turn the corner on his way home from work.

'Now then Jimmy boy what are you up to,' asked Georgie seeing the guilty look on the boys grubby face.

'It's Aunt Maude', he blurted out 'mother says she's dying.'

The statement hit Georgie like a bombshell making him run up the steps into the building and to throw open the door to their room in panic. His worst fears were realised, his mother lay on the bed her face ashen, her hair matted and dank and her eyes closed as if already in death. Hardly recognising the mother he had last seen only hours before Georgie reached out and grasped her limp hand.

'Mother, Mother!' he cried out in anguish, 'Mother!'

From the chair in the corner of the room where she had kept a vigil, his Aunt Jane rose to put a comforting arm around his shoulders.

'Aunt Jane, what's wrong, what's happened to my mother?'

'It's the dropsy Georgie, your mother's got the dropsy, and I don't think she will see the day out. I'm sorry young 'un.'

She let her arm slip off his shoulder as Georgie leaned forward, sinking to his knees, and Maude opened her eyes. She had hung on just long enough to see her little boy for the last time and though she did not really see him, knowing that he was there was a great comfort in her final moments and in a barely audible whisper, she said. 'Georgie, I haven't got long in this world. I love you.'

Georgie gripped his mother's hand, tears rolled down his cheeks and he whispered, 'I love you mother, don't go, stay with me.'

But it was no use, she lingered a while longer and as the night began to close in her breathing became more shallow, her heartbeat slowed and, inexorably, she slipped away leaving Georgie alone in the world.

Chapter 6

The small group stood around the open grave with heads bowed as the pallbearers carefully lowered the cheap wooden coffin into the ground. Father McManus stood to one side, his face sorrowful, dismayed at the death of one of his favourite parishioners. Maude and Georgie brought rays of sunshine to their weekly gatherings, she was a young woman who, no matter how hard her lot, always had a good word for everyone and now they were burying her.

Shaking his head slowly from side to side, he quietly mumbled a short prayer; with fingers bent, he made the sign of the cross, and as the pallbearers released their load, he began the committal, a ceremony he had performed so many times and had little trouble reciting from memory. In a final act, he reached down, picked up a handful of the dark earth and sprinkled it over the coffin lid.

'Ashes to ashes, dust to dust...'

The gravedigger lifted his shovel and began heaping the loose earth on top of the coffin, Maude was gone and poor little Georgie was an orphan and it was time for the small crowd of mourners to say their final goodbyes, Jane, Georgie, Ellen, James and Daniel Fremeaux together with two of Maude's friends from the Rookery. Of Billy Tyndal and his eldest son, there was not a sign.

'God bless you all,' said the priest turning towards Jane. 'I will leave you in peace now.'

'Thank you Father,' said Jane handing him the fee for his services. 'It was a wonderful send-off you gave her, I'm sure she has gone straight to 'eaven.'

'Indeed she has, indeed she has,' murmured Farther McManus pocketing the money. It was a sad occasion and he knew how difficult it was for the poor to raise money for a decent burial but he had to make a living just like everyone else. He said a few more warming words to the congregation and took his leave, his black cloak flowing wildly behind him as he went.

Walking over to Jane Daniel Fremeaux lifted his hat in a sign of respect. 'I'm so sorry you have lost your sister, she was my best worker you know, it's such a shame,' he said patting Georgie on the head and then he too was gone.

'Ere, there's nothing we can do now, you'll just 'ave to be brave Georgie boy,' said Jane wiping the tears from his cheeks. 'Don't know what we're going to do with you though, another mouth to feed an' no more money coming in will be 'ard but we can't leave you on the street can we? You're family.'

Ellen came to Georgie's side and held his hand. 'We'll look after 'im ma, don't you worry, we'll manage like ma says Georgie, your family.'

Jane looked at her daughter, she was a strange one young Ellen, always cheerful, nothing seemed to bother her and she was the best thief in the family. Perhaps she was right they would manage, Georgie was a strong lad and he had a job with the knife and scissor grinder.

Then she realised that he would not be able to carry on the trade because they lived across the river and it would be too far for him to travel every day. No, Billy would have to teach him a new trade to earn his keep.

Crossing the bridge leading into Lambeth, Jane and the children eventually reached the two dank rooms they called home and lying on the bed in the front room they found Billy Tyndal senior fast asleep and snoring his head off. The smell of stale alcohol rose like the morning mist from his prostrate form and Jane knew it would be dangerous to wake him in such a state. Likely, he would become violent and lash out at her and the children and he did not yet know that Georgie was coming to live with them.

'Be quiet, go in there and sit quietly,' she said in a whisper. 'I'll see what we have to eat and make some broth.'

Jimmy and Ellen led Georgie on tiptoe past their sleeping father and into the back room, closing the door so as not to disturb him and all seemed well until Ellen tripped over in the gloom and Billy Tyndal's eyes flickered into life.

'Wha... what's that' he called out, 'who's there.' He sniffed and rolled over, still unaware of the cause of the disturbance and for several seconds he laid still, his bloodshot eyes scanning the room until they fixed upon Jane standing not six feet from him.

'You woman, what d'ya think you're doing waking me up?' he said as his face contorted into a menacing sneer. He swung his feet over the bed and onto the floor ready to stand up, and Jane felt afraid, she had seen that look before.

'I bin to Maude's burial, I bin wiv the kids,' she piped up trying to take his mind off the violence he was contemplating. 'It was a nice funeral, fanks for giving me the money to pay for it; it was a lovely send-off she 'ad.'

It had cost Billy some of his drinking money and coupled with his throbbing headache the thought induced a rage and Jane could see what was coming.

'F...father McManus said you are a wonderful, generous man to pay for Maude's burial and said your place in 'eaven is assured,' she stammered, trying to calm him down and prevent him from thrashing her. 'Ere, why don't I make us all a nice 'ot broth.'

'Aye, do that you bitch before I knock the living daylights out of you,' he growled slipping on his shoes and getting to his feet. 'Where's Ellen and Jimmy?'

'Why, they are just in there, sitting quiet like, so as not to disturb you.'

'Hmm...' he grunted, feeling pleased that at least the priest had acknowledged his sacrifice, the thought helping his anger to subside. He went to the door of the adjoining room and pulled it open to reveal the three urchins sitting quietly on the grubby bed that almost filled the room. 'Oi, what's Georgie doin' 'ere?'

Before Jane could think up a plausible answer, Ellen piped up. 'He is coming to live with us dad; he is an orphan now an' got nowhere to go.'

That did it. 'What!' shouted Billy, 'he's coming to live with us, another mouth to feed and us as poor as church mice.' He turned towards his wife, took three strides towards her and lashed out with the back of his hand. He raised his hand again but before he had time to hit her again, the door burst open and young Billy, red faced and out of breath burst into the room.

Pickpockets and Zulus

'Peelers are after me, 'ere, stash this,' he said to his father pushing a small hessian sack towards him. 'It's last night's haul, some decent silver and a few pewter plates. I can't stop, if the police 'ave seen me they'll be in 'ere soon as you like. I'm off into 'iding down the far end of Whitechapel with Freddie an' Arnold till the 'ullabaloo quietens down. See ya,' he said scuttling back out of the room to run down the street. In the distance, the sound of a police whistle could be heard and young Billy wasn't hanging around to see if it was him they were after.

Billy senior forgot about Jane and Georgie, looked into the sack and indeed it did look a good haul, more than enough to pay for Maude's funeral and more drink. He grabbed a chair, pulled it towards the centre of the room and climbed upon it, reached for the ceiling and carefully lifted some loose plaster to reveal a small cavity. Hurriedly he stuffed the sack up inside and replaced the plaster, adjusting it until all that remained was a confused jigsaw of cracks. It had always been a safe hiding place and on the two occasions when the Peelers had come looking for stolen goods they had discovered nothing.

'Get me some food women?' he growled, the excitement of his new found wealth overriding the news of their new lodger. He had seen enough to know that his son had made a good haul and he had begun adding up the value of the sack's contents. There were two silver candlesticks, a carriage clock, three or four pewter plates, and a small box – a jewellery box by the look of it. What was in that box? He could only guess for now, but the other items, they might bring in excess of ten pounds and that constituted a good day's work.

Pickpockets and Zulus

'Right you three, out 'ere' he ordered. The children came out from behind the door, Ellen and Jimmy afraid of their father pressing up against the wall and Georgie, bewildered by the actions of his uncle simply followed their example. They stood silently looking at the floor and from behind Billy Tyndall, his wife pleaded with him not to hurt them.

'I'll not touch them an' you'll be alright woman, it was only a tap to keep you in order.' 'Now you three, what are you up to? If you've been burying Aunt Maude then you 'aven't been out thieving and 'ave nothing to show for today. It's a good job young Billy is as good at it as 'e is or we'd be bleedin' starvin.'

The three children dare not move as they watched the bullying master of the house take out his tobacco tin and roll himself a cigarette. 'Ah that's better, good healthy smoke always makes me feel better.'

For a few minutes, Billy sat quietly drawing on the cigarette thinking about the value of young Billy's haul. Yes, it was worth a few quid and if that little box contained some real jewellery, well it might be worth a lot more. That pleased him; it pleased him a lot, so much in fact, he became quite pleasant.

'Ere, 'ave a fag,' he said, offering the tin to Jimmy. 'Give your sister one it will do 'er good, an' give one to Georgie, I've got an idea for 'im.'

Jimmy and Ellen were adept at rolling cigarettes. They had been smoking on and off ever since they could remember and as Jimmy lit his, Ellen gave hers to Georgie, rolling another for herself. 'Pop it in your mouth then Georgie' she said, as she ran her tongue across the glue before the final roll. 'Aven't you smoked before?'

'No' said Georgie, a look of bewilderment on his face. He had watched people smoking many times but his mother had never smoked and so he had never tried to smoke himself.

'Ere' said Ellen taking it from his hand and pushing it between his lips 'go on light it.'

Georgie took the matches from her and scratched one across the roughened paper stuck to the side of the box and with some difficulty managed to light the end of his cigarette, his inexperienced hands allowing the match to burn down until it stung his finger ends.

'Ouch,' he said dropping the cigarette.

Ellen laughed, picked it from the floor, stuck it back in his mouth and struck a second match.

'Go on then, 'ave a drag, like this.' She put her own cigarette to her lips and sucked making it glow and a second or two later she blew the smoke back out.

Georgie tried it. Inhaling the smoke, he felt a strange burning sensation as the fumes entered his lungs for the first time, a shock to his system. He felt dizzy and convulsed into a coughing fit much to the amusement of the others but undeterred he persevered, copying his cousins as they puffed away on their cigarettes. Drawing smoke into his lungs at a slower rate he managed for a while, until he became dizzy once more finally convulsing in a coughing fit. Ellen watched with mild amusement as she finished her cigarette and she was not going to let Georgie's go to waste. Deftly she lifted the half-burned cigarette from Georgie's fingers and finished it herself.

Billy missed the performance with the cigarette, he was still deep in thought and, finally, looking up he said. 'The lads got a lot to learn an' I reckon we're the ones to teach 'im. Starting tomorrow we are going to get young Georgie 'ere to learn the tricks of the trade. Yes, he looks a bit more respectable than you two. We will get 'im some decent clothes with the money from that lot up there, and teach 'im 'ow to get 'old of some fine ladies silk 'ankerchiefs to earn 'is keep.'

The next day, Billy Tyndal senior set to work, showing Georgie how to deftly remove a handkerchief from a ladies pocket. He took his two youngest children and Georgie into a quiet corner of the rookery yard where he told them to act out the parts of the various players. His job was lookout and Ellen, as the most expert, would demonstrate her technique for lifting a handkerchief from a victim's pocket. Georgie watched with some fascination as James acted out the part of the victim while Ellen consistently picked his pocket without him knowing.

After an hour or more, Billy Tyndall showed Georgie how to detect where a purse might be kept and how to distract a person for long enough to take their valuables from them.

'We usually work with Jimmy here as the decoy, he will cause a diversion and then you pick the pocket Georgie my lad. Simple ain't it.'

Georgie wasn't so sure but he tried his hand and this time Ellen acted the part of the victim.

'Roll up roll up, hot chestnuts a penny for six,' called out James and Ellen looked his way.

'Go on, now's your chance,' said Billy.

Georgie sidled up alongside Ellen and reached towards her pocket thinking just how easy it was until

Ellen turned on him, grabbed his arm and shouted, "Stop thief".

Billy Tyndall shouted "police" and grabbed Georgie's arm, startling him further and leaving him unsure of what to do.

'There lad, that's what can happen if you get it wrong. The East End is crawling with peelers these days and we don't want you getting' yourself locked up now do we.'

'Frightened you did we Georgie?' asked Ellen with a grin on her face.

'You need to be careful Georgie, or the Peelers will 'ave you. Now let's try again and this time, before you even think about liftin' a purse, make sure you 'ave an escape route planned. My job is to look out for you three an' if I spots trouble I will warn you. Then scarper as fast as you can,' said Billy.

Repeatedly Georgie practised picking first Ellen's then James's pockets until he was reasonably proficient. Ellen watched with her sharp eyes and each time she felt that Georgie was making a mistake she would rush in and show him the correct way.

'It's about making 'em fink one fing while you do another,' said Ellen. 'It only takes a second and you are off and lost in the crowd but if one of those grownups grabs you then it's trouble and maybe prison. Don't forget that.'

Billy nodded his head in agreement and satisfied that Ellen was training Georgie well enough, left them practising to go and retrieve young Billy's haul from its hiding place. Lowering the sack to the floor, he pulled open the drawstrings and let out a low whistle of exclamation on seeing such a rich haul. There was still the little box to investigate and lifting the silver box from the sack he twisted open the lid and peered inside. 'You 'ave done well son, a proper good haul and these diamond earrings should fetch a pretty penny down at the Prospect.' He placed the box carefully back in the sack and went outside to tell the children he was going out on business and, left to her own devices, Ellen took great pleasure in taking charge, ordering the two boys about as if she were a school ma'am.

'Not like that' she scolded, putting the handkerchief back in her pocket for Georgie to try once more. 'Ere you show 'im Jimmy.'

This time Ellen began acting as if she were looking into shop windows whilst Jimmy walked nonchalantly by, taking his time, lifting the handkerchief just as she leaned over to examine something of interest in the window of the imaginary shop. Deftly James slipped his hand into Ellen's pocket and out came the handkerchief and as quick as a flash he stuffed it into his own pocket before walking briskly away.

'Ave you done it yet?' squawked Ellen.

'Course I 'ave!'

Ellen turned to Georgie. 'Well, did you see that? You will do that part when we go thievin.' So we've got the goods, what do you do next?'

'Pass it to Jimmy or you before anyone can search me,' said Georgie, a slight flush coming to his cheeks.

'Right, let's do it again then.'

They practised all day and then the next, until Billy senior turned up again a little unsteady on his feet and smelling of alcohol.

'Well,' he said, watching Georgie pick Ellen's pocket for the hundredth time, 'looks like you 'ave the 'ang of it my lad. We'll go up West tomorrow night an' see what we can get. Yes, I think I am going to make a nice little packet with you three. Has Billy turned up yet?'

'He popped in this morning, said he would be gone for a while. The Peelers are on to the gang and they are lying low for a while. He asked how much you got for the stuff he brought the other night,' said Jane busy washing some clothes in a large galvanised tub.

Billy looked at the floor, his eyes flitting about as he concocted a lie. 'Not as much as I had hoped, those beads in the jewellery box were not of the best quality, not by a long way an' I only got twenty pounds for the lot. Here, better take this,' he said pulling out a hand full of copper coins and passing them to her. It was almost twelve shillings, enough to keep them in food for a few days, pay the rent but he knew he would have to give young Billy and his gang members at least ten pounds or they would take all he had. Those boys were getting bigger and after the thrashing they'd given him for withholding what was rightfully theirs a few weeks previously, he wasn't about to test them again.

The following evening found Billy Tyndall leading his three charges along Drury Lane mingling with early evening theatregoers resplendent in their evening suits and top hats, the women, decked out in their finest and strutting about like peacocks. Yet these were not their targets, no their victims would arrive in private carriages and stopping close to the theatre entrance to allow their female passengers an easy walk. These were the rich aristocratic patrons who possessed the finest of silk handkerchiefs, the ones Billy knew would fetch the best prices.

Pickpockets and Zulus

Earlier in the day, Georgie's uncle had taken him to a second hand clothes shop on the Whitechapel Road, a place with a good selection of the kind of clothes Billy had in mind. He wanted the boy to look as respectable as possible, to be able to mix with the crowds without arousing too much suspicion and to get closer to their prey than any street urchin might. He was confident that Ellen and Jimmy would play their part helping Georgie whilst he, brave soul that he was, would size up the situation, give his instructions and retire to a safe place to keep a look out.

'Ellen, take these two over the road and get ready near the entrance while I go up there,' he said, pointing towards the junction leading to the river. 'I'll keep a look out from there and if I see anything I'll whistle.'

Ellen nodded, she knew his whistle all right and to his credit, he knew how to spot danger, saving her on more than one occasion from the Peelers. She watched him walk through the crowd and then she turned towards James and Georgie.

'Georgie' she said, grabbing his lapel and pulling him round, 'see that bridge over there, that's the Waterloo Bridge and that's where we go to make our escape. When you get an 'andfull, make your way across the river an' we will meet you on the other side. If things go wrong then still go over the bridge but 'aisty like, very 'aisty. We will be over there after you as soon as we can. Understand?'

Georgie nodded realising for the first time just what they were getting him into and he could do nothing except nod in agreement.

'Right,' said his cousin, 'you know what to do, and we've practised it enough.'

He nodded again and Ellen pushed past beckoning the two boys to follow her towards the carriage stand.

'Look,' said Ellen, using her eyes to point at a carriage where a groom was busy lowering steps for his passengers. 'There's two fat old ladies in there, should be easy enough for you to pick their pockets. Go on,' Ellen said, giving Georgie a nudge with her shoulder before grabbing Jimmy's hand and disappearing into the crowd.

Georgie felt excitement well up inside him. He knew what he was expected to do was wrong but what choice had he and anyway he was beginning to enjoy himself. He took a deep breath and slowly walked towards the carriage just as the groom reached up to help out the first of the women.

'My man,' said the woman addressing the driver, 'I expect you to be here when we return and I shall want you to take us to Claridges where we are to meet Lord Holmes. Make sure you know the way, the last driver got us lost.'

'Yes Lady Holmes, certainly,' said the driver touching the peak of his cap as the groom held out his hand to steady the woman and with some difficulty she managed to descend onto the pavement. Next, her equally well-endowed companion emerged from inside the carriage and with some effort, the groom managed to help her down.

'Come Penelope, let us enjoy a pleasurable evening,' said Lady Holmes straightening her parasol and from no more than six feet away Georgie watched. The two women were unaware of his presence as they made their way towards the theatre entrance, Georgie moved in alongside them with his heart beating wildly and then

Pickpockets and Zulus

Ellen emerged from the crowd to stand in the path of the Duchess remonstrating with the still hidden James.

'Oi you, gimme back my money,' she said swinging her arms wildly at Jimmy who was starting to emerge from the crowd. It seemed a fight was about to start, the crowd seemed to freeze for a moment before parting to give Ellen space and, taken by surprise, Lady Holmes stopped instinctively to avoid trouble. Ellen's antics drew the two wealthy women's attention, Georgie's cue, and unnoticed he moved close to the Duchess, running his hands ran over the folds of her coat feeling for her pockets, slipping his fingers deftly in to feel for the contents. Careful not to apply too much pressure, he gently but firmly grasped the handkerchief to draw it from the woman's coat and surreptitiously place it in his own jacket pocket.

By now, Ellen had caught hold of her brother and on cue; he broke free, running through the crowd with Ellen in pursuit, drawing onlooker's eyes. Georgie turned away from his victim, his first mistake. The commotion had drawn the coach driver's attention as well but from his vantage point, he had seen Georgie move a bit too close to Lady Holmes.

'Hey!' he shouted at Georgie, 'what are you up to?'

Georgie, alarmed, looked up at the driver not sure what to do and then he looked at the groom, a youth of around eighteen years old, bigger and stronger than himself. He might have bluffed his way out of the situation when first challenged but now guilt showed in his eyes and the groom, eager to prove his worth, leapt forward to grab him by the arm. Georgie's heart should have begun to beat a crazy rhythm and panic should have overtaken him but as the groom held him in a vice

102

like grip, he felt calmness. His own natural instinct for self-preservation, he saw things very clearly and knew exactly what he must do.

First, he stamped on the grooms foot, drawing a howl of rage and then he swung his elbow into the youth's ribs, forcing him to release his grip, giving Georgie just enough time and room to escape. The driver, watching events unfold had climbed from his seat and was about to use his whip on Georgie when the recoiling groom fell into him. He side stepped just enough to avoid being bowled over and managed to swing a fist close to Georgie's ear but he missed by a hair's breadth and Georgie was able to duck under a horses belly and escape across the street. Dodging pedestrians and carriages alike he disappeared into the darkness and within minutes he was onto the bridge and running towards the far side of the river with shouts of 'stop thief' still ringing in his ears.

'Georgie, over 'ere, quick,' it was Ellen waving him towards her. She had dragged Jimmy across the bridge, their agreed escape route, and now she spotted Georgie heading towards them.

'Come on Georgie' she shouted, encouraging him to run faster but Georgie needed no encouragement and he soon reached them. Together the three pickpockets ran as fast as they could and after a half a mile, their legs feeling like lead, they collapsed against a wall gasping for breath.

'Blimey, that was a close one' said Ellen breathing deeply and brushing her sweat soaked hair from her eyes, 'they nearly 'ad you there Georgie all right.'

It was a narrow escape but Georgie had never had such an exciting time in all his young life and now that he felt safe, he began to laugh aloud, releasing tension and infecting the others. Jimmy was the next to laugh, then Ellen and before long, the three of them were rolling about on the floor engulfed in mirth until suddenly, a shadow spread over them.

'What's going on?' said the sharp, familiar voice of Billy Tyndal. He had lost sight of them very early on in the chase and had made his way over the bridge hoping to catch up with his three apprentices and here they were rolling about on the ground laughing their heads off.

'Well, what 'ave you got for me?' he said sternly.

The three children stopped laughing and scrambled to their feet.

'Here' said Georgie sheepishly holding out the silk handkerchief he had taken from the Duchess.

'My, my young Georgie, this is the finest silk I 'ave seen in a long time, should fetch a pretty penny I think. Well done my lad, if you can lift a 'andkercheif once like this then you can do it again. Come on let's go a bit further an' see what you can do.'

A week after Georgie's first foray into the pickpocketing business, Billy Tyndal was returning home from visiting his fence in the back room of the Prospect of Whitby, the profits from the previous day's expedition safely in his pocket. He had a large grin on his face, testament to his self-congratulatory mood. His plan was taking shape, 'yes things are turning out very nicely thank you', he thought as he turned into Tanner Street and through the archway into the Rookery yard.

Several women were hanging out washing, he paused, leaning against the wall to roll a cigarette, and as he inhaled the smoke, he thought about his plans. The boy was shaping up well, he could see potential in young Georgie, and took another drag on the cigarette. Then, from a room above an argument broke out interrupting his peace, a woman shrieked and he heard the sound of a slap, then another and the argument was replaced by the sound of silence and Billy laughed. 'That's how to deal with them,' he said to himself flicking the half-finished cigarette deftly across the yard. He glanced up at the window as he passed and hearing no more made his way to his own abode.

'Oi, what 'ave you got for me to eat woman?' he said barging through the door.

'Not much, I 'aint got no bees left, you haven't given me any money for over a week. All we have is this potato peel soup. I'm just going to give some to those three,' she said, pointing with her thumb to the three figures sat on the wall outside.

'Well that'll 'ave to do for now but 'ere' he said holding out his hand 'if it's bees an honey you want here's half an Oxford Scholar' he gave her the silver half crown and grinned as her eyes lit up. 'I got some more for the rent an' after tonight I expect we will be in clover again.'

'Oh Billy, just in time, the rent man came this morning an' said if we did not have the rent by the end of the week we would be chucked out on the street.'

'Chucked out on the street? Humph, we won't be 'ere much longer if that Georgie keeps up 'is theivin.' '

Jane's smile disappeared as quickly as it had come. She knew what an evil man Billy could be when he put his mind to it and now he was cooking something up with poor Georgie. She thought of her dead sister, what she would think. Maude had always tried to be a good Christian woman, to bring her son up properly, to give him some sort of education and help him to improve his lot. What would she be thinking now that Billy Tyndal had control of Georgie's life?

'If Georgie keeps what up?' she said

'His good work, the lad 'as a talent for the work. My Ellen 'as it and Billy 'as it, they both take after me.'

'They both take after you and will finish up in prison one day, maybe even transportation.'

Billy was a hard man when he wanted to be and Jane could see young Billy becoming as wayward as his father and at times even Ellen seemed to be heading the same way. At least with Ellen there was the female thing, neither was able to stand up to Billy Tyndal alone but they watched out for each other in other ways and somehow they managed. She put the half crown in her skirt pocket, dished up a bowl of the watery soup for Billy, and three more for the children.

Chapter 7

The winter of 1871 was harsh but as the warmer weather of spring returned Billy Tyndal found himself sitting on a bench outside the Prospect of Whitby. He had purchased a clay pipe to go with his gin and as he stuffed it with tobacco, he reflected on the success of his little venture. Striking his match, he looked up to see Abraham Cohen, his long-time associate and fence, walking towards him.

'Ah, my friend,' said Abraham, 'can I buy you a drink?'

Billy Tyndal's eyes narrowed. 'That's very good of you Abe, I'll have a gin.'

It wasn't every day Abe bought him a drink, he was after something. A sharp and skilful scoundrel, he looked as if he could not afford to buy him a drink, shabbily dressed his lank hair hanging over his face and his long nose protruding like some vulture's beak. Yes, Abraham Cohen was softening him up for something.

'To a long and happy relationship Mister Tyndal.'

'What d'you want you old rascal?'

'Ha my dear there is no need to be rude, let us talk of business. I have been thinking, the quality of the goods you bring me is improving and my friends are very pleased. What say I offer you a little more for your goods if you can supply this kind of quality on a regular basis, hmm...?

'What exactly are you looking for?'

'Simply good quality goods, gold pocket watches mainly, they will bring you the best price. My friends have asked me to see what you can do for us Mister Tyndal,' he said as his dishonest eyes looked straight into Billy's and he tapped his long nose with his fore finger as if confiding a great secret.

'I will see what I can do, Mister Cohen, we are working the more affluent parts of city and I know the goods are of a better quality, I can see that and they will bring better prices. Am I right Abe?'

'Good...good, yes, I see you understand,' said Abraham, pouring the last of his drink down his throat. 'There are plenty of, shall we say, small time traders working the streets; I have too many silk handkerchiefs. Pocket watches Mister Tyndall, silver and gold items are what you should be obtaining for me.'

Billy Tyndall's eyes lowered a little, pocket watches, gold, silver, the fence was asking him to take more risk and he did not like it.

'And now I must leave you, I have some people to see at my shop. Goodbye for now my dear.'

Billy raised his glass to the old Jew as he shuffled off to his pawnshop, finished his own drink and called to the publican for another. He re-lit his pipe and considered Cohen's offer. Working deeper in the West End and around Theatre-land was bearing fruit, his idea of dressing Georgie in good quality clothes and mixing with the gentry was paying off but to go after the kind of goods Cohen was looking for would expose them to more risk and for once, his wife's words resonated. Abraham Cohen had set him thinking.

Billy did not sleep well that night, his mind full of ideas and worry. To work the West End properly, to lift valuable items would be much more difficult than their present line of work but the rewards were certainly more attractive and so, as he stumbled out of his bed and into the next room he made his announcement.

'Today we are going to Trafalgar Square, I 'ear the pickings are good, lots of strangers from out of town, sight seers they call them and their pockets are stuffed with gold watches.'

Ellen looked up from her porridge. Trafalgar Square? That was a long way off, what if they ran into trouble? They didn't know the back alleys so well and if they had to make a run for it, where would they go and with her mind working overtime, she took another spoonful of porridge. She did look up to her father but she also knew that he relied on her to see things through. Where was *he* when things went wrong? How many times had they to make a run for it to escape from the police or an angry victim and where was *he* when they needed him – gone. She looked at Jimmy and Georgie sitting at the other side of the table, both grinning at the thought of a new adventure.

'Sounds good Dad, how will we get there?' said Jimmy.

'Walk you stupid boy.'

Jimmy looked a little sheepish, he had no idea where Trafalgar Square was, he had only heard of it from friends and Georgie was too preoccupied with his breakfast plate, wiping it clean with his tongue. He didn't know where Trafalgar Square was either, but it sounded interesting.

'Will there be any ships there?' he asked innocently.

'Don't be daft, its miles from the sea and anyway the big ships can't get under the bridges,' said Billy with a frown. 'Come on, let's be off,' he said, marching out of the door.

The spring day was warm and sunny, and so with the prospect of improved spoils in the air, the little band of pickpockets made their way across London. Ellen soon forgot her anxieties as she looked at new and unfamiliar surroundings and after an hour, they were in sight of their destination, hot, thirsty and in need of a drink.

'Cor I'm firsty', said Jimmy to no one in particular, 'where can I get a drink?'

'Over there' said Georgie, pointing to a horse trough and laughing at his cousin.

'Leave it out, I ain't sharing wiv them 'orses.'

'You don't 'ave to' said his sister, 'there's a drinking fountain on the wall next to the trough.'

'Oh yes' said Jimmy, making a bee line for the pumping handle, rocking it back and forth until the water began to gush from the cast iron spout. He took several mouthfuls of the cool, fresh spring water and grinned at the others. They were thirsty too and once Jimmy relinquished his hold on the handle, they all rushed to get their fill.

'It's just over there, the Square,' said Billy stroking his chin.

The three children followed his gaze along a road, busy with traffic, trams and wagons, the air filled with noise and the aroma of horse droppings. Billy strode forward along the last wide stretch of Whitehall towards the Square and behind him followed Georgie and the others.

'Who is that up there?' asked Georgie, amazed by his first sight of Nelson's column towering into the sky.

'Nelson,' said Billy, 'it's Nelson's column.'

Georgie had heard of Nelson and Trafalgar, and looked with some wonder at the small figure standing at the top of the stone column but before he could dwell Billy Tyndall began giving them orders.

'Come on, let's go, Ellen, you keep a lookout for a likely trick and Jimmy, you can act as the stooge whilst you, Georgie my boy, do the business. I'll keep a look out from a safe distance.'

The little gang of pickpockets followed Billy to the Square, up the flight of wide stone steps to mingle with the crowds come to see the marvellous Nelson's Column. Billy had insisted upon pocket watches and the like, to follow the same routine, working as a close-knit team and with Ellen holding it all together. She was the brains, picking their victims and keeping her eyes open for signs of the danger but the square did not have the myriad of side streets for their escape and she felt uneasy.

The City's grand new attraction was busy with sightseers as Ellen and the boys pushed their way through throngs of sightseers, her bright intelligent eyes flicking this way and that, scanning the crowd for a trick. She soon spotted two women and after nudging Georgie in the ribs walked towards them to peer into their baskets and look for the tell-tale signs of a purse tucked away in their coats and her eagle eyes soon spotted one. The shape was almost imperceptible in the woman's coat pocket, but it was there. Easy, she thought and moving sideways out of the woman's vision, gave a covert signal with her dancing eyes, setting the machine in motion. First Jimmy moved forward past the women, pushing his way through the crowd before tripping himself up and sprawling on the ground. Taken by surprise the women's natural instinct was to swerve to avoid him and as she did, Georgie reached out and deftly withdrew the purse from the unsuspecting woman's pocket.

Several times more they picked pockets, lifting purses and anything else they could lay their hands on before slipping away into the crowd. However, things were not quite so simple, one of their victims, aware that she had been robbed, found a policeman near the Column and gave a good description of the thieves.

Albert Pawson was a good copper; he had been in the job for more than twenty years and seen most of what the underworld of London had to offer. He listened patiently to the woman, swinging his truncheon back and forth in a slow arc behind his back as she told him how a boy had tripped in front of her and how it was only minutes later that she realised her purse had gone. Constable Pawson pursed his lips; he remembered seeing a lad of similar description earlier in the day trip over in front of two women.

'Thank you for that information ma'am. I will keep a good look out for him.'

'Another one had her purse pinched Albert'? asked the burly recruiting Sergeant standing in the shadow of the Column.

'Yes, always the same story, some urchin distracting the victim whilst an accomplice picks their pocket, I must hear of it five or six times a day.'

'I wish I got five or six a day' said the soldier, 'if I did I could retire early.'

'How many have you hooked today?'

'Two' replied the sergeant in disgust, 'not enough to cover a day's wages.'

Not far from the two men and hidden from view by the crowd, Billy Tyndal spotted a well-dressed man looking a little worse for drink. The man was walking unsteadily towards the Column, his head thrown back as he surveyed the tiny figure high in the sky. He was wearing a top hat, carried an ivory-topped cane and Billy thought, 'he looks perfect for a few quid'; even the silk scarf around his neck would be worth something. But it wasn't the scarf that really interested him, more the gold chain hanging from the man's waistcoat, a gold chain that led to a handsome gold watch in his waistcoat pocket, and Billy Tyndal meant to have it.

'Ellen,' he called out to his daughter, Ellen, come 'ere. Look, that man over there,' he said, inclining his head. 'E's got a gold watch and chain inside his jacket. Go and fetch the others while I keep tabs on 'im.'

Ellen scurried off to tell Georgie and Jimmy who were playing marbles near the foot of the column.

'We got a gold watch to pinch boys' she hissed at them.

Pocketing their marbles, the two lads followed her back up the steps to where Billy was waiting.

'Ellen, you get up alongside that gentleman wiv' the top 'at, try and help Jimmy distract 'im' whilst you Georgie, get ready to lift the watch an' I'll keep a lookout for the Peelers,' said Billy.

It was a game they had played out many times, it had become second nature and so good were they that they had become blasé and allowed their concentration to lapse. Not far away Albert Pawson spotted them following a drunk and slowly moved in their direction.

He saw Jimmy first, recognising him from the description the woman had given earlier and now he could see Ellen and Georgie walking with him, all fitting the descriptions he had and he knew he was watching a pickpocketing team in action. The constable began to walk slowly behind the group, keeping an eye on their every move and through a gap in the crowd Billy Tyndal saw him but he was too far away from to warn his charges and decided his best option was to keep out of sight.

The drunken man was captivated by the sight of Nelson looking out over London and tilted his head further back as he got closer to it, unaware of thieves were closing in. First Jimmy tripped and fell against him then Ellen reached over to help her brother to his feet, apologising profusely to distract him, allowing Georgie time to slip his hand into the unsuspecting victim's jacket to feel for his gold watch. Georgie's hand closed round it and he lifted it from the waistcoat pocket but he could not quite slip the bar on the end of the chain through the buttonhole and snagged it. The man must have felt something for he gazed at Georgie with uncomprehending eyes at first, finally reacting as Georgie pulled the watch free.

'Stop thief,' he managed to shout.

Georgie turned to run but he had not seen Albert Pawson. The burly policeman reached out and grabbed hold of him as he passed, manoeuvring him into a head lock from which there was no escape and with panic in his voice Georgie called out to Ellen and Jimmy for help, but they had already vanished into the safety of the crowds.

'Get off me,' yelped Georgie 'let me go.'

'Not a chance my lad, your under arrest, it'll be prison for you I reckon.'

Prison, the thought was enough to spur Georgie into escaping the policeman's clutches and he almost succeeded, twisting, turning and finally breaking free only to run into the recruiting Sergeant. The commotion had alerted him, he had come to have a look and between the policeman and himself Georgie stood little chance of escape, firmly in their grip and going nowhere.

'Well done officer, that boy stole my watch. He had two accomplices you know,' said the drunk wandering towards them.

'Yes sir, I was aware of that but we have him and here is your watch,' he said, prizing it from Georgie's grip.

'What are you going to do with him?' asked the man.

'Take him to the police station and put him in a cell until the sergeant decides what to do. I expect after locking him up the assizes will deal with him. I will need your name and address as a witness, Sergeant will you hang on to the prisoner for me while I take down this man's particulars.'

The recruiting Sergeant nodded and tightened his grip on Georgie, finally stopping the boy struggling. Georgie's energy was gone and the thought of prison was beginning to weigh heavily on his mind. He had heard tales of prison from Billy Tyndal and Billy junior and those stories had made his flesh creep. The sergeant looked down at him as he gave up the uneven struggle and his body became limp, he was puzzled, there was something familiar about this boy.

'What's your name lad,' he said in a gruff voice.

'Georgie sir.'

'Well I'm blowed, you are Alex McNamara's son. I last saw you when I visited your mother.'

The sergeant held Georgie's face towards him for a better view. Yes it was Alex's son all right, he had grown since he last saw him, he was like his father though, the same strong features and those same steely eyes.

'Is your mother called Maude lad?' he asked.

'Yes, but she's dead.'

'Ah...' an understanding crossed the soldiers mind and he felt some compassion for the boy, the son of a fallen comrade, a sergeant like himself who had saved his life, a man to whom Sergeant Robert's felt he owed a debt and could be that this was the time to repay that debt.

'Will the lad really be sent to Prison?' he asked the constable as he finished speaking with the victim of the robbery.

'Spect so, a gold watch usually means prison or deportation. Why?'

'Listen Albert, I know this boy, I knew his father, he was my best friend in the regiment and no finer man you could ever wish to meet. We campaigned together in India, fighting right up to the Afghan border and Alex would be turning in his grave if he thought his only son was in this predicament.'

'Well 'e is and there's nothing you or me can do about it is there.'

'I think there is.'

'What?'

'We don't just recruit young men; we recruit boys as well. How old are you Georgie?'

'Fourteen sir.'

'Fourteen, just the right age and he said sir, that shows the boy has something about him. Let me have him and I'll make a man of him, more than any prison could and I will repay a debt I thought I would be never able to.'

'What debt?'

'When we were out in India Alex saved my life. We got in some tight corners on a few occasions and once I thought my number was up but this lad's father saved me.'

'Look, I can't just let him go, it's more than my jobs worth, I have a family to feed. Let's go down to the station and talk to the desk sergeant, I know what to say that might persuade him to put the boy in your charge. But listen, I have to get my paperwork right first, I cannot arrest someone and then nothing 'appens. Come on.'

The police constable, the recruiting sergeant and Georgie made their way out of the Square towards the police station on the Charring Cross Road. Georgie could do nothing, restrained as he was between them; he simply looked forlornly at the ground until, after they had travelled no more than a hundred yards, the Constable stopped beside a darkened alleyway.

'Right, in 'ere for a mo.'

Sergeant Roberts looked puzzled, defensive, a soldier's instinct making him wary.

'Don't worry, I just don't want anyone to see what we're doing. I got kids of my own, I know what it's like to be a parent, worrying about them, keeping them out of trouble. Listen, you want me to let the boy go, well I can see he's not a bad 'un, what if I let you 'ave 'im. For a small consideration that is, I have to feed and clothe my own family and it ain't easy. What do you say sergeant?'

'How much do you want?'

'Five bob.' Constable Pawson had a good idea of how much money the sergeant had on him. Recruiting sergeants provided the Queens shilling themselves, claiming it back with their commission when a new recruit reported to the barracks and today he would have at least that amount on him.

With little hesitation Sergeant Roberts pulled out his leather purse, loosened the drawstring, counted out five one-shilling pieces and handed them to a satisfied looking Constable Pawson. The policeman gave a cursory glance at the coins, stuffed them into his tunic pocket and without so much as a "thank you" left the sergeant and Georgie in the shadows to return to the main thoroughfare.

'Well Georgie boy, it seems you will not be going to prison after all. You have had a lucky escape and now you are going to join the Army. Well what d'you say?'

Georgie said nothing, bewildered by events all he could do was to look down at his feet. They were becoming very familiar.

Georgie had never seen a railway engine before, only heard an occasionally steam whistle from afar, so the scene at London Victoria was something of a wonder to him. Sergeant Roberts bought tickets for Chatham and smartly marched Georgie along the platform to the waiting train and Georgie eyes and ears became awash with new sensations. Trains thundered by, the noise from the steam engines causing him to recoil until eventually they reached the train for Chatham.

The sergeant smiled at him as he climbed aboard a train for the first time in his life, his face expressing curiosity and during the journey, they began to talk. The sergeant asked about his mother and Georgie told how she had died suddenly leaving him an orphan, how his Aunt Jane and Uncle Billy had taken him in.

'I 'ad nowhere else to go, uncle Billy said I had to become a pickpocket to pay my way or he would chuck me out on the street an' I didn't want that.'

'I understand lad, well those days are over now, let's hope the army makes something of you. I can see you are Alex McNamara's son and I reckon you will do fine.

'I never knew my father.'

'I know lad.'

'Tell me about him.'

Sergeant Roberts breathed in and cleared his mind, thinking back to those days when he and Alex just about ran the regiment along with sergeant Major O'Brien. He began with stories of their time in India, of the regiment travelling the length and breadth of the sub-continent and about the native people. He described strange customs, the heat of the day and the coolness of the mountains in the summer and of the tremendous downpours of rain known as the monsoon. By the time the train arrived at Chatham Georgie had learned something of his father and of the world outside the dark, claustrophobic streets of London.

'Look, we're just about here.'

The train passed rows of white tents, in the distance ships lay at anchor and before long, the train shuddered to a halt and the two of them climbed onto the platform amongst crowds of returning soldiers, noisy and irreverent and the buzz about the place left Georgie bewildered.

The sergeant led the way past the groups of soldiers, past several wagons and onto a dirt road leading to several large and plain looking buildings. Reaching a small wooden guard hut located near the entrance to the largest of the buildings, Sergeant Roberts burst in. Georgie followed and could see two men, who disturbed from their game of cards, looked up with surprise at the sudden intrusion.

'Sergeant Roberts reporting, I want to see the Sergeant of the Guard.'

The corporal looked lazily up wondering who was the stranger disturbing their peace, but Bill Roberts was more than a match for him. First he eyed him with a stern gaze then he turned his shoulder to reveal his stripes and realising at last the visitor outranked him, the corporal jumped to his feet, instructed the private to go and find the Sergeant of the Guard. For a few minutes, there was an uneasy silence until a voice boomed through the open doorway.

'Bill Roberts, well well, I haven't seen you for a while. How's the easy life in London?' said the Sergeant of the Guard.

'Hmm, easy life, I don't think so Sergeant White, and how's life treating you?'

'Can't complain Bill, anyway what are you doing here so late?'

'I've brought you a new recruit. Look, we haven't eaten all day, can you rustle up some tea and bread for us Chalky and then I want to talk to you, private like.'

'Aye, I think we can manage something. Come with me to the main guardroom and I'll get an orderly to fetch some grub, it's about time for my supper anyway.'

The three of them crossed the parade ground and climbed the broad steps to the entrance to the guardroom and Sergeant Roberts looked around at familiar surroundings.

'Nothing much changed since I was last here Chalky.'

'Naw, still the same old place, though the grubs got better. You will see. Private Jones!' he called out.

A soldier came out of a doorway several feet in front of them and stood to attention. 'Jones, get yourself down to the Mess and rustle up some grub for myself and Sergeant Roberts and the lad here will you.'

'Yes sergeant' said the Private, his boots clattering on the hard wooden floor as he disappeared along the corridor.

'Right, in here Bill' said Sergeant White, leading them towards a small office. 'Tell me what this is all about – unusual for you to bring a recruit in yourself.'

'A little unusual I grant you,' he said turning towards Georgie. 'Sit over there boy, on that bench and wait until I call you, understand?'

Georgie obeyed, crossing to the other side of the corridor as the two sergeants entered the room.

'Do you remember Alex McNamara?'

'Aye, I do. A good man, one of the best soldiers I've ever served with. Died of cholera didn't he, on that last skirmish before we came back home. Bad luck so near the end of the tour.'

'Yes he did and that's his only son sat out there. I don't think the boy saw much of his father.'

'Blimey Bill, what's he doing here with you, he can't be more than fifteen can he?'

'Fourteen I think, and he's with me to avoid being sent to jail.'

Sergeant Roberts explained the circumstances of his meeting with Georgie and the bargain he had made with the Police Constable in Trafalgar Square.

'I didn't have to do it but we look after our own don't we Chalky?' The other man nodded. 'Alex was my comrade out in India. He should have had a medal for what he did but it's too late now. The least I can do is to help his son.'

'So you've brought him here to sign on as a boy soldier.'

'That's right.'

There was a tap at the door and the orderly entered with a tray of beef sandwiches and a pot of tea.

'Your supper sergeant.'

'Thank you Jones. Take a couple of sandwiches and some tea for the boy and wait with him until I call you.'

'Yes sergeant,' said the Private, picking up two sandwiches and filling a mug with tea for Georgie.

With a mouthful of beef sandwich Chalky White managed to say, 'the regiment is under strength, any new recruit is welcome.' He swallowed and washed down the food with a swig of hot tea. 'I'll have a word with the Adjutant in the morning and have him put with the band boys until he's old enough to sign on proper. Well fancy that, Alex McNamara's son joining up. If he is half as good as his dad, he will be a credit to the regiment. And what about you Bill, what are you up to these days? Is it worth it being a recruiting sergeant? 'Bin thinking about trying that job for myself, perhaps in a couple of years, when my time's up.'

Bill Roberts laughed, putting Sergeant White straight on a few points and then the two of them reminisced about their time in India.

'I could do with a billet for tonight Chalky, if you can find somewhere for me and the boy and then I'll be off back to London first thing.'

'I'll arrange that. Jones!' he called to the Private, 'find a bed for Sergeant Roberts and to take the lad to the band boy's quarters for the night.'

At first, there was the muffled sound of people rising from their beds, then the sound of a thick Irish brogue reached Georgie's ears and he opened his eyes to see a dozen pairs of eyes staring back at him.

'Will 'ye look at dis lads, a stranger whit us during the noight.'

Pickpockets and Zulus

Before anyone else could speak, a door burst open and in marched two soldiers.

'Look sharp and make your beds ready for inspection!'

The room erupted into a hive of activity, those not already on their feet tumbled from their beds, dressed hurriedly and made ready for the inevitable inspection. Georgie didn't know what to do so he just copied what he saw, straightening the two woollen blankets and tucking their edges under the flimsy mattress and standing to attention as best he could. From the corner of their eyes, the rest of the boys viewed the stranger, weighing him up until band Sergeant Doyle marched through the open door.

'Ten shun,' called the Corporal.

Immediately the boys stood erect, arms stiffly at their sides, eyes straight ahead, no more inquisitive glances in Georgie's direction and the occupants of the dormitory stood in silence. Two N.C.O's began to move along the rows of beds, inspecting the young soldiers and their belongings until Sergeant Doyle came face to face with Georgie. No one had yet informed him of the boy's presence and in the best military tradition; he proceeded to embarrass the boy in front of his peers.

'What 'ave we 'ere, a new recruit? What's your name lad?'

Georgie remained silent, his face turning crimson and the sergeant repeated his question with a little more tenderness. 'I asked you your name. Speak up or you'll be peeling spuds for a week.'

'Georgie.'

'Georgie,' mocked the sergeant, 'Georgie what?'

'McNamara' said Georgie in a quiet voice, not at all sure what the sergeant was going to do next and he had no wish to antagonise him.

'McNamara is it? When I say what, your answer is "sergeant", do I make myself clear?'

'Yyy...es sss...ergeant,' stammered Georgie.

'Good' said Sergeant Doyle looking Georgie over for a few moments longer before moving on to the next bed where he proceeded to irritate the young Irish lad who had first spotted Georgie.

'Donovan, how many times have I told you to polish those boots of yours 'till you can see your face in them?'

'Tousands sergeant' replied the boy.

'Aye thousands and can you see your face in them? No and neither can I. I want those boots polished good and proper straight after breakfast and if I still can't see my face in them then you'll be peelin' spuds for the rest of the day. Understand?'

'Yes sergeant'

Sergeant Doyle reached the last of the beds and with his stick lifted the corner of a blanket, dished out some minor punishment and crossed the room to go through the same routine. When he had finished tormenting the young soldiers, he returned to a red faced and bemused Georgie.

'Well my lad, where did you spring from?'

Georgie cleared his throat and managed to say, 'er.., the recruiting sergeant brought me here last night. I'm to join the army.'

'Sergeant!' said the sergeant in an intimidating fashion. Georgie looked blank. 'Sergeant, you call me sergeant, understand?'

'Y...yes sergeant.'

125

'Good, well fall in for breakfast and in the mean time I'll find out what's going on.' The sergeant looked round the room to see if he had missed anything and deciding that he had not, ordered the band boys to stand easy and marched smartly back out of the room leaving the corporal to take charge.

'Troop fall in.' The boys moved to the centre of the room and formed two lines. 'Shun!' he said, bringing them to attention. 'Right turn,' they turned in unison, 'left right, left right' went the corporal and the troop moved off to the Mess hall for breakfast with Georgie bringing up the rear.

'Donovan, take McNamara here and get him some breakfast,' said the corporal. 'Sergeant Doyle said that he will come and collect him to get him kitted out.'

Patrick Donovan, like a good many of the soldiers in the regiment was Irish, escaping the poverty and starvation of rural Ireland to follow a well-trodden path by joining the British Army. Patrick was taller than Georgie, sixteen years old, with pale freckled skin, the red hair and the grey eyes of the Celtic race.

'My names Patrick, an' you are Georgie, I know that' he said with a grin, 'would ye follow me an' we'll get a bowl of porridge, might be some apples today, they're in season.'

Patrick had his own plate and utensils, found a bowl and spoon for Georgie and together they queued to have them filled with porridge before going to sit at a long wooden bench amongst the other boys. To the amusement of some, Georgie ate his food like a starved animal, his ordeal leaving him ravenously hungry and then he began to lick his plate clean.

'To be sure you're half-starved Georgie. Where the devil have you come from?'

Georgie looked up to see a row of faces watching him and with some embarrassment he said, 'London.'

'Where in London and what are you doin' here?' Patrick wasn't giving up easily.

'Near the river, just off Mile End Road.'

'And have ye joined up as a drummer boy?'

A drummer boy, Georgie still confused by the events of the past twenty-four hours had no idea what would happen to him.

'I...I don't know. I have to join up so they don't send me to prison or Australia.'

'Australia, that sounds like the penal colonies. What have you been up to?' asked the ever-inquisitive Patrick.

'Come on Georgie; tell us what 'appened' demanded a voice from across the table.

'Yes, tell us,' chorused some of the others.

'I was caught stealing a gold watch from a drunk in Trafalgar Square. A Peeler caught me and the recruiting sergeant bribed him to let me go, saying that I 'ad to join the Army.'

'Trafalgar Square,' said two boys more interested in the Square than the fact that Georgie was caught thieving.

'Why would a recruiting sergeant pay to have you released?' asked another.

'Because he was a friend of my fathers, my dad was in the regiment. He died in India.'

'So you are one of us young Georgie,' said Patrick, slapping him on the back.

The action made Georgie feel a whole lot better, accepted and after breakfast, he followed the band boys trooping out of the Mess hall and back to their dormitory. The young soldiers spent time gathering their equipment and then left for the parade ground where the drill sergeant was waiting for them. After a few short commands, the boys lined up and stood smartly to attention ready for the morning's instruction and Georgie watched from the sidelines until Sergeant Doyle appeared.

'McNamara, come with me and look sharp about it,' he ordered.

Georgie quickly fell in, trying to mimic the swinging arms as he went to the laughter of his newfound friends. First, they went to the recruiting office where he signed away his life until he was eighteen, No mention was made of the previous day's problem, Sergeant Roberts had made sure of that and with formalities complete, he followed the Sergeant to the quartermaster's store to be kitted out with a uniform and officially allocated his bunk in the dormitory.

An hour later, Georgie stood beside his bed surveying a neat pile of new clothes, and looked up to see Patrick Donovan walking towards him.

'The drill sergeant has told me to come and help you settle in the army way. You have to stow everything correctly or you will be peeling spuds in the cook house.'

Patrick demonstrated how Georgie should wear his day uniform; a grey shirt and high backed blue trousers with a red stripe running down each leg. The black boots were a slack fit for him to grow into and to finish off Patrick placed the Glengarry with the regimental badge on his head, tilting it to the right.

'Ha...don't you look different, now let me show you what to do with this lot.'

Georgie's full kit of a five button scarlet serge frock coat, webbing, haversack and buff leather Valise lay on the bed and he needed to stow all of them neatly in the small cupboard beside his bed.

'Give it another six months and some of your uniform might fit. Come on, I have to take you back to the parade ground.'

Georgie followed to begin his training, marching in step, left wheel, right wheel, quick march, slow march, a whole gamut of drills. He attended lessons to learn the basics of reading and writing, learned about guns and explosives and in his spare time, he polished his boots until he could see his face in them and at the end of the six months, he was taller and his uniform fitted him.

Chapter 8

Sitting cross-legged his spear lying across his knees, Nkosinathi squinted as the bright sunlight caught his eyes and he looked out across the valley to pick out each of his charges grazing amongst the long grass. He had grown tall; he was now almost six feet in height with broad shoulders and strong arms. At seventeen years of age, he had become proficient at stick fighting and as the eldest son still living in the village, was his father's chief herdsman. One by one, his elder brothers had left the village to go to the military iKhanda almost twenty miles away as cadets, to learn the ways of the Zulu Impi and Nkosinathi dreamed that one day he too would go to the Royal Kraal. For now though he served his father with his younger brother and half-brothers, looking after the herd from dawn until dusk and sleeping alongside his charges at night.

'Sibusiso my brother, go over there,' he called out, pointing with his stick. 'Some of the animals are beginning to stray too far. Go and bring them back.'

Sibusiso not far away stood and shook his spear in acknowledgement and then he ran to where Nkosinathi had directed him to retrieve those animals wandering off. Like his older brother, he too was growing into a fine Zulu youth. The outdoor life, the hardships they endured and the physical work they undertook made them physically strong, ready for the day when the King's messenger would arrive to summon them.

Nkosinathi watched his brother for a few seconds before reaching down to pluck a stalk of grass to chew and cast his eyes across the pasture towards the younger boys standing sentinel over the herd grazing quietly under the blazing sun. Spread right across the rolling hills, almost as far as he could see, the farthest of the animals were just black and white dots and he quietly congratulated himself. The herd was healthy, the rains had come early, raining as if it would never stop, soaking into the earth and now the grass was growing strong and lush and the herd was getting fat. These were good times, the milk would be plentiful and rich and Mondli would be proud of him.

Nkosinathi chewed on the stalk of grass, feeling a little bored because nothing much had happened during the day, the cattle were content and only a few had wandered off. The sun was hot and no one was interested in a stick fight, at least not with Nkosinathi for now, he was an expert and not easy to beat and the younger boys were wary of fighting with him. Strong and athletic he had gained a reputation as one of the best stick fighters in the kraal and they had no wish for him to split their scalps open. Sighing quietly he wondered about his elder brothers who had left the kraal to serve the King. For as long as he could remember it had been his dream to be part of an Impi, to dress in a warrior's kilt of fine cow tails, to carry his Assegai and the regimental shield. However, it was not his turn to leave the home Kraal just yet, he must wait until the King's messenger arrived though every Zulu youth had the right to override his father's wishes if he felt the time was right to serve the King and Nkosinathi had itchy feet.

'Yes I will, I will go to the nearest iKhanda and enrol as a Cadet,' he said aloud.

Tradition allowed for the youth of the nation to decide for themselves the time to become cadets and their fathers could not stand in their way. Still, it was polite to ask his father's permission and he would ask tonight before gathering his few belongings and leaving the village. Mondli was a proud man who had lived a full life, his wives had produced many sons, his herd was healthy and growing larger by the day and Nkosinathi believed he would not stand in his way.

There was always excitement when the herd returned, the younger children standing with their mothers, eyes opened wide at the sight of the lumbering beasts and youths ready with gourds to collect the milk. As the last of the cows entered the corral and the milking began Nkosinathi looked over the cattle one last time and secured the gate with plaited vines.

'The milk is rich tonight Nkosinathi,' said his brother Sibusiso, 'it will make good amasi.'

'I am pleased you are taking such an interest my brother, it may be soon that you are in charge of the herd and I want to leave it in good order.'

Sibusiso leant his head towards his shoulder a frown appearing on his brow as his brother's words sank in.

'You are leaving to kleza?' he said slowly.

'Yes Sibusiso, I have made up my mind to become a Cadet and go to the iKhanda. I will tell our father tonight and will leave tomorrow.'

Sibusiso gazed at Nkosinathi in awe, his large brown eyes telling their own story.

'I wish you luck my brother. You are a good fighter and I know you will be a good soldier.'

'And you my brother, you will take responsibility for the herd. Wear that responsibility well and serve our father and one day you too will become a warrior,' said Nkosinathi throwing his cloak across his shoulder and with some trepidation he made his way towards the hut of his father, finding him sitting cross-legged in front of his fire and poking a stick at the burning logs.

'*Sawubona*' called Nkosinathi, 'I have come to share snuff with my father.'

Mondli looked up, the light from the flames dancing across his shiny black face.

'*Sawubona* my son, you are welcome, come and sit a while.'

Nkosinathi took his place alongside Mondli and for a few minutes the two of them sat peacefully until Mondli at last broke the silence

'You have done well Nkosinathi. My cattle are fattening and the rains have done wonders for the milk yield.'

'Yes father, the grass was becoming too dry but now it is good.'

'Do you practice with the throwing spear; can you kill a rabbit at twenty paces?'

'Yes father, but not every time do I kill a rabbit.'

'You humble yourself, I know that you are the best with a throwing spear and, well, if you don't hit the prey every time then you must try and improve. To kill a rabbit with a throwing spear is no easy task.'

Pickpockets and Zulus

Nkosinathi remained silent, his decision to leave troubling him. By tradition, his father could not stop him but still, Mondli might not want him to go. He had been brought up to show respect for his father and he should at least try to gain his father's permission for the momentous step he was about to take. He wondered where to start and glanced at Mondli who was staring into the dancing flames of the fire.

Mondli was reflecting on his past life, he had been a warrior in the service of both King Dingane and King Mpande, his eldest sons were warriors of King Cetshwayo and he knew the time had come for his third son to think about leaving home.

'Nkosinathi you are very quiet,' he said reaching forwards to turn over a log.

The sparks swirled from the burning wood, the heat carrying them higher into the darkening sky and still Nkosinathi remained silent. He was plucking up courage to talk with the Chief of the Kraal, the one whom he had obeyed without question since he was born. He wanted to tell his father something he might not agree with and struggled to speak.

'My father,' he began, 'have I not served you well as your herdsman, have I not been an obedient son to you?'

Mondli smiled to himself, proud of this son who had grown tall, acquired the skills needed to look after the herd, to hunt and to fight with the sticks and now, he knew it was time for him to follow his destiny. His brothers before him and indeed he himself had one day come of age, left the home kraal to enter the army and he knew Nkosinathi's time had come.

'You have been an obedient son Nkosinathi and you look after my herd well. I am looking forward to a good year with you as my herdsman.' He watched Nkosinathi's eyes flicker as he teased him.

After a short pause Nkosinathi said 'Father is it not the destiny of every Zulu to serve the King?'

'Indeed it is my son.'

'And is it for me to serve also, father?'

'Yes it is,' said Mondli, 'since the time of the great Shaka, the duty of everyone is to serve the leader of our people and even I must be obedient, pay tributes and allow my sons to serve in his army.'

He could not stand in the way of Nkosinathi no matter how much he would have preferred the boy to stay and tend to the herd. 'You are of an age, you can go to the iKhanda and become a Cadet, should that be your desire my son.'

Nkosinathi's eyes lit up, Mondli was making it easy for him to leave. He had known that same dilemma when he too had sensed it was time to leave the village of his youth and had found it difficult to tell his own father.

Sitting a little straighter, his chest swelling with pride and confidence Nkosinathi said, 'father, thank you, it is time for me to go to the Cadet's iKhanda and to have your permission to leave the village makes me happy.'

'Yes my son, you have my permission to go, but first, tell your mother and sisters. My guess is that you have already told Sibusiso, for it is he who will now shoulder the responsibility of looking after the herd.'

'Thank you father, I shall leave tomorrow as the sun rises.'

The old chief smiled wishing he could turn the clock back but he knew that was impossible. 'Here,' he said, taking the small snuff filled horn from his ear, 'let us celebrate together your coming of age.'

Mondli pulled the stopper from the horn and tapped a little snuff into his palm and passed it to his son and for a time they sat in silence gazing into the flames. An hour later Nkosinathi walked proudly towards the boys hut to announce his imminent departure and then to the hut of his mother to tell her of his plans.

'Nkosinathi I wish you well, of all my sons only Sibusiso still remains in the village. I will tell Nozipho to visit you from time to time, for I know how difficult it is for cadets to find enough food. She will bring what she can. Go my son and may the spirits of our ancestors be with you.'

With a happy heart, he left his mother's home to spend a final night in the boy's hut and as the dawn broke, he was ready for the journey to the kraal of emaNgweni, a journey of fifteen miles towards the Mhlatuze River. He threw his cloak over his shoulder and picked up his soft leather satchel containing a little dried meat and maize for the journey. Lastly, he reached for his fighting sticks and made his way past the huts and as he left the Kraal, he saw that the herd was already beginning to leave for the pastures with the new herdsman in charge.

'*Uhambe hahle!*' said Sibusiso as he passed.

'Goodbye Sibusiso,' said Nkosinathi, slapping his brother's flat palm with his own in a token of farewell.

For a fit Zulu boy the journey to emaNgweni was neither long nor arduous and by mid-morning Nkosinathi reached the crest of a hill from where he set eyes on the royal iKhanda for the first time. It was a Kraal of over sixty beehive huts with a high wall of interwoven thorn branches, surrounded by an extensive area of cultivation and as he approached, a group of women working on the land gave him knowing looks. Nkosinathi was not the first Zulu youth to arrive from afar; in the past two days, half a dozen others had arrived to join the small group already assembled there.

'You have come to drink the King's milk,' called a warrior emerging from the entrance, more a statement than a question.

'Yes I have come to kleza,' replied Nkosinathi staring with some trepidation at the man, tall and muscular and in his hand, he carried a stabbing spear, a warrior.

'I am Ndukwana, the officer in charge of the cadets and I will instruct you until the King calls for you to join the other companies from amaKhanda throughout the land to form a new regiment. When that day comes you will receive your regimental name, but for now, you will look after the King's cattle in this iKhanda, and any other duties I give you. Find some space in that hut over there and for the rest of today you can go back out into the bush and collect fire wood.'

He waved his spear, pointing towards the hut, leaving the new recruit to fend for himself and Nkosinathi stood for a moment looking at his new home. Some youths were sitting on the ground not far away whittling sticks and he walked towards them.

'Hey you, what is your name?' asked one of them looking up.

'Nkosinathi.'

'Well, I'm Somopho, where have you come from?'

'My father is Mondli; his Kraal is half a day's walk to the West,' he said pointing behind him.

137

'I am from the Kraal of Dumisani, a day's walk to the North, come I will show you where to sleep.'

Nkosinathi thanked the youth who stood up to lead him to the entrance of the hut in which he was to sleep and dropping to his knees, crawled through the tunnel like entrance. Nkosinathi followed close behind, letting his eyes take a few seconds to become accustomed to the gloom. There were cooking pots and gourds arranged in a heap at one end but apart from that, the hut was devoid of anything save the small bundles of cadet's personal belongings arranged in neat piles.

'Come, I will find a place for you' said Somopho. 'Here,' he said, pointing to a space on the ground. 'Lay down your sleeping mat, this space will be yours for the rest of the time you are here.'

Nkosinathi did as Somopho told him and together they scrambled back outside to return to the other boys.

'We are all cadets; here is Bhekisisa, Lindani and Khulekani. We are to make spear shafts today whilst the others look after the herd and when they return we will drink the King's milk.'

Nkosinathi introduced himself and for several minutes listened as they chatted before he remembered Ndukwana's order. 'I must go and gather firewood, to cook our meal I think.'

Somopho chuckled.

'What are you laughing at?'

'You will learn, the only food we are allowed is to drink milk from the Kings' cows and then only after the people of the iKhanda have taken what they need. You will become very hungry here unless you are a good hunter or your family bring you food.'

138

Nkosinathi understood now the significance of his mother's words and thought about the meagre amount of dried meat and maize left in his satchel. It was all he had to eat, he had not realised that any food at the iKhanda was only for those living there. No matter he thought, he had killed small animals with his throwing spear and he would just have to keep a look out for small game, he would not starve, a Zulu Cadet could look after himself.

For the next few hours, Nkosinathi searched the surrounding bush, gathering firewood and taking it back to the compound just as Ndukwana had instructed him and in his search, he travelled several hundred yards into the bush. He remembered Somopho's words and they encouraged him to keep a watchful eye out for anything he could find to eat.

Slowly he moved through the undergrowth, looking for dead branches big enough for the fire and from the corner of his eye, a movement attracted his attention. A ground squirrel, busy rolling something round in its hands and he stood stock-still, watching the little animal. He could see that it was oblivious to him and carefully he lowered his load to the ground, taking a firm grip on one of his fighting sticks and cautiously he moved forwards. He could not hope to kill his prey outright, but he might stun it long enough to catch it in his hands.

He covered half the distance to the squirrel before it stopped chewing, raised its head and stood motionless to sniff the air. Nkosinathi was downwind of the animal and knew its eyesight was not good enough to spot him so long as he remained motionless and he felt relieved when the squirrel resumed chewing. The little animal seemed satisfied that it was safe and he crept ever nearer until, sensing rather than seeing him, the animal raised its head a second time and sniffed the air. It became alarmed and before he could react, it bounded off into the undergrowth.

'The spirits of my ancestors are not with me,' cursed Nkosinathi.

He had been so close and watching his dinner escape dismayed him, if he were to catch anything he would need to move much quicker. Muttering under his breath, cursing his poor hunting ability, he picked up his last load of firewood vowed that he would be more successful next time.

As the sun slowly slid towards the horizon, he watched cattle lumbering towards him, the king's herd returning for the night, amongst them some of the cadets. He stood and watched them pass, following the last of the beasts towards the Kraal and walked towards his new home to find Somopho and Lindani still whittling sticks.

'I have collected firewood and now I am hungry. Where do we get our food?' he asked a little naïvely.

'Be patient new boy, we will drink the King's milk as soon as we are allowed. Come; sit a while with us' said Somopho, a wide grin crossing his face.

'I nearly killed a squirrel today,' said Nkosinathi 'that would have fed us alright.'

The others laughed and Lindani said, 'nearly won't feed us Nkosinathi. We will soon see how good you are with the sticks.'

'I might crack your head with my stick tomorrow,' said Somopho laughing. 'I see you are not happy when we make fun of you, we make fun of all the new boys.

Soon you will become used to our ways. Ndukwana says that we should become strong on the inside as well as the outside; it will help us when the king calls us to Ulundi. Here, put down your firewood and come to watch the herd, we will drink the milk as soon as the villagers have taken their share.'

For the next few minutes, the cadets sat cross-legged near the corral, waiting patiently as royal attendants milked the cows. It was the hardest part of being a cadet, pangs of hunger gnawing at their stomachs yet they could not drink any of the milk. Nkosinathi watched the white frothy liquid filling the gourds and then came a shrill whistle, the signal for the cadets to feed.

'*Zi jubekile*, the King's cattle have been set apart,' chanted the cadets in soft voices so as not to startle the animal and as one rose up to quietly walk in amongst the cattle. Lindani beckoned Nkosinathi to follow him and once amongst the herd, the cadets squatted, two or three alongside each animal and began to drink milk straight from the cow's udders.

Nkosinathi gratefully sucked at the cow's teat, feeling the warm, nourishing milk enter his stomach and when he had finished he followed the other cadets back to their hut. It was dark and he was weary from his toil, his eyes felt heavy as he rolled out his mat and it was with relief he lay down to sleep after his first day as a Cadet.

The sounds of hoofs stamping the hard earth woke Nkosinathi from a deep sleep and for a moment, he wondered where he was. He rubbed his eyes, aware of the cadets leaving the hut and he rushed to follow them on his first day of training to become a warrior.

'Nkosinathi' said Somopho, prodding a large beast with his stick. 'Now you are here I can go out and look after the herd, you stay with Lindani and Khulekani and help them. Today they are crushing maize for mealie cakes. I will see you when I return tonight and you can tell me of your father's Kraal'

Nkosinathi felt disappointment, for had he not been in charge of his father's head, was he not a skilled herdsman, yet here he was about to do women's work. Having youths of his own age telling him what to do did not help either, making mealie flour was for his sisters not for him, his blood began to boil and his eyes flashed.

'Ha ha new boy! what are you upset about?' laughed Somopho. 'Are you afraid to do women's work? It is the first step on the road, we have to do everything for women are not allowed to fight, they can only accompany us on the march for a short time, and then we must look after ourselves.'

Nkosinathi looked down, a little ashamed at his reaction. Was this really the way to become a warrior? He nodded his acceptance and watched the herd pass by, tails flicking at the flies, splattering the ground with dung and Nkosinathi wished he were going with them.

Khulekani came towards him, sticks in one hand and a wooden hoe in the other. 'We are to go out to the fields to collect corn. You can take this hoe and remove the weeds,' he said, handing the implement to Nkosinathi.

Nkosinathi was puzzled, why was it that he had to work in the fields? Khulekani laughed at him, they had all felt the same when they had first arrived, but Ndukwana had decreed that they must.

Pickpockets and Zulus

'We all have to do it my friend; we are here to look after the King's herd and the iKhanda as well as to train as warriors.'

Deflated and hungry Nkosinathi followed the others out into the fields and after only a short time working his furrow, he began to realise that women's work was hard, harder than that of a herdsman and then, in the heat of the day, another of the new cadets came to work alongside him. They spoke little, working diligently amongst the rows of maize, digging out the weeds, and tossing them onto an ever-growing pile, until eventually he had had enough. Nkosinathi stood up straight, rubbed the small of his back and stood a while leaning on his implement. The other boy stopped and leaned on his hoe, grinning stupidly and then, unexpectedly, he dropped his hoe to the ground and strode over to where his fighting sticks lay. He picked them up brandishing them in challenge, a challenge Nkosinathi could not ignore.

Pleased with an excuse to stop work the two cadets began to circle one another, sticks in hand and looking for an opening to strike. Little by little, they probed, a thrust here a parry there and gradually they moved towards rough, uncultivated ground with a dry and uneven surface. Nkosinathi stumbled and his opponent saw his chance prodding a stick hard at Nkosinathi's midriff and forcing him to defend himself. Nkosinathi raised one of his sticks in defence and his opponent lunged at him, missing his midriff by a hair's breadth and losing his balance. It gave Nkosinathi the opening he was looking for and he crashed his own stick hard across his opponents back but the boy did not flinch, instead he again tried to jab at Nkosinathi.

The cadets were returning to the field to collect a load of maize and, silently, unseen by the protagonists, they closed up to watch from the sidelines eventually cheering on their favourite as the two gladiators parried back and forth. Twisting and turning they hit out at each other and after ten minutes, Nkosinathi's concentration began to weaken. The other cadet feinted to one side, managed to land a decisive blow to Nkosinathi's scalp and drew blood, the contest was over and Nkosinathi had lost his first fight.

The watching cadets cheered and slapped each of them on their backs for providing such sport. Before long other fights began to break out as each youth wanted to prove himself in front of his peers and Ndukwana, alerted by the commotion, strode across the field to watch. He was not about to put a stop to the fights, he wanted to see their fighting skills, to encourage them and watch the contests until finally ordering them to stop.

'You are keen to fight I can see that. Perhaps in two days, when your heads have healed we will begin some real training.' The cadets grinned, even Nkosinathi, his head as sore as it was, looked forward to some real military training.

Ndukwana drilled the cadets in the fighting techniques of the Zulu army, assigning them to company strength, showing them the formations they should adopt whilst on the move and what they should do when the enemy is sighted. They ran, they sang and they practised the technique employed for the short stabbing spears and occasionally Ndukwana allowed them to let off steam with bouts of stick fighting until one day, after a hard days' march, he addressed them;

'You cadets are looking after the Kings' homestead very well and he is pleased and now I think it is time for you to learn the regimental dance. When the King calls you to the royal iKhanda, he will expect a war dance, he will expect you to show how fierce you will be on the battlefield and so, after you have finished your chores we will form up on the parade ground and I will teach you your regimental dance.'

A few hours later, the cadets assembled, Ndukwana pushed and cajoled them into two lines facing one another before beginning his instruction.

'You and you' said Ndukwana pointing at one Cadet in each line, 'show me what you can do.' He began to clap his hands rhythmically and straight away, the two lines of cadets joined in. The two boys selected began to shuffle from their lines into the open space. Since childhood they had danced at festivals, weddings, burials and any ceremony that their village found as an excuse to make merry. They had known the beat of the drums ever since they could remember, the primeval rhythms of their culture was part of their being.

'You,' said Ndukwana.

The first Cadet stepped forward as commanded and leapt into the air as high as he could, landing gracefully on bended knees and touching the ground with his outstretched fingers.

'You' Ndukwana turned to the opposite row.

The second Cadet copied the first, leaping even higher and then both youths began gyrating to the beat generated by the clapping hands of their cohorts. Ndukwana watched with interest before sweeping his spear in front of him, ordering the dancers to return to the ranks. He selected two more cadets who sprang energetically out from their respective ranks and began to hop about on one leg, then the other before dancing across the space between the rows of Cadets. They made as if to throw an imaginary spear into the opposite rank in a show of aggression before retreating towards their respective lines.

Ndukwana's face was implacable, his expression giving nothing away as he watched each pair taking their turn. Eventually it was Nkosinathi's turn, paired with Somopho and their eyes met across the open space. The rhythmic clapping and an escalating show of violence increased both boys tendency towards belligerence and the dance became a challenge, a challenge to see who was not only the best dancer, but who would make the bravest warrior.

Somopho had been a Cadet longer than Nkosinathi; he was a year older and felt superior, his gaze held Nkosinathi's, challenging him. Nkosinathi responded, the blood pumping through his veins, adrenalin flowing and a feeling of fearlessness infiltrating his senses. Full of confidence he ran at Somopho, leaping almost his own height, seeming to hang in the air – a clear challenge.

Somopho was surprised at this aggression but not to be outdone ran several paces to confront Nkosinathi, leaping the last few feet, but he could not reach the height of Nkosinathi and he felt cheated. His blood was also running high and the thought of humiliation by a younger boy forced him to attempt one more leap but again he could not quite make the same height as Nkosinathi.

Ndukwana watched intently for this was just such a situation for which he had hoped. The cadets were competing to see who was best and he was able to judge who could lead and who could not. He looked along the lines of cadets and realised that the situation was in danger of getting out of control.

'Stop,' he shouted, thumping his spear noisily on the ground.

Immediately the clapping hands ceased their intoxicating rhythm and the two cadets looked sheepishly at him.

'I am pleased, you have performed well and now we will begin to learn the regimental dance and to perfect it before you leave for Ulundi.'

He clapped his hands twice and the cadets straightened their lines, Nkosinathi felt elated, he knew that he had jumped the highest and with a will he began to stamp his feet to the rhythm of the dance. First two stamps with his right foot then two with his left foot, and the opposing rows moved towards each other. Closer they came until, eventually, face-to-face, the fierce Zulu warriors with sweat pouring down their faces, glowered at each other and on Ndukwana's command sixty feet stamped the ground in unison and for a few seconds they shook their sticks at each other in mock battle before retreating to their starting positions.

For a further two hours they rehearsed these simple dance movements until they were exhausted. Ndukwana stood and watched, advising, inveigling the cadets and when they made mistakes, admonishing them. He was pleased because he had seen what he wanted to see, these cadets had the makings of an *Ibutho*.

147

Nkosinathi had been away from home for almost one cycle of the moon before his sister Nozipho appeared. She had walked from his father's Kraal carrying a bag of maize on her head and some dried meat in a satchel strung over one shoulder. Themba knew well of the hardships her son was enduring her eldest sons had suffered the same rigours and she knew that food would be scarce. Unless Nkosinathi could kill a few small animals or find berries and nuts in the bush he would be very hungry, it was the way of the army. Tradition dictated that the sisters of the cadets could visit periodically to bring extra sustenance and Themba had felt the time was right to ask her husband's permission to send Nozipho. She had prepared food the previous evening and as soon as it was light, she had waved Nozipho off on her journey to the Cadet's iKhanda.

By early afternoon Nozipho had come across the herd grazing out in the pasture and she asked the first cadet she met where she might find her brother. He directed her to the field of maize and as she approached, she giggled to herself at the thought of her big strong brother doing women's work.

'I see you little sister,' said Nkosinathi as she approached. 'I hope you have brought me some food, what have you in there?' he asked, pointing with his hoe at her shoulder bag.

'I have brought you mealie, and dried meat,' she said, unslinging her satchel.

Nkosinathi reached out his hand and placed it under her chin, applying just enough force so that she tilted her head up a little and her big brown eyes looked into his.

'Oh Nkosinathi, you look so thin. I should have brought you food earlier. I should have brought more,' said Nozipho.

'No my little sister,' Nkosinathi chuckled, 'this is the way of the Cadets. We serve the King, we look after his Kraal and his herd and twice a day we drink his milk, it is an honour. Sometimes one of us kills some small animal and we share it, we find tubers and berries in the bush, we survive but we are always hungry so please thank my father for this gift of food.'

Nkosinathi took the satchel from her. 'You should rest a short while Nozipho before you return home. Eat some of the maize and a little of the meat before you go, you will need your strength if you are to return home before dark.'

'Thank you my brother, but I have some food here,' and she opened her skirt to reveal a small leather bag. 'I have enough for the journey. Tell me Nkosinathi what it is like here, how do they treat you, what do you do? I have to tell all when I return.'

For half an hour they talked, Nkosinathi related details of his time at the iKhanda, told her what he had been doing, told of the new friends he had made; particularly Manelesi whom he said had been especially kind to him.

'That is Manelesi over there,' he said, pointing towards his friend watching over the grazing herd two hundred yards away.

'He was the one who directed me to you' said Nozipho.

'Hey Manelesi, come and meet my sister,' he shouted through cupped hands.

Nozipho looked embarrassed and made to leave but before she had gone twenty paces, Manelesi had reached them and stood in her path.

'This is your sister Nkosinathi?'

'Yes she is the youngest of my sisters and she has a temper so be careful or you might regret it,' laughed Nkosinathi.

'Boys, you are all the same' said Nozipho, embarrassment spreading across her face. 'I will leave now and I shall return soon with more food for you, and next time, do not tease me so.'

'Do not go yet little one,' said Manelesi looking down at her. She was a foot shorter, with the biggest brown eyes he had ever seen and they had him transfixed. 'Your father must be proud of such a daughter Nkosinathi, a girl that braves the wild animals to bring food to her brother, a girl that has such charm.'

Nozipho looked at the tall handsome boy who said such nice things about her. 'You are kind Manelesi, you have helped my brother, I shall tell my father this and you will be welcome in our village. But now I must go, for if I do not it will be dark before I reach home.'

'Yes, I understand it is dangerous for you to be alone in the dark. I shall ask Ndukwana if I can accompany you to make sure you get back to your Kraal safely,' said Manelesi and before either of the others could say anything, he ran off to find Ndukwana.

'What should I do Nkosinathi' said Nozipho turning to her brother, a little puzzled. 'Should I leave now or wait to see what happens with Manelesi?'

'Wait, I will feel happier if we can accompany you back home.'

Pickpockets and Zulus

Manelesi re-appeared a short time later, a sad look upon his face that told the story. Ndukwana had refused permission for him to accompany the girl back to her Kraal, for he would be missing for at least a whole day and would not be attending to the Kings household. 'But' he had said, 'I will arrange for her to spend the night in one of the women's huts and she may leave in the morning.'

Nozipho's eyes lit up because she did not particularly wish to return home immediately, nightfall might overtake her and besides, if she stayed she could watch what the cadets were doing.

'I am happy to stay a while,' she said.

'Hmm..., it is good that I know you are safe' said Nkosinathi, beginning to wonder what teasing he might have to endure from the other Cadets.

'I will show you where the women's huts are,' said Manelesi rather hastily. Nozipho accepted his offer just as quickly and Nkosinathi watched them go before returning to his weeding.

For more than two years Nkosinathi, Somopho, Manelesi and the others tended to the herd, repaired the beehive huts and constantly re-made the Kraals' protective outer wall of thorn bushes. Nozipho brought food when she could and each time Manelesi looked after her and from time to time other youths joined them until they were almost one hundred in number. Under the tutelage of Ndukwana, they learned the arts of a Zulu warrior, rehearsing the war dance, singing military songs and practising their stick fighting until the fateful day when the King's messenger arrived with his order to form a new regiment. His word was for the cadets to assemble near his principle residence to form a new regiment – 'the uVe.'

BOOK 2

Chapter 1

The Colour Sergeant's staccato words, 'Pre...sent arms',
echoed around the parade ground, the regiment
resplendent in red tunics and white Foreign Service
helmets, lifted their rifles and in well-rehearsed
movements finally held them stiffly in front of their
chests. Simultaneously a group of mounted officers
nudged their horses forward in front of the assemble
ranks and made their way to the centre of the square.

Onlookers, locals and soldiers families watched with
fascination at the display of discipline and order by the
soldiers of the Twenty Fourth Regiment of Foot. Then a
bugle sounded and from an archway in the Castle of San
Marcos, a contingent of seven soldiers marching in step
appeared. Six soldiers guarded a seventh who carried in
his outstretched arms, a scarlet cushion on which lay the
keys to the gates of the Rock of Gibraltar.

From the far side of the parade ground, amongst the
men of the Fourth Regiment of Foot an order bellowed
out and the rippling echo of rifles being presented
disturbed the still warm air and a party of soldiers
appeared from their midst to march smartly across the
parade ground. The two groups converged in front of the
officers watched by local dignitaries gathered to witness

153

the handing over of the keys, a symbol of the transfer of duties from one regiment to another.

The sergeants commanding the key parties barked orders to their men to "halt..., attention..., about turn..., pre...sent arms" and with much pomp and ceremony the keys were passed from the Twenty Fourth to the Fourth.

'Ri...ght turn, shoulder arms,' shouted the Colour Sergeant of the Twenty Fourth and the whole regiment turned, making a sound not unlike thunder as eight hundred boots stamped the cobbled ground and eight hundred rifles slapped against shoulders. The commanding officer and his company took up their positions and behind them; the bandmaster lifted his mace. With several movements he counted in Georgie and the other drummers who began a tap...tap...tap on their drums. The order "by the left, quick march" rang out across the square and the whole body of men and horses moved off in unison to the sound of "Men of Harlech", the regimental march of the Twenty Fourth regiment of foot.

'Blimey it was hot out there' said Georgie uncoupling his drum from the leather strap across his shoulder and letting it slide gently to the ground before wiping the sweat from his forehead and undoing the top two buttons of his tunic.

'To be sure it is,' replied Patrick Donovan, putting his brightly polished silver Cornet on the table beside him. 'It's a drink I'll be wantin' right now Georgie boy, what about you?'

Georgie grinned at the pale faced giant Patrick had grown into, red hair and piercing grey eyes, a man that stood out from the crowd. He was the tallest of the boys in the band and one of the best shots in the regiment.

He had trained with him at Chatham and they had become firm friends before transferring to the new regimental depot at Brecon, an isolated Welsh town in the midst of wild and hilly country. It was there that Georgie had learned to play his snare drum, to become a fully-fledged member of the regimental band, one of the best in the British Army and today they had shown just how good they were. Leading the parade from the barracks and back, their stirring military music had met with the approval of the assembled crowds and dignitaries alike and now that they were back in their barracks, they were able to relax. Patrick was waxing lyrical about the beer he was going to drink and Georgie was unbuttoning his tunic when the Band Master appeared followed by the Platoon Commander.

'Right men fall in; Lieutenant Pearson would like a word.' The bandsmen some sitting, some standing and some leaning lazily against the white washed walls were galvanized into action, forming a line and standing silently to attention.

'Men, you are aware that we are embarking for South Africa, how long we'll be there I'm not sure but some of you have been with the regiment for a number of years now and are reaching your eighteenth birthdays. You men can sign on for a further six years or you can take a discharge but I want to tell you that life in the British Army has never been better and the chance to see the world never greater, therefore, those of you who do wish to be discharged within the next six months will be left behind. The rest of you will embark on the steam ship Simoon at ten o clock tomorrow morning and I want you smartly turned out and on your best behaviour.' He paused for a few moments to look along the line of young bandsmen, saluted lazily and walked out of the room saying 'Carry on' to the Band Master.

'Fall out,' said the Band Master, 'Donovan.'

'Yes sir,'

'You're eighteen soon aren't you?'

'Yes sir, in a month sir.'

'And what about signing on for a further six years? Have you thought about that?'

'Yes sir I have, I'll be staying sir. There's nothing for me back in Ireland an' I fancy a look at South Africa sir.'

Band Master Burck smiled, pleased that Patrick was staying, for all his rough edges Patrick Donovan was one of the best Cornet players in the band and when they had the chance to play for the ladies at the regimental dances, Patrick could rustle up some lively Irish jigs towards the evenings conclusion. The result was always the same, the officers and their ladies left for home happy and content and he received the accolades.

'Good, good, well we're on the move soon and then we'll find out what South Africa is like. Anyone else thinking of leaving us?' he asked.

The soldiers didn't move, all those eligible for discharge seemed happy enough to sign on for another six years which made Band Master Burck a very happy man. With the band playing to a high standard, he would not have to worry about having to cope with a change of personnel.

'Corporal Harrington, take charge and get the men to sort out their kit for the move will you. The instruments are to be packed in the hold for the voyage, so can you organize that?'

'Yes sir' said the corporal.

'Looks like there will be no drinkin' tonight Georgie boy,' whispered Patrick out of the corner of his mouth.

Georgie just grinned, he did not have the drinking habit yet and at almost seventeen years of age, it would be another year before he had to make the decision of whether or not to sign on as a man for a further six years. He picked up his drum, began to pack it in its cloth bag and wondered, there was no real decision to make; he was alone in the world, his only family was the Army.

As he slipped the drum into its Hessian bag his mind drifted back to the time when he had completed his six months basic training. The platoon was allowed a few days leave and he had joined some soldiers on the train into London to try to find his Aunt Jane and her family. Arriving in London, he had left the station and walked the old familiar streets back to Lambeth where he Ellen and James had spent their time picking pockets and he wondered how and where they were. He had crossed the bridge, passing street sellers, the costermongers barrows and the grim buildings of the South Bank, eventually reaching the familiar tenement block on Tanner Street. He had banged on the door of Aunt Jane's room until eventually a scruffy looking woman had opened it. He smiled to himself at the memory, "scruffy" he remembered thinking, in fact most of the people he had encountered since crossing the river had looked "scruffy". Army discipline was having its effect, making a man of him as the recruiting sergeant said it would.

'Whaddya want?' she had snarled at him.

'I've come to see my Aunt Jane. Does she still live 'ere?'

'Naw, no one called Jane lives here. This be my an' my man's abode now.'

'Oh, perhaps you know where I might find them then?' he asked slightly taken aback.

'Naw, don't know nothing,' she said and slammed the door in his face.

He remembered how dejected the woman's words had made him feel. Uncle Billy, Aunt Jane and their three children, for all their faults, were his only family. He had left the building, descended the steps onto the street and sat for a while on the low wall wondering what he might do when a voice from behind said;

'Is that you young Georgie?'

He had looked round to see the old man who lived on the first floor standing in the doorway. He had never really known the old man, simply seen him shuffling back and forth occasionally.

'Yes sir,' he had said, bringing a smile to the old man's face.

'Well you certainly look different boy. Smartened up a treat, and filled out. You're going to make a fine specimen when you finally stop growing. Don't look so puzzled lad, I've seen you many a time with that no good Billy Tyndal and I know you were a livin' with them. I was with the Ninety First, in the Crimea you know, we fought at Balaclava. I was a soldier for nigh on twenty years before I came back to London. It's good to see the Army's made something of you son.'

They were kind words indeed and from a man he didn't really know. 'What's happened to Aunt Jane and my cousins?' he had asked.

'I don't really know, only that there was some commotion with the Peelers a couple of months ago and

I haven't seen them since. I can only guess they had some trouble with the law and I am not surprised they not be about these parts. I've not seen any on 'em in two months and don't suppose anyone else has either. They've made themselves scarce I reckon, disappeared for a while like.'

There was nothing else Georgie could have done, he did not have the time to tramp the streets looking for them but thought he would at least have a look outside the theatres and drinking establishments they had frequented. He found a bed in a lodging house on the Mile End Road and spent the following day trudging round his old haunts and up to Trafalgar Square but could not find any sign of them. The recruiting sergeants were still there but Sergeant Roberts was not one of them.

Chapter 2

The sweat ran down Georgie's' forehead, dripping onto the end of his nose where it briefly remained before evaporating in the hot African sun. He stood rigidly to attention, his drum hanging loosely at his side and his drumsticks clasped in his right hand. He had stood in the same place for almost an hour, his back ached and it seemed that the speeches would never end. First one dignitary then another addressed the watching crowd until finally the President of Cape Colony stood up to speak.

'My Lords, Ladies and Gentlemen, I have listened to the words of our distinguished speakers and I can only add that these are momentous times in the history of our Colony. Building this new Parliament building to uphold democracy in these lands will be a great achievement of which we should all be proud. I therefore declare the laying of the first stone complete.'

It was exactly twelve noon and at that moment, a Royal salute from the castle guns boomed out across the bay launching a ripple of applause and cheering from the assembled crowd. Band Master Burck turned to face his bandsmen, raised his baton and with a gentle curving motion he led them into a rendition of the 'Hallelujah Chorus.' As the sonorous tones of the brass instruments drifted across the square, the celebrations continued and then the dignitaries led the parade along Cape Town's Main Street followed closely behind by the band to the applause and cheers of colonials and Africans alike. There was a feeling amongst the people of the Cape that the colony was finally coming of age.

The discovery of diamonds at Kimberly had brought newfound wealth to the colony and that in turn attracted all manner of men seeking their fortunes. The white population was growing, the new Parliament building would give them stature and they felt the Government back in Great Britain was finally noticing them.

Georgie was unaware of the greater politics of Cape Colony he was a simple soldier who enjoyed life in the Army. He had friends and comrades, interesting occupations for part of the time and here he was on his second posting, experiencing the delights of South Africa.

'Georgie, how's about a last drink before we leave civilisation?' said Patrick, packing his instrument away.

'Sounds good to me Patrick, I ain't got a lot of money left though.'

'Where we're going I don't think you'll be needin' money, there's no pub out in the back of beyond. What about you lads?' he said to the other bandsmen. 'How's about one last drink and a cuddle with one of those native girls?'

They all laughed, Patrick was a character and could get a party going at the drop of a hat and it would be no more than a day or two before they left Cape Town to head up towards the Vaal River. A bunch of renegade white men, Germans, Fenians and disgruntled Boers were agitating against the authorities in Cape Town and rumour had it that there was unrest amongst the diggers in the diamond fields. The Regiment was going to Kimberly to quell any rebellion, and if there were rebellion then it would be their first taste of action.

'Come on boys, lets dump this lot,' said Patrick pointing to their instruments, 'let's hit the town, I know a couple of good bars where they will look after us.'

The young soldiers took little convincing and were soon walking towards the docks for a last few hours of leave before they headed into the barren lands of the Great Karoo. Their first port of call was the Lord Nelson Inn; a modest stone built structure that was a favourite of the Royal Navy.

'Good day to you landlord, 'tis a fine day to be sure,' said Patrick walking into the bar room rubbing his hands together.

The landlord nodded and began to fill tankards with his homemade beer, the finest in the port and the soldiers settled down at a long wooden table leaving Patrick to pay.

Dickie Henderson chirped up 'I heard we're going to fight natives and we'd better be on our toes because the county's wild up there.'

'To be sure we'll sort the bastards out' said Patrick, depositing the last of the tankards onto the bench. 'I fancy those diamond fields, could be some pickings there for a soldier.'

The others laughed 'you won't have time to go looking for diamonds, we'll be soldierin' all right' said one. 'Aye, an' who knows where we'll fetch up, chasin' 'oten tots' said another. They picked up their tankards and for a while, there was silence, the only sound that of beer pouring down dry throats and then suddenly, they were all talking at once and so it went on for the rest of the evening. The beer flowed freely; they talked of the coming campaign, women and the sights they had seen in this strange new land. Georgie was enjoying the banter but by the end of the evening, the alcohol left him the worse for wear and it seemed an awful long way back to their barracks.

Resplendent in red and blue uniforms, shouldering their new Martini Henry rifles, the regiment marched smartly to the railway station and the start of the expedition, but the railway track meant for the diamond fields had only reached Wellington, forty-five miles away.

'I'm thinking of volunteering for the Mounted Infantry Georgie mi boy, what do you think of that?' said Patrick squashed between Georgie, half a dozen other soldiers and the window.

'Can you ride a horse?'

'Can I ride a horse? Nope, but I'll surely try. I bin lookin' out of the window and to be sure, this country is too big to be walking round. I will learn to ride a horse soon enough and will not be wearing my shoe leather out', he said with a grin. 'Are ye comin' with me Georgie boy?'

'I can't Patrick, you know that I can't volunteer for anything 'till I'm eighteen and that's another six months or more,' said a bemused Georgie.

'Well they have been asking for volunteers to form a mounted section and I'm pullin' your leg, I used to ride a pony on the farm back in Ireland and I reckon I could handle one of those colonial nags,' Patrick added, looking out of the window and noticing that they were

163

almost at their destination. 'Not long now lads, I can see tents.'

The train arrived in Wellington in good time and Georgie's company joined the main body of the army. Originally, the band had remained behind in Cape Town for the ceremony of the laying of the first stone for the new Parliament building, but now they had caught up. Descending from the carriage Georgie slung his kit bag over one shoulder his rifle over the other and together with the rest of his platoon, marched the short distance to the military camp.

'This doesn't look too hard does it?' said Dickie scrutinizing the scene. 'The pace those mules go we shouldn't have much difficulty keeping up',

'See that line of hills in the distance,' said a corporal, 'we will have to find a way up there with this lot.' He nodded towards a vast array of wagons and mules spread out across the open country. 'There won't be any roads you know, look' he said pointing to several wagons. 'You'll find out soon enough what real soldiering is like, when we have to start hauling them by hand because the mules can't manage.'

Dickie's face changed from bright, breezy to dark and stormy in a fraction of a second as the realisation that perhaps it was not going to be so easy after all dawned upon him.

Cone shaped tents soon began to spring up like a field of daisies as the newly arrived soldiers made camp for the night. After an inspection by the Colour sergeant and an officer, the men trooped off to the field kitchen for their evening meal and after washing it down with a mug of hot tea, out came the tobacco.

'Here Georgie take a pipe full,' said Dickie offering his pouch.

'Where is it we're supposed to be going?' said Georgie, tamping the tobacco in the pipe bowl.

Dickie Henderson was a sharp individual and invariably he was the first one with any news about the regiment and if anyone knew what was going on, it would be him.

'We're off across what they call the Great Karoo to Griqualand where there's supposed to be some sort of rebellion by the miners. With a bit of luck we'll be in the diamond fields and maybe we might pick some up along the way!'

'I read a bit about that in the newspapers,' said Georgie. 'I didn't know we would get to the diamond fields though. Blimey, we might all become rich if we find diamonds.'

Around their little camp fire several pairs of eyes shone brightly, sparkling diamonds uppermost in their thoughts because finding a large enough diamond could be a one-way ticket out of the Army and towards the good life. But the night was cold, and the soldier's soon forgot about diamonds, their immediate priority was to keep warm as they managed only a fitful night's sleep.

The sound of reveille roused them at four in the morning, damp and cold air greeting them after their first night under canvas. Tumbling out into a grey and unwelcoming dawn the soldiers struck camp to the sound of angry mules protesting as their handlers forced them back into harness. They ate a hasty breakfast and then loaded the wagons with all the paraphernalia of an army on the march and finally the column began forming up, the drover's whips cracking over the ears of the angry mules.

The early morning mist was giving way to drizzle and the cold air made them shiver and it was not long before the track, firm enough to begin with, began to turn into a quagmire. Hundreds of wagon wheels and mule hooves churned up the mud, the cracks of the bullwhips became more frequent and the misery of an army on the march set in. Eventually the rain did stop and the sun rose high enough in the sky to warm them and the wagons began to spread out across the countryside, each drover finding his own route over firmer ground towards the distant hills. The soldiers marched in companies, their rifles slung across their backs and after a week, the mountains began to tower over them. The terrain changed markedly, the ground began to slope increasingly upwards and the pass known as Bain's Kloof came into view.

It was supposed to be a proper road with the promise of easy passage but the rain returned and when they began to attempt the ascent, mud and running water made progress pitifully slow. The wagons became too much for the valiant mules straining in their harnesses, even the encouragement of the drover's whips had little effect on them. They slithered and stumbled; wagon wheels skidded and stuck in the soft mud forcing the soldiers to lend assistance. Grabbing hold of the spokes of the wheels the men heaved with all their might, forcing the them to turn, backbreaking work, but slowly bit-by-bit the wheels did began to turn and the mules reached solid ground.

'Ere, you men,' the corporal called out to Georgie's section 'get your shoulders be'ind these wagon wheels and shove.'

The soldiers laid their weapons and equipment on the ground and flung themselves into the backbreaking work of moving the wagons, slipping and sliding alongside the mules.

'I tell you Georgie lad, I'm for the Mounted Infantry as soon as I can. Have you seen them riding by, easy as you like and here we are bustin' our guts.'

Georgie pushed hard against the wheel with his back against the rim until he felt it turn and the mules took the strain. The soldiers stood back at last blowing their cheeks out as they recovered from the ordeal and as Georgie salvaged his rifle, he noticed a group of riders following further down the slope.

'I'm not so sure they have it that easy Patrick look there' he said, nodding his head towards the group of horseman, each on foot and pulling at their horse's bridals. With heads and necks stretched forwards, their eyes bulging in fear the horses resisted as their riders tried in vain to coax them up the incline. The soldiers pulled hard on the reigns shouting encouragement until suddenly, one of the horses slipped in the mud and slithered sideways, the stricken animal kicking out in panic and almost taking off its rider's head as he dived out of the way. 'I think there's more to it than you think Patrick.'

Patrick was unmoved, keeping his eye on the cameo as he recovered his own rifle and stood watching the Mounted Infantrymen advance up the slope.

Pickpockets and Zulus

'That was nothing; any horseman worth his salt could have done that. You watch Georgie he'll be on that nag soon enough whilst we're still wearin' out our boots.'

Sure enough, within half an hour the horses had reached firmer, level ground, and the soldiers remounted to trot off along the lines of wagons to the envy of some watching infantry.

'Come on you lot, keep moving,' called the corporal and after a difficult and demanding climb the Army of the Vaal eventually reached the top of the pass and made camp for the night.

'That was quite a climb,' said Georgie filling his pipe.

'Aye and I hear it is just as bad going downhill, they say it's a steep and dangerous decent towards the Breede River for us tomorrow,' answered Dickie, the font of all knowledge.

For two hundred miles, the column wound its way north, surrounded by towering mountains before making a second ascent onto the vast plateau known as the Great Karoo, an unending expanse of shale and sandstone. The landscape was uninteresting, covered in sparse vegetation, bleak and broken only by an occasional hillock or dried out riverbed. However, the army of redcoats was becoming skilled in moving the wagons across virgin terrain and with the flatness of the high plateau; they began to make a decent rate of twenty miles a day. Spread out over a wide area each wagon made its own track and for the soldiers and progress became easier except for the swarms of maddening flies that descended upon them. Such distraction caused by the flies coupled with their inadequate tunics, too hot by day and barely warm enough at night only added to their discomfort and hardship.

'I knew we would have a bit of a time of it,' said Dickie one night, 'but I didn't expect my balls to freeze off!' None of the men laughed, they were all experiencing the same sensation.

'I tell you Georgie,' said Patrick in a quiet voice, 'I tell you, it's the Mounted Infantry for me to be sure. Are you with me?'

'It's tempting Patrick, but I can't ride a horse. What good's that?'

'They'll teach you, pretend you can ride if you're asked and I bet in a couple of days you'll be ridin' like a proper Lancer to be sure,' he said, a wry smile lighting up his face and a tired Georgie simply nodded agreement.

The column plodded on for another week until finally, after three hundred and fifty arduous miles, it reached Hopetown where the army made camp on the banks of the Orange River. Pitching their tents the army received orders to rest and recuperate for a few days, the field kitchens were fired up to provide decent hot food and the pickets dispersed to vantage points.

Georgie had lost weight, all of the men had and he pulled his belt one more notch tighter to prevent them slipping and felt his stomach heave. Quite a few of the men had suffered from diarrhoea and now it seemed it was his turn. Dropping the tent pole he was carrying, he made his way to the latrines as quickly as he could to gain some relief.

'Where are you rushing off to?' shouted Dickie, pulling on one of the tent's guy ropes. Georgie did not reply, he was feeling quite ill and had only one thought in mind, he was not well and his visit to the latrines confirmed it. His next port of call was the medical officer, and the queue outside his tent was a long one.

'Right my lad, what's your problem?' asked the orderly. 'By the look on your face you've got what most of the rest of today's patients have.'

'Upset stomach and I'm losing weight I think' replied Georgie in a quiet voice.

'Aye, I thought so,' said the man in a matter of fact voice, 'here drink this, it should help.' He poured some white chalky mixture from a large jar into a cup and passed it to Georgie who gulped it down in one go. 'If it hasn't cleared up by tomorrow afternoon come back for another dose. Next!' he called out, dismissing Georgie with a nod of his head.

'I hear you got the runs Georgie boy,' said Patrick when he returned to their tent. Georgie could only nod; all he wanted to do was to lie down and go to sleep. The trek from Cape Town had taken its toll on not just him but many of his fellow soldiers and the chance of a rest was very welcome. All they needed now was a good fight with the enemy and they could call themselves veterans.

Georgie slept well that night and woke from a deep sleep feeling much better, managing to eat a small breakfast of dry bread and sitting with his fellows outside the tent he watched a party of mounted men bringing in a line of horses, strung one behind the other.

'Well Georgie my boy, I have to tell you that I will be leavin' you soon. Do you see the horses, well l will be up and ridin' one of them soon enough.'

Georgie looked up at his friend, not really grasping the big Irishman's words.

Pickpockets and Zulus

'I have volunteered for the Mounted Infantry and I'll be off learning to ride and fight like a cavalryman so I will.'

'Blimey, so you've gone and done it? What about the band, can you leave so easily?'

'To be sure I can, it is a war zone we in, and its fighting that matters, not blowing. I've had my permissions an it's off that I am.' Patrick ducked into the tent and five minutes later emerged in full uniform, carrying his equipment, his Martini-Henry slung casually over his shoulder. 'It's goodbye for now boys,' he said with a wave as he turned and walked towards the picket lines of the mounted section.

For several weeks, the Army recuperated, trained and waited in anticipation for orders to march on the rebels. Back to full health, their equipment and guns in tiptop condition they were eager for a fight, show these colonials what they could do to an enemy. However, news of their presence alongside the Orange River had panicked the rebels who had requested a meeting with the Governor of Cape Colony, Sir Henry Barkly and had quickly come to an agreement to lay down their arms and to disband their organisation. The troops were not going to have to fight after all.

The news of the rebel's capitulation created mixed feelings within the ranks, the soldiers were trained and eager for a fight but on the other hand, a few days of relaxation was very welcome. Within days of the agreement with the rebels, the Army of the Vaal crossed the Orange River into Griqualand West and struck out towards the Modder River and no sooner had they crossed the river than rumours began circulating that perhaps they would have their fight after all. Intelligence received by the high command suggested that Fenians, who hated the British and all that Britain stood for, would oppose their crossing of the Modder.

The order came to double the night guard and during the day, the newly formed Mounted Infantry scouted far ahead of the slow moving column. Amongst them was a slightly uncomfortable Patrick Donovan, his buttocks sore and red as he acclimatised to the saddle.

'Private Donovan, lean forwards a bit more, you will find it more comfortable,' shouted Lieutenant Browne. 'I thought you said you could ride a horse.'

'To be sure I can sir, the awkward beast is just getting used to me sir. He's the one that can't ride,' said Patrick grimacing.

Lieutenant Browne swung his horse away from the struggling Irishman and nudged it forward with his heels. Edward Browne had only had two weeks in which to train the volunteer infantrymen in the art of riding a horse and began to wonder if some of them would ever become competent horsemen. Most of the soldiers could indeed ride, ex farmers and liverymen and he knew that with such men the enterprise could be a success. Even at this early stage the Mounted Infantry were showing their worth, scouting out well ahead of the slow moving column, on picket duties during the hours of darkness, the eyes and ears of the Army.

Patrick had bluffed his way into the Mounted Corps and for a while, he struggled to hide his lack of ability on a horse but his training had begun in earnest once the Army had acquired enough horses. The Boer farmers, initially hostile and not prepared to sell their animals, had soon changed their minds at the sight of the British government's money. Realising they could almost name their price, they were suddenly more than willing to sell and the Mounted Infantry section expanded.

The soreness associated with their extended time in the saddle was not the only problem for the new recruits, serge trousers were wearing thin and Lieutenant Browne took a leaf out of the Boer farmer's book. He arranged for the issue of brown corduroy as a substitute for the blue serge and during their initial training, discovered that the long barrelled Martini Henry rifles were too cumbersome for use in the saddle and after some experimentation had them replaced with the shorter and more manageable Snider Carbines. It had been an idea of his and Lieutenant Carrington's for some time to form a mounted section, to give the regiment more mobility and an ability to scout well ahead of the column. As soon as he had heard that Lieutenant Carrington was looking for fellow officers to help form the Mounted Infantry he had jumped at the chance and slowly but surely Lieutenant Browne was whipping his command into shape and after one particularly gruelling patrol deep into hostile country, he reported to his superior, General Cunynghame.

'Sir, we have made a broad sweep across country and I have to report no sign of hostile activity towards the river,' he said with some pride in his voice.

'Very well Lieutenant, your Mounted Infantry are becoming useful. How are the men performing, I hear that one or two of your men are, shall we say, not quite in the league of the Lancers. Hmm...?'

'Quite well sir, they need to practice their riding a bit more but generally they are competent enough. They will never compete with regular cavalry, but then we never expected that they would.'

'Quite, quite. Tomorrow I want you to reconnoitre the far bank and if it looks safe enough, cross over and see what you can find. Carry on Browne I want a few more words with Lieutenant Carrington here.'

'Yes Sir, thank you sir,' said Lieutenant Browne saluting before he walked out of the tent as pleased as punch.

Patrick was standing alongside the picket, a mug of hot tea in his hand and he reached out to slap the nearest horse on its rump.

'To be sure my arse hurts, like I've been sliding down a mountain. Will you look at that, the bugger didn't even flinch, what chance has my arse against that?'

Georgie smiled at the comical Irishman. 'Well you were determined to get on a horse you stupid Irish bastard. What did you expect? Anyway you told me you could ride a horse.'

'I can now Georgie lad and as soon as my soreness wears off, I will be as happy as a pig in shit. You ought to try it, sitting up there you can see all manner of things and your feet don't hurt none.'

Georgie had wandered over to the picket line to see Patrick, billeted for now with the mounted section and not part of his unit any more. 'Have you seen any sign of the enemy yet?'

'Naw, not a thing, me and the lads are wondering if there really is an enemy. We should have seen something by now I reckon. Lieutenant says we should be somewhere near the river tomorrow and that's where we are expecting them.'

Pickpockets and Zulus

The following afternoon, Lieutenant Browne sat high in his saddle holding his field glasses and scanning the ground ahead of his troop when he noticed a flash of light. He concentrated his vision on that one place for a while - there it was again. They were approaching the River Modder and if the rebel faction decided to attack, then it was likely to be there, a place where the column would be at its most vulnerable.

'Keep your eyes peeled. You four move over there a couple of hundred yards and you four over there, the rest of you spread out in skirmishing order,' he said waving his arm to emphasise his instructions. 'We will move towards the river at walking pace.'

The troopers took up their positions, two sections of four men riding out to protect the flanks the rest strung out across the open ground, moving to within a few hundred yards of the riverbank. Lieutenant Browne called a halt and lifted his binoculars to his eyes, as he had done every ten minutes since seeing the flash of light. Carefully he scanned the brush on both sides if the river, sweeping slowly from side to side but there was nothing to see.

'Sergeant, take four men and make for that bluff over there, if we hit trouble I want you in a position to give covering fire.'

'Sir' said the sergeant, nodding towards Patrick and the other men of his section, indicating that they should follow him. The riders spurred their animals forward and the party trotted away to the vantage point ahead of the main body.

Arthur Morgan and Frank Williams had volunteered with Patrick from the first battalion and the other two men of the section, Barney Smith and George Allen were from the Second battalion. Initially there had been some light-hearted rivalry between the men, but the weeks of training and their patrols had formed them into a well-drilled unit and reaching their objective, they dismounted, leading the horses into a hollow. Quickly and efficiently they handed their horses reigns to the designated handler, Frank Williams, before taking up their positions. Carbines at the ready, the sergeant led his men up the slight incline to the summit of the hillock where they had a good view of the river crossing and the opposite bank. If there was anyone waiting for them, they were confident that they would spot them.

'To be sure there's nothing moving' over there,' said Patrick to himself as he scanned the brush on the far bank. He lifted the Carbine to his shoulder and adjusted the sights for two hundred yards, peering along the barrel for a target.

'What's that?' whispered Barney traversing his gun barrel towards some bushes on the opposite bank. 'The leaves on those bushes moved.' Both men froze. 'Sarge' hissed Barney, 'over there, something in those bushes.'

The sergeant looked in the direction of the trooper's gun barrel, lifted his field glasses to his eyes and scanned the bushes for any movement. There it was again, almost imperceptible but enough for him to be alarmed. 'Steady lads; wait for my order to shoot.' He blinked in the strong sunlight, focusing his field glasses on that small area of vegetation that might conceal an ambush and his body stiffened as he picked up a movement. The leaves vibrated rapidly for a second or two and then all was still once more.

'Get ready,' he said.

176

Pickpockets and Zulus

Patrick peered along the barrel of his gun, his sights adjusted and his finger wrapped around the trigger. He was ready, this was going to be his first taste of real action and he wanted to make sure his shot counted. Then suddenly the movement in the bushes increased and all of them could see exactly where the enemy was and the tension increased, becoming almost unbearable. Then, suddenly a large dark shape appeared and Patrick began to wonder just how big the enemy was. Why didn't the sergeant give the order to fire?

'Steady boys, hold your fire, it's a Reindeer and there's another one right behind.'

For a moment nothing happened, the soldiers lay prostrate, squinting down the barrels of their guns, then, all at once two large wild animals crashed out from the bushes where they had been happily feeding and the men burst out laughing.

'Sarge' said Barney, 'Reindeer live at the north pole not here.'

The sergeant looked round at him, 'a slip of the tongue, I meant Gazelles.' They were not Gazelles either; a pair of Oryx had been grazing in the undergrowth and had decided to make their way down to the river to drink.

'All right then, no sign of an ambush, I had better report to the lieutenant,' said a slightly embarrassed Sergeant Murray.

The troopers returned to the horses where a bemused Frank Williams enquired as what was all the laughter about.

'What did you see? Is there any enemy over there?'

Still chuckling to himself Barney said 'No we don't think the Fenians are over there but the sergeant's spotted a herd of Reindeer.'

The others started laughing again until Sergeant Murray silenced them with a stare. 'Never mind that, Barney, ride over to Lieutenant Browne and tell him what we've seen and tell him we are going over for a look.'

Barney mounted his horse and cantered off in search of the lieutenant whilst the others followed the sergeant into the river to test its depth and the strength of the current. One by one the horses slid down the river bank and the disturbed Oryx quietly trotted away back into the bush and once safely across, the troopers fanned out to scout inland for five hundred yards or so before the sergeant called them back. Retracing their path, they reached the riverbank and there on the far side, Lieutenant Browne and the rest of the Mounted Infantry were waiting for them.

'Nothing to report sir' said the sergeant, 'we've had a good look over the other side for about a quarter of a mile and found no sign of the enemy.'

'Good, good' said the lieutenant, 'we'll cross over and have a better look round and if you're right we'll head back to camp and tell the General that we don't think that the Fenians are here after all and that should please him.'

Chapter 3

'They're across,' said Dickie Henderson, walking alongside wagons towards the rear of the column. 'I can see at least a dozen wagons on the other side of the river. It's been a lot easier than we expected hasn't it?'

The other soldiers alongside the wagons nodded; they were at a bend in the track and had a clear view across to the river. Their job was to protect the wagons at the rear of the column and guessed that any ambush would probably start without them and if there was going to be an ambush it would have to be soon. But there was no opposition to the Army of the Vaal and they crossed the river in an orderly fashion, the rebels had capitulated and the crisis was over.

'There won't be any fighting. Politicians from Cape Town have negotiated a truce' said Dickie in a matter of fact tone as the men settled down to eat their dinner.

'You seem to know everything Dickie. What do you think we will be doing next?' asked Georgie as he returned from the field kitchen with a full mess tin.

'Well some important person joined the column today and rumour has it that the General is moving to Kimberly' said Dickie, stuffing his pipe with tobacco.

'I didn't think we were going anywhere near Kimberly?'

Pickpockets and Zulus

'That was yesterday's rumour Georgie, today the rumour is that the General and his staff will be moving to Kimberly and the regiment will follow. You watch' he said, lighting the pipe.

As usual, Dickie was right; they struck camp the following morning, loaded the wagons and marched towards the mining camp of Kimberly. The soldiers were eager to get back to some sort of civilization, two months in the wilderness had sapped their energy and the promise of canteens and maybe some girls had its obvious attractions. In fact, they themselves were an attraction because it was not every day that Kimberly welcomed the British Army. Miners and their dependants lined the route into town people of all shades and colours but mostly they were black, the labourers silently, inquisitively watching as the soldiers resplendent in their red and blue uniforms. The natives amongst the crowd had never seen anything like it and as the marching soldiers neared the town, the atmosphere changed. More and more white faces appeared, the crowd grew more dense, the cheering became louder and the soldiers grinned with pleasure.

The General ordered them to make camp on the outskirts of the town; he wanted his men looking their best, instructing the Colour Sergeants to make sure that every soldier under his command appeared smart and well turned out. He meant to impress the colonials who had said from the outset that an Army from England would not be able to cope with crossing the Great Karoo, but they had done it and he wanted to show them the mettle of the British Army.

'Patrick, what are you doing here? I thought that you would be grooming your horse for the parade later today',' said Georgie sitting outside his tent sewing a tear in his jacket.

'Oh, I did that hours ago, she's feeding now and after an hour or two's rest she will be as fit as a fiddle and you Georgie, how did you enjoy your little walk from the Cape?'

'Well the good news is my boots are still in one piece.' They both laughed and Georgie put down his sewing to greet his friend. 'What's it like riding a horse in the Army? I have only seen you boys once or twice passing through camp; you are always out on the plains or up in the hills'

'That's the job Georgie. We go and have a look to see what's in store for you lads don't we.'

They laughed again until Patrick's face took on a more serious look. You should think about joining us Georgie. It's a fine life in the saddle and you get to see an awful lot more, and better still it sure saves on shoe leather.'

'Maybe later, it's not long to my eighteenth birthday and then I will have to decide whether or not I'm staying in the Army.'

'Well for a couple of stray's like us Georgie there's not much else is there?'

Georgie grinned, it was good to see the brash, tough Irishman again, he had missed him since he had joined the Mounted Infantry. Patrick was right though, what else was there? it was either the Army or to go back to making a living on the streets with Aunt Jane, if she was still there and that seemed impossible, he not heard a thing about them since the day he had returned to London in search of them. No, the Army was his life now and soon he would have to decide whether to sign on as a man or not.

'Tell you what Patrick, if there are any vacancies in the Mounted Infantry after I sign on again let me know.'

Patrick's eyes lit up, 'bejasus I will, to be sure, we'll have a grand old time together Georgie boy. Anyway I need to be off, I have to saddle up my nag for an inspection before the parade and our sergeant can be a hard man if he wants to be.'

Patrick strode off towards the picket line to ready his horse for the parade and Georgie watched him go, screwing his eyes up. Patrick seemed to be walking strangely, 'must be all that horse riding he had been doing,' he chuckled to himself.

General Cunynghame had received instructions from Cape Town to intimidate any miners contemplating rebellion with a show of strength and to make his headquarters in the town itself. To emphasise this point, he had decided to march his troops into town as a spectacle but more importantly, as a show of strength. The soldiers would march from their camp on the outskirts and assemble outside the Town Hall where the General and a few loyal Burgers would address the crowd. It would be enough, he believed, to keep any thoughts of rebellion out of the minds of the troublemakers.

The band had hauled their instruments across the Great Karoo and now proudly led the parade of soldiers marching in step; their rifles sloped lazily against their shoulders. A rousing cheer from the inhabitants of Kimberly met them as they approached the outskirts of the settlement; anyone and everyone who lived within ten miles had turned out to line the short route to the town square. It was not often such an event took place in this remote, rough town and they had come to see the spectacle of uniformed soldiers and to listen to the speeches of the dignitaries.

After an hour, the proceedings ended and the band played 'God Save the Queen.' Those of English lineage together with a smattering of Welsh and Scots joined in, singing at the top of their voices, watched sullenly by Boers, Fenians and the other malcontents. But it was a resounding success; the General was pleased with his show of strength, the response of the crowd of ordinary people but most of all by the subservient posturing of the town's Burgers. His Army of the Vaal had shown them who was in charge and as a reward, offered most of the soldiers the rest of the day to themselves. The band boys took little persuading to lay down their instruments and unfasten the top buttons of their tunics to cool down.

'This is the life,' said Dickie, stretched out on the scrubby grass, hands clasped together behind his head. 'I could do with a few days of this, what say you Georgie?'

'Aye, it's grand,' said Georgie sitting against a tree smoking his pipe. 'What's the latest Dickie, how long will we be here d'you think?'

'Dunno really, haven't heard anything but my guess is quite a while, a month maybe. I read in the local paper that the High Commissioner is coming to sort things out and until he does I reckon we'll be stayin' here.'

'I think I might go a little mad if we have to stay that long. It's bad enough living in tents all this time, no decent latrines or a bathhouse and not much to do. Why, we don't even drill these days.'

183

'Tell you what,' said Dickie, I wouldn't mind getting hold of a pan and a shovel and having a go at looking for some diamonds. Just think what I could do if I found a big one.' His eyes rolled skywards at the thought of becoming a rich man.

'Mm..., that sounds like a good idea Dickie.'

Georgie drew another mouthful of smoke through his pipe, crossed his legs and listened to Dickie rambling on about finding diamonds. Diamonds indeed, what did they know about looking for diamonds - where would they look? Before Dickie could say any more a subaltern disturbed them.

'Where's your Platoon Sergeant lads?' he said.

'Oh, what's up Thomson, what's going on?' asked Dickie, inquisitive to the last.

'I'm supposed to tell the sergeants not privates,' he said smirking.

'Oh look, I seem to have rolled a spare cigarette. Well would you credit that? Would you like it Mister Thompson?'

The man grinned, held out his hand to take the precious item and secreted it in his tunic pocket. 'Well now, could you direct me to your sergeant, private, I have to inform him that the platoons are to muster in order to receive the two months back pay owed.'

'Ah..., I do believe you will find him over there,' said Dickie pointing to a group of men sat around a table and playing a game of cards. 'See the one with his braces off his shoulders, that's Sergeant Murray.'

'Thank you Private' said the subaltern, grinning broadly and walked away.

'So that's how you do it you crafty bugger,' said Georgie.

Before Dickie could answer him, they heard a familiar voice.

'Well boys I'm back whit you again.' It was Patrick; he dumped his knapsack and rifle on the ground and squatted beside Dickie pursing his lips. 'Looks like the Mounted Infantry are no more and I'm back walking with you lads again.'

'What's happened Patrick?' asked Georgie.

'They disbanded us, selling off the nags; I tell you it was good while it lasted.'

Patrick slipped off his jacket and took out his pipe and tobacco.

'So tell us about it Patrick, you seemed to like being with the mounted section,' said Dickie.

Two other men from the platoon came and sat down near Patrick, wanting to hear his tales, far-fetched as they might be. He span them a yarn or two about his brief episode as a Mounted Infantryman, making them roar with laughter as he described the time they came across the 'Reindeer'.'

'D'you know we are getting some back pay Patrick?' said Dickie.

'Now that sounds like a good idea. When the devil will this be happening?'

'Soon we think, they are telling the platoons sergeants to muster the men, pretty soon I think,' replied Dickie.

'Bout time, I've nought left but a few ha'pennies,' chimed in Fred Murray who had been listening to Patrick's tales. 'And Dickie here says he's going panning for diamonds.'

Pickpockets and Zulus

'Diamonds eh?, well I never. This is as good a place as any if it's diamonds you're looking for I suppose. How the hell are you going' find them?' queried Patrick.

The following morning, Tuesday, they lined up outside the paymasters tent for their eagerly awaited back pay and by Friday, it was the platoon's turn for a forty-eight hour pass. There was nowhere else to go and spend their money but in the flesh pots of Kimberly itself and the men looked forward to it with relish.

'To be sure we'll have a good time Georgie my boy,' said Patrick as they left the camp for the walk into the town. 'Will you look at all those piles of mud? I wonder how many diamonds they get out of a pile of muck like that.'

Georgie was not listening; his attention taken up by the sights and sounds of the mining operations along the road. For as far as he could see piles of earth and rocks littered the countryside, the waste from the diggings and amongst these heaps of earth black labourers in no more than a loincloth toiled away with shovels and pick axes. It looked to be back breaking work and Georgie was not really sure the rewards merited such effort.

'Do you still want to go panning Dickie?' asked Georgie. 'You might have to live there,' he said, pointing with his thumb towards a shack made from left over packing cases and sheets of corrugated tin. 'I think I'd rather stay under canvas than live in one of those.'

'Of course I do. I tell you it only needs one decent diamond to make a man rich, anyway those huts are for the blacks not the white miners. The blacks do all the work and the miners take all the profit,' added Dickie.

Perhaps it was not a bad idea after all thought Georgie as they arriving at the outskirts of the town, an area where the lean-to sheds and homemade shacks of the labourers gave way to more permanent structures of sawn wood and stone. They walked towards the centre of town and entered the main square full of Boer ox drawn wagons laden with produce for sale to the thousands of miners come to Kimberly to seek their fortunes.

'Here lads, this looks like a likely pub. Is it here we will have a drink because I'm parched dry with the dust.' Patrick pointed to a two-story building with a veranda running round two sides. Dickie and Georgie started to walk towards the entrance and behind them, Patrick let out a guffaw. 'Ha lads, I'm thinking that the pub is the lean to. That one looks more like some sort of business building to me.'

Georgie stopped walking and looked more closely at the structure. The sign on the door read 'Kimberly Mining and Assay Office,' the one on the lean to read 'Martha's Bar.' Patrick, forever the first to spot a watering hole grinned broadly and walked towards the black hole that was the entrance to Martha's Bar.

'I'm with you Patrick,' said Fred Murray, marching in after him.

'Barman, six beers if you will, the first round is on me lads,' said Patrick to the soldiers surrounding him.

The beer arrived in bottles, there were no glasses or tankards, and when the barman told Patrick the price, he almost collapsed. 'I'm sorry' said the bar tender 'you must be new here. I do not set the prices. In this god-forsaken place, everything has to come from the coast.

Do you still want the beer because if you don't someone else will have it.'

Patrick looked a little crestfallen, counting out the money from his meagre army pay and took the bottles.

'Well this place is not much fun if you don't have plenty of money, that's for sure.'

The others were not too happy either because it would not be long before each one of them had to stump up the same amount and with each bottle costing a days' pay, they were not going to have many days out like this. They took their bottles and sat at one of the tables at little glum at the realisation they may not be able to have such a good time after all until the barman, probably more worried that they might start a fight, advised them that they could obtain cheaper liquor on the far side of town, towards the shanties. Taking his advice, they left the bar with the expensive beer and made their way across town to find a hostelry with half-decent prices.

'Here look at this, let's try this place,' said Dickie wandering towards a shack standing on its own with strings of beads for a door.

In the gloom, they ordered beer from a sullen barman of dubious origin and began to enjoy themselves, a second bottle helping them on their way and they had soon forgotten about the price of beer, except Dickie Henderson, that was. He watched his pennies very carefully and sitting to one side he mentally calculated how long he thought their money might last until a voice broke into his thoughts.

'You men are part of the Army that's come to town?'

Dickie looked across at a scruffily dressed man of about fifty years of age with a bushy unkempt grey beard. 'Yes mister, we are.'

'And how long do you reckon on staying?' asked the man.

'We don't know, could be a week or it could be a month. We probably will not find out until it's time to leave anyway. What d'you do in these parts?' enquired Dickie pulling out his tobacco ready to roll a cigarette.

The old man's attention transferred to the open leather pouch, all conversation on hold as he eyed its contents.

'Would you like a roll up?'

'That's mighty fine of you.'

The old man held out a gnarled and dirty hand and Dickie passed him his tobacco pouch watching as the old miner dug his scrawny fingers into the soft mound of tobacco. He took a rice paper and proceeded to roll a cigarette deftly between his fingers much to Dickie's amusement.

'You are certainly an expert at rolling cigarettes.'

The man twisted his head a little towards Dickie and closed one eye as if imparting some secret.

'Here, take your tobacco,' he said passing the pouch back to its owner.

'Are you a miner?' the man nodded his head. 'I've been thinking that we might try our hand at a bit of digging if we're stuck here for a while. Is it easy enough to start looking for diamonds?'

The miner looked at him and placed the rolled cigarette between his lips. 'Got a light soldier?'

Dickie pulled out his matches and lit his own cigarette before passing the burning match to his new friend.

'I'll tell you a bit about mining because of your kindness soldier. Bit lonely out there with no one to talk to fer weeks on end.'

'Mind if I sit a while, I'd be interested to hear more about mining.'

'Ahh...yes, good to have someone to talk with,' said the old man taking a puff on his cigarette.

Dickie picked up his bottle and pulled his across chair to the next table unnoticed by the rest of the group and for the next half hour he listened to the old miner as he related tales of digging for diamonds and Dickie noticed that not once did he mention the whereabouts of his activities.

'Do many of you find diamonds then?'

'A few.'

'Have you found many?'

'One or two, not enough to get rich on.'

Dickie was beginning to ask searching questions, trying to glean at least some information on the whereabouts of the diamond finds but the old man was canny and was less prepared to answer Dickie's questions.

'Tell me' said Dickie, changing the subject, where can we get cheaper beer than this? It seems that if you don't strike it rich in these parts then you can't afford a good night's drinking.'

The man shrugged his shoulders. 'Best stay away from the diamond quarter or the centre of town. Cheapest drink is the home brewed native kind.'

'Where might we find that?'

'Head back that away and keep a lookout fer an open doorway with a lot of noise and smoke. Be seein' you,' said the old miner getting to his feet. He picked up the small sack by his chair and walked out of the bar with not so much as a glance at Dickie.

'Who's your friend?' asked a soldier.

'Funny bugger, a miner, I asked him about mining.'

'What did he tell you?'

'Not much, but he did tell me where the cheap drink is.'

'Bejasus, let's be finding it then chirped in Patrick.

'Yes, come on Dickie show us where' chorused some of the others, eager to get their hands on cheap beer. Dickie told them what the miner had said and within minutes, they had drunk up and were filing out of the bar ready to look for an open doorway with noise and smoke.

'Hey soldier mans,' said a black youth of about sixteen years of age appearing as if from nowhere. 'You want cheap beer and girls?'

The soldiers stopped in their tracks and stood looking at the boy.

'Did you say cheap beer and *girls*?' asked Patrick.

'Sho man, here is a cheap beer place,' he said waving his arm towards a rundown building, 'an they got girls.'

The young soldiers needed no persuading, crowding into the dim interior of the makeshift pub they ordered beer at half the price of white run establishments. Homemade and potent, but by now their taste buds and their concentration had deteriorated to the point where it did not matter.

'You should be Irish Georgie because you certainly have the luck. How much was that lot?'

Georgie laughed, 'Sheep enough Fatrick,' he said slurring his words and looking round to peer into the gloom. They were the only white men, they had not noticed that the rest of the clientèle were exclusively black when they had come in but the beer was cheap and allowed them to extend their day of freedom a little longer.

'Well lads do we want some girls?' asked Patrick in his own inimitable way.

'Bloody right, said a voice from the gloom', 'Aye' said another.

'Whell then, here lad,' he called to the boy lingering by the doorway, waiting, and asked him about the girls.

'I go see boss' he said disappearing into the darkening night and by the time they had finished their drinks he returned with several black women of various shapes and sizes. Just what the soldiers wanted and each of the women took hold of a soldier's hand to lead them them like sheep out of the bar and into the night air.

'Georgie, there is no ladies left for you, here boy, find my friend a girl for he's missing out,' Patrick called to the youth. Georgie looked embarrassed. 'What's the matter Georgie, have you not done it before? Well now's the time to start, my friend here will find one for you. I'll see ye back here in a while,' he said as the last of the girls pulled him away.

Georgie sat and watched his fellow soldiers disappear one by one and the woman running the establishment began to light oil lamps hanging from the roof beams to alleviate the gathering darkness. Georgie leaned back against the flimsy wooden wall, alone, his head feeling slightly fuzzy, and his thoughts focusing on the rigours of the march when three roughly dressed white men entered the bar. One had very broad shoulders and sporting a thick black beard, he looked as strong as an ox. He carried a satchel slung across his shoulder and as he went to the makeshift bar for their drinks his companions sat near Georgie.

'Hey, soldier boy,' one called to Georgie.

Georgie looked across at them; these were serious looking men, weather beaten, dirty and had the hands of men who knew hard labour.

'Since your mates have left you all alone come over here and let me buy you a drink' said the broad shouldered man returning with their beer.

Georgie felt unsure about accepting the man's offer, he was alone and not sure where Patrick and the others were or when they might return.

'Another beer,' one of them called out to the native woman.

'Where are you from soldier?'

'London,' said Georgie with some apprehension.

'London eh? I haven't been back there for ten years. I grew up in the East End; my father had a pub on the Mile End Road. Let me introduce us, this is Clarence and John and I'm Marty.'

'What's your name?'

'Georgie.'

'Well Georgie, pleased to meet you, come and sit here. It's not every day I get to meet someone from back home.'

Georgie stood to his feet and took his chair to the men's table just as the woman arrived with his beer.

'Whereabouts in London do you hail from Georgie?'

'Spitalfields mainly, but I lived with my aunt in Southwark for a while when my mother died.'

'You'll know the Mile End Road then?'

Georgie nodded,

'Did you ever come across the Duke of Wellington public house during your travels?'

Georgie's eyes lit up. He remembered very well the Duke of Wellington, he had stayed there when he had returned to Spitalfields to look for Aunt Jane and Ellen and his no good Uncle Billy.

'Yes I know the Duke, stayed their once, on my first leave. Nice place as I remember, I think the publican was a man with a fine military moustache.'

'Well I never,' Marty was obviously pleased, 'that sounds just like my dad. I wonder how he's managing these days. Like I say I haven't been home for ten years or more.'

Just then, the young boy Patrick had sent for another girl returned followed by a dusky, well-made female.

'I got you girl bass, she good girl, she only six English pennies,' he said.

Georgie felt embarrassed and could do nothing but stare at the girl. He had never been with a woman before and although the prospect intrigued him, he had no idea how to handle the situation but help was on hand. The three diamond miners dug into their pockets and each tossed two pennies onto the table. 'There you are soldier, we've had some luck today and we're happy to share it with you, just make sure you come back here so's you can tell me all about London,' said Marty.

The girl reached forward and took hold of Georgie's hand, the boy picked up the coins from the table and Georgie disappeared into the night, just as his companions had. The three men grinned at each other, called for more drinks and chatted for a while in low voices until interrupted by Patrick who had returned to the bar.

'To be sure Georgie boy must be getting serviced,' he said looking round the room.

'Don't worry about your mate; he's in good hands,' said Marty as his two compatriots guffawed.

'Thank you for that I think it's the lads first time so I don't think he'll be long in coming back.'

The men in the room laughed aloud, the soldiers began to return in dribs and not long after Georgie appeared with a large grin on his face.

'Well my lad you look like you've been to heaven,' said Patrick with brotherly smile.

Georgie said nothing his smile fading, replaced by a look of embarrassment and an ever-reddening face.

'Let me buy you boys a drink,' said Marty changing the subject, waving to the woman at the bar, 'We've had some luck today and when we do, we share it around for a while.'

'That's good of you,' said Dickie, 'this diamond mining business must be profitable?'

'It can be, but we can go for a long time between finds and then it's not so good. We've been prospectin' along the river and we've had one or two good finds haven't we?' he said to his friends.

'The ground is full of diamonds but you have to know where to look,' said the one called Clarence. 'It's not as easy as some folks make out. Why, thousands have turned up here in Kimberly, expecting to be rich men within the first week. But most are spent up after six months without a find and disappear as quickly as they arrived.'

'Clarence is right lads, If you are thinking of a little prospecting whilst your here, why I'm sure we can help. We have some old equipment, shovels and the like, that we are prepared to sell you, aren't we?' said Marty turning to his two friends.

Clarence and the other man, John, nodded agreement, it would be useful to get rid of their old sieves and shovels for some cash and these soldiers looked gullible enough to pay over the odds.

'I tell you what, why don't we bring you the equipment here tomorrow night and we can agree a price and better than that, we can tell you where you might find some diamonds. Here,' he said, pulling a wallet from inside his jacket. 'You will need this and I am prepared to sell it to you.'

Dickie's eyes lit up 'what is it?'

'Without one of these you will not be able to dig. It's a claim, a registered claim.'

Through the haze of alcohol, Dickie began to imagine the biggest diamond that ever found in South Africa and it was going to be his. He had already forgotten the old miner, his caginess about where to dig for diamonds believing that these men were much more forthcoming.

'How much you will want for the shovels and sieves?' he asked, unable to contain himself.

'Well I don't rightly know but they were expensive, best that money could buy,' said Marty noting the looks in the soldier's eyes. He saw greed taking hold and all he had to do was reel them in. 'I know, what if we let you have them for half of what we paid for them, what d'you say to that?' he said slowly, trying to keep a straight face.

'And you will show us where to dig?'

'Yes we'll do that. This claim form shows you where and we can sell you that as well,' he said, folding the piece of paper and putting it back in his wallet before any of them could read what it said. 'Now, what about another drink?

Clarence pulled some coins from his pocket to buy the soldiers more drinks. Inebriated to say the least, they were intrigued at the prospect of finding diamonds and were ready to part with all they had for the chance get their hands on some diamonds and none more so than Dickie Henderson.

Marty smirked as he totted up in his head how much they could get rid of their surplus equipment for. If he could persuade these soldier boys to part with some money he would be happy and, if they were prepared to buy the tools, he felt sure they would buy the claim. The soldiers were drunk and missed the secret look he gave his companions, all that is except for Patrick who had a true Irishman's capacity for drink and who noticed their sly exchanges.

Leaning on his shovel, streaks of sweat running down his grimy face, Patrick looked exhausted. 'To be sure I could do with a drink Georgie.'

Georgie looked up from his work, the big circular patched up sieve held firmly in his hands as he swirled it in a slow, circular motion. 'That's all you think about you big Irish wolfhound. We'll have a drink when you find your first diamond.'

'It's a week we've been digging here an' my chuvel is nearly worn through,' said Patrick planting the blade firmly in the ground and leaning on the handle. If I'd a known it was going to be this hard I would of stayed home and been a navvy on the railways, at least there is always a pub around in England. I knew those miners were leading us on – bastards.'

Marty and his crooked friends had conned the soldiers out of most of their collective back pay, arranging to meet them the following day with their surplus equipment and the claim certificate. As on their first meeting they had plied them with drink as they discussed the deal and when the soldiers became tipsy enough they reached an agreement, none more eager to see it through than Dickie Henderson. Somehow, Patrick had forgotten the looks he had witnessed the previous evening, swept along by the enthusiasm of his comrades, but ever since that first back breaking morning the spectre of Marty's grinning face had haunted him. He thought about it again and wished he could punch it until some shouting disturbed his thoughts.

'Yes! Yes! Whoopee!' shrilled a voice from a few feet away. 'I've found one! I've found one! The drinks are on me tonight boys.' It was Dickie Henderson jumping up and down like a lunatic and waving his arms in the air like a windmill.

His fellow workers stopped working to gather round and see what the commotion was all about and finally Dickie's exuberance subsided. He opened the palm of his hand to reveal the smallest diamond ever found in Kimberly

'Look 'he said, rubbing it on his trousers and holding it up to the sunlight, 'a real diamond. Come on boys lets go and see what it's worth and I'll treat you all to a drink.'

The soldiers needed little persuading, any excuse to down tools and finish early for the day was very welcome. Before leaving the diggings for the distant cluster of corrugated sheds that was Kimberly, they hastily washed the mud off their tools, cleaned themselves as best they could in the river, put their shirts and tunics back on and were soon striding towards the town.

'Here, this one looks likely,' said Dickie marching ahead, eager to find an assay office and discover the diamond's worth.

The door to a small lean to shack was ajar and above it was a sign reading 'Isaac Lewis, Diamond Dealer,' but before they could enter that same door flew open and their benefactor of the previous week stormed out with a face like thunder.

'It's Marty the miner,' said Patrick, recognising him. 'How the hell are ye Marty?' he said cheerfully, but Marty was in no mood for niceties.

'Theivin' robbin' bastard, offered me half of what my diamonds are worth. I haven't worked myself to death to make him rich. No, I'll find a dealer that will pay me what they are really worth. Anyway how are you managing?' he said to Patrick, his eyes narrowing.

He had expected trouble if the soldiers ever came upon him and his associates again but here they were as friendly as could be and it had already dawned on him that they were looking for a diamond buyer and by simple reasoning, he deduced that they must have found something.

'You've had some luck already boys?' he said slowly.

Patrick had not known what a fair price was for the digging utensils, it had seemed steep but Dickie was so eager to lay his hands on the implements and he had persuaded the rest of them to stump up their back pay. To be fair to him thought Patrick, it looked as if it was beginning to pay off. If they realised a decent price for the diamond they had found, then they might re-coup most, if not all, of their outlay – as long as they walked past the pubs. First though, there was a score to settle with Marty.

'To be sure we've hit the pay dirt thanks to you and your mates. We found the ground full of diamonds.'

Still the proverbial thick Irishman thought Marty, his mind beginning to work overtime, how he wondered, could they have found diamonds in a place they had worked unsuccessfully for months. It was not often he was outsmarted but, unknown to him, he had met his match in Patrick.

Patrick understood it all as he watched Marty's face change, the free drinks, the instant friendship, the price of the substandard tools and the worthless claim. But they had found a diamond and Patrick decided that it was payback time.

'Let me shake your hand sir, you have made us rich and I can't thank you enough. Why that little bit of river must be worth thousands of pounds with all those diamonds lying there.'

Suddenly the alarm bells were ringing in Marty's head. Perhaps they had not worked out the claim after all and he had sold it for a pittance. He would have to take it back off these soldier boys.

Georgie and the others were a little puzzled at Patrick antics and began to give him funny looks. Where *were* the diamonds he was talking about? Georgie knew his friend well enough and after catching his eye realised that he was up to something and he turned his back on him. He needed to be left alone to see through his ruse and so, looking straight and Dickie and the others with a stern gaze he quelled any questioning.

Pickpockets and Zulus

'We did not find anything in the riffer where you sent us, no it was a barren stretch but we worked our way inland a little an' we found some rich pickings. We can't sell them here because we can't be carrying all that money about whit us on the march. We're leaving soon an' me an' the lads here have decided That we will get a better price back in Cape Town. So there you are, we should thank for our good fortune an' one day we'll be back to carry on working our claim,' said Patrick his face deadpan, and to the greedy swindling miner, convincing.

'If it's such a good find why don't you stay and dig?'

'Because, sir, if we deserted the Army we would be shot an' that is a good enough reason for me not to stay here when the Army leaves.'

Gradually the others began to cotton on to Patrick's plan murmuring agreement that it was better not to be shot as deserters and to leave with the Army, utterly convincing Marty. Nevertheless, where had these soldiers been digging? He could look around for fresh diggings after they left but it could take months and abandoned diggings littered the landscape. Then an idea occurred to him, but he had to tread carefully, they appeared unaware that he had swindled them, so maybe he could fool them again.

'It seems a shame that you can't stay and find more diamonds. I have an idea, why not let me buy the claim back off you, you show me the location of those diggings with these diamonds and I will give you a good price. It would save you worrying about not being here and you would have something to show for your endeavours. What do you say?'

'I would say that's a fair offer sir but we will need to talk about it, just a minute.' Patrick waved his comrades towards him and led them out of earshot of the drooling Marty.

'Listen lads, this Marty and his mates swindled us with the chuvels. If you leave it to me I'll get as much out of him as I can before we go back to Cape Town. I heard that we are moving out soon, soon as the general has sorted out these colonials. What do you think lads?'

'I'm with you Patrick,' said Georgie.

That was enough for the rest of them; prospecting was back-breaking work with little or no reward and they all nodded agreement. Patrick walked back towards Marty.

'Sir, my mates are not too happy in giving away the secret of our little find, there might be riches beyond our wildest dreams under the ground and we can't give up the secret at all at all.' Patrick's eyes, still deadpan, did not betray his true feelings and to Marty, he still appeared the thick Irishman. However, these soldier boys might be gone in a matter of days and the secret of their find with them. He just had to get that claim back, had to find out where they had made their discovery and do it without parting with any money.

'Look, I've got a nice little bag of uncut diamonds here worth at least two hundred pounds. If you show me where the diggings are you can have them, what d'you say soldier?'

That clinched it, calling him "soldier", the man was taking him for a stupid, green soldier boy and that made Patrick more determined than ever to take the bag of diamonds off him.

'To be sure sir it's a deal, Georgie an I will take ye there now if ye like?'

'Right, just give me a minute and I'll let Clarence know that I'll be delayed for a while.'

Marty left the small group and walked between two buildings at the far side of the street to find his associate and the soldiers still had a diamond to sell.

'We'll try here shall we?' said Dickie looking at the diamond buyer's office. 'I have no idea what it's worth but if we don't like the price we can try another.'

'Why don't you try them all and see who will give the best price?' said one.

'I bet the buyers are all working together to keep the prices down,' said another.

'You're right there Fred, but I wouldn't worry too much about the price just get what ye can,' said Patrick, noticing Marty's return and putting his right index finger against his nose in a gesture to indicate he had a plan.

'Everything's sorted; Clarence and John will meet me in the bar when we get back, so let's go.' Marty began walking down the street towards the river followed by Patrick and Georgie, leaving Dickie and the others to find a diamond buyer's office and after two hours of walking they were in sight the riverbank.

They walked, mostly in silence, Patrick spending the time thinking through the possibility of a trap because he had glanced around occasionally, his training in the mounted scouts making him aware of possible trouble and trouble there was. Clarence and John were following them. Still some way behind, at a safe distance and using the bush as cover, Patrick had caught fleeting glimpses of them and guessed what was coming. Marty must have told them to follow and he was sure they would try an ambush at some time. He reasoned that until Marty discovered the whereabouts of the diggings, he would not risk springing his trap and until then he and Georgie were safe enough. He managed to catch Georgie's eye and mouthed the word "Trouble" and Georgie tilted his head in acknowledgement.

'Well, where is it?' demanded Marty, 'where is this find? I can't see any fresh digging about here.

'You won't, it's in the rifer, look there, that's where it started but the big find is away over der' he said, giving no positive indication in which direction the diggings were.

'You said you found them near the river bank, not in the river. If you want these diamonds then you had better show me where,' Marty demanded.

'Not so fast, let's be seeing the goods first, I told you the river bank to keep it a secret; we didn't want anyone knowing the exact whereabouts.'

Marty pulled a small soft leather bag from his pocket and spilled twenty or so small and uncut diamonds into his hand. 'There you are, now show us where to dig.'

'Give me the diamonds first,' said Patrick.

The man replaced the diamonds in the bag and handed it over, confident that he would soon have it back.

'This way,' said Patrick heading along the riverbank, through some undergrowth and to a flat area where the soldiers had been digging earlier in the week. 'Here is where I found the first diamond and later when the boys joined me we found lots in the river just there,' he said, pointing at a pronounced bend in the river. Purely by chance, unknown to Patrick, prospectors often found diamonds where a river changed its direction, where the flow slackened, where it deposited silt and sometimes, diamonds. That was the clincher, as far as Marty was concerned Patrick was telling the truth and now it only remained for him to retrieve his diamonds.

'Put your hands up,' he said pulling a revolver from inside his jacket, 'put your hands up and give me back those diamonds. Clarence, John,' he shouted to his accomplices.

'Sergeant Bains, glad you could make it' said Patrick to the imaginary soldier approaching Marty from behind. Marty could not resist the temptation to glance round; his accomplices were not yet close enough to help him and if there was someone behind him he had better dispose of him as quickly as he could. He half turned before realising that it was a trick, but in that split second, Georgie managed to leap forwards and gripped Marty's wrist tightly in both hands, forcing the barrel of the gun skywards. Marty panicked and fired, the shot echoing across the river and from the bushes Clarence and John rushed to Marty's aid. Three against two and the soldiers were not even armed. Clarence pulled his revolver out and took aim but Georgie had managed to wrestle Marty's gun from his grasp and in one slick movement swung it round and aimed it straight at Clarence's head. The miner did not have time to take aim and in that split second he became convinced that he would lose any exchange and he lowered his weapon.

Marty rushed at Georgie in an attempt to take back his gun but Patrick was ready for him, smashing his fist into Marty's face and knocking him to the ground his boot then placed firmly across Marty's neck to pin him to the ground. Clarence had faltered long enough, Marty was helpless, that convinced John that the game was up and as he turned to run, Clarence followed.

'Let them go, the silly man should have waited till his friend's arrived,' said Patrick, a grin spreading across his face and under the pressure of his boot, Marty began spluttering and coughing.

The two soldiers laughed aloud before Patrick made Marty stand up and remove his trousers, using them to tie him securely to a tree and then he gave him a mocking military salute before throwing Marty's gun into the water.

'Well, that was the best day's work I ever did Georgie. They think they know where the diamonds are now even though they have had to pay us for the privilege but it will be six months before they realise that there ain't no diamonds and we'll be long gone by then.'

Georgie could not fault Patrick's logic and eventually, when they returned to the town to meet up with the others, they visited the diamond buyer. Overcrowding his tiny office with half a platoon of soldiers was shocking enough but when they presented him with a handful of diamonds he was more than surprised. Instantly he recognised the diamonds, grasped the situation and realised that perhaps he had better not ask too many questions.

The order to strike camp for the return journey to Cape Town came a day later and the soldiers flush with their success, set about breaking camp.

'Where's Dickie?' asked Georgie looking around. The tent was ready to drop, the guy ropes were slackened, each man was ready to let the ropes slip through his hands and collapse the canvas neatly onto the ground.

Fred looked up, "I think 'e might 'ave absconded'

'What do you mean?'

'Just that, he's pissed off.'

'What?' said Georgie.

'Are you deaf or daft, he's deserted, said he's going to make his fortune from diamonds and the Army can get stuffed,' said Fred.

'Aw blimey, I knew the diamonds had turned his head but I didn't think he'd be stupid enough to become a deserter.'

Chapter 4

It was the day after Christmas Day 1876, a busy day for a Regimental band expected to entertain the local townspeople. They began in the public park at mid-morning playing Hymns and Carols shaded by some Keurboom Trees, their pink blossoms and fragrant scent adding to the occasion and they began with a rendition of 'Silent Night.'

'Well done men, let's make sure we play just as well tonight for the Prime Minister and some of his Government, we want them to know that the Band of the Twenty Fourth is the best in the British Army do we not?' said the bandmaster.

'To be sure we will sir,' said Patrick, always the one to speak up, 'and what about New Year's Day sir? We will give 'em an evening to remember.'

The other bandsmen laughed at Patrick, their star performer who, amazingly, was their best cornet player and they were all looking forward to the biggest party of the Cape Town calendar, the Regimental New Years' day Ball. Always a grand occasion, an opportunity for the officers of the regiment to entertain the local dignitaries and the well to do of Cape Colony, a time to network and after the success in Kimberly it promised to be a party to remember.

Pickpockets and Zulus

By eight o clock on New Year's Day the dance floor was awash with officers in their best uniforms and highly polished boots, their ladies in their flowing ball gowns of silk and taffeta and a local gentry that could not match the soldiers for smartness. But some of the colonial women were easily the equals of the military wives and Georgie watched with fascination from the corner of his eye as they swirled past the band stand. Garlands and ribbons adorned the room, large flower arrangements surrounded the bandstand, their African colours balanced well against the reds and blues of the officer's uniforms. At the far end of the room tables covered in bright white cotton tablecloths supported an array of delicacies and in attendance, soldiers from the catering Corps, orderlies turned out in white uniforms, attending to the every need of the officers and their guests.

From his vantage point on the bandstand, Georgie caught sight of dancers gliding past, some adept in the dance steps of the day and some not so adept and inwardly he chuckled as some of the colonials stumbled clumsily by in their attempts to emulate their hosts. An Officer and his lady caught his eye, the man stiff and erect, the woman ill at ease, elegant yet appearing to have some difficulty with the dance steps. She was a dark haired beauty, well proportioned, her gown flattering her figure and her hair cascading over her shoulders made her stand out. He watched foe a few seconds until they disappeared into the crowd, his concentration focusing back on his music.

The waltz finished, the men bowed, the ladies curtsied and partners were exchanged for the next dance and as the band master counted him into the next piece of music he tapped out the rhythm on his drum. The party was in full swing, the dancers, energetic and animated as they went through the dance sequences and from the corner of his eye, Georgie again saw the woman and her dancing partner.

She was very good looking and she seemed familiar and yet that could not be, she was with an officer, a class to which he did not belong. Following the music, he could not look at her for long, just a short glance each time her partner swung her away. She *was* familiar, but where from, the problem intrigued him so much that he began to stare and then she was facing him, looking straight at him and a shock of recognition shot through him. It was Ellen the cousin he never expected to see ever again, what was she doing here.

'Georgie,' whispered Alwyn the bass drummer, 'why have you stopped playing?'

The shock of recognition had caused Georgie to freeze momentarily and it was only Alwyn's prompting that brought his concentration back and Regaining his composure, he hoped that his faux pas had not go unnoticed but Bandmaster Burck was glaring at him and he dare not look again for Ellen. Trying to concentrate on his music his mind was in turmoil as he wondered how Ellen could possibly be here in Cape Town and with an officer. The soldier was at least a lieutenant and from his brief sighting, not of the Twenty Fourth Foot, his dress uniform was blue not red.

Suddenly, from the swirling crowd of dancers she re-appeared, at first with her back to him but as her partner swung her round their eyes met, any doubts he may have had that it was Ellen soon dispelled. She had recognized him he was sure, bewildering him, forcing so many questions to the front of his mind but before he had time to catch her eye again they had passed by.

The dance ended, the bandmaster was tapping his baton on his music stand, instructing the musicians for the next dance, and Georgie dare not appear lacking for a second time. The revellers held hands and the band struck up the first bars of the military two-step and the mass of happy, laughing and drunk people performed the dance as well as they could. Back and forth, they danced and Georgie searched amongst them for Ellen and then, out of nowhere, she appeared, her bright blue eyes staring straight at him and her black hair curled and shining like he had never seen it before. She was a beautiful woman, that he could not deny, but how had she made the transition from the street urchin to an officer's lady?

'To be sure that was a pretty woman as kept lookin' at you Georgie,' said Patrick, folding his music away as the officer's and their guests dispersed. Georgie said nothing, he was perplexed, it was years since he had last seen his aunt and cousins, years since he had even thought much about them and now here, in Cape Colony, was Ellen and on the arm of an officer.

'Are ye listenin' to me?'

'Er, what, I...I'm listening, yes, what did you say?'

'Begorrah, the boy's smitten. Well Georgie are you going to tell me who the young woman is that has turned your head?'

Georgie looked up, not able to hold a proper conversation for the time being. 'Erm...I can't, not now Patrick,' he said packing his drum into its bag.

He picked up the sheave of music and left the stage to walk the short distance to their barrack room, his mind in turmoil and Patrick watched him go, puzzled because had never seen Georgie in such a state. Was he in love with this mysterious woman or was he going down with something? The big Irishman shook his head, picked up his cornet and followed his friend, finding him sitting on the edge of his bunk deep in thought.

'Well, it seems you've got something Georgie. Are ye going to tell me what's wrong with you?'

Georgie looked up, 'have you got any beer?'

'Now that's more like it. Aye I have picked up a couple of bottles on my way past the tables. Albert Taylor, a mate of mine was servin' on tonight and he passed me a couple of bottles and some left over sandwiches. Here let's have a little party on our own.' He took the beer and food from his music bag and held out a bottle to Georgie. After a pause, Georgie looked his friend in the eye.

'I've had a shock tonight.'

'That was plain enough to see.'

'The girl is my cousin Ellen. I have not seen either her or my aunt and uncle since the day I was collared in Trafalgar Square. I haven't told you everything about my life before I was forced to join as a boy soldier. Well Ellen and me and her younger brother James used to work the streets and trams, pickin' pockets and stealing anything we could lay our hands on. Ellen was good at it, very good, in fact she was the best. She looked after me and we used to bring in enough to feed the family and pay the rent and keep her no good father in drink.'

'Soo..., it would be a shock to see her turn up here tonight then. She looked a darlin' little thing mind.'

Georgie ignored Patrick's remark. 'How could she have transformed herself so much and be with an officer, a Cavalry Officer?'

'Aye, now you mention it, I think he might have been Cavalry.'

'I couldn't speak with her, but she recognised me I'm sure. I'm baffled by it all, how can I find her, how can I find out what's happened to them all? They are my only family.'

'Don't look so sad, but you've got me there,' laughed Patrick taking a swig from the bottle, lightening the mood a little. 'Tell me what you can. I'm interested to know where my mate comes from.'

Georgie relaxed, finished the bottle of beer and began to tell Patrick all about his life before he joined the regiment. His mother, his Aunt Jane and his cousins and Billy Tyndal, leaving nothing out and the more he related to Patrick the more the big Irishman said 'well I never.'

During the following months army life followed a familiar pattern, parade ground drills, guard duty in and around the naval base of Simon's Town and helping move stores from ships docked in the Naval base to the Military camp on the outskirts of town and then, in early August, an order came to move up country to King William's Town. Not the long, strength sapping trek of the previous year when they crossed the Great Karoo, but passage by sea to East London and then a forty mile train journey to Williams as they called it and it was there, at the end of a band practice Georgie first heard rumours of war.

'I'm telling you Patrick there's trouble brewing in the Transkei, there's a couple of different tribes at each other's throats an it'll be us that has to sort it out,' said Alwyn Cosgrove to an attentive Patrick Donovan, recently promoted to Lance Corporal and Corporal Alwyn Cosgrove saw him almost as an equal.

'I'd heard that rumour, d'you think there's any truth in it?'

'I was talking to Sergeant Jones this morning and he'd heard from his mate with the General's staff that a tribe of Xhosa have fallen out with their neighbours. It seems that a while ago their chief asked for guidance from his Witch Doctor and the Witch Doctor told him to sacrifice all their cattle, destroy their crops and then they would find salvation, so that's exactly what the stupid bastard did and then of course they bloody well starved. He told me that they had been resettled up on the coastal strip by governor Wodehouse right next to their sworn enemies the Gcaleka and now it looks as if they are at each other's throats, so we can forget going back to Blighty for a while.'

'We might see a bit of action then,' said Lance Corporal Donovan rubbing his hands together. 'We've done a fair bit of soldierin' but there hasn't been any real fighting has there. Did you hear that Georgie, looks like we might get a chance for a bit of fighting after all.'

'Let's go and have a drink in the mess, we might get to hear a bit more of what's going on,' said Corporal Cosgrove.

'I'll catch up with you later Georgie, I'm off for a drink with the corporal here.' Patrick picked up his instrument, saluted the Bandmaster and disappeared.

Pickpockets and Zulus

'We're off to the mess for a drink as well Georgie are you coming?' said Angus, one of the horn players. Georgie took little persuading, a beer was a good idea and together with several of the band members he walked towards the mess tent, their main topic of conversation the rumour spreading rapidly through the camp.

'Boys, will ye join us?' called out Patrick when he saw them.

Georgie and Angus bought some beer and came over to Patrick and the corporals' table.

'A celebratory drink I think. The lad's signed on and will be staying with us?' said Patrick.

'Yes, I was eighteen last week and I had a word with the Adjutant.'

'So you've decided to stay in the Army have you Georgie?' asked Corporal Cosgrove.

'Yes, I've got nothing to go back to in Blighty and I quite like it in the Army.'

'Good lad, well you will be pleased to know that I've volunteered you for a new Mounted Infantry section starting up soon,' said Patrick with a grin. 'The General wants some Mounted Infantry because the natives are stirring up trouble. Before you arrived, the Sergeant came round lookin' for volunteers an' I thought, sounds like a lot of marching. I prefer sitting my arse on a horse and with you signing on, I thought you ought to be up there with me.

'But I can't ride a horse Patrick. What good would I be in the saddle if I can't ride?

'Don't worry about that, I couldn't ride very well when I started but it comes easy enough, an' if they get

215

one of dose proper Cavalry men to show us how, why tis easy enough.'

So that was it, decided, Georgie had signed on for a further six years and now Patrick had volunteered him for the Mounted Infantry knowing full well he couldn't ride.

Miles away out amongst low-lying Boer farms, a young Lieutenant leaned on a corral fence and watched as a string of horses paraded past.

'How much d'you want for them?' he asked the Boer farmer.

The Boer stroked his thick grey beard, his eyes watching his animals and to all appearances, he appearing a little slow of wit yet his brain was busy. He knew very well that whenever the Army came to town there was a good chance to make money. He had done it before, hiring out a wagon and a few mules and now they wanted to buy horses.

'For all of them, one hundred pounds,' he said.

The lieutenant sucked his breath through his teeth. His orders were to buy horses for the best price he could, but dealing with the canny Boers was proving a difficult task.

'Look, I've been buying horses for ten pounds each, what would you say if I pay twelve pounds for each of these beasts?'

The farmer was used to negotiating with the army and sensed that this officer was desperate for his horses. He took out his pipe and started filling it, allowing the tension rise a little.

'Dees are good stock, dey not cavalry horses I give you that, but are hardy and will survive easy enough where you'll take dem.' He paused again and took out a match to light his pipe. 'Fifteen pounds each and we have a deal.'

The lieutenant looked over the horses once more; it was not his money, it was government money and he was eager to begin training his small force. With the six horses in front of him, he would have a full complement and for the sake of a few pounds, he was not going to hang around any longer, but one last try, 'eighty five for the lot?'

The farmer lit the tobacco, hiding his glee at such a high price and nodded his head, 'it's a deal,' he said through the cloud of smoke beginning to rise from his pipe.

The two men shook hands and the lieutenant turned to the paymaster accompanying him, instructing him to draw up the bill of sale and to pay for the horses. When the transaction was complete, he was able to lead his small party and the string of newly acquired horses back to camp and the following day the volunteers arrived to begin training.

Patrick Donovan and an apprehensive Georgie McNamara were amongst the new recruits together with Barney Smith and Frank Williams, members of his platoon who had also volunteered.

'This should be fun Georgie,' said Barney, 'I hope you've got plenty of camphor for the sore arse you'll be getting afore long.'

'What do you mean?' said a startled Georgie.

'Take no notice, I have a large tub of the stuff and I bet Barney has too, haven't you?' said Patrick.

'I have that, an' I'll let you have some Georgie, don't you worry'

They reached the horses tethered to a lines strung between stout tree trunks and joined several more volunteers.

'Right you lot,' barked the sergeant in charge, 'fall in and lets 'ave a look at you.'

The two Lieutenant, Carrington and Clements, in overall charge of the new unit turned from their private conversation and approached their recruits for a brief inspection before beginning training.

'Sir, the men are present and correct,' said the sergeant saluting smartly.

'Right men,' began Lieutenant Carrington, 'I'll introduce myself and Lieutenant Clements here and we'll tell you what's expected of you. I'm pleased to see one or two familiar faces, which should make the task of turning you into an efficient fighting force a little easier.'

Sitting in the saddle for the first time and holding tightly onto the reins, Georgie felt awkward. He pressed his feet firmly into the stirrups to hold his balance; his legs tight against the animal's sides and he wondered what to do. The horse was docile enough and once he got it walking round riding it did not seem too difficult but when they began to practice the trot he felt a panic rise in him and wondered what Patrick had got him into.

'Relax a little Georgie will you, the horse will feel your tension and it won't be a happy horse at all,' said Patrick. 'Just let your knees bend a bit an let those reins slacken off a little, the poor horse thinks you're tryin' to slice its head in half.'

Lieutenant Clements could see Georgie was having some difficulty and rode up alongside him. 'Have you never ridden before trooper?' he asked.

Before he could answer, Patrick chipped in. 'To be sure he has sir, but twas back in England before the Regiment came overseas and he's a bit stiff. Give him a bit of time an' he will be raiding like one of them jockey fellers sir.'

'Thank you Lance Corporal Donovan, I can see when a man has never ridden before, leave him to me will you.'

'Yes sir, thank you sir,' said Patrick riding off before he got himself into any more trouble.

'Right trooper, what's your name?'

'McNamara, sir',

'Well trooper McNamara you are obviously not used to horses and that's not much good to me is it?'

'No sir',

'Never mind, you've got to start somewhere and it's my job to turn you into a useful Mounted Infantryman. We are not Cavalry, we have a different function, but we're no good if we can't ride are we trooper?'

'No Sir' said Georgie with some nervousness. Was the lieutenant going to discharge him and send him back to the Regiment he wondered?

'We'll learn to sit correctly for starters...'

Georgie need not have worried for Lieutenant Clements was a good teacher and did not intended to discharge him, he needed all the volunteers he could get and knew from Georgie's army record that he was an excellent shot, an important attribute. He would persevere with him until he was comfortable on a horse and for the rest of the day drilled Georgie in the skills of horse riding and within a week, he was riding passably well.

'Barney, give me some of that Camphor, my arse feels like it's on fire and the inside of my legs sting like mad,' said Georgie sidling into the tent.

'Drop your trousers,' said Barney reaching for his backpack, 'rub some of this on it'll soon get rid of all that redness. Crickey you have got it bad.'

'Thanks' said Georgie walking stiffly across the tent. 'I hope this bloody soreness wears off soon, it's not much fun is it Barney?'

'Don't worry, it'll clear up in a day or so, your hide will toughen up and you'll forget all about it.'

One morning, a mile or so from camp it was Georgie's turn to show what he could do. Nudging his steed forwards knees pressed tightly against his horse's sides he released the reins and lifted the Snider to his shoulder. He took aim and fired off a round at the target a hundred yards away.

'Missed, but you're getting better,' said Lieutenant Clements, 'I want you to come past a little faster next time and see how you do.'

'Lieutenant Clements?'

The lieutenant twisted in his saddle to see a Cavalry Officer sat astride a large Bay.

'Captain Jameson?' he asked, saluting.

'At your service' replied the Captain, returning his subordinates salute. 'I've been watching your men as I rode through the camp and they seem competent enough horsemen. Wouldn't last five minutes in the Cavalry though,' he snorted. 'Still they're not supposed to be Cavalry are they lieutenant?'

'No sir, they are being trained to be our forward eyes and ears. We don't expect we'll ever have to fight as a

Cavalry regiment but if your training methods will help to make us a more efficient fighting unit, then I should be most grateful sir.'

'Quite, quite.'

'Sergeant, bring the men to attention will you, I'd like to have a few words with them,' said the lieutenant.

Within minutes, the mounted troopers assembled in line ready for their commanding officer to address them and from the corners of their eyes, they watched the officers approach, none more so than Georgie. He was sure he recognised the uniform; the colours were the same as those he had seen at the New Year's Eve dance, he was the same officer who had danced with Ellen. What was he doing here, and where was Ellen?

'Men, this is Captain Jameson of the Seventeenth Lancers, he has been seconded to this unit for a short time and will be teaching us some Cavalry drills. I hope that he will help turn us into a more cohesive fighting unit and tomorrow we will begin working up the drills. Would you care to address the men Captain Jameson?'

'Fank you Lieutenant, I will, yes.' Clearing his throat the cavalryman looked along the line of soldiers. 'I am Captain Jameson of the Seventeenth Lancers and it is my job for the next few weeks to assist the lieutenant here wiv your horsemanship and teach you a few Cavalry manoeuvres. Now my experience is with proper Cavalry of which you are plainly not, therefore it is my intention to concentwate on your riding skills more than anything else. Your principle weapon is, I believe, the Snider Carbine and as such the lieutenant is perhaps more qualified than I to give instruction on that weapon. Well, I will leave you until tomorrow morning when we will see how good you are on horseback. Lieutenant!'

'Thank you Captain, carry on Sergeant.'

Georgie had not taken his eyes off the Captain, puzzled as to how his cousin had ended up with such a man, if indeed it were he, and began to wonder if Ellen had accompanied him to King William's Town.

He did not have to wait long for the answer. Two days later, Georgie and the rest of the troop were returning from exercises out on the plain. It was late afternoon and the horses, tired from the days exercising, were walking slowly along the main street of King William's Town. From doorways and windows, townspeople watched them ride by and standing alone outside the Victoria Hotel was a woman with a parasol. Georgie was riding near the rear of the column and as the troop passed, he saw her face, only at the last minute recognising her.

'Hello Georgie.'

'Ellen,' said Georgie, touching the front of his helmet in salute, not daring to say more, prohibited as he was from communicating with an officer's wife without her husband present, cousin or not.

'Who was the woman who said hello to you Georgie', asked Barney riding alongside him.

'Oh...it's err...Captain Jameson's wife I believe.

'How do you know her Georgie?'

Embarrassed, Georgie did not know what to say, simply muttering something about meeting her and her husband at the New Year's Day ball and just in front of them Patrick looked straight ahead and for once did not say a word.

Bang..., Bang, Georgie let off two shots as he rode his horse at the gallop past the target, an old wooden door propped up against a pile of rocks. The fifth time he had done the manoeuvre that day and each time he had improved his aim, each time he had felt more at home in the saddle. They had undergone extensive training with the horses for six weeks or more and were showing a marked improvement, close to being competent enough to take to the field, according to the sergeant.

'Bravo trooper,' Lieutenant Clements called out watching from his horse, pleased, very pleased with the progress the troop had made. He had to admit that it was due in no small measure to the pompous Captain Jameson, an expert horseman who had drilled the troopers incessantly in horse riding skills.

'The men are coming along well don't you think Captain Jameson?'

'Reasonably well, reasonably well, vey are obviously not Cavalry material, bit rough round the edges,' he said rather snootily.

Lieutenant Clements sighed inwardly; he was used to the Captains' haughty remarks about the superiority of the Cavalry and new it was futile to disagree.

'I fink I have done just about all I can wiv your chaps Clements, I shall make arrangements to return to Cape Town next week, so if there is anything more you need me to do...'

'No, I think you have done all you can, it's up to the men now to perfect their riding techniques, their primary task of using their rifles is up to me and my drill Sergeant. No, I think we can let you go Captain,' he said in an acerbic tone that was lost on the pompous Captain.

Lieutenant Clements had become more and more frustrated with this stuck up Cavalryman as the weeks had passed, but he did have respect for his equine abilities and he felt it best they part on good terms.

'Well I say lieutenant, it is only right that I invite you to dinner with myself and my wife one evening, shall we say Monday next, at eight? I will reserve a table in the hotel dining room, not quite the West End but it will have to do.'

'Thank you Sir, I look forward to that' said Lieutenant Clements, looking forward more a parting of the way and being able to take his troop out into the field. Rumours were rife of trouble up in the Transkei and he expected that the army might soon have to keep the peace between the warring factions. He saluted and rode across the parade ground to where his troops were already unsaddling after their days training and amongst them were Georgie and Patrick.

'Georgie, we're allowed out of camp for this evening an' me and some of the lads are going into town tonight for a little drink, are you with us at all,' he said, lifting the saddle from his horse.

'Yes, I could do with a drink, haven't had one for a couple of weeks.'

'A couple of weeks! What's wrong whit you, are you poorly?'

They had been friends a long time, been together in the Army for over four years and Patrick could see that the Captain's wife was troubling Georgie. He had had told him that he believed that she was married to the captain and Patrick guessed he was a little withdrawn because he wanted to talk with her, catch up on the news but she was an officer's wife and off limits, talking to her privately could prove very difficult. For his part, Patrick could see that she was certainly a stunning looking woman.

Two hours later, the horses groomed and fed, the soldiers strode towards the town for a few hours leave, the lieutenant's reward for the progress they had made before finally going out on patrol.

'Down here lads,' said Patrick, leading the them towards a neat wooden building in the Dutch style. The Trafalgar might be a Dutch style building but it was an English style pub and run by a tough ex Sergeant Major from the Royal Artillery. He was a man who had fought in the Crimean War, a popular character with the troops and his stories of an earlier age made the hairs on the back of the young soldiers necks stand on end.

Noisily they made their way past the Victoria Hotel and some instinct made Georgie look up. A figure of a woman was looking out of a first floor window and he recoiled seeing Ellen looking down at him and smiling before withdrawing behind the curtains. Georgie could not help wondering about their past lives, young James, running the gauntlet of angry crowds and dodging the law. It all came back to him and he looked towards the window and saw again. She waved discreetly, thumped the clenched fist of her left hand into her right palm, bending her thumb back to indicate direction – she was telling him to meet her at the rear of the building and Georgie understood, their signals of long ago not forgotten.

In the bar of the Trafalgar, the soldiers were drinking beer and smoking, their conversation loud and boisterous as they enjoyed a few hours of freedom. The bar top had been set up to represent the positions of the opposing forces at the battle of Inkerman, mugs and empty bottles stood in neat rows and their host was enthralling the soldiers with tales of battle. He had been there and no one in the room could dispute the truth of his stories. The soldiers listened, argued and offered their own take on the battle and Georgie picked his moment. Slowly he sidled towards the open doorway, waited until an argument erupted and the soldier's attention was completely on the battle, then he slipped quietly out of the room and into the gathering darkness.

Pressing against the wooden wall of the building he silently made his way to the rear of the hotel and from the shadows, a slim female figure emerged. She had a shawl held tightly over her head and she reached for his hand, pulling him deeper into the shadows.

The first thing Georgie noticed was her aroma, gone were the stale smells of the East End, in their place a delicate perfume and when she let the shawl slip from her head he could see she had changed almost beyond recognition. Her complexion was smooth, lightly tanned, well-kept long black curls lay provocatively across her shoulders, and when she spoke, the transformation was complete; she wasn't dropping her H's.

'Georgie, we thought you was gone to Australia on a prison ship, we h...eard nothing of you. Last we saw of you was the Peeler taking you away. What happened to you?'

He told her of events after his arrest. 'There was a recruiting Sergeant who knew my father and he persuaded the policeman to let him take me into the Army. After my training, I had some leave and I came looking for you but you had gone all of you, even the old man who lived upstairs knew nothing. I asked about you in the street and the pubs but you had all just, vanished.'

Pickpockets and Zulus

'No we didn't just vanish we had to go on the run. My stupid big brother really got us into trouble, he and his mates robbed the house of a Member of Parliament and he brought the roof down. Every peeler in London was on the lookout for us. Turned out they had been watching Billy and his mates for a while and knew who they were. Anyway, mother was pregnant again, after all that time, and dad had lost it, he couldn't keep off the drink and was caught picking some woman's pocket. Luckily, he only got six months in Newgate but worse was to come. They caught up with young Billy and his gang, they got ten years hard labour in the penal colony in Australia, then mother died in childbirth and I had to look after young Jimmy. It was hard at first but an old man gave me a job in the kitchen of his big house and James helped with the h...horses. I 'ad to do fings though, I can't tell you about that. Anyway, I was wearing decent clothes and mixing with the crowds on my day off when I met Clarence, him you've been training with. He took a real fancy to me and I could see it was a chance to escape from the old man so I put on me best be-havior and he really fell for me. He thinks I come from a well to do family who made money out of the clothing trade so he puts up with a few rough edges – but I'm working on them Georgie boy.' She paused for a moment and cast her eyes over him. 'You're looking well, I'm so glad I've found you because we really haven't got anyone except each other have we?'

Bewildered but happy, Georgie said, 'no we haven't and I've often wondered what had happened to you. Now I know but listen, if I'm caught with an officer's wife I could be in big trouble. Your husband might disown you and then where would you be? How can we

227

keep in touch, I hear you're leaving next week and you could be going anywhere.'

'I'll write you Georgie, I know your regiment and believe it or not I've learned to read and write.'

'Blimey,' said Georgie, his face beaming.

Chapter 5

A slight rustle to his left distracted Nkosinathi and swivelling his eyes he caught an almost imperceptible movement of the elephant grass. He turned his eyes to look to his right, not daring to move his head in case the movement revealed him to the enemy and his heart beat with excitement. Alongside him lay fifty more warriors; all fit young men, all feeling the same emotions, waiting in anticipation.

Nkosinathi and his cohort had lived in the military iKhanda for almost two years and trained hard to become warriors. Barefoot they had marched for miles across the rough ground, toughening up the soles of their feet and learning the killing techniques with their stabbing spears, the *Iklwa,* the Zulu weapon of choice ever since the time of Shaka.

Beside him each warrior held his shield, spear ready, the air tense and only ten or twelve feet away the enemy were within reach. To a cry of *"Usuthu"* the warriors leapt to their feet like coiled springs and charged forward into the oncoming soldiers. Their shields crashed into those of the opposing forces, pushing them back. Nkosinathi's cohort seemed to be prevailing but then the grass in front of them parted to reveal more of the enemy force and eventually the weight of numbers counted. Nkosinathi and his platoon were about to be overrun when, from the left another body of soldiers concealed in the undergrowth sprang up to reinforce Nkosinathi's group and for almost two hours, the two sides clashed shields.

It was hard, hot work and because the regiment was in training they were forbidden to use their spears in anger, simply shaking them threateningly at each other. It was a realistic exercise to drill the warriors in the art of stealth warfare but they must not draw blood, a sign of their discipline. Back and forth, the sweating pack forced each other first one way and then the other until eventually the Induna called a halt and the exhausted men collapsed to the ground.

'You have done well, the King has been watching you, and he is pleased. You are to return to the Kraal and to take a black bull from his herd to slaughter for your reward. Go and prepare your feast and tomorrow you will be allowed to leave to visit your families,' said the Induna.

A great whoop went up from the men who, without a word of command, formed themselves into ranks and began the famed loping run of the Zulu army. They were happy, first to feast on one of the Kings bulls and then that they could go home. Singing the regimental song the tall, fit and impressive body of young men made their way back to the Kraal.

'Nkosinathi, we are to leave for home tomorrow and I will come with you,' said Manelesi.

'Oh and why would you visit the Kraal of Mondli before your own,' asked Nkosinathi, knowing why his friend wanted to visit.

Pickpockets and Zulus

Looking slightly embarrassed Manelesi cleared his throat and said, 'My father has spoken with your father and they have agreed that I can marry your sister. When I am released from the King's service I will marry her.'

'Is this true Manelesi?' teased Nkosinathi, deciding to have some fun at his friend's expense. 'Is my sister happy to know that one day she will marry you?' He could see the embarrassment on Manelesi's face, he was suffering and Nkosinathi was enjoying the moment.

Manelesi was a fine strong Zulu warrior but he was nothing when it came to women and he simply stood looking at Nkosinathi until finally, his eyes dropped and Nkosinathi let out a bellow of laughter. He pushed Manelesi's chest with both hands sending him stumbling backwards, alerting the other warriors, perhaps a fight was developing, and they began to gather round. But they were disappointed as Nkosinathi held up his palms in friendship and Manelesi did the same.

'Nozipho?'

'Yes.'

Before Nkosinathi could say more a cry went up from the coral as a black bull was turned loose, trotting out towards open countryside but did not get far. The warriors nearest the doomed animal leaped onto it, grabbing hold of the long fearsome horns and through weight of numbers, forced it to its knees, turning it over onto its back to lay, thrashing out with deadly hooves. Surging forward, twenty men took hold of each limb and the ten muscular young men gripping each of the bull's horns began twisting the animal's head until finally, a loud crack signalled the breaking of its neck.

Swiftly the warriors butchered the carcass into large joints to hang over a great fire and as the meat blackened, the warriors filed past each cutting a piece from the joints.

'You will leave the King's Kraal and return home. The word will be spread when you are next to assemble here,' said the Induna walking amongst the feeding soldiers.

This was good news, the King was formally disbanding the regiment so they could return to their villages to help with the harvest and to see their families. The past few years, had taught them some hard lessons and now they were fully fledged Zulu warriors, a state of being they had coveted since childhood.

'When did you meet my sister?' Nkosinathi asked Manelesi, as they trotted side by side across a wide expanse towards Mondli's Kraal.

'At the festival of the Reed Dance, for the first time when I was young, it was the only time we could meet and each year we have talked, talked of many things and the last time she said that I could speak with her father.'

For a while they fell silent, the only sound was that of their feet pounding the ground as the miles passed until eventually they came in sight of Mondli's Kraal and inquisitive villagers working in the fields looked up to watch their approach. A stranger or a returning warrior always brought news of the kingdom and the wider world and they were eager to hear the news.

'Nkosinathi, my son,' said his mother with pride in her eyes. 'They have told me that it was you approaching and this one, he is a son of Nongalaza, brother to Siphiwe I think?'

'Yes, it is so mother.'

'And why is he visiting our Kraal?' she asked, a twinkle in her eye, for she knew very well why he had come and she knew that Nongalaza was a rich man and that he would pay a high price for the hand of her daughter and make Mondli very happy.

As a guest in the Kraal, Manelesi knew that as his father's representative he must show respect to Mondli, but more than anything he wanted to see Nozipho. But Nozipho was working in the fields when the men arrived and she did not know of her brother's arrival until a girl called out, 'Nkosinathi returns and he has someone with him, a warrior.'

Her heart skipped a beat and, eager to see if it was Manelesi, she ran all the way to the kraal, elated to see that the tall young man standing beside her brother was he.

'Little sister, look who I have brought to see you, teased Nkosinathi and for once Nozipho did not scold him, but she did tell him to keep his distance while she spoke to Manelesi. The two of them walked for a while to stand by the coral, chatting and catching up on the latest news and then, when he felt confident Manelesi told her what she had been waiting to hear.

'I am going to ask your father to let you marry me Nozipho,' he said suddenly, 'but I must return home soon, I will leave first thing in the morning when the sun returns. I will ask Nkosinathi to find me somewhere to sleep and I will return with your dowry as soon as I can.'

Nozipho listened quietly, knowing that marriage between then could not happen for a long time, maybe years, not until the King gave his permission. She looked at him with her big brown eyes, tracing his features and inside she felt a warm glow.

'I will wait for you Manelesi, go, talk to my father and seek his permission.'

Manelesi looked down at her and felt happy but at the back of his mind was the fear of asking her father to marry him. Later that evening he sat with Mondli at his fire and they talked until at last Mondli allowed him to broach the subject of the bride payment. Manelesi had his father's permission to conclude an agreement and when they finally agreed the price, Mondli took his snuff horn from the slit in his ear lobe and they sealed their bargain.

Tell your father I am happy with the price in cattle and one day I will welcome you back to take my daughter.'

Early the following morning Manelesi said farewell to Mondli and Nkosinathi and walked with Nozipho to the entrance of the Kraal. A few precious moments together was all they had before he set off on the road to his father's Kraal and with a happy heart, he reached out and touched her fingertips, looked into her eyes and then set off on the long loping run that would eat up the miles.

Outside Mondli's hut, father and son sat together, Nkosinathi relating his experiences at the Kings iKhanda, answering his father's questions.

'Your friend, Manelesi, son of my friend Nongalaza, he came with you from the iKhanda.'

'Yes father.'

'Hmm...., there was a reason for him to visit my village, he wants to marry Nozipho one day and his father is wealthy with a large and healthy herd. We have agreed a good price for your sister, she is worth a great many cows and he is willing to pay my price. That makes me very happy my son. Now, tell me more about your time at the iKhanda, it makes my heart happy to go back to the time when I too was a young warrior.'

Mondli leaned forward, tapped a small amount of snuff from the horn onto the back of his hand, and passed it to Nkosinathi and not far away, on clear ground at the front of the kraal, Nozipho worked threshing ears of corn ready to make the flour for the mealie cakes and beside her mother smiled at her obvious happiness.

'So daughter, you have a suitor?'

'Yes, Manelesi told me yesterday that when the regiment receives the King's permission to marry then he will make me his wife and I have told him that I am very happy for that.'

'Do not forget daughter that the King may not give his permission for many years and you might be past child-bearing age. Is it not be better to marry an older man who has been released from the King's service? He will have cattle of his own and you will be able to have many children.'

Nozipho's expression changed from one of happiness to that of anger. 'Mother, I do not care if I have to wait for Manelesi or that he may not be rich; I want to be with him. He has spoken with my father and has agreed a bride price in cattle.'

Themba knew not to antagonize her feisty, single-minded daughter. When she made up her mind about something, it was not easy to sway her. Themba would play a waiting game; she did not want to see her daughter become too old before the King allowed her to marry Manelesi. It was all very well agreeing a bride price but it might be years before the King gave his permission. No there would be other suitors...

Nkosinathi woke from a deep sleep, something had disturbed him and opening his eyes he could see nothing, the interior of the hut he was sharing with the herd boys was pitch black. He listened, it was the sound of cattle stamping the ground had alerted him and their snorting signalled distress. He knew that something was very wrong and as his head cleared, he caught the faint smell of smoke and sat bolt upright thinking that one of the fires flared up during the night. He jumped to his feet, kicked his sleeping mat away and felt his way towards the entrance to investigate the disturbance. The smell of smoke grew stronger as he emerged and he became aware of a faint yellow glow intruding into the darkness.

He shivered in the cold morning air as he looked around for the source of the fire but there was nothing; the yellow light was coming in through the thorn-bush wall. He ran to the Kraal entrance and pushed aside the gate and there not two hundred yards away he saw the source of the flames. The tall, dry grass in the pasture was burning furiously and was coming towards him; the village was directly in the path of a wildfire.

His heart missed a beat, disaster was about to strike and he ran through the village shouting and slapping the walls of the huts with his spear to alert the sleeping villagers. Threading his way through the huts, he made his way towards the corral, the safety of the herd uppermost in his mind and as he reached the fence, he saw that he was no longer alone. Youths from his hut had heard his shouts and had run to the corral to save their precious herd. Mondli and some of the elders of the village appeared and stood bleary eyed and bewildered as the younger members of the community dashed recklessly about.

Two youths lifted the top bar off the gate and scrambled to remove the second one, Nkosinathi and three more of them waded in amongst the cattle, encouraging them to leave, the wooden shaft of Nkosinathi's spear becoming a cattle prod. Gradually the reluctant the animals began to move, complaining, snorting but at least they were moving towards the compound entrance.

'This way, take them out and round the side of the Kraal away from the flames' shouted Nkosinathi, abreast of the lead animal. He prodded its neck with his spear shaft, slapped its back and guided it from the corral, the others began to follow and through sheer determination, Nkosinathi managed to coax the near half tonne lead animal up to trotting speed. Behind him, the herd boys were beating the rest with their sticks and before long, mooing, trumpeting cattle were trotting through the entrance of the Kraal and away from the flames to safety.

'Over there,' shouted Nkosinathi, pointing with his spear. 'Up there onto the higher ground. Get them out of the way of the flames.'

He looked back, it was still dark, the oncoming fire was beginning to illuminate everything in an orange glow and he could hear the dry twigs crackling as the fire began to engulf them. Eventually the last of the animals passed by at a lazy trot and Nkosinathi could see the boys would manage to reach the high ground before the flames overtook them and he turned his attention back to the village. The thatched roofs of the huts were vulnerable to fire and if one ignited then the fire could rapidly spread throughout the Kraal and destroy it.

Racing back through the entrance, he saw that the whole village had turned out to watch the oncoming wall of flame. Mondli appeared in the midst of a crowd of women and began to order them to find anything they could to fight the fire. His face was grim, very aware of impending disaster, his whole world was on the brink of destruction.

'Nkosinathi, the herd, what is happening to the herd?' he asked.

'The herd is safe father; I have made the boys take them across the front of the fire to safety on the high ground in the north pasture. We must save the huts now. We need water and brooms to beat out the flames when the fire arrives.'

'Will the fire reach here?'

'Oh yes father, very soon.'

As if to re-enforce Nkosinathi's prediction the first of the sparks flew over the thorn bush barricade to fall amongst the huts. Each person, male or female, young or old held something with which to beat the out the flames and it was not long before the dry thatched roofs began to burn. The stout compound fencing would resist the rapidly moving wall of fire for a time but the beehive huts were another matter and within a very short time, the first sparks began to land on the thatched roofs. As they began to burn, the villagers frantically beat the flames with anything they could lay their hands, a desperate attempt to save their homes that was beginning to look increasingly futile.

'Quickly, fetch climbing poles.' Mondli shouted to some of the older men.

They were beating out flames but could not reach the fires high on the roofs and those were beginning to take hold.

'Let me father.'

Nkosinathi leapt up and grasped the thatch, pulled himself onto the sloping roof and was able to reach the fire to beat at it with his bare hands. he frantically extinguished the fire with a broom passed to him but from this vantage point, he could see many more huts were on fire. The villagers were doing their best to contain the many small fires that were breaking out but some huts were beginning to succumb, their thatch engulfed in flames and the smoke billowing out across the Kraal.

'Nozipho, get the children away from here, they will be burned if they stay,' said Themba, her face streaked in soot and sweat.

'Children, here' Nozipho held out both hands to a small group of very young children, 'come we must find shelter.'

'Over there,' shouted Themba, 'over there, in the centre of the Kraal is the safest place. Go, take them there.'

Themba turned back to her firefighting whilst Nozipho took the children away. 'Here' she said to two girls standing nearby and watching their mothers, 'come and help with the little ones.'

The three of them gathered as many young children as they could and led them towards the open spaces at the centre of the Kraal and then Nozipho left them to return to the mothers and bring their young ones to safety.

Outside the Kraal the fire had closed in and driven by a wind of its own making, had swiftly swept past, leaving only the smouldering grass and several burning huts in its wake. The villagers were exhausted by their efforts but there was still work to do, if the huts still burning were not dealt with there was still a real danger the whole kraal would be destroyed and hurrying between the burning huts, Nozipho would not stop, she looked and listened, searching for any children missed in the panic. Then she heard it, somewhere nearby, a baby crying and then the hut suddenly ignited and thinking nothing of the danger, she dropped to her knees and began to crawl inside.

'Nozipho!' shouted Nkosinathi from the rooftop, 'Nozipho, come back, don't go in there, the roof is alight.'

But it was too late, the girl disappeared inside and at the same time the roof began to burn fiercely. Nkosinathi slid from the roof on which he was working on to chase after her. He reached the hut just as the roof began to weaken, the blazing beams buckling and ready to fall in. He tore at the narrow entrance tunnel with a strength he did not know he possessed, ripping away the interleaved twigs and small branches until he had created a hole large enough for him to reach inside.

Nozipho had found the baby and coughing from the smoke, her eyes streaming she tried to get out just as Nkosinathi reached inside the inferno to grab hold of her. He felt her shoulder but before he could catch hold, the roof fell in and Nozipho screamed out in fear. She took the full weight of the collapsing roof and

Nkosinathi had little choice but to dive in amongst the falling debris. Tearing at the burning thatch with his bare hands, he eventually managed take hold of Nozipho's arm to pull her and the baby clear of the flames. He dragged at Nozipho, her arms still clasped tightly round the baby, and then the rest of the roof collapsed, some the burning debris falling across her head and shoulders, setting her hair alight. She screamed out in pain forcing Nkosinathi to redouble his effort and by sheer luck he pulled both her and the baby clear as the whole of the hut erupted in flames

'My baby, thank you, my baby,' called out the mother picking up the child and running to safety, leaving the stricken Nozipho to fend for herself.

'You brave girl Nozipho,' said her brother, 'we must get you away from here. This looks to be the last hut on fire and there are plenty of people to put it out.' He reached down and gathered up his sister in his arms, lifting her effortlessly and carrying her to safety.

The fires burned for a few more hours, destroying several huts and leaving blackened grass stretching for almost as far as the eye could see. A few trees still stood but it was a scene of desolation, an alien landscape, but at least the herd was safe. The herd boys had not stopped where Nkosinathi had told them, but had kept the animals moving all night until they were well out of reach of the fire, everyone had survived with no more than a few minor burns, that is except for Nozipho.

For three days, Nozipho lay on a bed of soft skins her mother had prepared for her and Themba sat with her bathing her wounds, applying a soothing mixture of herbs and a crude form of calamine given to her by the Witch Doctor. The burns were severe to her head and

241

shoulders, most of her hair had burned away leaving the skin on her skull raw and badly wasted. Her shoulders had caught the full force of the burning roof as it had collapsed about her, but worst of all was the injury to her eye.

'You are a brave, brave girl,' said Themba, tears in her eyes as she looked down at her daughter, seeing nothing but a bundle of rags. Themba lifted a shell with a little water, lying on the mat alongside Nozipho and put it to the girl's lips. To see her like this was heart-breaking, she was normally a happy energetic girl who worked hard from dawn until dusk and now she seemed helpless. Everyone agreed that she was courageous in her actions and the spirits must have been looking after the baby.

'Mother' Nozipho managed to whisper, her first words since the fire.

'How do you feel daughter?'

'Mother, it hurts a lot but it is better than before. Will I still be pretty?'

'You will always be pretty Nozipho. No one is as pretty as you.'

Nozipho forced a weak smile, closed her eyes and drifted into sleep, she was getting better but her disfigurement would be with her for the rest of her life and her mother began to wonder what Manelesi would think. Would he still want Nozipho for his bride? It seemed that he was her only hope of a husband after all.

She soon found out, for on hearing the news of the fire and the heroics of Nozipho, Manelesi made the journey to their village. Nkosinathi saw him coming from the rooftop of a hut he was repairing, a lone figure loping along towards the Kraal.

'Manelesi it is good to see you. You have come to see Nozipho?' a question he need not have asked.

'Yes, I have come to see her and to offer my father's condolences to Mondli. I have been many miles away to the north hunting with my father and it was only yesterday that a messenger came from our village and I heard of your tragedy'

'She is in that hut there with our mother,' said Nkosinathi, pointed, his saddened eyes avoiding those of Manelesi.

Manelesi crawled into Themba's hut and once his eyes became accustomed to the gloom he was shocked by what he saw. Nozipho, hair missing, the scabs of dried blood on her scalp and shoulders, one eye closed, the eyelid stuck fast, was a forlorn sight lying on the mat. Manelesi felt repulsed and he knew then that he did not want to marry her, no longer was she the girl he had fallen in love with, but a creature of the spirits.

'You are well Nozipho?' he asked.

'Do I look well you warthog,' she snapped, her spirit returning, 'if I was well I would not be lying here like a baby now would I?'

It was still Nozipho; perhaps he had judged her too cruelly.

'Where have you been, the fire was a week ago and you only come now. What kind of husband will you make? I might change my mind,' she said, anger in her voice and still unaware of how badly she had been burned. No one had told her and she was not well enough to figure it out for herself and she had no idea her hair might not grow back or that the scars forming on her face and shoulders would leave her disfigured for life. It would be several more days before she could leave her sick bed but even now, events were conspiring against her.

The drought had left the grass tinder dry to burn easily, depriving the cows of their much-needed fodder and the fire had partly destroyed the maize crop. It would not be long before the villagers would begin to go hungry and to some it seemed that the spirits were angry, something needed doing about it and the Sangoma knew exactly what that was.

Always on the lookout for advantage, the tall musty smelling Witch Doctor approached his chief.

'Mondli oh great one, you have led your people for many years, graced us with your wisdom, fed us from your herd but now we are in the grip of the great spirit's wrath. The spirit of our ancestors is displeased; this spirit brought the fire upon us and is slowly destroying our crops. The spirit must be appeased.'

Mondli was as much afraid of the spirit world as any Zulu and was not about to argue with this conduit to the underworld.

'What do you know? What should we do?'

The Shaman dug into a crocodile skin pouch hanging from his waistband and pulled out his divining bones.

'The bones will tell us the source of the evil that has befallen us and, of the remedy.'

He began a slow, circular dance, chanting some unintelligible verse as he went. The hair on Mondli's neck began to stand up. He was afraid of only two things in this world; the power of the Witch Doctor and the power of the King and at this moment, the Witch Doctor had his attention.

'I see the spirit of your father Mondli.'

Mondli's knees felt weak. Communication with his father meant that the spirits were indeed angry.

'He tells me that it is his own blood that gives the spirits displeasure. One of his own blood must give up their life.' He became silent, eyes closed and rocking his head back and forth – waiting.

Gripped by the suspense, Mondli could not help himself. He was the Chief of the Kraal, leader of his people and yet the Sangoma held him in his hand and he knew that he would have to do whatever the diviner said.

Unable to remain silent any longer he said, 'What must we do to please the spirit of Belial, my father?'

The Sangoma's eyes opened, the drugs he had taken dilating them and with his face covered with a white powder giving him a most sinister appearance. He lifted his medicine stick, stretched it out before him, like a pointer, straight at Mondli and made him flinch.

Between the huts, the villagers watched and held their breath because it was with his stick that the Sangoma communicated with the spirit world and the pointing stick often meant death. Nkosinathi stood in the background and watched, puzzled as to what might happen, whom would the Sangoma single out for death? He was sure that it could not be him but even so, he still he felt a weakness in the pit of his stomach.

The stick began to move, swinging in a slow arc, projecting fear like a bolt of lightning through the Kraal. From side to side it went, followed by a hundred pair of eyes until finally, it came to rest. An audible intake of breath from the audience revealed that the stick was not pointing at them. It was pointing towards Themba's hut, but Themba was not the one singled out.

'The girl Nozipho, she is the one, she must die, only then will the spirits be placated.'

Mondli looked down at the ground, relieved that he was not to lose a wife for he needed them to plant crops and to bring in the harvest; to lose one of them would be a further tragedy. Nevertheless, what of his daughter, what about the cows he was to receive in payment for her hand in marriage, what should he do about them?

Raising his arms in a gesture of obedience he said, 'Belial, father I hear you, your bidding will be done. Nozipho will be put to death tomorrow evening as the sun sets, tell the slayer,' he said. 'Prepare a feast for tomorrow. When the sun leaves the earth we will celebrate our salvation with the spirit of my father.'

He clapped his hands, dismissing the villagers who were very happy to return to the business of rebuilding the Kraal.

'You may take the first blood of the cow to be sacrificed,' said Mondli to the hovering Sangoma.

The Witch Doctor bowed his head in acceptance, pleased he still held sway and as the darkness began to close in, he slinked away to his lair.

'The spirits say that it is Nozipho that offends them. I do not understand how, for she does no harm to anyone and she saved the life of the youngest amongst us.' said Nkosinathi.

Manelesi stood beside him and said nothing, it was the way of the Zulu and they accepted these things though he was troubled. Ever since he had first seen Nozipho, he had wanted her but now he had rejected her, why? She had scolded him for that, he knew of her bravery, she was special and now they wanted sacrifice her to appease the spirits. His heart felt heavy for although he would be free to marry another he could not let her go. What should he do?

'Nkosinathi, my friend...' he began, falling silent before he could finish.

'What?'

'I...I think I should be the one to take Nozipho's life. She was to be mine in life and it should be me that ends that life.'

Nkosinathi nodded; there was logic in Manelesi's words.

The Kraal was quiet, Mondli sat by his fire watching it flare up, following the sparks with his eyes as they rose up into the air. He was sad to be losing his favourite daughter but he knew that to please the spirits was more important.

Sitting opposite his father, his face illuminated by the flickering flames Nkosinathi spoke. 'Father' said 'I have never asked you for anything have I?'

'No, I believe not.'

'Nozipho is my sister, my friend Manelesi here, was one day to take her as his first wife. Father, would you let Manelesi take her and sacrifice her to the spirits?'

'Manelesi has told me that he will give you three cows as payment for her. She will only be his for one day and he believes three cows is a generous payment.'

Mondli stopped poking the fire, his stick motionless in thin air as the words registered. He had begun to believe that he would never see any cattle for Nozipho, yet to let this young warrior have the honour of despatching his daughter would solve many conundrums. First, it would appease the spirits, secondly Manelesi would for a short time, have his daughter and thirdly he would receive three cows.

'It shall be so, Manelesi will take her to the Lake of the Crocodiles and there, as the sun sets, he will send her home, I have spoken.'

Manelesi sat quietly listening to the pronouncements and later, with a heart heavy, told Nozipho of the Witch Doctor's pronouncement and her father's decision. He watched as she calmly accepted her fate, a true, proud Zulu woman and in that moment, he realized he should never have forsaken her.

He left her that final night, sleeping soundly and in the morning the two of them walked out from the kraal and towards the Lake of the Crocodiles. To begin with, Nozipho walked several paces behind Manelesi with her burned and sorrowful head held high, her good eye fixed firmly on the road ahead and watching from a gap between the huts Nkosinathi felt sad. He could not understand how his sister could have been the one to disturb the spirits as he watched the two of them. Manelesi standing tall, his shield in one hand and his spear in the other and Nozipho, a small hunched figure struggling along behind and hanging from Manelesi's waist, the knobkerrie he would use for the execution.

Once they had lost sight of the village Manelesi waited for Nozipho to catch him up and they walked side by side.

'Your father said that you must be sent home to your ancestors as the sun sets. He has allowed me the privilege,' he said lowering his head. He had seen many of his fellow Zulus put to death, to pacify the spirits, mostly for trivial transgressions and now it was his turn to become a slayer and his heart was heavy at the thought.

'It is the will of my father and I must obey him' said Nozipho, in a quite matter of fact manner.

'You are brave little one. You put great warriors to shame with your actions.'

'I am a Zulu, it is the will of our fore fathers and it is the way of Shaka. What else should I do?'

Manelesi's mind was in turmoil, he fell silent and for the next few hours, they walked alongside each other uttering not a word. By late afternoon, they reached the river and walked along its bank until the ground rose up towards low overhanging cliffs and the lake of the crocodiles, the place of execution.

'The Crocodile Pool is this way,' said Nozipho.

Manelesi looked at her and felt a surge of feeling. He loved her more than anything and soon they must part until it was his turn to cross the great black river to the spirit world.

'I will make a fire and cook some of the meat I have brought for my journey home. Do you want some?'

Nozipho shook her head. 'Why would I want to eat when I am to die?'

'I am sorry, little one; it is the will of our ancestors. The Sangoma has consulted them and they have decreed that you are the one they want,' said Manelesi, unconvinced by his own argument.

'Hmm...perhaps the Sangoma was more interested in the payment he receives for such a thing. He will have my bones for his magic.'

'How can he? you will be consumed by the crocodiles.'

'He has been following us. I thought you were a fine warrior warthog. Haven't you seen him?'

'Yes I know the Sangoma is following us and I know that he will try and collect some of your bones for his spells. He will grind them down, mix them with herbs and sell the potion to the villagers. We have a Sangoma in our village that is just the same. I did not want to distress you.'

Nozipho shuddered visibly; realisation of the fate awaiting her beginning to crack her resolve.

'Do not worry little one, I have a plan, I am not about to lose you.'

Her head jerked up and her eye met his. She said nothing, her wounds and the exertion of the journey had tired her.

'Lie down and sleep a while,' said Manelesi, his eyes scanning the bush and two hundred yards away, in a hollow surrounded by Mimosa bush, the Sangoma crouched, waiting for the darkness, the time when he would venture forth to witness the death of Nozipho and to collect anything of her body that he could scavenge from the crocodiles.

Three hours later Nozipho awoke with a thirst as she had never known but to her delight the stinging pain in her scalp was no more than a light throb.

'Manelesi I am thirsty, give me some water.'

He jumped up and leaned over her to reach for the water gourd, felt her warm skin against his, inhaled her perfume and watched with fascination as she gulped down the water.

'I am hungry, I will eat something,' it was more an order than a request.

Manelesi smiled to himself, opened his shoulder bag and took out some meat for her. He had decided not to light a fire; it would make it too easy for the Witch Doctor to find them.

'Little one I will tell you of my plan and you must listen carefully...'

The sun became a deep red, its lower limb almost touching the tops of the distant mountains when Manelesi stood up and beckoned Nozipho to follow him. They climbed the shallow slope to the cliff edge to see before them the deep water of a lagoon, home to a congregation of crocodiles and after walking along the edge of the cliff for fifty yards Manelesi called a halt.

'This is the place little one, do as I have told you. Do not be afraid.'

She looked up into his eyes and he could see that she was afraid but more than that, she was prepared to face her death.

'Kneel here and face the water.'

Nozipho took a step forward and sank to her knees as he told her, head bowed in submission.

A short distance away, several pairs of eyes watched the event unfold, the Sangoma and the pool's inhabitants. The Witch Doctor had begun to wonder if Manelesi was indeed going to carry out the sentence and speculated on what he might extract from Mondli when he told him of the warriors disobedience. Nevertheless here they were at the appointed place and he could see the execution was about to happen.

Crawling slowly on his hands and knees through the bushes, he made his way towards the edge of the cliff, stopping no more than thirty yards from the couple. Carefully he parted the bushes to gain a better view, aware that he was no match for the warrior should

Manelesi see him and become angry. He watched knobkerrie rise high and for a few seconds it hovered in space before crashing down onto Nozipho's scull. There was a sharp crack and her body tumbled from sight over the cliff edge. He heard the splash as she entered the water and then, after a period of silence, came the thrashing of powerful tails. All the Sangoma could think of at that moment was the prize of a young female's body parts.

Manelesi sank to the ground in sorrow and for a few minutes remained still and silent, reciting a short prayer before standing to his feet. It was practically a moonless night, almost pitch black and by the time he had gathered himself together to walk away, the narrow crescent of the moon barely illuminated the scene.

Waiting in his hideaway, the Sangoma was becoming impatient and impulsively broke cover, creeping towards the cliff edge. Peering over into the gloom, he could see nothing and he decided to hide himself in a thicket once more until the morning light. Crouching down he thought how quiet it was, he had witnessed the execution and yet he could not understand why the crocodiles were so still. After a while, he could not contain himself and decided that he would go down to the water's edge to see what he could find.

In the darkness, some distance away, Manelesi lay flat on the ground overlooking the pool arm outstretched. He leaned further over the ledge feeling for Nozipho's hand and felt her touch, good; she was where he had told her to be. He felt her fingers grasp his wrist, he tightened his hand around her slender limb and using all his great strength he hauled her up onto firm ground. He felt good; his plan was working and

Nozipho was safely back with him but what of the Sangoma, if he should catch sight of them, if he should see that Nozipho still lived then all was lost.

Before she had dropped to the ledge, Manelesi had told her to pick up two large stones. As he swung the knobkerrie to the ground beside her, she had banged them together, mimicking the sound of the club crushing her skull, then, dropping onto the carefully selected ledge six feet below. Manelesi had told her to toss the rocks into the water, hoping that the diversion would fool the Sangoma into thinking it was her dead body. Then she crawled along the ledge towards the waiting Manelesi who had lifted her up and once she felt safe she had thrown her arms about his neck and planted kisses all over his face.

They had to get away as quickly as possible the darkness would hide them for only so long and he wondered where they could find safety. He had heard of a Norwegian mission station at Mfule where fugitives had often found shelter and he had decided to take her there. It meant a dangerous trek of at least ten miles in darkness, through territory he knew little about and there were wild animals to contend with, moreover, there was still the Witch Doctor.

At that moment the Sangoma, fully occupied with his descent down the steep cliff, did not have any thoughts of trickery in his mind. He believed he knew where the girl had fallen into the water; he had heard the club strike her, the splash as she fell into the lagoon and he wanted to get there as quickly as he could before all her body parts disappeared. Concentrating on the place where he believed she had gone into the water he scrambled over the cliff edge but in his haste, he caught his foot in an exposed root. His forward momentum was too great for him to react, his ankle twisted badly as he fell and head first, he slid down the muddy bank, coming to rest within a foot of the water.

Crying out in pain, he tried to stand but his leg must have broken just above the ankle and he could do nothing but pause on his hands and knees. However, he had landed almost exactly where he wanted to be, the place where the crocodiles had taken Nozipho. Indeed it was exactly where she had thrown the rocks into the lagoon and the noise had attracted the crocodiles. They had not eaten for a long time and were hungry and now they had his scent, and with a great thrash of its powerful tail one giant male reared up from the depths to clamp the Witch Doctor's head in its powerful jaws, to drag him into the water and then a second crocodile joined him. Between them, the beasts began the death spin, tearing the body to pieces, turning the waters of the lagoon red, all that was left of the Witch Doctor.

Chapter 6

Georgie's platoon finally received orders to move, the potential for unrest between the Gcaleka and Xhosa becoming all too apparent. The army was preparing to move and Georgie was using his few hours leave to gather some of the essentials he would have difficulty in obtaining once they were out on the move. It had been raining; the road was too muddy to walk on so he used the wooden sidewalk and as he passed a small haberdashery shop the door opened and a woman came out. He was preoccupied with his chore and did not notice her until a soft female voice whispered 'Georgie' and he turned his head in surprise.

'Ellen.'

'Hello Georgie, how are you this fine day. I hear you are all leaving soon.'

'Yes, tomorrow. I'm looking for a few things to make life a little more comfortable.'

'Like what?'

'Well, er... Camphor,' said Georgie a little embarrassed.

Ellen smiled, she knew very well what the lotion was for, wasn't she married to a cavalry officer. 'Anyway I can't be seen talking to you for long Ellen, you're an officer's wife.'

'Awe, don't be such a prude Georgie, Clarence ain't here now. He's been sent up country so I think we can 'ave a chat now and again can't we?'

He grinned at his cousin as her façade slipped for a few moments her East London accent returning to the fore.

'How long will you remain in William's?' he asked. 'The natives are getting restless again. Is that where Captain Jameson has gone, to see what they're up to?'

'He didn't tell me, anyway I don't really care so long as I gets 'is pay' she said with a self-satisfied smile on her lips.

'You've landed on your feet gel, I'll give you that. Do you love him?'

'Eh, shut up Georgie, love's got nofin' to do with it, he's a good man and he looks after me, that's all I care about. Without him, where would I be? And you,' she said, 'look at you. You've turned out well enough Georgie, army life seems to suit you and don't forget where my brother is right now, breaking rocks in Australia and we could be with him,' she said, her voice softening as she settled back into to a more cultivated style.

'So, where do we go from here Ellen, will you stay an officer's wife? I signed on as a man six months ago so I will in the army a while longer. Who knows, we might see a bit more of each other.'

'Of course, I can't deny it's an easier life than we used to have eh, Georgie? And you, make sure you write, you're all I've got that I really care about. I'm happy enough with Clarence and I know that he loves me but you and me are blood Georgie.'

Pickpockets and Zulus

'You and me are blood,' mouthed Georgie to himself as he sat motionless in the saddle. For so long his only family had been the Army and here was Ellen telling him they were blood, and of course they were. His mother and father were both dead, he had no siblings and her family had all but disappeared from the face of the earth, neither had much family to speak of, she was right.

His horse pawed the ground, bringing him back to his senses and he snapped his head up to look around. It would not do to be caught napping, not since the Xhosa had shown how dangerous they could be. His patrol had reached the edge of the forest, the wooded ravines with their steep rocky outcrops made ideal ambush country, too dangerous for them to venture any further.

They had been chasing the Gcaleka warrior chief Sarhili for days, a crafty adversary who was giving them the run around, striking when they least expected it. Each time they had him and his men in their sights they simply melted away into the thick, impenetrable forest and these rocky ravines were no place for the horses. They were calling it the Ninth Frontier War, skirmishes, low-level battles had been going on for months and now the Government was trying to negotiate a peace with the Xhosa paramount chief, Sandile but younger, more aggressive tribesmen had pushed him aside. They had never felt defeat at the hands of the Europeans only tasting success at Gwadana where they had killed several police and panicked the colonists. This had forced the Government to send the Twenty Fourth Regiment of Foot, a naval contingent from HMS Active and a few marines to help the colonial volunteers and their native levies.

Hard pressed though they had been on occasion, the colonial forces had won a resounding victory at a fortified mission station. They had driven the rebels off with heavy losses and it seemed that the emergency was over but now the Ngqika tribe was rebelling and had allied themselves with the remnants of the Gcaleka army.

'It will be getting dark in an hour or so,' said Lieutenant Clements. 'Sergeant Donovan, signal to the rest of the units that we are returning to camp.'

'Yes sir,' said Patrick, newly promoted to sergeant.

He took called to the trooper carrying the heliograph to set the device and flashed a signal to the other sections of Mounted Infantry spread out across the countryside and one by one they rode towards the lieutenant's position to regroup ready for the ride back to camp.

In the mess tent the soldiers were greedily consuming their dinner when Patrick appeared and joined them.

'There's a rumour that we're going to do a sweep through Gcalekaland to the coast. To be sure it is feasible boys. I have just come back from seein' the lieutenant and he has told me to get you lads ready to move at four. Looks like we will be scouting ahead of the column.'

'Aye no doubt we will,' said Barney, 'we might see some action this time instead of panning for diamonds. I wonder what happened to Dickie, if he ever did get rich.'

'He might not be rich but he sure as hell won't be able to show his face again. They'll hang him if they catch him,' said Patrick.

He seemed to be taking his duties rather seriously thought Georgie; he would not normally worry about a deserter, certainly not one who had been a friend.

'What do you think Patrick, where are we going?' asked Georgie.

'Well we're leaving Ibeka with in a day or so and we'll be under the command of Colonel Glyn. I think they will want to follow the Qora river to the sea and catch a few Gcaleka along the way.'

The soldiers sitting at the table listened, pondering the implications of Patrick's words for no more than ten seconds before the cards came out, all thoughts of fighting forgotten.

In the cold, damp morning air steam drifted from the horses' nostrils and Georgie's horse stamped several times on the hard ground, annoyed at being disturbed. Georgie took no notice, throwing the saddle up onto its back and reaching under its belly to fasten the strap. He reached up to catch hold of its reigns and rubbed his hand along the horse's neck to calm it before mounting ready for another day's patrol.

It was the first day of the push up into Gcalekaland in pursuit of Sandile. Patrick had been accurate in his assessment; they were to be part of the Central Column, a mixed bag of Redcoats, Bluecoats from the Navy and some colonial troopers, together with six hundred Mfengu warriors dressed in a variety of uniforms. The British soldiers looked on with apprehension at this rag tag bunch of natives dressed in old tunics or simply a blanket thrown over their shoulders, bare footed and lightly armed. Some carried ancient firearms as well as their Assegais and with their flamboyant headgear, a collection of colourful feathers, they seemed easy targets to the Infantrymen apart from a piece of red cloth tied about their foreheads, the only feature to distinguish them from the enemy. Passing them and the main body of troops leaving camp on foot, the detachments of Mounted Infantry rode out to scout ahead of the column.

'Alright, Sergeants Donovan and Jones, take your men about half a mile out to the flanks. The rest of you stay with me' said Lieutenant Clements. 'Keep your eyes peeled and do not go shooting at shadows.'

The two sections broke away to ride out to the flanks whilst the rest of the Mounted Infantry spread out around the lieutenant to make a sweep in search of any Gcaleka hiding in the brush, all day scouring the undergrowth, fighting not the enemy but swarms of flies sticking to their sweaty faces. It was an exercise repeated daily across a featureless landscape broken only by clumps of brushwood and by the fourth day, they were deep into Gcalekaland and nearing their first objective, a fork in the river.

Lieutenant Clements ordered Patrick to take his section, Georgie, Frank Williams, Arthur Morgan and John Allen, to search the left fork whilst he took the remainder of his men along the right fork and alongside each party trotted some Mfengu Levies. These natives were expert trackers who hated the Gcaleka and whose job was to search the tangled bush where the horses could not go. As the morning wore on the vegetation increased in density and the ground became more uneven forcing the troopers to slow their mounts to a steady walking pace. From time to time Patrick would hold up his hand and they would stop, look and listen for any sign of the enemy and alongside them the Mfengu would slip silently in and out of the bush looking for tell-tale signs. Eventually they reached a wooded incline and Patrick called a halt.

'Frank,' hissed Patrick, 'stay still.' He gestured to the others to pull up their horses and all five mounted men sat quietly, listening, not even a bird sang and then the sound of a breaking twig disturbed the peace. There was someone or something hiding in the bushes up ahead and slowly, silently, the troopers unslung their Carbines. The leader of the Mfengu Levies moved his Assegai slowly in a sweeping movement before him, a signal to his warriors to spread out. Shoulders hunched in anticipation, the tribesmen quietly slipped passed the stationary horses and riders to disappear ghostlike into the bush on both sides and minutes later shouting and gunfire echoed from the undergrowth.

The Mfengu had found the enemy, the bush ahead vibrated with unseen violence, shouts, gunshots, screams, and then silence. Georgie felt his horse flinch and quietly patted its neck in reassurance. Then it started again as the Mfengu found more of the enemy and he felt his blood run cold as he heard terrible screams came up ahead as more men died and then there was a strange hissing noise. The Mfengu were celebrating their kills.

Georgie sat bolt upright his body tense, his gun at the ready and from the corner of his eye he caught a glimpse of a man running across some open ground. The man was without a red bandanna and must be the enemy he thought. Instinctively he raised his rifle to his shoulder, guessed the range and trajectory and let lose a shot. He was not sure he had hit him because the man did not falter in his haste to escape, crashing on into some aloe bushes, coming out on the far side. Georgie opened the breechblock and flipped the rifle with a twist of his wrist, releasing the spent cartridge and from his ammunition pouch deftly slipped in a fresh one. This time he took proper aim and fired at the running man who was by now at extreme range but his aim was true. The man's head jerked forwards, his arms splayed out and he managed two more paces before crumpling, lifeless to the ground.

Two Mfengu warriors pursuing the fugitive appeared from the bush, saw the man fall and ran on towards the corpse hissing through their teeth. Georgie was in no doubt he had killed his first man and felt elated as adrenalin pumped madly through his veins, but he did not feel like hissing, simply satisfied that he was doing the job for which he was trained.

'These Mfengu are buggers when they get going aren't they Georgie,' said Barney as the patrol turned back towards the column. 'That was one hell of a shot you pulled off.'

Georgie pursed his lips and nodded. 'I thought I got him with the first shot but that second one certainly finished him.'

'It did. I'm sure you got him first time, but boy, did he keep going,' said Barney.

'Georgie I've never seen such good shootin' said Patrick with a look of admiration. 'If you can keep it up we'll soon have this war over.'

The soldiers laughed, releasing tension, it was the first time they had seen any real action and the first time they had seen a man killed. As for the native levies, from the number of trophy ears they carried back, it appeared they had despatched many more Gcaleka out of sight of the Europeans. To them it was currency because the more ears they returned with, the more meat they would receive as reward for their services.

The following day the scouts entered the Manubi forest and searched in vain for an enemy that simply was not there. Their first contact with the British had convinced the Gcaleka to retire to a safer place forcing the column to push on over ever more difficult ground, eventually reaching the Qora River. It was a chance to rest the horses whilst the sappers made rafts from empty barrels to float the wagons across and during the ensuing weeks, they swept through Gcalekaland capturing cattle, burning Kraals and killing more than a hundred warriors. However, Sarhili, the main reason for them being there had evaded them.

'I hear that road back to William's is cut off,' said Frank sitting on the ground opposite Georgie, his Carbine in pieces as he cleaned the mechanism.

'I was talking to Corporal Jones of D Company earlier today' said Georgie, his own gun in a similar state. 'He told me he had overheard two officers talking. Intelligence reports suggest that Sarhili and his warriors have given us the slip and gone westwards towards the Kei River.'

'If he has then we will be heading back to Ibeka, you mark my words,' said Frank.

Georgie thoughtfully rubbed the loose parts of his gun with an oily rag, Frank was usually right about these matters.

The patrol moved over the veldt and up an incline to and vantage point and Patrick scanned the horizon, the flat palm of his hand against his forehead to shield his eyes from the sun.

'I saw some sorta glint over there I'm sure,' he said, lifting his field glasses to his eyes, concentrating for several minutes more on the area of interest but could not detect any movement. 'I'm sure there is something, come on, we'll make for that ridge for a final look and then it will be time to head back to camp.'

They moved off in single file, Patrick leading the way picking his way across the rocky ground. Their orders were to head for the new base camp being constructed at Centane, to report there as a forward scouting party. At that same instant, four miles away, just about, where Patrick had scanned with his binoculars, a large party of Ngqika warriors were resting after a twenty-mile march, their leader sitting cross-legged on the ground and chewing on some dried meat. His name was Khiva and he had not long since met with Sandile for a council of war. They had decided to make an assault on the Redcoat's camp at KwaCentane and out of sight of the patrols, the warriors massed in the ravines and kloofs, thousands of men awaiting the order to begin the attack.

'Khiva, oh great one,' said a warrior approaching his leader, 'a messenger has arrived from Sandile.'

'I see him,' said Khiva, standing to his full six feet, his muscular chest glistening from the animal fat rubbed on him by the Witch Doctor as protection against the bullets of the Redcoats. 'You have news.'

The messenger dropped to his knees in front of Khiva, holding an ox tail out in front of him to show he was indeed come from Sandile. Averting his eyes from the warrior chief, he recited the message.

'Our great leader Sandile is gathering the clans in the Nyumaga valley. You are to wait here until the main force is in position.' He went on to describe the strength and disposition of the rebel forces, told him of the plan to surround the camp at KwaCentane and the signals for battle.

'You have done well, eat our food and drink some of our beer before you return to Sandile. I have a message for you to take to him. Tell him we are ready to fight the Redcoats, to destroy them or die gloriously. I have spoken,' said Khiva.

He left the still prostrate messenger and walked towards his warriors, lifting his Assegai high above his head, a demonstration of his authority and a signal for his Indunas to gather together to hear the order of battle. He swept his spear back and forth to demonstrate the order of attack, its sharp polished blade briefly reflecting the bright sun light.

Across the valley Patrick decided that it was time to head for the camp, they had seen nothing of the enemy and to go further into the hills as darkness approached would be folly. He turned his horse towards the setting sun and after an hour, just as the first stars began to appear high in the darkening eastern sky, the troopers arrived at the camp.

'Here, take my horse Georgie. I'm off to report to the officer in charge, tell him there's nothing to worry about,' said Patrick slipping deftly from the saddle.

Alongside Georgie, Frank dismounted and began to loosen the straps on his saddle before preparing to give the animal a feed and a good rub down.

'Do you think they are out there Georgie? We've seen neither hide nor hare of any Gcaleka for days now. I reckon they've had enough and we won't see them again.'

'I don't know, but I was talking to one of the Mfengu after that encounter in Gcalekaland and asked him what he thought.'

'What did he think?'

'Well, if I understood him right he said that the Gcaleka consider this as their homeland and wouldn't give it up easily, army or no army. He said that there were plenty of them in the forests, enough to form a decent sized army and he expects them to return sometime.'

'Sometime when?'

'I don't know, but I tell you what, we had better be on our guard 'till we get back to Williams.'

'Stop speculating you two and let us get some dinner, I'm starving,' said an agitated Barney. 'If they are out there then we would have seen them. There wasn't a sign of anything so forget those buggers for now and let's go eat.'

Frank smiled at Georgie, 'he thinks of nothing but his belly, does he?'

Patrick was waiting for them at the mess tent. 'Come on lads, you've earned your dinner today. I've seen the Captain and he thinks that they will be attacking in the next few days, he's had reports of sightings from other patrols and he wants us back out at three 'o' clock in the morning.'

The hungry troopers looked at each other, they would not get much sleep tonight and it had just started to rain. Their tent was water proofed from above but they could not hold back the ground water once it decided to infiltrate and it had rained heavily two nights before soaking the ground and with today's downpour, they would likely have to sleep in mud.

They were right about the mud and after a few hours of fitful sleep, they struggling out of their tent, bleary eyed and ready for the day's patrol. Saddling the horses first, they left them to grab a quick breakfast of coffee and porridge before leaving camp to patrol the approaches from the north.

The rain did not let up, and long before the sun rose over the coastal plain, the weary troop dismounted for a rest. It was a dark night, but not totally so, the half-moon illuminated the countryside enough to discern any movement over open ground but they would have no hope of seeing anyone concealed in the bush until the sun rose.

'We'll stop here a while and rest the horses,' Patrick said, 'listen out for anything you can boys.'

He reached into his saddlebag for his water bottle and took a long drink.

'What's that?' hissed Frank, spinning round.

Patrick almost choked with surprise as, immediately in front of him, the bush parted to reveal a party of black warriors forcing Patrick to let go of his water bottle in panic and reach for his carbine. The other soldiers rapidly hoisted their guns to their shoulders ready for a fight but to their great relief each of the approaching men had a red bandanna tied round his forehead.

'*mole-WAY-nee*, how are you?' asked the leader approaching the soldiers, a huge grin on his face, his white teeth shining in the moon light.

'We are well,' said Patrick recovering his composure, and in a mixture of tongues interspersed with his thick Irish lilt, he learned of the approach of a large war party that these men had spotted during the night. They thought there was upwards of a thousand warriors making their way to the south west of the camp.

'We go now' said the Mfengu leader, 'must tell headman Up-chaa' he said, pronouncing Captain Upcher's name with an elongated syllable.

As quickly as they had appeared, the Mfengu scouting party disappeared back into the bush, only their feathered headdresses visible above the long grass as they darted away.

'Com'on lads, I think we should be getting back to camp as fast as we can. If'n the Gcaleka are heading round to the southwest we are in the wrong place right now to be sure,' he said remounting his horse.

The others followed suit and the party of scouts raced back to camp with the news. The Mfengu, although on foot, could cover the uneven ground and pass through the bush at a faster pace than the riders and by the time Patrick's patrol arrived back at camp the news was out and men were rushing about in preparation for the impending attack.

It was not yet six 'o' clock in the morning and already Infantrymen were crouching motionless, watchful and uncomplaining in the mud of the rifle pits. Georgie noticed the two artillery pieces were already in position covering the south and west of the camp and the naval contingent were busy preparing their rocket tubes for action.

Patrick led his troop to the picket line and dismounted, handing his horses reigns to Georgie.

'I'm away to get orders Georgie. You stay here with the horses until I get back an' if it is to be a fight I do not want to miss it,' he said, unable to conceal the excitement in his voice.

Disappearing between the tents to look for a superior officer Patrick left his men standing silently in the drizzle. Georgie shivered, the rain had penetrated his jacket and he was feeling the cold, he sniffed and looked around. Strange, he thought, there were a lot more horses tethered to the picket lines than when they had left. Lieutenant Carrington's men had ridden in to reinforce the beleaguered garrison, making a welcome sight to Georgie and his comrades.

Patrick returned after ten minutes, followed a short time later by Lieutenant Carrington, now the senior officer who had come to take charge of all the mounted men.

'Sergeant Donovan.'

'Sir' Patrick said, saluting the lieutenant.

'Donovan I suggest that you get your men ready for some action. Reports are coming in of a large movement of men heading our way and we want to be ready to receive them don't we?'

'Indeed we do sir.'

Two miles away in the Mnyameni bush, an army of three thousand warriors had assembled and dancing about in front of them was their most revered Witch Doctor. The shaman sprinkled his magic potions and offered a foul smelling liquid of bulls gall and monkey blood to Khiva and his leading warriors. The sun had just begun to show itself above the distant mountains and Khiva gave his command to his Indunas to disperse and rally the warriors ready to begin the advance on the redcoat's camp where Lieutenant Carrington was pacing about in a state of animation. The forward vedettes had reported the Xhosa approaching and the Colonel had ordered them to retire to man the defences and he was becoming agitated.

'Damn it, I will bet any man that they will try their hit and run tactics again. We must not let that happen, we need to bring them on to the guns.'

Standing up straight he adjusted the collar of his tunic, strode quickly towards a group of officers and after a short heated discussion, returned with a look of determination on his face.

'Appleyard' he called out to his second in command, 'get the troops to mount up. Lieutenant Clements, you and your men can fall in with my light horse.'

He snapped out more orders and within minutes, the fifty troopers of Carrington's horse had assembled with their mounts, Patrick, and Georgie, together with the rest of the Mounted Infantry joined them and the whole body rode out to meet the Xhosa army. Half a mile from camp Lieutenant Carrington ordered his men to spread out in five man sections and probe the countryside for any sign of the enemy. Moving forward at a non-too cautious rate they crossed a stretch of open country and reached a hilly area with ravines and kloofs running up into thick vegetation, classic ambush country.

They did not have long to wait to engage the enemy, after penetrating no more than two hundred yards into the bush the first shots rang out. Hidden behind large boulders the first of the attacking Xhosa emerged to engage the approaching horsemen, black uniforms of Carrington's horse interspersed with the Redcoats of the Mounted Infantry. It was enough to send the warriors into frenzy, gone was their tendency to avoid full-scale engagement and instead, in far superior numbers, they came on.

Georgie, Patrick and the others slipped their Carbines from their shoulders and on Carrington's order, fired into the black horde. Georgie saw three or four warriors fall as well placed shots found their mark and beside him he heard Frank exclaim, 'got 'im' and again 'got 'im.' The Xhosa were unfazed, moving rapidly towards them, threatening to overwhelm their positions if they stayed much longer but Carrington knew what he was doing.

Pickpockets and Zulus

His plan had always been to entice the enemy to charge his position in numbers and now it was time to initiate an orderly retreat back towards their front line. The bugler sounded the retreat; the soldiers fired one last volley, mounted their horses and rode quickly to the base of the ravine where they dismounted once more. The pursuing Xhosa had taken the bait, unable to resist chasing a retreating enemy they came whooping and shouting down the steep sides of the ravine straight into the guns.

'Cease fire, remount!' shouted Lieutenant Carrington.

'Remount,' echoed the sergeants, the bugler sounded the order again and the troopers swiftly swung themselves back into the saddle, turning to fire one last volley before they galloped out of range of the onrushing horde. The ground was flat in front of the camp's defences and there was no need to dismount this time, the troopers could steady themselves enough to take a proper aim from horseback. Georgie wheeled his horse round, levelled his rifle and fired several rounds at the black figures bearing down on them. He saw many fall under the withering fire of the Carbines and this time, Carrington led the retreat at full gallop, past prepared trenches concealing the infantry crouched down and ready.

From their vantage point high above the developing skirmish, Xhosa warrior chiefs and their Indunas waited, ready to order more concealed warriors to join the attack on the retreating Europeans and around them, a low throaty rumble of expectation came from the warriors. Irrepressible in their desire to join the fray they could not resist the urge to attack and at last, Khiva shook his spear, pointed it towards the retreating horsemen and the warriors surged forward. In the light of the early morning sun, the defenders could easily see the Xhosa army advancing towards their positions. Ahead of them, the mounted men were racing back into camp, to tether the horses, grab their Carbines and ammunition before reinforcing the forward defences.

Regular Infantry and Native Levies were manning most of the barricades and as the mounted soldiers joined them a cheer went up. They took their places amongst the wagons, bags of flour and potatoes and watched as the first of the combined force of Xhosa and Gcaleka neared the forward trenches. The Infantry put up a barrage of firepower; the attacking ranks of native warriors fell like flies to well-aimed shots. Then it was the turn of the seven-pounder and the rocket launchers of the Naval Brigade. Carrington's plan had always been to bring the enemy onto the guns and now those same guns began to spit out their deadly fire. However, the range was still too great and they were not having the desired effect.

Ahead of the rifle trenches, Xhosa warriors positioned to take the brunt of the defenders fire began to falter, but the lack of success from the field guns, the greater numbers of their fellow tribesmen arriving renewed their determination, and once more, they came on.

'Jesus, will ye look at 'em all,' said Patrick in amazement. 'We had better be ready for some serious work if they get this far.'

Georgie's heart rose into his mouth and around him the native levies begin to panic. On either side of him, the Mfengu Levies were deserting their posts in the face of the mass onslaught of seemingly unstoppable Xhosa and then, fifty yards from the forward trenches, the charging horde finally came within range of the big guns. This time when the order to fire came, the shots found their targets, great holes appeared in the ranks of Gcaleka warriors and after only three salvoes, the charge broke down. Unsettled the attacking formation ground to a halt and from the defenders a great cheer rose up. A bugler sounded an order to the Infantry to join the fray and out of the forward trenches, two hundred white pith helmets emerged with their breech loading Martini Henry rifles and within seconds demonstrated the firepower of a modern army.

The front rank of warriors collapsed completely as two hundred lead bullets a minute found their mark. It looked to be a resounding victory but the smoke from the guns drifted across the battlefield and a morning mist began to rise obscuring the defenders vision. The shooting stopped and it was with baited breath that the Redcoats paused to see if the enemy had fled. Gradually the smoke and mist began to clear and it became obvious that the Gcaleka had regrouped and were still a determined enemy.

During those sightless minutes, some warriors had dared to creep closer to the trenches of the Infantry but as the mist lifted they were exposed, sitting ducks and were shot dead. Then it was the turn of the artillery and at a reduced range the seven pounder guns more readily found their mark and it wasn't long before the mass of black warriors disintegrated and finally began to retreat. It was a signal to the remaining Mfengu to turn the tables on their bitter foe and, scrambling from their cover, they chased after the retreating Xhosa.

Pickpockets and Zulus

'Come on men,' shouted Lieutenant Carrington, 'after
them.' He raced towards the picket line, sprang into the
saddle, with one slick movement wheeled his horse
round, and spurred it into action. Behind him, his men
and the Mounted Infantry followed suit and at full
gallop, they raced past the field guns, past the slit
trenches to the cheers of the Infantrymen and out across
open ground. Thundering over the bodies of the dead
and dying natives, they headed into the bush after the
fleeing Xhosa. Carrington led from the front, his sword
slashing furiously at black half naked bodies and when
he could not reach with the blade, he used his revolver.

Patrick was shrieking some Gaelic war cry as he rode,
hands free, shooting his Carbine at any target he could
find. Georgie was right beside him picking off fleeing
Xhosa and the fight continued for several more miles.
They chased the fleeing army right down to the river
until forced to pull up the horses and allow a few
fortunate tribesmen to escape.

'Bloody hell,' said Georgie. 'Those poor buggers
didn't stand much of a chance did they? Still, they would
have made short work of us if we hadn't stopped them.'
He had never seen so many dead bodies; the Mfengu
had made sure that any Xhosa still on the field were well
and truly dead.

Returning to camp the soldiers hitched their horses
to the picket lines strung between trees, unsaddled the
horses and slipped on their nose bags before they
themselves settled down for breakfast. Georgie and the
others looked forward to some hot food and a short rest
but no more than five minutes later a bugle sounded the
alarm. Jumping to their feet, they left the half-eaten

breakfasts and ran as fast as they could to the picket lines.

A small Xhosa force to the north of the camp, motionless atop a ridge, was inviting attack. An overzealous Captain, who had played little part in the morning's events, decided that he would take a troop of police and fifty Infantrymen to repeat Carrington's trick of luring them onto the guns. The force had left the confines of the fortified camp and made its way towards the enemy under the eyes of Captain Upcher standing on elevated ground and watching through his field glasses.

'Damn the stupid ass,' he was heard to say, 'he's walked into a trap. Look there are more Xhosa ready to outflank them and there, look, even more of them in the bush. Carrington!' he shouted, 'get your men out there, try and extricate Captain Grenfell and his men.'

'Let me have a look sir,' said Lieutenant Carrington holding out his hand.

Captain Upcher handed him the glasses.

'Those men will be cut to ribbons once the trap closes. Over there, look, can you see them in the trees?'

'I can sir. I see what we must do. I will get my troop organised immediately. Thank you sir,' he said, handing back the glasses and striding off towards where his Frontier Light Horse waited for orders. His own horse was ready and putting his foot in the stirrup, quickly mounted.

'There is a force of Xhosa up on the ridge offering themselves as bait for any headstrong officer that wants to make a name for himself and believe it or not Captain Grenfell has gone after them. It is plain to see that he is heading into a trap and we are to rescue him,' he said waving the troop forward.

'What about us?' asked Lieutenant Clements as he drew level.

'Yes, fall in you men. You acquitted yourselves well this morning and I am glad to have you along.'

'C'mon lads, we're not missin' out on a bit more fun are we now?' said Patrick, reaching for his horse's reigns.

He was the first to mount, the others not far behind and Lieutenant Clements was soon leading them after the Frontier Light Horse for the second time that day, the thunder of the horse's hooves raising a cheer from the watching Infantrymen. The assisted by pulling a wagon from the fortified line to allow the horses through and then the riders made short work of the flat ground in front of the camp and were soon climbing the slopes leading up to the ridge to the sound of gunfire.

However, unseen by the riders and lying flat in the hollows of seemingly empty ground hundreds of warriors waited until the time was right. As the unsuspecting horsemen climbed higher and higher, the trap was sprung. A shout from somewhere in the midst of the bush signalled the hidden warriors to rise up and within seconds, all hell broke loose. Shots were fired from ancient guns, spears flew through the air and almost immediately caught some of the leading horsemen, their screams echoing across the valley as they fell to a frenzy of stabbing spears. Those that could hang on long enough and manage a retreat from the mayhem retreated past the column of riders following on behind them.

'Dismount men,' shouted Lieutenant Clements.

277

His troopers slid to the ground, leading their horses towards any cover they could find to offer smaller targets for the warriors to aim at. Ahead of them Carrington kept going, believing they could contain the enemy but from out of the long grass came yet another group of warriors, running to outflank them and dangerously exposing the Mounted Infantry at the rear of the column. Outnumbered ten to one, their training suddenly came to the fore and they rushed to form defensive groups, firing at the attacking native soldiers. Georgie and some of the other troopers were already ahead and understanding their predicament, they turned to meet the threat.

Dismounting, they handed their horses reigns to Barney and then Patrick led Georgie and Frank towards the enemy. Finding some cover behind a rocky outcrop they crouched down, lifted their Carbines to their shoulders and took aim at men appearing from out of the long grass and from behind boulders. Things were getting serious, even a grim faced Patrick was silent for a time, weighing up the situation.

'Georgie, if we can hold this position long enough we can prevent them getting round the back, then we have a chance. Pick your targets men and let's give them something to think about.'

Georgie understood, if they could cover the approach of the Xhosa and shoot fast enough then they might keep the enemy at bay. Firing off a few rapid shots seemed to work well enough, picking off any Xhosa that came near, the rest holding back. Patrick moved position, slid alongside Barney for a better line of sight and keeping up a steady rate of fire, the three of them managed to hold off the enemy until a squad of Infantry came to their support.

A few yards away one of Carrington's troopers attempted to re-mount his horse but two Xhosa warriors sprang out of the long grass and drove their Assegais into the animal's chest. The beast's front legs buckled and the trooper sprawled straight in amongst the Xhosa who came at him ready for the kill. Georgie saw the man's predicament and took aim at the lead warrior, killing him with his first shot but immediately a second warrior was on the stricken man. The trooper had managed to get to his feet, pull his rifle from the scabbard and attempt to drive the butt into his assailant's chest, but the blow was not decisive and the Xhosa warrior lunged with his spear ready for the kill. This time Patrick fired, killing the attacker and allowing the trooper to scramble away to relative safety.

The worst was over, a withering fire from infantry and their repeating rifles forced the Xhosa to retreat, Carrington had extracted Captain Grenfell and most of his men and the Mounted Infantry had not lost anyone in the melee. After a brief pause, the Mfengu levies raced silently forward after the retreating Xhosa to press home the advantage and a secure a new collection of ears.

The fighting soon subsided as the Xhosa retreated into the kloofs and ravines ahead of the pursuing Mfengu, the Mounted Infantry sections regrouped to make their way down the sloping ground past the bodies of the fallen Xhosa to cover the withdrawal of the infantry before heading back to camp.

'How are you feeling Patrick?' asked Georgie when they finally dismounted.

'On top of the world Georgie my boy, on top of the

world. Didn't we give them a good hiding today to be sure.'

'We did,' said Georgie, glad still to be in the land of the living. 'I wonder what else this place has in store for us?'

BOOK 3

Chapter 1

The two women gripped each other's hands as they crept cautiously out from the bush and slipped noiselessly into the cold waters of the river. The night was dark; it was difficult to see more than a few feet in front of them and they knew that crocodiles lived somewhere along this stretch of river but their fear drove them on. They waded into the cold waters, felt the current tugging at them, trying to sweep them away and clung to each other in desperation.

'Mpansi, hold my hand tighter, I do not want to lose you in dis river.'

'I am frightened,' said Mpansi, her body shaking with cold and fear.

'Not much further, we must get to the other side and then we will be safe.'

From somewhere Mpansi found the strength she needed and together the women waded deeper into the water moving cautiously one foot in front of the other. Chest deep, their bare feet slipping and sliding across the flat, weed covered stones, they felt for toeholds on the uneven riverbed.

Mpansi was the younger of the two, eighteen years old, a wife of the old chief for less than six months and she had hated every minute with him. She had been obedient to begin with, administering to his needs and then one day, she had met a young warrior and an animal passion had consumed them. They had met more than once at a secret place until a Shaman discovered them and the Witch Doctor, ever on the lookout for advantage with his chief, had told of the indiscretion and Nokuthala, the second wife of the headman had overheard their conversation. She had warned the younger girl, learning then of her unhappiness and she too was unhappy at being pushed out by her husband's other wives and together they had decided that they would escape their husband's clutches together.

'We must cross the river to the side of the white-man and then we will be safe,' Nokuthala had said as they had slipped quietly out of the Kraal.

No one saw them leave, they escaped unchallenged and as quickly and as silently as they could, they ran into the bush. Travelling through the darkened, dangerous night, they made their way to the river, fearful of every sound in the night and now they were almost across.

'We will go to the Norwegian mission and live there, I know of fugitives that have found sanctuary there and our men folk will not cross. The King forbids anyone to cross.' Nokuthala had said.

Mpansi gained strength from Nokuthala's words as she felt the waters tearing at her, strength that she herself did not possess and then she stumbled, her feet slipping on slime-covered rocks. Unable to hold her balance, she disappeared beneath the surface but Nokuthala held her tightly in her grip, reaching under the surface with her free hand to grabbed hold of

Mpansi's hair to haul the squealing girl back to her feet. Cold, wet, and coughing up a lungful of river water Mpansi held onto Nokuthala until the water level began to drop and finally they made it to the opposite bank to collapse sobbing with relief.

'Mpansi, be strong. Come, the mission is in that direction I know.'

Nokuthala reached out a hand to the shivering Mpansi, helping her to her feet and for two hours, the women walked, first along the bank of the Buffalo then inland until the mission station came into view. It was a wooden, white washed structure and alongside it stood the missionary's house, the home of the Reverend Paludan Bröder and his wife Inga. They were from the Norwegian missionary service, living and working together in this part of the world for more than twenty years. Over the past year, they had seen many Zulus fleeing the persecution and brutality of their society to seek sanctuary in this little white building and The Reverend Bröder was just leaving his house of worship when he saw the women approach.

'Welcome to our church,' he said.

The two Zulu women stopped and stood looking at him, not knowing how to answer.

'Welcome,' he said again.

He could see the women were uncertain of him but he persisted in welcoming them, opening the gate to allow them in.

'Where are you from children? I do not recognise you,' he said in the Zulu tongue.

Nokuthala found her voice. 'We have come from across the river.'

Paludan had lived amongst these people for long enough, King Cetshwayo's kingdom could be a hard and cruel place at times; swift and violent death hung over his subjects constantly. The King had absolute sway over his people and if he was displeased or a Sangoma advised him the spirits needed appeasing, then someone usually paid with their life.

'You have travelled all night children, you must be hungry. Come, I will find you some food and you can rest a while and tell me your story.'

The power and cruelty of the Zulu nation was legendary and advance warning of impending trouble from these fugitives was priceless. He knew well enough of the border disputes between Cetshwayo and the Boers, of the commission set up to mediate, aware also that the situation was becoming volatile. Rumour had it that the British wanted to invade Zululand and it was common knowledge that if they did Cetshwayo would resist.

He beckoned the women to follow him towards the little house where he told them to sit on the grass and wait. He disappeared inside and within a few minutes returned followed by a native girl carrying two gourds of mealie.

'This is Nozipho; she too came to us from Zululand and has lived...'

He stopped in mid-sentence, shocked at the expressions on the faces of the two fugitives. They lifted their hands to cover their eyes and began wailing.

'Stop it,' he said, 'have you no manners.'

Nokuthala pulled her hand from her eyes and looked down at the ground unable or unwilling to look at Nozipho.

284

'This one has been invaded by the spirits,' she said.

'No she hasn't, she was burned when her hut caught fire. She has lived with us for a year and has become a Christian, a good Christian, as I hope you might one day.' Paludan frowned, the native's superstitious beliefs were difficult to counteract the spirits took the blame for everything and made his job more difficult.

Nozipho seemed unmoved, she put the gourds in front of the women and without looking, turned and walked back to the house her shoulders hunched. She had not had much contact with her own kind for quite some time and had become used to her disfigurement. The Reverend Bröder and his wife were kind, they had dressed her wounds when she had arrived and nursed her back to health. They accepted her deformity and the few natives that came to church and the mission school treated her kindly. However, Nokuthala and Mpansi knew nothing of her and their superstitious beliefs had taken hold.

Nozipho reached the house and picked up the broom to begin sweeping the floor, her head hung low, a tear forming in her eye.

'Nozipho, what is the matter?' said a voice from behind her, but Nozipho kept sweeping, pretending not to hear. 'Come child, don't be upset, what is the matter?' Inga repeated.

The girl finally turned towards Inga, Paludan's wife and a typical Scandinavian woman who was so different from the natives with her pale skin and blonde hair. Inga had felt, rather than seen Nozipho was upset and was about to ask why when Paludan walked into the house.

Pickpockets and Zulus

'Inga, we have two visitors from across the river, I'm afraid they have been unkind to Nozipho and we must show them the way of Jesus Christ, let me try to gain two more converts for the church.'

On most days they turned the church into a school where Paludan and Inga could give some form of rudimentary education to the native children and young adults, a difficult task for it was not in the Zulu nature to sit still for long. To Inga's delight some of the younger ones seemed to be receptive and capable and Nozipho particularly, was a good student. She had impressed Inga with her ability and today she decided to let the girl read the bible to the assembled class. Nozipho stood from her bench and took the bible from Inga, holding it open to begin reading in her quiet, lilting voice, her gentle tones imparting meaning to the word of God.

'What is happening in the wider world husband?' asked Inga joining her husband as he read a day's old newspaper under the shade of the big Mimosa tree. 'I see you have spoken to the women that arrived yesterday. Are they from Zululand?'

'Yes my dear, they have run away, fed up with life on the far side of the river.'

'And what news of Cetshwayo?'

'They do not know much of that situation. They told me that the warriors have been called to Ulundi and that could mean the King is preparing for war. Look, here is Nozipho with the tea.'

Nozipho was carrying a pot of tea and some scones on a silver tray. She placed it on the small table and made to pour the tea, until Inga said, 'here Nozipho, I will carry on serving, and you can go and read your bible for an hour until I call you.'

286

Nozipho managed a crooked smile, the burned skin on the side of her face tight, preventing expression of her full range of emotions. H er damaged eye was recovering slowly and she remained cheerful, having a special beauty all her own and after she had placed the tray on the table she went back towards the house. Paludan turned a page and read for a few minutes before looking up at Inga.

'There is trouble brewing I think and Sir Henry is convinced that there will be a confrontation with Cetshwayo. He has asked the British Government for extra troops. I do not understand it, only a few months ago the boundary commission found in favour of Cetshwayo. Why would he want to stir up trouble when they found in his favour? It's those English empire builders, mark my words, they want his land as well as everyone else's.'

'If it comes to war Paludan, what shall we do? We are on the border, any attack by the Zulus might bring them here and what about Rorke's Drift, what about Otto, what will he do if the Zulu's attack?'

'My dear, I cannot believe that Cetshwayo will attack, not if re-enforcements arrive and he sees the European's fire power. John Dunn will tell the King, he has Cetshwayo's ear and Cetshwayo trusts him.'

'I hope you are right Paludan.'

The next few weeks were uneventful, except for the rumours. The Reverend Bröder and his wife had lived on the border of Zululand for twenty years helping the natives, teaching them the Christian way and it had been a peaceful enough existence. The wars between the Boers and Xhosa were a distant memory but something was stirring, something terrible seemed to be happening and one day, in late July, an expression of the changes taking place presented itself. Inga was with Nozipho preparing breakfast when she happened to look out of the window, a movement attracting her attention. Standing on tiptoe she looked again and Nozipho's inquisitive eye following her gaze. For a minute they both looked out of the window quite not sure what it was.

'Something is moving amongst the Sunflowers, I can't make it out,' said Inga.

She looked again and took a sharp intake of breath as, through the row of tall plants, she saw two Zulu warriors.

'Paludan!' called Inga in terror, 'Paludan! come quickly.'

Her anxious tone alerted Paludan who dropped the bible he was reading and strode quickly from his study towards the kitchen.

'There, look,' said Inga

Paludan peered out towards the tall flowers and sure enough, he could see two Zulus discussing something and was equally shocked because they were carrying war shields and that worried him. The warriors parted the sunflowers and made their way straight for the front door of the house and then Paludan saw two more coming from the direction of the river.

'Stay here, I will talk to them whilst you fetch the gun. If anything happens to me, shoot them,' said a stern Paludan.

Hurrying to the front door, his heart in his mouth, he prepared himself to confront the intruders, men dressed for war, and in his experience when Zulus arrived unannounced, dressed in military garb, it usually meant only one thing – death. He swung the door open to reveal at least half a dozen warriors. Shocked, realising he could not hope to fight them off and that there was no escape he took a step back. Their leader glowered at him, a man he recognized as Mehlokazulu, the chief son of Sihayo Nokuthala Zenzele whose father was the Zulu Induna responsible for the security of the frontier and he wondered why he was here in such an aggressive manner.

As a man of God, Paludan realised that this might be a moment in his life when faith had to carry him through and was about to speak when Mehlokazulu thrust him aside, sending him crashing against the flimsy doorframe. Two more of the Zulu warriors pushed past and strode into the hallway looking this way and that. Systematically they kicked open the doors to the study and living room, entering with their Assegais at the ready and after cursory inspections, they began to converged on the kitchen. Paludan became worried that Inga might pull the trigger, perhaps killing one of them but surely, that would be the end of them if she did. He must stop her, he called after them in their own tongue.

'Warriors of the great Zulu people, what brings you to our church?'

Mehlokazulu paused at the kitchen door and turned back towards Paludan.

'I am the son of Sihayo Nokuthala Zenzele the guardian of the Kings border and I am searching for those that have brought shame onto our house,'

It was enough; he had paused just long enough for his tone to warn the women hiding in the small kitchen and behind the door, Inga looked at Nozipho for inspiration.

'I do not think they have come to kill us. They are looking for someone I do not know who. Better to put down the gun Missy,' whispered Nozipho.

Inga needed no encouragement and slipping the rifle out of sight behind a cupboard, she was just in time. The door burst open and Mehlokazulu stood there glowering, looking straight at Inga and for a brief moment stopped in his tracks looking her up and down, not sure what to do and then his eyes fell on Nozipho a girl of similar stature to one of his father's wives. He soon realised she was not the object of his search, her deformity singling her out and as his eyes flicked across her features he knew she had angered the spirits and he wanted nothing to do with her.

'The ones we look for are not here, come,' he said turning away from the women, quickly retracing his steps towards the front door and from the open door Paludan watched them go.

'Oh Paludan,' was all Inga could say.

'They are going to search the church. They are looking for fugitives and they must have crossed the border against the will of Cetshwayo and I know there will be repercussions in Natal,' said Paludan.

Inga said nothing; she was watching the warriors pulling open the door to the church and after they entered, she heard a piercing scream. Then Mehlokazulu re-emerged followed by a warrior dragging Nokuthala who flung her to the ground. Next Mpansi appeared, held by two more warriors and she to joined Nokuthala on the floor.

Inga drew in her breath and held her hand to her mouth as she watched. 'Should I fetch the gun' she heard herself say.

'Where is it?' he asked.

Inga told him and he ran to retrieve it as the two women watched events from the open door. Mehlokazulu was standing over the two prostrate forms and saying something but they were too far away to hear and then he raised his spear. Paludan had returned with the gun and lifted it to his shoulder in readiness, expecting the worst but Mehlokazulu, with his back to them, shouted something and set off at a run. He leaped effortlessly over the fence and, followed by his men, disappeared into the long grass.

Paludan raced towards the two sobbing women and helped, first Nokuthala and then Mpansi to her feet.

'Are you all right, what did their leader say?'

'He say we are bad people, he say he should kill us but we are not who he is looking for,' said Mpansi still shaking.

'Where are the others?' asked Paludan, there were more of you in the church. Oh no, had they killed everyone?

He ran through the open door to find the church empty, returning outside, looking all around and to his great relief saw his congregation peering at him from amongst the maize plants in the field behind the church.

A week later Paludan received a copy of the Natal Witness and sitting in his favourite spot in the shade of the Mimosa tree he lit his pipe and took his glasses from his pocket to begin catching up on the Colony's news. He had heard rumours that trouble was brewing and now here it was in black and white.

'Inga, Inga,' he shouted.

'What is it Paludan, why are you calling for me?'

'Read this,' he said, passing the newspaper to her.

She read for a minute or so. 'Oh. That explains things. They were looking for the runaway wives of Chief Zenzele and it was his son, Mehlokazulu who came here wasn't it.' She read on, a concerned look spreading across her face. 'They found the runaways and took them back across the river to Zululand and they executed them, his own mother, what kind of heathens are they?'

Chapter 2

Parting the flimsy lace curtains and brushing aside the hair from her forehead Ellen looked down to the street below. She felt lonely. Clarence left her alone for weeks on end whilst he was off on some mission or other and when he did return he would not talk about what he had been doing. She did not love him she was sure, she never had, he was her passport to a better life and she felt that she would go mad if she did not find something to do.

A few people were walking along the wooden pavement, the odd carriage passed by, not enough to hold her interest for long. There was usually some movement of military personnel and equipment along the main street in King Williams Town, but not today, it seemed. Then she saw a small contingent of mounted soldiers in their red tunics and white helmets in the distance and watched them approach, counting them, twenty five riders, six on black horses, one a grey and all the rest riding brown horses. At least she had some distraction.

She watched the troop enter the main street, their horse's heads hanging with fatigue and the soldier's clothes dusty from their journey. She guessed that they must have been out on patrol for some time and be glad to be back in town and like any young woman; she admired their rugged good looks. Invisible behind the lace curtains, she took the liberty of watching them more closely as they passed, her eyes darting from one handsome face to another. As they drew level with her vantage point, her attention settled upon a weather beaten man in his early twenties. He wore his helmet at a casual angle and sat squarely on his saddle, it was Georgie, no doubt about it.

She felt so pleased to see him that she involuntarily pulled the curtain wider, the movement catching Georgie's eye, and by the grin spreading across his face, he seemed just as pleased to see her. He had grown a beard; a scruffy beard that really did not suit him but the sergeant riding beside him was another matter. He could grow one, the lower half of his face sporting the most luxurious red beard, one that any woman would love to stroke.

Georgie winked and looked away before the lieutenant saw him and from beneath her window, she heard a man's voice call out. 'Hey Donovan, I have some news for you, I'll see you in the mess tent.'

The soldier with the red beard lifted his arm in acknowledgement.

'What was that all about, what's Sparkey want?' asked Georgie.'

'To be sure I have no idea, he has his ear to the ground does Sparkey so he must of heard something about what is going on. A lot could have happened; it's been almost three weeks.'

It had, one of the longest patrols they had done. They had ridden up along the middle drift towards Alice and the Tyumi River before heading north to Queens Town, patrolling a great arc of country, an uneventful exercise and they were glad to be back in Williams, looking forward to few beers and a meal that was not only bully beef.

They reached the military camp on the outskirts of town, Patrick tied his horse to the picket line and dropped the heavy saddle to the ground.

'To be sure your legs are taking the shape of that old nag of yours Georgie, I reckon you couldn't stop a pig in a passage,' he said with a grin.

The other soldiers laughed, Georgie simply shrugged his shoulders, at least his buttocks and the inside of his legs didn't get sore anymore.

'Sergeant Donovan,' he said.

That was enough to gain the attention of the rest of the section. It wasn't often that Georgie addressed Patrick by his full title.

'Sergeant Donovan,' he said again, 'if I call you a bastard Sergeant Donovan, you'll put me on a charge. Isn't that correct Sergeant Donovan?'

The troopers attending to their horses paused and listened to Georgie with complete attention, his tone of voice suggesting confrontation.

'To be sure I would, no one calls Patrick Donovan a bastard an' gets away with it.'

'Mm...but if I only think you are a bastard then there isn't anything you can do – is that right Sergeant Donovan?'

Patrick looked puzzled for a moment. 'Noo...I suppose that if ye only think it then there is nothing I can do.'

'Good,' said Georgie, 'then I think you're a bastard.'

The silence was tangible, Patrick stood motionless as the full meaning of Georgie's statement sank in. What would Patrick do to Georgie after a remark like that, thought the collective mind of the rest of the section, he could have him peeling potatoes for a week. Patrick didn't even consider a punishment, he simply threw back his shoulders and burst out laughing, joined in short order by the rest of the men. After weeks on patrol, enduring tough conditions and sleeping under the stars, they were due some light relief.

Patrick tilted his head towards his friend and narrowed his eyes for a few seconds, enough to warn Georgie to watch out and then a grin spread across his face.

'Come on Lads, let's get these poor nags sorted out,' he said, and set to work with a will to give his worn out horse a good rubdown and a feed.

The horses were in a poor state after working so hard and were in need of a break just as much as the troopers were. Each man attended to his own mount, grooming it, looking for parasites and finally they slipped nosebags over the horse's ears and sat on bales of hay for a rest and a smoke, yarning and telling jokes. When the horses had eaten, they removed the nosebags and replaced them with a generous helping of hay before heading for the mess tent and their own dinners. They were interested in only two things right now, a good wholesome meal and, after a clean-up and a shave, a night out in Williams.

'I'll not be coming with you tonight Georgie, I reckon Sparky has some serious news so I'll be heading for the Sergeants mess. I'll see you later.'

Patrick knew that if Sergeant Barry Sparkes had something to tell him, then it would be interesting to say the least, for if one man knew the workings of the British Army it was Sergeant Barry Sparkes.

Sergeant Sparkes put the two tankards of beer on the table and sat down. 'Cetshwayo has been given an ultimatum Patrick; he's been up to no good lately. You'll have missed some of the news whilst you were out on patrol.'

'We heard a rumour when we passed through Queens Town about ten days ago. Something about a raiding party chasing after some women'

'More than just women, they were wives of Zenzele, Cetshwayo's Induna and the chief responsible for the security of Zululand's boarder along the Buffalo. There was a commission a few months back looking into border disputes with the King and I believe part of the settlement was that his warriors could not come across the river into Natal, nevertheless, they have. It was one of Zenzele's sons with a raiding party that crossed over and took the women off to have their sculls smashed in.'

'What do you think might happen Sparkey?'

'I haven't finished yet. It seems that another party of Zulus surrounded two government surveyors working along the border. They were held for a while and released unharmed but I've heard that the powers that be are using these two incidents as an excuse to invade Zululand and whip that upstart Cetshwayo.'

'Where did you get all this from?'

'Never mind that Sergeant Donovan, just think on, we could be moving out soon – up to the border. Here, let me fill our glasses.' He reached across the table and picked up Patrick's glass and while Sergeant Sparkes went for more beer Patrick mulled over what he had just heard. They hadn't done much soldiering to begin with;

parades, inspections and incessant drills, but after their experiences in the Amathole mountains he knew what it was like to be fighting the natives and the Zulus had a fearsome reputation, a different proposition to the Ngqika.

In the Trafalgar, Georgie, Arthur, Frank, and a few troopers from the Mounted Infantry were letting off a little steam, well into a rendition of 'The Wagon Loafers.'

'Glory glory hallelujah,
glory glory hallelujah,
glory glory hallelujah,
wait till we get home...'

Several of them were musicians and some were Welshmen, their singing worthy of any music hall in England. It was stirring stuff and spirits were high but Georgie had something else on his mind, the proximity of the hotel making him think of Ellen.

At that same moment, Ellen was sitting in her room reading the local newspaper, she could hear the soldier's bawdy songs drifting up from below and eventually becoming bored with her reading, she went to the open window. For several minutes she stood there, eyes closed thinking of home, wondering what had become of her family and her mind turned inevitably to Georgie. She opened her eyes, bored, fed up of being cooped up in her room and decided to go for a short walk along the street and back, stretch her legs and take in some air.

Georgie had broken away from the crowd, deciding to stand outside in the cooler air and have a smoke. He walked a few paces from the entrance of the Trafalgar, leaned against a wooden veranda for support, and rolled a cigarette. He popped it between his lips and felt for his matches, looked up and there was Ellen, walking out from the hotel.

'Ellen,' he called in as discreet a voice as he could.

'Georgie, what are you doing here? Silly question wasn't it,' she laughed.

Georgie looked at her and said nothing, simply lighting his cigarette and taking a lungful of smoke. He glanced around and seeing that they were alone said, 'do you want a roll up?'

'Clarence thinks I don't smoke but you carry on.' She paused and looked him up and down for a few moments. 'Well, go on Georgie, haven't had a fag for ages. Don't you look a picture with your tan, you're a lot different from the pasty faced boy I once knew,' she said taking his tobacco pouch off him.

Georgie grinned 'you don't look so bad yourself cousin.'

'I'm glad I've seen you Georgie. You know there's trouble brewing with the Zulus don't you?'

'A little bit. The men were talking earlier about it. What do you know?'

'Well, all I can tell you is that it looks like a proper war. Clarence has been gone longer than normal and I think he has something to do with it. I have become friendly with some of the local women. Their talk is mostly about the money their husbands will make from a war, supplying the Army, hiring out their wagons and the like. There is even talk of them taking land from the Zulus so that must mean war mustn't it?'

'It looks that way Ellen.'

'Be careful Georgie, you're all I've got now.'

'What about your husband, doesn't he count?'

'Not really. I hardly ever see him these days; he's always away with the General or somebody important. I get a bit lonely at times and if it wasn't for you I think I might try and go home, but there's not much there for me either.'

Ellen, not normally one for emotions, seemed a little sad thought Georgie as he watched her rolling her cigarette. He felt a little sorry for her, he had his job as a soldier but she did not seem to have much to do other than being married to an Officer and it appeared that perhaps life with Captain Jameson was not so exciting after all.

'Can't be seen smoking this, not in the street Georgie, come on let's go round the back. You can keep look out for me eh...just like old times. Who was that sergeant I saw you ride in with today? The one with the fine red beard'

'Ha!' She had taken Georgie by surprise with her question. 'That's Patrick Donovan, my best friend. He's a likeable Irish rogue. Do you want to meet him? I could bring him to the Trafalgar tomorrow night if we can get time off. You sound in need of a bit of cheering up and Patrick's the one for that.'

'I know what I will do, I shall announce that you are my cousin and invite you both to tea in the hotel dining room tomorrow. At four 'o' clock, what do you say Georgie?'

'Sounds like a good idea.'

'Come on, outa sight I'm dyin' for this fag.'

Sure enough, at four 'o' clock the following afternoon two smartly dressed and clean shaven troopers of the Mounted Infantry walked into the lobby of the Victoria Hotel, removed their battered pith helmets and waited patiently.

Ellen had seen them approach from a seat near the window of her room; she was nervous, excited and happy as she got to her feet. She hadn't experienced much in the way of male company since her husband had gone off on one of his jaunts and she was looking forward to meeting Patrick. Picking up her fan, she left her room, traipsed down the stairs in a quite unladylike fashion and walked into the lobby to find the soldiers waiting. She felt her heart skip beat as her eyes took in the smart red and blue of their uniforms but Patrick looked different, he had shaved off his beard leaving Ellen a touch miffed but she soon got over her disappointment and greeted them with a friendly smile.

Georgie thought she looked striking in her high bodice dress; white with a faded pattern of pink roses and Patrick was intrigued. He had caught glimpses of her from a distance, heard a lot about her from Georgie and now here she was in the flesh, a beautiful woman.

'Georgie, I'm so glad you could come and this must be Sergeant Donovan,' said Ellen holding out her hand to him.

'Pleased to meet you ma'am' said Patrick, his charm beginning to show through.

'Come, sit with me a while and we will talk and I will order some tea and cakes.'

'Bejasus cakes is it?' exclaimed Patrick, 'to be sure I haven't eaten a cake since I left my poor old ma back in Ireland.'

301

Ellen smiled, he was not quite as handsome without his beard, but he more than made up for it with his brogue.

'Do they not serve cakes in the mess, Sergeant Donovan?'

'Not at all, the best we get is a hard biscuit. You have to dunk in you tea so's to not break your teeth.'

Ellen giggled; his accent, so different from that of Londoners and Georgie, even after years of kinship still smiled at Patrick's abstractions. He was pleased she had arranged for them to meet and in such a way as to satisfy protocol and he could see that Patrick had lifted her mood already.

Ellen did most of the talking, isolated as she was living in the hotel she wanted to know all about Georgie's life in the Army and of Patrick's life back in Ireland. Eventually, after swearing the big Irishman to secrecy, she told a little of her and Georgie's early life in the East End. Patrick listened without interruption because he had heard it all from Georgie but unlike Georgie's version, there was no mention of her father or elder brother. She had forged a new life for herself and if any knowledge of those two vagabonds ever reached Clarence, she might lose all she had gained.

'And what will you do now Ellen? We are to move up to the border country in the next few days and you will be on your own again.'

'I'll be all right Patrick; some of the military wives are training to be nurses. They say that if there is to be war then there will be wounded men to care for and I have volunteered my services,' she said looking straight into Patrick's eyes. They had been flashing unseen messages

between each other for some time, their exchanges more
telling than any heliograph.

Chapter 3

Standing on high ground commanding the approach to the Royal Kraal of Ulundi the Praise-Makers waited. Clothed in ceremonial cloaks and carrying staffs of blackened hardwood festooned with the skulls of monkeys they watched intently as the small black dots, first seen several hours before, grew larger. Eventually the warriors, summoned by the king, began to arrive and it was the time of the Praise-Makers, time for them to address the soldiers, time to sing out their message.

"*Oye oyeye!*", 'You are the lion warriors, you are the sons of Shaka come to rekindle his spirit. Cast out the cowards, cast out the white men, sing your praises to the great King Cetshwayo.'

'*Hho! Hho! Eya ehhe!*' sang the warriors in reply, resplendent in feathered headdresses, animal skin kilts and their regimental shields held high. As far as the eye could see, warriors were streaming towards the Royal iKhanda of Ulundi, the capital of the Zulu nation to assemble before their King.

Cetshwayo had been unhappy ever since his Indunas had returned from the great Indaba with the British. The result was not what he had wanted nor expected, an ultimatum from the very people he had once called friends. War was inevitable and he knew it, the British

Army had been re-enforcing for months, ready to invade his kingdom. The sons of Sihayo had given them an excuse and now the British wanted them handing over for trial. If he acquiesced, he would seem a coward to his people, a mere puppet of the white men; an act that would bring shame down on his house. Worse than that was the demand to disband the Army, the source of his power, the glue that held his kingdom together. No, he would not, could not acceded to their demands and so he had summoned his advisors, trusted Indunas and generals, the wisest of the Zulu elders and together they had decided that if it was to be war, then the Impis should be summoned.

A Praise-Maker stood upon a large boulder, gesticulating, waving his arms, exaggerating his movements and calling out to the passing regiments.

'The King is great; Cetshwayo is a lion to his people. He will take the Redcoats like a snake by the tail and snap off its head and you, the uVe, will bring victory,' he sang out.

The warriors grinned happily, 'Hho! Hho!' they replied, shaking their spears in defiance. The day they had dreamed of had arrived, the day the King would finally commission the regiment into his Army and reaching the crest of a small hillock, they saw before them nestled in a slight depression, Ulundi, the great capital of the Zulu King. Nkosinathi's heart lifted for he had never seen such a sight and tomorrow the whole of the Army would assemble there for the first time in many years.

The uVe was the youngest of Cetshwayo's regiments, fit men in their early twenties, easily impressed by the promises of their leaders. Their Induna sang out a command, and as one the uVe chanted '*Ingonyama* – he is a lion' and the sound of almost a thousand spears slapping hard against shields, rippled through the air like thunder. Their pace quickened, they closed ranks and the well-drilled uVe closed in on Ulundi.

From all corners of the Kingdom, upwards of thirty thousand Zulu warriors descended upon the capital, summoned by the royal decree. Their Indunas, telling them of the British Army massing along the Natal border, even now crossing the Buffalo into Zululand and that they would meet them in battle and destroy them.

Aside from the warriors, scouts were reporting seeing columns of soldiers and their transports crossing the border, fording the Buffalo river at Rorke's Drift, another near the estuary of the Thukela River and a third column to the north near the Inyezane River. However, it would come to naught when the Impis of King Cetshwayo defeated the British just as they had defeated enemies before – the ghost of Shaka was with them and the glory days would soon return.

In the Royal Kraal Cetshwayo sat on his throne surrounded by his chief advisers – strong men, warriors by nature, men who counselled war. The King knew much of the White Man 's army, he feared their guns and for a long time he had managed to reign in the more headstrong amongst his generals. This time though, the threat to his Kingdom was real, his advisors had seen for themselves the approach of the Redcoats, their huge wagon trains struggling in the mud and across the fords. Their progress was painfully slow across the Buffalo; it was an army of pasty faced, round-shouldered youths, immobile, hardly a match for the swift attacking formations of the Zulu Army and these men believed that perhaps the British Army was not so powerful after all.

'Oh great leader,' began a Praise-Maker, 'unshakeable Lord of the land, battle-axe of the nation, with the strength of an elephant...'

Cetshwayo waved him away, he had serious matters to attend to and the Praise-Makers words were for the masses not for him. Sitting on his throne of rosewood and leopard skins, he fixed his eyes on some invisible creation in the near distance, giving an appearance of someone uninterested in the proceedings, but his mind was racing as he weighed up possibilities. He considered his strengths and weaknesses, he had spoken with his advisers, spies and generals and all had their own point of view, but the consensus was war.

The Zulu King did not really want to fight; his army did not have the guns that would ensure success although for years he had instructed his people to acquire guns and ammunition asked his friend, John Dunn, for guns. The White Man John Dunn had brought him guns but at the same time had advised him of the power of the European's guns and the havoc they could cause. For all his cajoling and planning, his army was still mainly one of spears and knives and in his heart of hearts, he feared for the future.

At last, his eyes focused, his mind came back to the present and he lifted his spear and stood to his feet. He was tall, arrogant and confident, every bit a King and as he looked out over the Kraal, out towards the surrounding hills he saw the men who would secure his crown making their way towards the Royal homestead. He had heard from his scouts that the British had destroyed the Kraal of his trusted advisor, Sihayo, killed one of his sons and driven off his cattle. It had begun, there was no turning back, and the *amabutho* must be prepared for war.

On they came, never ending columns of proud, half-naked warriors singing the regimental war songs that boasted of their prowess in battle. They streamed down from the hills in their regiments onto the Mahlabathini plain and those already there whistled, chanted and slapped their shields in welcome. The newcomers responded in like fashion until the whole area in front of the Kraal was crowded with so many men that Nkosinathi and the uVe struggled to find enough open ground for their camp. By nightfall, most the army had arrived and for as far as the eye could see their cooking fires caused the night sky to glow a dark orange and after arranging their sleeping mats, the Impi lay down to sleep. Caught up in the excitement of the occasion, the warriors found it difficult to manage more than a few hours' rest before all too soon, the sun rose, and the King summoned them to hear his words.

'Oh warriors of the Zulu nation you have been summoned here to hear of the danger approaching our lands.' Cetshwayo paused for a few seconds as the echoes from his powerful voice dissipated. He held his spear high above his head, his great hands clasped tightly about its shaft. 'The White Man's army with the scum of the Xhosa are at this very moment crossing the Buffalo. You are fearless, you are obedient and I tell you now – go and kill the invaders. Go now,' he shouted and from somewhere in the packed regiments a lone voice called out *'Oye oyeye!,'* in reply thirty thousand voices sang out *'Uhlaselaphi na! E! E! E!,'* and thirty thousand feet stamped the ground sending a human shock wave across the plain.

Cetshwayo and his Indunas had spent much of the night locked in discussion finally deciding upon the plan of attack. The regimental commanders received the King's instructions and the *Izinyanga* the specialist war doctors, started the process of cleansing the regiments of evil spirits. They began the process by digging pits on the bank of the Mfolozi River ready to receive the regiments.

'Nkosinathi it is our turn to be cleansed, the *Izinyanga* will give us extra powers to fight the White Man,' said Somopho.

Nkosinathi looked up from whittling the stick in his hands. Since the King's speech, he had not paid much attention to the proceedings, his mind wandering, thinking about his father and his half-brothers who were here somewhere amongst the army in their own regiments. He thought of his dead sister, Nozipho, the bravest of the brave who had saved the little children at the cost of her own life then Somopho's words cut his thoughts short.

'I am coming,' he said and jumped to his feet.

The regiment made its way in a narrow procession towards the waiting *Izinyanga*, the most powerful medicine men of the Zulu nation, their job to cleanse the army of spiritual impurities. Manelesi fell in beside Nkosinathi, the ranks of young uVe warriors following on behind the iNgobamakhosi and the uKhandempemvu, the best regiments in the army. They were about to have the evil spirits purged from their bodies, magic potions and rituals would protect them from the White Man's bullets, they would be invincible.

Emerging through the dongas and across the grassy plain, they crowded along the riverbank to wait their turn for the *Izinyanga* to cleanse them. The potions were evil smelling, their ingredients a closely guarded secret and each man closed his eyes as he drank the foul smelling liquid his body rejecting the potion almost as soon as consuming it. It made them feel sick and quickly they made their way along the line towards the open pits to vomit involuntarily, spewing out the contents of their stomach, purging themselves of the evil spirits lurking inside.

Eventually, late in the afternoon, the doctoring ceremony was complete and the whole army gathered inside the Kings Kraal, many spilling out from the parade ground, to fill any open space. A great mass of powerful black bodies, adorned in only the minimum of clothing ready for war – real war. The regiments formed up in order of seniority and at the centre, sat on his throne of leopard skins, Cetshwayo prepared himself for the final send off. Wives, advisers and generals surrounded him and when he felt the moment was right, he rose to his feet.

'Warriors of the Zulu nation,' he said, his commanding voice echoing across the Kraal, 'we are invaded by the white men in their redcoats and the snivelling tribes that hide behind the skirts of the white Queen. They come to take our land and our cattle under false pretences and we will resist them.' He lifted his arms skywards, a sign that for once, the warriors could view his personage without fear of death. "*Bayete*" I salute you, "*Bayete*".

"*Bayete*" roared out the eager soldiers.

'My soldiers, you are the boldest in the land, go, slay the invaders,' he bellowed, his arms sweeping across his chest and stretching out as far as he could reach, signifying that the doctoring was complete, the speeches made and the order given to begin the war.

'You are a lion, you are a herd of Buffalo – we will kill them all,' chanted the massed warriors. 'Oh great King you can depend upon us to drive the White Man away,' they sang, and one by one regiments were singled out to pass before the King, eventually the turn of the uVe, the most junior regiment. Nkosinathi felt the blood coursing through his veins, the excitement of the occasion lifting his spirit higher than it had ever been and as he passed close by the royal personage, he knew that he had no fear of death and would gladly lay down his life for his King.

'I will kill many red soldiers,' said Nkosinathi to Manelesi walking beside him.

'I will kill many red soldiers as well,' Manelesi replied.

'And so will I,' came the call from Lindani and Khulekani and together with Somopho the young warriors marched off to the meet the British, singing their war songs, able at last to fulfil their dream.

The King decided that some regiments should make their way to the coast, to counter the threat of a British column seen by the scouts making its way towards the delta of the Thukela. Two more were sent north to where a third column was detected, but the bulk of the army was to make its way to the White Man's mission station at Rorke's Drift. The lumbering Boer wagons could easily ford the Buffalo there and it was where the largest of the invading columns had already crossed. Each day spies were returning to Ulundi with news of its movements and the King realised that he must destroy this army first.

'Conserve your strength, do not go hastily to the battle,' the King had said, and so they covered the ground, not at the loping run of the Impi, but a steady march forward and by sunset on the first day they had crossed the Mahlabathini plain. The regiments bivouacked for the night, eating food carried by the younger boys and girls who would stay with them until their supply ran out, then the regiments would be on their own, foraging for what they could. The King had told them they would not need to carry a great deal of food because once they had defeated the Redcoat Army they could gorge themselves on the White Man 's supplies.

Nkosinathi spread out his sleeping mat amongst the warriors and lay down, slipping into a deep and dreamless sleep. It had been a momentous day and had left him very tired and all around him warriors lay down to regain their strength to cross the Mfolozi and before dawn Nkosinathi felt a hand on his shoulder.

'My brother, it is your turn to look out for the regiment,' said a warrior returning from his guard duty, 'go there by those trees and stand guard until day break.'

Without saying a word Nkosinathi rose to his feet, rolled up his sleeping mat, picked up his shield and spear and headed off into the darkness and for the next two hours sat cross legged against a tree to peer into the night. He listened for the sound of danger, but there was nothing. Such a large body of men held no interest for the predators of the night and the British Army and its patrols were still far away. Now and again, he heard the familiar sounds of wild animals up in the hills and in the grey dawn, the army came to life. The fires, damped down for the night, suddenly flickered brightly abd the army breakfasted before marching towards the river.

'We will see the Redcoats soon,' said Somopho, a statement rather than a question.

'I will kill many of them,' said another breaking into a personal war dance, imagining the battle to come, stabbing and twisting, demonstrating how his Assegai would split open the enemy.

Many miles away across the plain, another army moved slowly towards a great misshapen rock, colourful in their red and blue uniforms their standards flying in the warm summer breeze. Behind the van came a line of native soldiers, conscripted, coerced, paid handsomely for their allegiance. Strung out for five miles or more behind them was a vast array of ox drawn wagons, the food and ammunition supplies for an army on the move.

Reveille had sounded before dawn, instigating a hustle and bustle of the organised chaos that was a British Army on the move. They had been camped for a week at Rorke's Drift, bored and suffering the trials of the Natal weather, the overpowering heat mixed with torrential downpours dampening spirits but now, at last, they were moving.

To an impartial observer, the chaotic antics of the soldiers of Queen Victoria contrasted starkly with the disciplined warriors of Cetshwayo but the difference was superficial for the Zulus were simple people with simple weapons. Although the long, twisting wagon train made slow progress across the muddy plain, it carried the weapons of war that the Zulus could not hope to possess. Ammunition counted in millions of rounds, field guns, rocket launchers and the Martini Henry repeating rifles.

Georgie lifted his pith helmet from his head, wiped the sweat dripping into his eyes with the back of his sleeve, and turned in the saddle to look back at the column. The band had stopped playing; the only sounds those of the jangling brass fittings on the horse's tack and the crack of the voorlooper's whips. He halted his horse for a few moments and stood up on the stirrups to shift his weight, smiling to himself as he caught a faint strain of 'Men of Harlech' wafting up from the rear. Many of the men of the first battalion were Welsh and although some of them left a lot to be desired when it came to soldiering, they could certainly sing.

Arthur Morgan and Frank Williams drew level with him. 'It's a fine day for fighting Zulu's Frank.'

'I heard their army is on the move somewhere in these parts,' came the reply, 'I reckon we'll be at 'em soon enough.'

'Aye, and give 'em a good thumpin' said Arthur, stroking his beard. Georgie smiled as he remembered Ellen swooning over Patrick's red fuzz only to be disappointed when she had seen it shaved off. Patrick was only a few yards ahead of them sporting the beginnings of a new one and he thought that should please his cousin.

'What do you make of that Frank?'

'Bit of rough country coming up I think, I wouldn't be surprised if we are ordered to go and have a look at it.'

Pickpockets and Zulus

No sooner had he spoke than the lieutenant came trotting back along the column towards them to reign in alongside Patrick and hold a brief conversation.

'The General's orders, he want us to ride on ahead and scout the trail for Zulus. He reckons that there is an army heading our way. Come on lads, follow me.'

They took little persuading, the journey had been uneventful so far, mostly a slow slog to the river but at least they were on the move, in Zululand proper and could expect some hard riding. Georgie reached forward and slapped his animal on the neck, kicked his heels into its flanks and encouraging it to follow Patrick's steed. Behind, Barney, Frank and Arthur fell into line and soon they were one mile, then two from the agonisingly slow moving wagons. Riding steadily for two hours across flat and uninteresting terrain, they eventually reached the Manzimnyama River.

'Dismount men and let the horses have a drink,' said Patrick, pushing his helmet to the back of his head and taking a pair of binoculars from his saddlebag. He lifted them to his eyes and began to scan the countryside.

'See anything Sarge?' asked Arthur.

'Yes, a small Kraal over there.' He took the binoculars from his eyes and held them out at arm's length indicating the direction. The troopers followed his gaze and in the distance, on their side of the river, they made out the rooftops of some low lying native huts, faint wisps of smoke rising from the cooking fires.

'All right, we'll take a look over there I think,' said Patrick. 'I'll give Nelly here a drink first and partake of one myself.'

Five minutes later the party re-mounted and followed the riverbank, Patrick nearest the river, Georgie three hundred yards away, the other three filling the gap in between. Slowly they moved forward until the Kraal came into view and when they were within half a mile, Patrick ordered a halt and scanned the place with his field glasses and satisfied, waved his men towards him.

'I think there is only a few women and children in there so I don't expect much trouble, but still we'd better be careful. Georgie, you and Frank get up there on that hillock and cover the rest of us.'

The two troopers turned their horses towards the high ground and trotted off whilst Patrick, Barney and Arthur spread out and moved slowly towards the Kraal, a small affair, no more than a dozen huts surrounded by the ever-present thorn wall and through the open entrance, they could see several women and children milling corn. The soldiers, Carbines at the ready, moved cautiously towards the natives who, on seeing them approach, stood up. Fifty yards from the entrance, Patrick waved to Georgie and Frank to make a sweep around the perimeter before they moved in any closer.

Unseen by the soldiers, a hand holding a knife, carefully cut a hole in the side of one of the huts, just big enough to watch them approach. A sharp pair of eyes peered out from the gloom, watching the five Mounted Infantrymen come together and ride towards the entrance. He noted their attire, their weapons and the condition of their horses, for that was his job, Nokuta was one of Cetshwayo's best spies, the King's eyes and ears on the frontier. He had spent most of the previous year slipping over the border and back, mixing with the whites in their towns and settlements, watching the military build-up and reporting to the King. He knew he was watching the beginnings of the invasion and these soldiers would be the first of many.

The soldiers rode into the Kraal, pointing their guns at the Zulu women, keeping a watchful eye for signs of a trap, but there was nothing. The centre of the village had a corral holding around twenty head of cattle, not many, this Kraal was on the edge of Zululand, well away from lush pastures and within ten yards of the small cluster of Zulus, they halted, Carbines at the ready.

'Does anyone speak English?' asked Patrick.

'Yas boss, I can a little,' said a plump woman.

'Whose Kraal is this and where are the men folk?'

'Diss is the Kraal of my husband Ngqumbazi.'

'And where might he be now?'

'He is called to Ulundi, to the Kings Royal Kraal. He take all the men with him.'

'Hmm...' mused Patrick, looking her over. Her rotund appearance suggested that she did not do much work and he guessed that she probably was a chief's wife and telling the truth. He thought about searching the huts but decided against it. Should he order the men to set fire to them? He had no specific orders to do so and looking at the children clinging to their mothers he felt he did not really want to, but the cattle were another matter. He did have orders to bring in as many animals as he could to deprive the Zulu army of succour.

'Arthur, you and Frank help me cut out these cows. Get the women and children out of the way Georgie,' said Patrick pulling on his reigns.

He kicked his horse forwards and reached down to unhook the Kraal's primitive gate and after a few shouts and whistles, the soldiers had the herd trotting out from the pen, mooing and grumbling as they went.

'Come on Georgie, you can leave them now.'

Georgie nodded, glad to be relieved of the task of looking after women and children, not a job he relished. Only a few yards away, Nokuta cut another hole in the thatch to watch proceedings, relieved when they left and yet puzzled that the soldiers did not seem interested in searching the huts. If they had been Zulus, he was sure he would be dead by now and the huts ablaze. He watched them drive the cattle out of the Kraal and when they were well away he crawled out of the entrance tunnel and slipped away to report what he had seen.

'There's the ford,' said Patrick as the came upon the expanse of flat shallow water. 'We'll stop here and rest the horses. Take the animals into the water for a drink and you two get over to the other bank in case some of them decide to leave.'

The soldiers took to their tasks, herding the thirsty cattle into the shallow water, dismounting to leading their own mounts to the water's edge. In the distance, the vanguard of the approaching column was in sight, a red smudge and above it a cloud of brown dust, raised by the thousands of plodding hooves.

Within an hour the first of the column reached the ford and behind them, spread out across the uneven, trackless country, were the wagons. The mounted soldiers arrived first followed by ranks of hot and tired Infantrymen, the men, the oxen; all were thirsty from their morning's exertions and found the river a welcome sight. The horses drank at the water's edge, the Infantrymen spread out along the riverbank to drink and to fill their water bottles and the wagons were outspanned to give the oxen a rest.

318

Pickpockets and Zulus

'Sergeant,' called the Major in charge. 'Get your men back in the saddle; we'll take care of these animals for you. Your orders are to scout ahead towards that mountain over there.' He pointed towards a strangely shaped hill in the distance. 'That, my dear fellow, is Isandhlwana and that is where we have been ordered to make camp tomorrow night, so off you go.'

Several miles away the Zulu army was heading in the direction of that same hill, sent there initially by Cetshwayo to avenge the destruction of his Induna's Kraal. The regiments had made steady progress since leaving Ulundi, moving at the speed of light compared to the lumbering oxen of the enemy and in the lead Ntshingwayo, their able and resourceful commander. Sat high in the saddle he surveyed the landscape, wondering what the Redcoat's plans were and how he could bring them to battle. Seventy years old and fit enough to run with the Impis he was a clever and capable general. He looked up at the gathering storm clouds, thick, black and beginning to blot out the sun, he felt the first drops on his face and then the heavens opened. The deluge obliterated the marching Impis for a while but when the storm passed and the skies cleared there they were, unflinching, marching towards the enemy and Ntshingwayo turned to his regimental commanders.

'The army moves well my Indunas; it will not be long I think, before we meet the enemy. Look at them, no army in the world can resist us; we will be victorious and save the nation from the invaders.'

Pickpockets and Zulus

A murmur of approval rose from the Indunas, each of them responsible for one of the King's regiments, each eager to demonstrate the prowess of his own regiment.

'Oh great General, soldiers approach,' said one, pointing to a group of warriors two hundred yards away and heading towards them. Two six-foot warriors gripped a shorter, older man between them, holding him firmly and as they reached Ntshingwayo's group, his own bodyguard stepped forward to take the man, throwing him to the ground in front of the commander. The man got to his knees covered in mud and with a look of disgust on his face.

'Oh great Commander, great bull elephant of the army I am Nokuta the Hyena of the night, why do your men treat me so?'

'Ha, Nokuta, I know of you. Have you have news of the British?' Ntshingwayo was pleased that such a renowned spy should find him and laughed aloud at his predicament.

'I do.'

'Speak.'

Still on his knees, Nokuta, the Hyena of the night, spoke. 'Oh great one, I have seen the first of the Redcoat scouts on this side of the river, he pointed behind him. 'They come to destroy the homesteads, to take the cattle. I did not see many, only a scouting party. I think that they are a day, maybe two days, away from here. They will make for the hill of the cow's stomach, of that I am sure.'

'Then so will we, you have done well Nokuta the Hyena. Rest a while then go to Cetshwayo and tell him your news,' said Ntshingwayo dismissing both the spy and his bodyguard with a short backhand sweep of his hand. 'So, they make for Isandhlwana. We will make haste towards that place and eliminate them. Indunas of the Impis, go to your regiments, tell them that we go to the mountain of the cow's stomach.'

Chapter 4

The Mounted Infantry squadron arrived at the foot of the rock and in the distance could see the infantry heading towards them. They were the advance party and temporarily under the command of a major whose job was to determine the best place for the bivouac and to begin to mark out an area for the camp. He had already sent a contingent of native horsemen out to a perimeter several miles away when he approached his regular mounted troops. The time was not much past three 'o' clock, the sun was just at its hottest and in the distance a huge cloud of dust marked the progress of the wagons. It looked as if it would be another hour or two yet before the first of them rumbled into camp but by then, the major thought, the engineers would have determined its basic layout and they could begin stockpiling stores and equipment.

'Lieutenant Clements, take your men up into to those hills over there and set up some forward observation posts and keep a sharp lookout for these Zulu chaps. I will deploy some vedettes once we get sorted out and the infantry get here but I think you chaps are our best bet for now. We need a bit of a warning if the beggars show up what.'

The lieutenant saluted and turned his horse towards his troop, singling out his sergeants for their orders, Patrick being no exception, and with a wry grin on his face, Patrick called out to Corporal Jones, an antagonistic Welshman.

'Jonesy, the lieutenant says you have to fall in with us for a while.'

'That would be lovely you big Irish....'

'Now then Jonesy I don't make the fun of your nationality now do I?'

Corporal Jones's face cracked into a broad grin. The two had known each other for years, their banter always a source of amusement to the other ranks. Corporal Jones was from Tonypandy in the Rhondda Valley and as proud a Welshman as you could ever meet.

'Ser-geant Donovan when have I ever made fun of your home land?'

Patrick looked at Jonesy and said nothing, his mind on his job, if there were any Zulus creeping about up in the hills then they would probably be the first to know and from the rumours beginning to spread there was certainly something going on and he didn't want to be caught out. Other sections of Mounted Infantry were beginning to peel away and head into hostile country to keep a watchful eye on the approaches to the camp. Pulling his reins in tightly he turned his horse eastwards towards the mountains some ten or twelve miles distant, signalled Corporal Jones to fall in with his section and together the ten riders left the shadow of the rock to ride out to their new positions.

'Arthur, you and Frank ride up there, look that hill to our right. I think you will be able to see a fair way down the valley from there. Georgie, Barney, and me will go over there and keep a lookout from the big hill. Jonesy, take your lads up onto that high ground over there,' he said, pointing to a low flat topped hill some distance away to their left. 'Post lookouts and make sure you don't lose sight of one another in case they surprise us.'

'Oh, all-right ser-geant' said Corporal Jones in his melodic welsh voice, 'any-thing you say.'

Georgie watched and listened with amusement, sometimes it sounded as if these two were speaking a foreign language and he found it particularly hard to understand them when they began to argue. Today though, there was no argument, both were good soldiers and both aware of the danger they faced. He leaned forward and patted Blackie's neck, watched her ears flick and then, thoughtfully patted the Carbine's butt protruding from his back, two very necessary components for his survival in this hot, dry and dangerous land. He looked up at the sky, clear and blue with no sign of the rains they had experienced of late and then across the plain to distant hills before kicking his heels into his horses sides and nudging her on after Patrick and the others.

'Fancy a biscuit or two?' asked Patrick as they reached the crest of the hill giving them a panoramic view of the valley.

'I do,' said Barney, 'not eaten much today.'

Patrick dismounted, passed his reins to Barney and lifted slung his rifle from his back, placing it against a large rock and then he felt in his bag for his field rations, half a dozen hard biscuits and a water bottle. In similar fashion, Georgie dismounted and handed his reigns to Barney and took out his dry biscuits and water bottle, placing them on a rock.

'Here, let me help you tether the horses Barney. I'm sure you could do with a drink.'

'Could I, why half my water has gone already, at the rate I'm going there will soon be none left,' he said, slipping from his horse. The other troopers passed their reigns to him and between the two of them, they pulled the horses out of sight to tether them to some bushes before re-joining Patrick munching on a biscuit and scanning the horizon with his field glasses.

'Nothing that I can see boys but that don't mean the buggers are not out there,' he murmured. 'Take your rifles and keep a look out from there, and there,' he said, pointing to flat rocks a few yards away, an ideal place to lay flat, unobserved and to watch the approaches.

For the next few hours the soldiers remained motionless, their eyes constantly on the lookout for any movement and as the sun sank lower and the shadows lengthened Barney spotted a cloud of dust in the distance. Patrick lifted his field glasses to his eyes and adjusted the focus of the instrument.

'Ours, looks like it might be our relief,' he said, turning a watchful eye back towards the hills.

From the direction of the camp, a troop of Mounted Infantry emerged from the dust haze heading towards them and Patrick stood up to wave and draw their attention.

'Where's Sergeant Donovan?' asked the lead rider as the troop neared the first man.

'Over there' said Frank, pointing to Patrick visible amongst some low bushes.

After a brief conversation Patrick told the relief patrol what they had seen – nothing, and waved to his men to come to him. 'Time to go boys, come on.'

The new day had not yet dawned when Reveille brought the sleeping army back to life. Georgie rubbed his eyes and yawned, not believing that he had to rise so soon, the ground was hard and uneven and his back felt a little painful. Once on his feet he was soon himself again and eager to join the others for some breakfast and within half an hour they were riding past the hustle and bustle of the new camp and out onto open ground. Most of the wagons had arrived the previous day and now the drivers were cracking their long whips, rousing their animals to make the return trip to the Drift and squads of Infantrymen were moving about preparing to dig defensive works.

Once clear of the camp perimeter Lieutenant Clements halted the troop to issue his instructions to the section leaders, detailing their duties for the day and from the camp, another column of at least a hundred riders appeared, the Natal Native Contingent, a hotchpotch commanded by Māori Browne, a larger than life Irishman.

Auxiliary troops drawn from the native population were of unknown calibre, generally poorly armed and likely to bolt as soon as the fighting started but amongst them was a large body of disaffected Zulu warriors. These men were an altogether different prospect, looking to all intents and purposes to be Zulu warriors distinguished only by a red bandanna tied about their heads. Most had a grudge against Cetshwayo, escaping his clutches and crossing the river into Natal and for one reason or another, they were glad of the chance to fight back, volunteering for service more out of revenge than the pay.

Patrick had already made fellow Irishman Māori's acquaintance and as the column passed he saluted Patrick.

'The top o the marnin' ti ye.'

'Sor' said Patrick as he swung his own arm in salute. Another day had begun and Patrick ordered his and Corporal Jones' sections to merge and together they headed out towards the distant hills.

'Make sure you have your rations and water for we might not be back till late,' said Patrick.

'Bit late for that isn't it sarge,' said Arthur.

'Looks like another boring day,' added Barney.

Georgie swung round in his saddle. 'Don't you believe it, I bet those Zulus are not far away. Did you notice yesterday, hardly a living thing was moving? Something's up'

'Naw, they're keeping out of our way till we're deep in their territory, when we have stretched lines of communications. That's when they'll strike,' said Arthur.

'Will you listen to the general 'ere' said Barney with a laugh. 'You've missed your way Arthur.'

Several miles to the north the Zulu army was closing in, spread across a wide swath of countryside with the senior regiments leading the way and Ntshingwayo at their head. He had forsaken his horse and was leading by example, loping along at a steady, strength-preserving pace at the head of his army. Since leaving Ulundi, he had received a constant stream of reports from spies and scouts tracking the enemy and ahead of his him, a group of warriors were rapidly closing in. The warriors carried the shields of the uKhandempemvu, one of his best regiments.

'Ntshingwayo, Lord,' said the leader, 'we bring news of the enemy, of the Redcoat invaders. They have made camp in the shadow of the great rock. Their horse soldiers are spreading out across the plain. They did not see any of us Lord.'

Ntshingwayo raised his arm in acknowledgement; he did not speak for his mind was busy working out his strategy, his next moves in this great game of cat and mouse dictated that he would need to gain the element of surprise and overwhelm the enemy. The King had charged him with the defence of the Kingdom and he must not fail. He had divided the army in two to protect it from surprise attack, sending half under the command of MavumMengwana, the King's favourite, a few miles to the west. They had marched since before dawn and as the mid-day sun became unbearably hot he decided it was time to rest, give him the opportunity to survey the landscape and to consult with his staff. Already he had decided to take the army up into the hills, to hide them in the hollows and depressions of the high plain, out of sight of enemy patrols.

He grasped his chin in thought, had not the wise men counselled against battle the following day. The InSangoma had prophesied a major astronomical event, warning him of the moon's phase, of an eclipse and the danger it might bring. It would not be a day to fight, resting the men before battle would be the better option.

Well to the rear of the lead party the uVe marched, higher and higher into the hills and could see clearly in the distance the great rock with the strange shape. The young warrior friends, Nkosinathi, Somopho, Lindani, Khulekani and Manelesi marched together, spirits high.

'Oh Khulekani, Somopho, my brothers soon glory will be ours soon we will fight the White Man and drive him from our lands,' said Lindani. He ran a few steps and launched himself into the air, demonstrating his prowess as a warrior.

'*Bayete*, we will be great,' sang the others, infected by his enthusiasm.

'Nkosinathi, how many will you kill?' asked Khulekani, his shiny white teeth barred in a grin.

'All of them, I will kill them all, *Hi, Hi, Hi*.'

'We will kill them all,' chanted the warriors and before long a great roar went up from the whole regiment, and they would have broken into their regimental song if it were not for the Induna turning angrily upon them.

'Has not Ntshingwayo told us to be like a lion seeking its prey, should we not be silent and invisible to our enemies?' he said.

The warriors hung their heads and quietened down, each of them aware of Ntshingwayo's orders, realising an admonished before a battle would bring shame on the regiment. In silence, they marched, following the line of the hills, keeping below the level of the ridges and out of sight of enemy eyes. To an observer they were a terrifying sight; muscular, fearsome warriors with painted faces, spears and shields and moving in total silence. They picked their way skilfully through thorn bushes and over sharp rocks until eventually, they reached flat ground where the regiments recombined to enter the valley of the Ngwebeni stream, its steep sides affording anonymity. As they progressed through the dongas they began to secret themselves amongst bushes and rocks, behind any cover they could find, the army becoming a silent black mass to settle down for the night.

'It will be dark soon, Nkosinathi,' whispered Manelesi, 'soon we will fall upon the enemy.'

His eyes shone brightly, it was the pinnacle of a Zulu man's life to be victorious in battle, the rewards well worth the struggle. A successful warrior might receive land from the King, permission to build his own beehive hut, perhaps even to marry and wear the coveted headband of a married man and Manelesi considered of all these things until the face of Nozipho interrupted his thoughts. He could see her, hear her voice as if she were there; the Nozipho he had once known, not the disfigured wretch he had saved from the crocodiles. What had become of her he wondered, had she survived, where was she now?

'Here, share the last of my meat,' said Nkosinathi pulling a few strips from his shoulder bag. It was the last of their food, the camp followers, the young boys, women had left them days ago, and all they had left were scraps and the knowledge that soon they would gorge on the food of the White Man. He passed a few morsels to Khulekani, Manelesi, and the last of the food he offered to Somopho, but to his surprise, Somopho declined.

'I am making ready for battle. To eat now is to risk evil spirits entering my body,' he said solemnly.

The others looked at him aghast, should they fast too? Pangs of hunger were gnawing at the walls of their stomachs, if to eat before battle angered the spirits then perhaps they should resist the temptation and it was with troubled minds they looked upon the morsels of dried meat. Before they had time to decide, the InSangoma appeared, chanting and swinging their medicine bowls, ghostlike, their faces painted white to ward off the spirits.

'Take these leaves and chew them for a long time,' said one, handing a few small leaves to each warrior. 'The leaves have magic in them; they will protect you in battle, make you brave and strong, the medicine from these leaves will deflect the white-man's bullets.'

Nkosinathi reached up and took some leaves from the outstretched hand, so did Khulekani and the others. Somopho was the last to hold out his hand, a sad look on his face for he realised that he could have eaten the food, the Witch Doctors had come to ward off any lingering evil spirits. Somopho's friends read the expression on his face as they popped the last of the meat into their mouths. Their strong white teeth showing as they grinned broadly at his obvious disappointment and Somopho watched them with a feeling of deflation he started to chew on the Dagga leaves

Sitting motionless in the saddle, the troop of Mounted Infantry looked out across the deserted valley, watching for movement from their vantage point high on a ridge. A magnificent vista stretched out before them, the valley sides were carpeted in lush green foliage and contrasted with the flat dusty landscape of the Isandhlwana plain and In the distance, shimmering in the heat haze, they could see a few isolated Zulu Kraals dotting the landscape. From below came the tap, tap, tapping of a Ground Woodpecker and high overhead a kettle of Buzzards circled and twice Patrick's horse pawed the ground, breaking the spell of silence. He lifted his field glasses to his eyes and scanned the valley for the umpteenth time that day, looking for enemy movement, searching for a possible trail down to the floor of the steep sided krantz.

'There is nothing down there that I can see, what do you think Jonesy?' he said passing the glasses to Corporal Jones.

The Welshman lifted them to his eyes and swept, first the valley floor and then the ridges on either side.

'No-thing Ser-geant Donovan,'

'Hmm...' mused Patrick, 'it certainly is quiet.'

He had decided to keep clear of the few settlements and concentrate on hiding places in the many gulleys and amongst the sandstone cliffs that abounded. He led the troop forward, down towards the plain carefully picking his way amongst boulders and loose stones and after few miles of relatively flat country, they began to climb again and proceeded in single file along a narrow gully until late in the afternoon they came across a small stream.

'Frank, you and Barney get up there,' said Patrick pointing, 'near that tree and keep a sharp lookout. We do not want catching with our trousers down do we? Jonesy, send a couple of your men over there, by that big rock and we will let the horses have a drink and rest a while we can and have a chew on a biscuit or two.'

The men dismounted, unslung their Carbines and handed the reins to Georgie before scrambling to their posts.

'It's too quiet for my liking Jonesy,'

'It is a lit-tle bit qui-et I'll give you that Ser-geant Donovan.'

'You can call me Patrick when there are no officers about.'

Jonesy grinned, he was making fun of the Irishman but his humour soon faded as, "Bang...Bang" two shots rang out in quick succession from above.

'Sarge, there is a load of them up 'ere' shouted Barney. "Bang" another shot rang out. The horses were startled and began to pull back hard against their reigns. Georgie and Tompkins from Jones's section held on managing to calm them. The last thing they needed was to lose their mounts so far from camp.

'Stay here you two,' ordered Patrick grabbing his rifle and running across to join the lookouts.

"Bang...Bang" a trooper fired back and then a yelp from further up the valley as a bullet found its' mark. For a few elongated seconds there was silence and then, high up near the ridge, a fusillade of fire as the Zulus began a concerted attack. They seemed to be well armed but their aim was high, their bullets whistling harmlessly overhead.

At the sound of the first shots Georgie had instinctively ducked, holding the horses reins tight in his hands, afraid that they might bolt. After a few seconds he realised the Zulu's shooting was wildly inaccurate and guessed that they had no idea how to set their sights but they must have believed their shots were telling because they became bolder, exposing themselves as they made for better positions.

'There, look, two of them,' shouted Patrick as black shapes emerged from the undergrowth poised to throw their spears. "Bang" one of them went down, hit in the chest, the other let fly his spear straight a Jonesy, missing him by a whisker. "Bang", down he went. Higher up the slope, amongst the trees, the soldiers heard yells and shouting from some Zulus near the ridge giving their position away and Patrick directed the trooper's fire in that direction. They were outnumbered, that was sure, the crackle of gunfire from above telling its own story and Patrick decided that a rapid retreat was in order.

'Come on boys, give them a couple of rounds and let's be off.'

On his command, the well-drilled troopers fired two rounds in quick succession before sliding back down the slope breathless and sweating from their exertions. The soldiers appeared in a mad rush forcing Georgie to briskly hand out their horses reins and with something between an efficiency borne of many months of training and panic, they were quickly back in the saddle. With a mixture of men's shouts and the whinnying of unnerved horses, they retraced their path to open country to put some distance between themselves and the Zulus.

'Phew that was a close one,' said Patrick to Corporal Jones as they slowed their horses to a gentle trot.

'Well I think we put paid to a few of them Patrick. It remin-ded me of my child-hood throw-ing rocks at the lads from Maerdy up the Rhon-dda.'

Patrick looked at Jonesy and shook his head, mad Welshman.

The rest of the day did not pass without further indecent. During the ride back to camp, they detected several small groups of Zulus, probably forward scouts, commanding high ground and as the day wore on it became evident that the Zulu army was somewhere in the vicinity and two hours later, in the glow of the setting sun, the weary soldiers returned to the base camp. It had been a long, hot day and they knew that there would be no let-up in the near future.

Pickpockets and Zulus

Patrick left his section grooming and feeding the horses and went to make his report to the headquarters staff where he learned that they were not the only ones to have engaged the enemy. Reports had come in of sightings of larger groups of Zulus high in the hills and his suspicion about the closeness of the Zulu army seemed to be borne out.

'Any news of the Zulus Patrick?' asked Georgie when he returned.

'Well not really. I don't think they know where the Zulu army is, only scouting parties like the ones we had the run in with. Major Reed said he thought the General would go for a closer look tomorrow. Let's get these horses sorted out an' get ourselves to the mess tents, I'm starvin.'

Daylight was still hours away when Georgie saddled his horse. The night sentries were being relieved, Infantry detachments were moving out to their defensive positions and the mounted vedettes were beginning to return. It was raining again, light, wet rain, the sort that seemed to penetrate anything and everything and Georgie shuddered as the cold morning air penetrated his tunic.

'Another day chasing shadows Barney?' he said, more as a question than a statement.

'I don't think they were shadows yesterday. Very real Zulus if you ask me.'

'I didn't see much of them from where I was,' said Georgie a little sheepishly. 'Perhaps I'll have better luck today.'

'They were a brave bunch I'll give them that. I'm not so sure all this talk about them being a walkover is so right – and don't forget there are a lot more of them that there are us.'

Just then a major of the Second Battalion approached and saluted, Lieutenant Clements returned the salute and stood to attention, listening as the major gave him his orders. After a brief conversation, they saluted; the major left and Lieutenant Clements called his section leaders to him.

'Mount up men, we've got orders to move out, looks like Māori Brown is in a spot of bother again and we have to go an rescue him and it seems the General wants to go and look for the Zulu Army,' said Patrick.

The troopers mounted their horses to fall in behind him and head towards a column forming up on the edge of the camp. Several hundred yards further out, they came upon Infantrymen of the Second Battalion, the General had decided take a large force to go and look for the Zulu Army.

'Looks like we're going out to look for a fight Barney,' said Georgie.

'Aye, I reckon we are,'

'Hey, Thornton' said Georgie, spotting a soldier from the band. 'What are you doing out here?'

'Hiya, Georgie, we are coming as medical orderlies. They want us as stretcher bearers in case we get into a fight.'

'What, all of you?'

'Just about, only bandmaster Bullard and the little drummer boys are staying in camp,' he said.

Bemused, Georgie waved a goodbye and swung his horse around. 'Not often the band is told to come out with us is it?'

'No, just think if you had stayed with the band you would be carrying stretchers today Georgie instead of having a comfortable ride.'

The two men chuckled, they knew the bandsmen well and were glad to have them along and experience had already taught them that sometimes it could be harder riding than marching.

Patrick sat in his saddle watching the Second Battalion begin to move, there had been no bugle this morning, no shouted command just, simple orders in matter of fact voices. The General had decreed that the force should move out under the cover of darkness and as quietly as possible because the previous day's reports of Zulu scouting parties watching them had made the command wary. Indeed, within an hour of the force leaving camp Zulu scouts were running back to Ntshingwayo with the news.

The Zulu commander had slept for no more than two hours, sitting with a leopard skin around his shoulders in the midst of his army. The first of his scouts had reported to him less than ten minutes before and quietly he mulled over their intelligence. The British had divided their army and were coming out to look for him, well they must not find him, not today, for the omens were not good for fighting. To fight during the passage of the eclipse might provoke the spirits but he still had to instruct his commanders in the order of battle.

'Zibhebhu, MavumMengwana,' said Ntshingwayo, calling the first two by name. 'Our scouts are reporting a major development and I want to make clear what I have in mind. Indunas of the King's regiments, I have received word that the enemy has sent out a large part of

337

their army to look for us – a mistake I think. I do not want to meet in battle just yet for the omens are not good; the moon is not in our favour for another two days. Then we will meet them and eat them up.'

A murmur of approval spread through the assembled commanders.

'We will leave this place and outflank them, get between the part of their army heading this way and their camp. Either force will be no match for us; we will destroy them one by one. Zibhebhu, you will take command of the reserve regiments.'

Zibhebhu looked as enthusiastic as he possibly could but still his disappointment showed. The probability of his regiment taking an active part in the forthcoming battle seemed limited and he would not have the chance of glory.

'It is as you say Ntshingwayo,' he said solemnly.

Ntshingwayo spoke for a quarter of an hour outlining the battle plan, how he wanted them to deploy their regiments and after a further hour of discussion, he sent them away to begin the day's manoeuvres. His strictest instruction being that the warriors should remain hidden from the sight of the enemy until he alone gave the order to attack.

Sitting in a depression in the hillside, Nkosinathi and the warriors of the uVe dozed or chewed incessantly on their Dagga leaves, awaiting their orders.

'Nkosinathi, we are moving,' said Khulekani, nudging his elbow into his friend's ribs.

'Uh..., what?' muttered Nkosinathi still half-asleep.

'Get up, we are leaving here.'

Nkosinathi became fully awake and scrambling to his feet, slung his shield across his back and picked up his weapons. No guns for them, the uVe, they carried only the traditional Assegais and throwing spears, but it would be enough to defeat the enemy. A signal from the Induna and the well-disciplined regiment moved silently across the uneven ground and up the dongas towards the plateau.

Chapter 5

The soldiers remaining in camp had not long settled into their routine when sound of distant gunfire forced them to abandoning their breakfast. The remaining Mounted Infantry and the men of the Natal Native contingent set off to patrol the plateau, to sweep the dongas and gullies that criss crossed the ridge and watching them were Ntshingwayo's scouts. Spread far and wide, their reports filtered back in a steady stream to the Zulu commander and it was only a matter of time before he knew of every movement of the enemy.

Such a large force leaving the enemy camp earlier in the morning had intrigued him. Why split the army in two? It did not seem logical for an enemy to divide its force and to leave their camp poorly defended, was he missing something, if he were he would find out what it was and during the morning, the news of the enemy's movements convinced him that there was nothing problematic about the British General's decision to split his force. To him it appeared he had simply blundered and he would profit from it.

'MavumMengwana,' said Ntshingwayo quietly to his second in command, 'we have an opportunity my friend, an opportunity given to us by the spirits of our ancestors.'

MavumMengwana's dark eyes burned beneath his bushy eyebrows. The King had charged the two of them with the conduct of the campaign, both were experienced and shrewd warriors and MavumMengwana could see as plainly as Ntshingwayo the weakness in the enemy's strategy, a weakness they could exploit.

'Send for Mehlokazulu and three more of the Indunas with horses. I want trusted men to go and see what those at Isandhlwana are doing.'

'It shall be so,' said MavumMengwana, pleased his commander was doing as he would do.

MavumMengwana clapped his hands twice for his bodyguard and ten of his best warriors appeared ready to do his bidding. He told half of them to look for the Indunas, to give them their instructions and the rest to accompany him back to his place at Ntshingwayo's right hand.

'MavumMengwana, what would you do now?' asked Ntshingwayo.

'I would begin my advance; I would send out our right horn now. They have a long way to go to encircle the camp. They must come from behind that hill,' he said pointing with his spear, 'and I would want them in position when we send in the chest.'

'And what about the left horn?'

'Wait, wait until it is time to send the chest forward. They have less distance to cover, the uVe are younger and fleeter of foot than the iNgobamakhosi, they will complete their task quickly and then all will be in place to destroy the Redcoats.'

Ntshingwayo nodded solemnly at his friend's assessment, for it was the way to victory and for

MavumMengwana to think the same thoughts meant that it must be right and in an instant he had decided.

'We will do as you say, we will send out the iNgobamakhosi and the uNodwengu brigades to circle the rock of the cow's stomach. We will keep the rest here for a while and then we will advance, but not today. The omens are against battle, the eclipse will happen and the spirits will not help us. Send the Indunas to me as soon as they return.'

He left MavumMengwana and, followed by his own bodyguard, made his way to the crest of a small hill to survey the plain below. His plan was simple – he would not risk the centre of his army, the chest of the bull until the horns had closed round the enemy camp, only then, when the time was right would he send his veteran regiments into the attack. He was well aware of Europeans firepower; he did not want to sacrifice his Impis too cheaply but he would do what was necessary to please his King.

The party of Natal scouts made their way slowly up the steep donga, their horses carefully picking their way over screed and boulder strewn slope. The leading horseman nudged his mount forward through some thorn bushes and closely packed vegetation, the only path he could take. The rider was more preoccupied with saving his corduroy trousers from tearing than looking for the enemy and momentarily his concentration lapsed, he failed to keep a good lookout and then his horse snorted, jerking up his head and he pulled on the horses reigns, calming the animal but it was enough. The nearest of the resting Zulus looked over the vegetation to see what the noise was all about and seeing the horse soldier cried out '*Ayye*', to alert the resting army.

Startled by the cry, the trooper looked across to where the sound had come from and was horrified to see and hear a thousand men jump to their feet. He realised immediately what he had stumbled upon and the shock of it literally caused him to freeze, his jaw dropped open and his eyes were wide with fear. Within seconds, his adrenalin kicked in spurred him into action, wheeling his horse away from the danger about as the tranquil green vegetation gave way to an angry blackness.

'Get back, the place is crawling with 'em' he shouted. 'Come on, turn round, there are thousands of them. Hurry up.'

His voice became louder, he screamed in blind panic and the line of scouts strung out along the donga looked up at him, the gravity of the situation beginning to dawn upon them. Almost as one, the line of horses turned and began to retreat along the path, the sound of gunfire and bullets whistling overhead re-enforcing the warning.

Among the ranks of Zulus, a low throaty murmur began to spread as they came to life. They had made contact with the enemy and conditioned as they were for battle, doctored by the medicine men and eager to fight they could not contain themselves. First, those nearest the disturbance began to rush after the retreating horsemen and then the whole army rose up and in their midst a dismayed Ntshingwayo. He realised that the situation was changing fast, his soldiers had the scent of prey in their nostrils and there was no stopping them. The headstrong warriors chasing after the enemy were disrupting his plans and he needed to think fast.

Standing to his feet, his cold black eyes darting every which way, Ntshingwayo realised that he might lose control of the army and quickly decided to go with events. He called for runners to take his orders to the Indunas to order them to begin their attack as they had planned and he prayed to the gods that his strategy was right because there was no stopping his warriors now — the battle had begun.

Nkosinathi held his shield high above his head as he

ran towards the ridge, the air streaming across it making him feel that he was about to fly like a bird. The whole of the uVe regiment was there, poised to descend the escarpment, their Induna frantically cajoling, threatening them, trying desperately to hold back their excited charge, but his efforts were in vain. Right across the hills and dongas the Zulu warriors were appearing, infected by that first low, throaty call to arms and were in hot pursuit of the fleeing enemy.

Eventually, the well-trained, obedient warriors responded to their commanders, but it was too late to stop the attack, the warriors had their tails up and were ready for a fight. Ntshingwayo's runners were delivering his orders to the Indunas even as they attacked and reaching flatter, firmer ground, the regimental commanders managed to make their warriors take up the formation drilled into them year after year. The uVe was to be part of the left horn together with the uNdi regiment, the younger, less experienced warriors and ones that knew no fear. Excited, adrenalin and the drugs in their blood, they advanced chanting their battle cry "*Usuthu*", their deep voices carrying across the open Veldt towards the enemy.

As they advanced, the defenders began falling back and for an hour, the Zulu army closed in on the British camp in the shadow of the hill. Thousands upon thousands of eager black warriors, their shields held proudly across their chests, assegais held threateningly moved as one. Behind them, on high ground, Ntshingwayo sat astride his horse watching the battle unfold and from his side his most senior Induna spoke.

'It begins my General.'

Ntshingwayo looked round, shielding his eyes from the sun with his hand and watched as the two discs high in the sky converged and the sky began to dim.

'Did we not foretell of such an event, oh great General of the Army. Did we not say that you will today win a great victory for the Zulu Army, a victory to rival those of the father of the nation, the great bull elephant Shaka,' said the Sangoma not six feet away from him.

The Witch Doctor had prophesied many things and this prediction was beginning to unfold just as he had said and today he foretold that Ntshingwayo would be victorious. Ntshingwayo looked back towards his army, his mood lifted, and he allowed himself a rare smile. He had dreaded engaging the enemy on just such a day, believing the omens to be against him, but from the reports of his scouts, he was beginning to think that the day would indeed be his.

'Yes Bheka, your prophesy has come true, I know now that nothing can stop us crushing the Redcoats.' His smile disappeared as quickly as it had begun for there was serious business to attend to, he could not fail his King.

Almost a quarter of a mile away, marching side-by-side, Nkosinathi, Manelesi, Khulekani, Lindani and Somopho were in high spirits and feeling invincible, nothing could stop them. All around the Zulu army was in full flow, an awesome sight, advancing towards the poorly defended camp and they could smell blood.

The forward vedettes looked on in horror as the full impact of what was about to happen dawned and began to fall back. Horsemen were despatched to the camp to report the news of the approaching Zulus and in the hills the sound of gunfire signalled the first engagements with the Zulus. Then a bugler sounded the withdrawal and along a wide front, vedettes began to fall back, dismounting, kneeling and firing, hastily re-mounting and falling back several hundred yards before repeating the manoeuvre. Some Infantrymen and field guns were brought forward to try to re-establish a more solid defence and for a time they held the Zulu advance, but not for long.

Nkosinathi and the warriors of the uVe regiment emerged from a gulley to intermingle with the battlefield's darkening haze created by the eclipse and drifting gunpowder clouds. The effect of the drugs administered by the Sangoma had dulled his senses, in the distance dark shadows danced to the sounds of battle and there was only one thought in his head, to kill Redcoats.

'*Usuthu*', cried the Induna. '*Usuthu*' replied the thousand voices of the uVe and they surged forward into the White Man's guns. Volley after volley ripped through their ranks and several of Nkosinathi's comrades fell mortally wounded but still they advanced. With shields held out in front of them, Assegais ready to stab and kill they flung themselves at the enemy and soon the charging regiment of Zulus turned the line of Redcoats. The sound of a bugle cut through the din of gunfire and war cries, the redcoats retreated, halted, turned and fired one last time before the first of the Impi overwhelmed them. Stabbing and slashing at the soldiers, the Redcoats had no choice but to return the compliment with bayonets and in the maelstrom of writhing bodies and slashing steel the Zulus gained the ascendency, overcoming the red soldier's resistance.

Suddenly the ground in front of the advance erupted. The defenders had finally deployed their field guns; gaps began to appear in the line of advancing Zulus, ten or twenty warriors killed in each short, violent act. Limbs and heads were ripped from their bodies as the hot steel erupted in their midst and the attack faltered. From the right of the uVe's charge, a detachment of mounted native horsemen making their way back to camp from skirmishes further out, came sweeping through, killing and wounding many as they passed.

It happened quickly and the warriors had little chance of retaliation but a passing rider's horse came within feet of Nkosinathi and instinctively he dug his Assegai deep into the animal's ribs. The stricken animal continued its run for a few more yards until blood spurted from the wound and it sagged to its knees, its rider toppling forward and onto the ground. Nkosinathi leapt forwards and with a powerful lunge, sank his spear between the man's shoulder blades, its razor sharp tip passing completely through his chest. The Sangoma was right, his medicine was potent, driving the evil spirits from Nkosinathi's body, making him stronger and immune to the white soldier's bullets and with one last stab, he finished the job. It was his first kill and he was elated

'Come Nkosinathi, we still have work to do,' said a voice from behind. It was Manelesi, grinning from ear to ear, dressed in a red tunic he had taken from a fallen British soldier.

'Where is Khulekani and Somopho?' Nkosinathi heard himself ask.

'Somewhere around, I saw them stabbing a Redcoat.'

'And Lindani, have you seen him?'

'No, Lindani, I have not seen him since we began the charge.'

348

They did not dwell, the Zulus had created a momentum that was impossible to halt, *"Usuthu"* they cried again and again overrunning position after position, killing Redcoats until all lay dead from the thrusts of the Zulu spears.

On a small hill overlooking the plain, an Officer of the Natal Native Contingent sat motionless on his horse listening again for the sound that had first attracted his attention. There it was, the distinctive sound of heavy guns drifting across the hot, empty plain and was coming from the direction of the base camp. He lifted his field glasses and studied the landscape, his gaze moving ever nearer to the horizon and then he saw it, a puff of smoke, then another, rising slowly from amongst tiny white dots. He squinted and adjusted his sights, he was not able to see them clearly but he knew they were the tents of the base camp and then he saw a black smudge and he knew then that the camp was under attack.

'A black smudge I'll be blowed, that's the Zulu army,' he said to himself. 'Lieutenant Cummins' he called to one of his officers, 'take this message to Lord Chelmsford up ahead will you, and don't hang about.'

In the thick of the battle, the uVe surged forward howling blood-curdling obscenities at the retreating Redcoats and killing many of them. Nkosinathi and Manelesi worked their Assegais feverishly, stabbing their blades deep into any of the enemy they found, dead or alive. The British soldier were not easy to kill, brave to the last, shooting at them until their ammunition ran out and then thrusting their bayonets clean through the hide shields of the warriors. A final volley of lead whistled close by and missed Nkosinathi's head by a whisker, forcing him to crouch and then he was up again and charging forwards for the final fight. The fatigue of the march and lack of sleep during the past few days was beginning to catch up with him. The drugs administered by the Sangoma were wearing off, the danger he faced suddenly became real and a natural instinct for survival took over.

His bravery had diminished not one iota, but he began to think for himself a little more and to his left he saw cover affording him the chance to get closer to the line of soldiers shooting at them.

'There look, a gulley we can crawl down and attack the guns. Our Assegais will be more than a match for them at close range,' he called to Manelesi.

There was no answer.

'Manelesi,' impatiently he turned to his friend but Manelesi could not answer.

He was lying flat on his back, motionless, eyes closed as if in death and Nkosinathi growled like a wild animal. The sight of his friend on the ground unnerved him, a determination to avenge his friend's death overtook him and his strength returned to spur him on. Fearing nothing he ran, his body stooped, to the donga before any of the defenders saw him. The native soldiers were already close to panic and were starting to bolt as he emerged from the long grass followed closely by several more of the uVe. They jabbed at the fearful natives with their spears, swung knobkerries viciously about their heads and quickly despatched the laggards. A burly Redcoat Sergeant, his helmet missing, his trouser leg stained with blood, equally fearless levelled his rifle at

Nkosinathi and fired. The bullet should have killed Nkosinathi, except that he was not alone in rushing the position. A fortuitous lunge from a spear passed straight through his neck at the crucial moment, knocking him off balance, spoiling his aim and the bullet simply grazed Nkosinathi's shoulder opening a long shallow wound.

The Red coat was stout, as brave as any man that day and with blood spurting from his neck wound he turned away from Nkosinathi to make one last lunge towards his killer, his bayonet piercing the warrior's pelvis and the two of them fell to the ground in an embrace of death. Within minutes, all the defenders of that small enclave were either dead or fleeing for their lives with a horde of warriors chasing after them and it was Nkosinathi's chance for a trophy. He paused just long enough to remove the sergeant's jacket and slipped it over his own shoulders before chasing after his comrades. They were only yards from the camp, pouring in for the final kill, easily overrunning the last few defenders and killing them and they began to ransack deserted tents and wagons. It was all over, the Redcoats were defeated, a few had escaped, a few more were making their last stand down towards the river, but it was over.

Nkosinathi felt tired and hungry as he picked his way through the destruction of the camp looking for anything he could find to eat. He was lucky; he stumbled across a field kitchen where he managed to scavenge some dry bread and quenched his thirst from the remains of a half-destroyed water barrel and then he looked at the proof of a great victory. Littering the camp were half-naked native and European corpses, their stomachs slit wide open in the Zulu way, dead horses lay amongst the tents and wagons the blood of slaughtered oxen soaking the grass. On a day such as this, the victors spared no living thing.

Eventually the blood lust abated, there was nothing left to kill, and the warriors began to dance with joy. They wore their defeated enemies red jackets and white helmets, they looted the tents, searching out the White Man's drink and Nkosinathi was happy. His wound stung but it was bearable and looking down, he held out the sleeves of his new jacket to admire it, his reward for the effort he had put in and for the service he had afforded his King. He found a helmet lying forlornly under a wagon and reached for it, a once proud white helmet, defaced with the earth, sweat and blood of battle, its shiny metal badge dulled. He held it up and after a cursory inspection placed it firmly on his head.

'Nkosinathi,' it was Somopho.

Nkosinathi looked at his friend. 'Manelesi is dead I think. He died a brave warrior.'

'And Khulekani what news of him?'

'I have seen him, some of the uVe have found the White Man's drink, he was with them and he did not recognise me. His eyes were clouded and he could not speak.'

'Will you help me to find Manelesi and send him home like a true warrior?'

'I will,' said Somopho.

Wearily, the two warriors walked past comrades picking through the wrecked camp looking for anything they could carry away, some tents were on fire and the Zulu soldiers had begun destroying anything they could not carry away.

Pickpockets and Zulus

'Somopho, you have no trophy, could you not find anything?' asked Nkosinathi.

Somopho pretended not to hear, he had a dark secret, and dare not tell of his cowardice in the face of the guns.

'Here, he is somewhere here I think,' said Nkosinathi, looking at the faces and clothing of any Zulu they came across, and there were many.

Eventually he found his friend where he had seen him fall, lying on his side, his hand still clutching his Assegai and nearby, his shield with a large hole in it. Nkosinathi and Somopho stood for a moment, looking down at the body of Manelesi. The fingers of his left hand twitched, perhaps he was still alive and Nkosinathi knelt beside his friend, to put an ear to Manelesi's mouth and felt a light breath. He *was* still alive, but only just.

'He lives but I do not think he will last until the sun returns,' said Nkosinathi.

'We will put him in the river,' said Somopho in a matter of fact manner.

'It shall be so,' said Nkosinathi reaching for Manelesi's shield.

Between them they lifted the body of the fallen warrior onto his shield and carried it through the Nek where the last of the fighting had so recently finished and on towards the river. They were not alone in their endeavour, other warriors were taking their fallen comrades to the river also, to send them on their way, back to their ancestors. It was the custom for those not expected to survive and standing on the bank of the river the two warriors lay down the shield to stand for a while, remembering their fallen comrade in arms.

'Goodbye Manelesi, my friend, my kind and caring friend,' said Nkosinathi and together he and Somopho tipped the shield. Manelesi's limp body slipped down the sloping riverbank to fall with a splash into the fast flowing stream and within seconds, the current swept him away to join his illustrious ancestors.

Chapter 6

The news was less than reassuring, the reports from the forward scouts suggested that the base camp was under serious attack and the estimated numbers of the Zulu army was far in excess of anything the Staff Officers had anticipated. Lord Chelmsford was not a happy man as he rode out to a vantage point with his senior officers to see for himself the clouds of smoke, the black smudges on the landscape indicating the overwhelming numbers of the Zulu army. He had no choice but to return to Isandhlwana and support his beleaguered garrison.

A mile or more away, heading north east and away from the main column, Patrick and his troop spread out in skirmishing order, blissfully unaware of the desperate fight in the camp. Their orders were to scout the country further up the wide valley and search out the Zulu army. Most of the Mounted Infantry were there, covering the whole width of the valley and up into the low-lying hills on either side.

'It's quiet,' Patrick said to the lieutenant riding alongside him. 'We have not seen one Zulu, man or woman, all mornin' sir.'

'Hmm...I'll admit I do not like it Sergeant Donovan. There should be at least some scouts out, but as you comment, nothing.'

'D'you think they are up here sir?'

'Well if you want my opinion, then no, I don't. Then that begs the question, where the bloody well are they?'

Both men fell silent, Patrick looked across at the distant mountains and the lieutenant lifted his field glasses to scan the valley from side to side and was about to make a comment when the sound of galloping hooves disturbed the peace.

'Sir, compliments of the General,' the rider blurted out. 'Your orders are to return to the main column.' He paused for a few seconds. 'The camp is attacked, the Zulus are not here.'

Patrick and the lieutenant looked at each other and said nothing.

'Sergeant, gather your men, instruct them to fall in behind me. Bugler, sound the recall,' said the lieutenant.

The eclipse had run its course and the heat of the day had returned to its normal thirty degrees and they were almost half way back to the rock when Patrick called a halt and took out his field glasses for a better look. Those poor bastards, they must be having a tough time of it, he thought, aware how severely outnumbered they were but then they had guns against spears didn't they.

He scanned the countryside, nothing but thorn bushes, grass and the occasional mimosa tree, not a sign of any living thing. He lowered his glasses for a moment and looked around at the troop spread amongst the long grass and it dawned on him that there was no gunfire. Until now, they had been too far away to hear or see much but the camp was less than three miles away, surely he would have heard at least the field guns. His mouth felt dry, he whipped the glasses to his eyes and concentrated hard on the camp. There was smoke but

356

not from the guns, more like burning wagons but he was sure he saw men in red moving about and then he caught sight of a shadow moving in the bush maybe four hundred yards away. He could not make it out exactly, vegetation screened whatever he had seen and the heat haze was blurring his vision, it could be anything from Zulus to a Rhinoceros.

'Georgie, there is something over there,' he said pointing.

'What?'

'I don't know, you and Barney go take a look, we'll wait here a while.' He stretched in his saddle for a better view, watched as Georgie and Barney picked their way across the rocky ground until suddenly there was a flash and the sound of a gunshot.

'Bejesus,' exclaimed Patrick, 'tis some of those bloody Zulus, I can see them now, come on lads.'

He spurred his horse forward and low in the saddle he rode hard after Georgie and Barney, catching up with them just as the group of Zulus spotted them and began firing spasmodically in their direction. Georgie felt rather than heard the first round as the bullet sped overhead and quickly made a decision to get out of the way of any further pot shots.

'Quick, down here Barney,' said Georgie, finding a hollow a few yards in front of them.

He swung one leg off his horse as he went and jumped the last few feet, pulling on the reins to slow the animal. Patrick and Barney were right behind him and soon all three were out of the view of the enemy.

'How many Georgie?' asked Patrick.

'I think I saw about eight or ten but I'm not sure.'

'Here take the horses,' ordered Patrick, handing his reigns to Barney. 'I'll take a few shots at them.'

He slipped his Carbine from his shoulder and scurried forward followed close on his heels by Georgie and the two of them found some ground affording better cover. Lying flat on their stomachs, they wriggled forwards and gained a better view of the enemy. Carefully reaching forward, Patrick gingerly parted the grass and saw a sharpshooter taking aim at the rest of the approaching troopers. Georgie guessed the distance at one hundred and fifty yards and set his sights accordingly, aimed low and let off his first shot. The man crumpled as the lead smashed through his sternum and Georgie turned his attention to the others.

'Good shooting Georgie' said Patrick, 'I reckon you got another of the buggers.'

Frank and Arthur arrived, sliding in alongside Patrick and Georgie and all four let fly at any target that presented itself.

'I'm sure we got another couple but they don't make a lot of noise when hit. Hold your fire for a moment lads.'

For five minutes, the soldiers scanned the bush for more Zulus, the only noises to disturb the peace, the occasional snort of a horse and the low moans of wounded natives.

'I reckon they only have spears and clubs for weapons now. We've got rid of the guns, let's mount up and give em a fright,' said Patrick setting off on a crouching run towards the horses.

The troopers followed and climbed back into their saddles and with carbines at the ready, headed at a gallop towards the thorn bushes covering the Zulus. It took less than fifteen seconds to close to within spear throwing distance and it was clear that if there had been ten of them, only five remained. A big warrior appeared, coming at them and ready to throw his Assegai but a shot to the head sent his lifeless body sprawling to the ground then his comrades attempted to put up a fight and they too died just as easily.

'Phew, that was interesting,' said Barney, his cheeks bright red from a combination of excitement and heat.

Patrick slipped to the ground, holding his gun ready for any trouble and one by one, inspected the bodies for any sign of life. Three were spread-eagled on their backs and obviously dead but he had to use his boot to turn the other two over. They were older than he had expected and from the two empty whiskey bottles lying on the ground, they were probably drunk, dead drunk; no wonder they were so easy to kill. He looked again at the bodies, they were wearing articles of clothing that could have only come from the bodies of dead British soldiers and his heart sank. Those poor bastards of the First Battalion, the Zulus must have wiped them out, where else could items British soldier's clothing have come from.

'Right, that evens up the score a little, but there's more to do, come on,' he said, gritting his teeth.

The dead Zulu's war trophies had not gone unnoticed by the rest of the troop and it was in sombre mood that they rode towards the ill-fated rock. Within the hour, the forward scouts had reached the outskirts of the camp and the full horrors of the day's events soon became apparent to the troopers. As they picked their way past the bodies of soldiers of the Twenty Fourth lying amongst their own entrails, recognisable only by the braces hanging from their backs. The Zulus had stripped them of their tunics, slit open their abdomens to release their spirits and leave them sprawled where they had died. Black bodies lay about in groups, limbs missing, headless, where cannon shot had ripped through their ranks.

In their rampage through the camp, the Zulus had destroyed everything, horses, oxen littered the open ground, and behind them, the once orderly white tents lay torn and burned. Some of the Boer wagons had survived the onslaught, too large and heavy to destroy, the only remnants of the British army to remain untouched.

When the Mounted Infantry arrived at the outskirts of the camp, the lieutenant ordered them to close up for the final approach and several hundred yards or so in front of the camp he called a halt.

'Sergeants Donovan, Jones, Appleyard and Davies take your men and spread out a little just in case there are any Zulus left in there. I do not want any surprises. Keep a sharp lookout and do not stray too far, it will be dark soon.'

The sections broke away from the main body, Patrick led his men four hundred yards to the north of the camp. Georgie and Arthur nudged their horses forward and moved away fifty or so feet onto some higher ground to sit motionless, their eyes fixed upon the rock.

'Rider coming Sergeant,' called Barney, pointing to a lone horseman.

'Where's the lieutenant Sergeant Donovan, I have his orders,' said the officer when he reached them.

Patrick saluted and pointed to the group of horsemen. 'You'll find the lieutenant over there sir.'

'Thank you Sergeant, carry on,' he said, spurring his mount forward.

'There's the column Sarge,' said Barney excitedly, his eagle eyes always first to spot change.

'And here comes Lieutenant Chatt' said Georgie.

'Compliments of the General Sergeant Donovan have your men spread out and under no circumstances are you to approach any nearer to the camp. The column will be here fairly soon and we are to stay out here for the night, so keep a good lookout and await further orders.'

'Sir,' said Patrick, saluting and the lieutenant moved on towards the next section in the line. Patrick hung his head in a silent prayer for a few moments, well aware as to why the General had ordered them to stay away from the camp.

An hour later as darkness fell, a bugle call rang and almost immediately, there was the boom of one of the field guns and a shot flew over their heads into the camp. More guns joined in, first one shot then another and another until after a quarter of an hour the General was satisfied that there would be no resistance and ordered the advance.

The long line of horsemen sat motionless as advancing infantry companies marched past them bayonets at the ready and then the native auxiliaries and in darkness they entered the camp. The Zulu army, a volunteer militia, had decided that they preferred to go back to their Kraals with their booty rather than take on the remainder of the British Army, disappearing and leaving the camp deserted.

The order came to form a defensive square and slowly the mass of infantrymen straddled the road and moved slowly forward in the dark, only their nostrils giving any hint of the carnage as they stumbled over cold stiff forms. There was nothing to be done for the fallen; all the soldiers could do was simply lay down on the grass, sticky with the blood of friend and foe alike to try to get a few hours' sleep. The mounted men serving as lookouts were relieved for a few hours and just before midnight, Georgie and the rest of his section dismounted on the outskirts of the camp and tried to gain a few hours respite.

'Can you smell that?' he asked Patrick as they led the horses in the dark past the burned out tents and overturned wagons. 'You know what that smell is don't you?' Georgie repeated.

'I can guess.'

Far out on the plain and in the hills the returning Zulu army was exhausted; the march from Ulundi and the battle had drained their resources, silence replacing the boisterousness of only two days before. Nkosinathi was typical, hungry and tired he sat amongst some aloe bushes with Somopho and Lindani, resting for a while.

'We attacked a line of Redcoats,' said Lindani, recounting the fighting. 'Their guns spat fire and death but still we ran at them, Khulekani leading the way, I saw him fall and then we reached the soldiers. They died bravely, and those that ran away we hunted down, stabbing them, making them squeal like pigs.'

Nkosinathi said nothing, he did not need to, his friends were telling the same story he would have and he was so hungry that his exuberance had deserted him. It *had* been a great victory and King Cetshwayo would be pleased with them but he had lost two good friends,

Khulekani, the bravest of the brave, and Manelesi, the kindest and most thoughtful of them all. The battle was over, the Redcoats resistance broken, every one of them left in the camp and on the slopes of the rock, killed. They had plundered the tents and wagons, found a little food and some liquor, Nkosinathi was the proud owner of a red tunic jacket and a pith helmet with its metal badge, and he longed to see the beehive huts of his Kraal.

Before the journey home, they had performed one more task. Picking their way through the fallen, they searched for Khulekani, finding him lying with arms outstretched and still clutching his spear. The top of his skull was missing where the bullet had smashed through the bone, but he was still recognisable. The warriors stood in silence, one picked up his shield and together they placed it over the body in token burial.

The Manzimnyama, normally a quiet backwater was unusually full for the time of year, the summer rains had been heavy. Looking into that same, fast flowing stream late on the previous afternoon Nkosinathi and Somopho had said their last farewell to their comrade in arms. A single, powerful bullet had smashed Manelesi's left arm, fracturing it beyond repair and he had slipped into unconscious but the cold water revived him enough for him to splash out with his good arm, enough to keep his head above water. An instinct for survival had taken hold, the cold water slowed his metabolism, stemmed some of the bleeding and it was all he could do to keep his head above water long enough to take gasping breaths.

On the edge of consciousness, he braved the river, his will to survive dominating everything until he eventually

363

tipped over the edge of a small waterfall and into a wide, still lagoon. For a time he managed to open his eyes, nausea filling his head and with one last effort, managed to kick his legs hard enough to reach a hanging branch, pulled his broken body into shallow water and drifted into oblivion.

Chapter 7

Inga pleaded with Paludan to leave the mission station as soon as news of the approaching Zulu Impis had reached them but Paludan was having none of it, his faith in the almighty unshakable. He guessed, shrewdly, that Cetshwayo would not allow his men to cross the river into Natal and they would be relatively safe.

'Inga, we have devoted our lives to serving God in this backward country. We have come to convert the heathen to the way of God. To run away now will tell them that their spirits and their Witch Doctor s are a stronger force than Jesus. No Inga I cannot leave, but you must.'

She looked at him, her brave, courageous Paludan, every bit of him descended from his Viking ancestors and yet he was a gentle, caring man, one who always put others first and the love she felt for him reasserted itself tenfold. She had proved strong and resilient in their adopted country and she knew that she could not, would not leave him to face his destiny alone, so they remained together on the edge of the mayhem that was Isandhlwana.

On the day of the battle several of the native contingent who had escaped or deserted, Paludan did not ask, came by looking for food and water telling harrowing tales of the Zulu attack, the retreat of the Redcoats and of the savagery. Paludan and Inga had listened with dismay wondering if perhaps they had made the wrong decision to stay but no Zulu warrior appeared and so Paludan decided to go out to the river to look for survivors. He had asked for some of the natives living and working with him to come but the fear in their eyes gave their answer. Only one brave soul did not falter, Nozipho.

'You have been kind to me great white God talker.'

Paludan smiled to himself. She had heard him praying aloud on several occasions, her inquisitiveness getting the better of her and she had asked him what he was doing.

'I am talking to God my child.'

Her good eye had looked at him and she had whispered 'you are talking to God? You are a God talker. Ooh, you are more powerful than the Sangoma for they do not talk directly to the spirits, only through medicine and sacrifices.' From then on, she knew him as the God talker.

Together they walked along the river bank looking for signs of life but only dead bodies floated past, men beyond salvation and they were about to return to the mission when Nozipho stopped dead in her tracks. She sensed something, Paludan stopped too, unsure of why.

'There, look,' she said, 'over there, is that someone in the water, someone I think who is alive.'

Paludan looked but saw nothing, Manelesi's body was partially submerged, his head obscured by vegetation but Nozipho had seen him. She retraced her steps, and then, more clearly, she saw a Zulu warrior slumped against the far bank.

'There master, look.'

'I see him. We must cross the river, it is shallow just there, I can see rocks under the water, a bridge of sorts.'

They crossed the river easily enough, wading through shallows and jumping from rock to flat rock but it was a different matter trying to get Manelesi from the water. Nozipho was so absorbed with the task and Manelesi so weak and drawn that she did not recognise him at first. Only when they had dragged him further into the shallows and rolled his body clear of the water did she finally look at him. It was a familiar face but it was not until his eyes flickered open for a few seconds that she realised who it was, leaving her speechless.

The missionary could see that Manelesi's wretched arm would need a doctor and slipped off his jacket, undid his shirt to tear it into strips for a bandage. First, he must stop the bleeding and wrapping a stone in the cloth winding it tightly about the upper arm, above the break to stem the flow and then he carefully straightened the break to strap the useless arm to the unconscious Manelesi's chest.

'I will stay with him child, you run back to the Mission and fetch the cart and some of the men from the fields. Tell them they must help us this time, and we have not seen any warriors, tell them that.'

'I will,' whispered Nozipho.

She was not about to lose Manelesi a second time and for a fleeting moment she looked down at him, his eyes shut as if in death. She was determined that she would not let that happen and running as fast as she could, she splashed across the ford and set off towards the Mission.

'Mistress Inga,' Nozipho shouted as she approached the house, 'Mistress Inga come quick.'

Inga picked up the gun and looked out through the net curtains, Paludan might have put all his faith in God but she reserved some of hers for the gun. She saw Nozipho but there was no sign of her husband – what had happened, where was he?

'Mistress Inga, come quick we have found Manelesi, come,' she gasped, hardly able to get the words out.

'What is it, where is Paludan, who is Manelesi?' asked Inga emerging from the house.

'He is my man and he is safe mistress, we have found him but he is badly injured. I have come to fetch the hand cart and anyone who can help.'

'Wait Nozipho, wait just a moment. I will put on a pair of my husband's trousers; it will be easier for me than this dress. Here, take this she said handing the gun to Nozipho, wondering who this Manelesi was and within minutes, she was back dressed in a pair of Paludan's trousers.

'I have come for the cart mistress, and someone to help me.'

'There is no one here, they were working in the fields earlier but something spooked them and they've gone, fetch the cart, I will help you.'

Nozipho passed Inga the gun and ran to the shed where Paludan kept a handcart and after throwing the gun and some cartridges into it, Inga took hold of one of the handles, Nozipho the other and the two women pulled it out through the gateway.

Zulu people are not only physically strong but also seem to have an inbuilt ability to overcome sickness and injury more easily than the white race and Manelesi was no exception. They spoon fed him nourishing broth, changed his dressings several times and he began to recover. Meanwhile, as news of the British defeat at Isandhlwana and subsequent triumph at Rorke's Drift filtered through, some of the Mission station's previous inhabitants began to return. News filtered through of the Zulu army leaving the area, the panic of the settler population subsided and Paludan felt he could send for the doctor in Dundee and two days later, the doctor appeared on horseback.

'It's a bad break Paludan,' he said examining the wound, 'you have made a decent job of strapping it up but it's too late for splints. The bone is shattered and there is a risk of gangrene, the only thing I can do is to amputate. Tell your girl to boil some water and I will need bandages. Have you a stout wooden table I can use to work on?'

'Yes, you can use the one in the study. I will have it moved here. Will that do?'

'Yes, I anticipated the patients' injuries from the brief description you wrote in your note. I have some chloroform and carbolic acid with me – let's get to work.'

They spent an hour preparing the patient, Paludan and Inga helping the doctor whilst Nozipho scurried back and forth with the hot water and bandages and finally, they were ready. Manelesi had recovered some strength, though he was still relatively weak and was conscious when they lifted him onto the table. He offered no resistance but his eyes were wide with apprehension and fear until Nozipho's calming words settled him down and once the doctor had administered the chloroform he made short work of the operation.

'Thank you doctor, it's not everyone that helps the natives, especially after Cetshwayo's belligerence.'

The doctor lifted his cup to his lip and drank some of the tea Nozipho had brewed and looked pensively at Paludan.

'They didn't laager their wagons you know and Chelmsford split his force into two – stupid.'

They drank their tea in silence for a few minutes, alone with their thoughts before the Doctor finally took his leave, shaking Paludan's hand and as he rode out of the gateway with a wave to Paludan and Inga, it crossed his mind that if the Impi did return, then he may never see them again.

Lying in the darkened room Manelesi was still very weak. Not knowing where he was and with almost no recollection of his ordeal, he struggled to understand his predicament, even his memory of the battle vague. He drifted in and out of consciousness for a time but each day the pain lessened and he grew stronger eventually noticing the native girl who regularly came to feed him and Paludan who came to see him, explaining in his poor Zulu how they had found him. He refrained from mentioning the Zulu victory, Manelesi did not ask, and by the end of the week, he felt well enough to stand and decided that he would try.

Swinging his legs over the bed he propped himself up with his good arm, feeling for the floor with his feet but the pain from the amputation became too much and he cried out. Nozipho, alerted by his call, burst into the room to find Manelesi slumped awkwardly across the bed and in danger of injuring himself. She caught hold of him and too heavy for her to get into the bed, she lowered him to the floor, kneeling beside him before reaching for a damp cloth to wipe the perspiration from his brow.

Slowly he opened his eyes, he looked straight into hers yet still recognition did not dawn.

'Why is it always night?' he whispered.

Nozipho understood, it was the curtains, always drawn shutting out the sunlight and to a Zulu that meant the spirit world. She went to the window to draw the curtains apart to let in the daylight to illuminate the room – and her.

She turned back towards him and lying flat on the floor, squinting his eyes to adjust to the brightness, taking in the surroundings and then he looked at her. He focused on the bright eye staring back at him, recognition of sorts beginning to stir. Her face was familiar yet her deformity obscured her true likeness, yet she *was* familiar and then it hit him.

'Nozipho?' he said weakly.

'Yes Manelesi, it is me, Nozipho,' she said, lowering her gaze.

'What has happened? Where are my friends, the battle, wwh...at happened?

'Do not worry about the battle, I do not know what happened, I do not know where your friends or my brothers are, I do not know anything except that you are safe and that I will make you well. I will bring you some food and make you well.'

Nozipho brought him a bowl of mealie porridge and sat watching as he fed himself for the first time, wolfing it down, a sure sign that he was on the mend and she was delighted.

Eventually the invalid left his bed for longer and longer periods and for a while was morose, realising he could no longer fulfil his destiny as a warrior and then one day, sitting in the garden and almost back to full strength, Paludan came to sit beside him.

'Nozipho,' he called, 'Nozipho, come and sit with us for my command of the Zulu language is not complete and I will need an interpreter.'

She was very happy to oblige and hurriedly pegged the last of the clothes she was hanging out before sitting on the grass in front of the men and looking up at Manelesi knowing that she loved him and yet sure he would not want her with her scarred face and useless eye.

'Manelesi you have come to us by the will of God and it was with his help that we brought you back to health. When we found you, you were closer to death than any man I have known.'

Nozipho helped where Paludan's vocabulary failed him and between them they spoke to Manelesi about the great battle in which he was wounded, the effects of the conflict and finally to tell him he was welcome to stay at the Mission for as long as he wished and Paludan would help him find God. Manelesi nodded his understanding as far as he could, for he knew nothing of the white-man's God.

'It is time for you to join us in our worship and to learn of the teachings of the prophet,' Paludan faltered, unsure of how to say what he meant and looked to Nozipho for help to explain his thoughts.

'This man is a God talker, he speaks straight to God, the InSangoma of the Zulu cannot do that and what is more his God is gentle, asking for neither sacrifice or for payment. I have lived here since you saved my life Manelesi, and now their God has helped me save yours. Is that not a better way than killing. Remember the smelling out, the executions for only small transgressions? These things do not happen here.'

Manelesi looked at her; obviously she believed what she was saying and although he had only been at the Mission for a short time he could see that it was a very different world from the one he had grown up in.

'I do not know what to say little one. I am glad that you are safe and I am glad that you saved me.' He laughed aloud. 'I am a warrior of the Zulu nation and yet my life was saved by a girl, perhaps I know too little of the spirit world, perhaps I should learn of the white-man's God after all. Can I be a God talker?' he asked Paludan.

Paludan smiled, 'Yes we are all God talkers and God listens to what we have to say. You shall come to the service on Sunday, sit with Nozipho and she will show you what to do.'

Chapter 8

Alone in her hotel room, Ellen read the note received that same morning from Clarence, writing to inform her that shortly he would arrive back in King Williams. She had not seen him for almost six weeks and felt apprehensive at his return, she was bored living in the hotel room and was becoming increasingly unhappy. Although thankful to Clarence for helping her escape the poverty of the East End of London, she did not love him but she was still dependent upon him for almost everything.

She paced slowly back and forth, wondering if perhaps she should go and take some air, walk for a short while. she looked out of the window and into the street seeing several people, two women talking, a local man riding past on a horse. In the distance, a large troop of mounted soldiers was entering town and from her vantage point, she watched the horses walk slowly along the street. To her surprise, riding at the head of the column was Clarence, his blue Lancers uniform standing out from the red tunics of the troopers. He looked thinner and as he passed, he took a cursory glance towards her window, the lace curtains masking her from his view. He did not see her and once he had gone by, she carefully parted the curtains to look again at the

374

troop. At least a hundred men she guessed, and she wondered if Georgie and Patrick might be amongst them.

Her hidden eyes flitted from one sunburned face to another, unfamiliar faces mostly until eventually her gaze came to rest on a face she knew well. Georgie and alongside him Patrick who had let his beard grow and her heart leaped at the sight of it.

An hour later a cursory knock at the bedroom door announced Clarence's arrival and in he walked.

'My dear, I'm so glad to see you.'

'Clarence, I only received your letter this morning. Er... what a nice surprise.'

'Yes, quite, I have a few days leave here in Kings.' He dropped his small battered valise onto the bed and looked his wife up and down. 'Perhaps we can catch up on a few things,' he said, a blush of embarrassment spreading across his cheeks.

Ellen knew what his idea of catching up meant and she did not relish it one bit. 'Oh, Clarence, I'm so sorry but it's the wrong time of the month, I cannot possibly oblige you.'

He lowered his eyes to hide his disappointment. He did not really understand a woman's ways; he knew only that once again she had rejected him. As a soldier he was fearless but in the company of his wife, a mere mouse.

'Well, perhaps we can do other things; let's dine out at the best restaurant in town tonight. How about that?'

'Oh Clarence I would love to.'

At least he was giving her a chance to dress up, to show off in front of some of the officer's wives, something to break the boredom. She had agreed to marry Clarence only because he spoiled her, took her to places she could only dream of, fine restaurants and to wear clothes that were not grubby, patched or pawned, to travel in the coaches she could only chase after as a youngster.

'We could go to the East London Hotel, they have a fine French chef there I am told,' she said.

'Splendid, I will take a walk there right this minute and reserve the best table' said Clarence, feeling a little better.

Ellen watched him go and catching her reflection in the mirror she wondered for a moment just who this woman was staring back at her. The face was pretty and her hair hung down to her shoulders, just as her mother's did, but the look in her eyes was one of sadness. Then she remembered her mother with some fondness, those times in the rookery, on the streets looking for victims. She would still be there if it had not been for that chance meeting with Clarence and she looked again in the mirror. She had noticed the glances some of the officers had given her and wondered what might have been if it had not been Clarence.

'I say old girl, would you like some more of these wonderful vegetables, such a change from bully beef y'know,' said Clarence spooning more onto his plate.

'No thank you, I am feeling quite full and I don't want to miss the wonderful desserts they have here. Tell me about the war Clarence, I've heard a lot of rumours.'

'This war is getting dirty,' he said, laying his knife down on his plate. 'We have been humiliated by the Zulus. Quite unexpected you know.' He paused, dug his fork into a carrot, glanced around the room, and lowered his voice. 'Lord Chelmsford is determined that next time we will win, no question. You've probably wondered what my part has been in all this.'

Ellen looked at him; she had a mouthful of food and was, thankfully, unable to speak, but his prolonged pause allowed her to swallow. 'Yes Clarence, I have often wondered what an officer without a regiment was doing in Africa.'

He was not sure whether she was being sarcastic or not but continued. 'I've been on a fact finding mission for the Lancers. My orders are to reconnoitre the country and to ascertain as to its suitability for a Cavalry wegiment to operate. I've been with Colonel Evelyn Wood's column most of the time, scouting to the north.'

'Did you see much fighting?' Ellen asked.

'No not really, the blighters were concentrated down on the plain of Isandhlwana and didn't come near us.'

'What has happened to the men with Lord Chelmsford's column, the ones that weren't involved in the massacre?'

'Oh, they are guarding the border until the re-enforcements from England and India arrive. Some are here in Kings, part of the escort, Mounted Infantry and some irregulars.'

Ellen remained silent. She knew very well that some Mounted Infantry were at the base, Georgie and Patrick amongst them.

'I advised the Command of the Seventeenth Lancers that the country is not good for the horses. I have recommended they acclimatise before joining any campaign, and my dear, I shall not be long without a regiment, the Seventeenth are advancing from the Cape in good order at this very moment and should be here within a day or two. Until they get here I have some leave due, so come on old girl, let's have some fun,' he said, colouring up once more.

'Clarence, you promised you would teach me to ride a horse, perhaps we could do that tomorrow.'

His eyes lit up, nothing would give him more pleasure than to take her riding. Apart from the enjoyment of the ride, his fellow officers had assured him that horse riding was a good aphrodisiac.

'Splendid my dear, splendid. I will arrange it as soon as I can.'

In the military compound at the edge of town, the British Army was functioning as normal, the infantry drilling and parading, the mounted soldiers grooming their horses and effecting repairs to broken equipment.

'Corporal, see if you can find some decent tack for the horses, I've snapped both of the stirrup straps and I do not want to be riding all the way back with short straps.'

Georgie looked at Patrick; they were having many equipment failures, and most of the troop needed some replacement. His own saddle was in poor condition and he jumped at the chance to visit the quartermaster's store, a chance to stretch his legs and catch up on some of the camp gossip.

'Permission to be excused Sergeant?' said the newly promoted Corporal McNamara.

'Excused corporal,' said a grinning Sergeant Donovan.

Georgie lifted his saddle onto his shoulder and was about to walk to the quartermaster's store when he spotted Clarence in his cavalry uniform with a woman by his side, Ellen. She looked good in her riding clothes;

no longer the street urchin he had known as a youngster in Spitalfields and although he would like to speak with her he could not acknowledge an officer's wife in front of her husband. Not so Patrick, he had the gift of the blarney and he called out.

'Good mornin' to you sir, is it horses that you'd be lookin' for, one for yourself and one for your lady for she looks dressed for a bit of riding.'

'Yes Sergeant, I would be obliged if you could find a compliant animal.'

'Sir' said Patrick, finding it difficult to tear his eyes away from Ellen. 'I'll be back in a few minutes whit a nice little filly.'

He put down the tack he had been inspecting and made his way to the corral, calling a native groom to him on the way.

'Here lad, cut me out that grey,' he said, pointing to a pretty little grey horse no more than twelve hands high and ideal for a woman.

The native boy jumped in amongst the horses and within no time was leading the grey towards Patrick. 'Let us see what we can find in the way of a saddle for the lady,' he said pointing to the tack store.

'Here you are sir, a pretty little horse and I found a lady's side saddle to boot,' he said with a grin.

It was the first thing he had done for Ellen and it left him feeling pleased as he waited for Clarence's approval who was busy running his hand across an animal's chest and showing little interest in the sergeant. Patrick took the opportunity and risked a glance at Ellen and their eyes met for an instant.

'This will do Sergeant,' finally Clarence said in his customary dismissive tone. 'Thank you Sergeant, I can manage, that will be all.'

Patrick was powerless to do anything but obey and turned back to his own horse, watching the officer and his wife ride slowly across the parade ground. Taking a deep breath, he ran his hand along his horses back and was about to fill his pipe when Georgie returned.

'Hey Patrick look, I've been issued a new saddle and you have a new pair of stirrup straps. It seems the Zulus have really upset the General because he has issued orders that he wants the Army to have the best equipment. There have been too many failures because of sub-standard workmanship by greedy colonials.'

Patrick looked at his friend, not hearing a word, his eyes out of focus, his mind troubled with thoughts of Ellen.

'What's up Sarge?'

'Nuttin.'

'How long do you think we will be here Sarge? I hear that re-enforcements for the Twenty Fourth are already on their way from England to bring the regiment back up to strength,' said Georgie stuffing his own pipe with tobacco.

'And a fine lot a lads they will be I expect. They will need a bit of training before we take on those savages again,' said Patrick with unexpected vehemence.

Georgie was surprised at Patrick's outburst and was still pondering the reason why as he brushed his horses' hindquarters. 'Well Blackie, you do look well after your rest and some oats,' he said. The horse turned its head towards Georgie as if it understood and he slapped her hindquarters. 'Let's have a look at your shoes,' he said dropping to one knee.

'There, that should do it,' he said as he let go the last of her hooves.

He looked round to see that the rest of the troop was taking a break leaning against the rail and filling their pipes. Patrick was with them and so he walked over to them and was about to speak to Patrick when a woman's voice called from some distance behind them.

'Here Sergeant, will you take my horse.'

'Ellen my dear, do not address a common soldier directly. I will give any orders needed. Here, you two, take these horses and return them to the stables,' said Clarence dismounting.

He reached up to help Ellen from her horse but she avoided his grasp and slid deftly from the saddle, only increasing his ire. 'That's not the way for an Officer's wife to behave' hissed Clarence, 'you should allow me to help you down.'

'I can manage quite well on my own Clarence; I don't need any help thank you.'

She almost said "from you" but did not need to, everyone there could see what she was thinking and for Clarence it was the final straw. During the mornings ride Ellen had parried Clarence's advances and if he thought riding acted as a mild aphrodisiac he was very much mistaken.

'You will do as I say,' hissed Clarence, his emotions beginning to run out of control.

'I will not,' said the defiant Ellen.

It was enough to set Clarence ablaze, he lifted his riding crop took a stride towards Ellen with the obvious intent of thrashing her, but his were not the only emotions running high. A certain lovesick Irish Sergeant was witness to the proceedings and he sprang into life, placing himself between Ellen and her angry husband.

'Sir, it would be a terrible thing that you should hurt the lady, especially in front of all the men,' he said casting an eye over Clarence's shoulder towards the troopers.

Clarence spun round and realising that "common soldiers" were witness to the event looked Patrick in the eye, his arrogance slowly replaced by a more sinister aspect of his character. Here was a Sergeant of Foot questioning his authority, standing between him and his wife, humiliating him in front of the men. Patrick saw Clarence's reaction, realised that he may have gone too far, and quickly tried to calm the situation.

'Sir, if it will please yourself, the Corporal an' me would be only too pleased to take the horses off you.'

To the outside world, Patrick had simply moved several paces and politely asked to look after the horses but to Clarence it was a declaration of war and, one day, he would see this upstart hang.

'Yes, sergeant, take them for grooming and feeding and I will deal with you later. Come my dear, time for us to return to our room.'

Ellen too had noticed the menace in Clarence's voice and sensing trouble for Patrick and Georgie she altered her demeanour. Pretending to be unaware of the undertones, she held out her hand to Clarence and said 'Why of course Clarence, it will be pleasant to have a change of clothes and freshen up for dinner.'

Clarence reacted positively, his reddened face returned to its former light tan and he reached for her hand, guiding her towards the rough pathway and away from the corral. As she passed the soldiers, she nodded her head.

'Thank you for your help sergeant,' she said looking straight into Patrick's eyes. He responded and they both knew that it was not finished.

'That was a bit risky Patrick, wasn't it?' said Georgie relieved that his friend was still in one piece. 'Confronting an Officer like that is Court Marshal offence, he could have you lose your stripes and spend years in a military prison. Thank goodness that clever bastard is an Officer in the Lancers and not the Twenty Fourth. With a bit of luck we might not see him ever again.'

Patrick looked a little downcast. 'Aye, maybe your right.'

'I thought you moved a little too quickly, what is it Patrick, is it Ellen, do you have designs on her? Good God man you cannot chase after an Officer's wife, they will hang you for that.'

'Now did I say anything about the lady, did I? I was only doing my duty to protect the lady from harm. I would do it for any woman,' he said with unconvincing bluster, but it was enough to shut Georgie up.

'Now let's be off to the mess for a drink, I need one after that.'

'You and me both, you big daft Irish fool.'

'Oi, now who's over stepping the mark?'

Patrick looked across the corral and shouted to a group of native stable lads 'Here, come and take these horses, and under his breath, 'to hell whit the Lancer's horse, let's get some dinner.'

Together strode across the parade ground towards the mess tents, Georgie relieved that they had survived the encounter with Clarence but Patrick's thoughts lay in a different direction. Those beautiful blue eyes were still boring into the centre of his brain.

Clarence watched the vanguard of the Seventeenth Lancers enter camp and with a nod or two, reacquainted himself with his fellow officers. It had been a long, slow process acclimatizing the horses to the African climate and now they had finally arrived. The cavalrymen found an area to string their lines, tether the horses and when they had finally finished feeding and grooming them, Clarence spent some time swapping stories and learning about their journey from the Cape. The officers were in high spirits and decided that before they moved into Zululand, a regimental dinner would be in order.

It pleased Clarence, it would be a time to reacquaint himself with his fellow officers and show off Ellen and it was in high spirits he returned to their room to find Ellen washing. She looked up from the bowl of cold water, picked up the towel, began to dry herself and before Clarence could speak she scolded him.

'What am I to do when you leave, how long will you be gone?',

'Well you are still my wife even though you have made it plain enough that we have very little in common. I was about to tell you some good news. The regiment will be holding a dinner tomorrow. I thought it might cheer you up a little.'

Ellen stopped drying herself, her eyes less angry, she had done some thinking since their encounter with Patrick and realised just how much she relied on Clarence, she had grown up the hard way, not schooled in the art of acquiring a husband of independent means.

'Oh a dinner, a chance to dance.' Her demeanour changed and she turned on her charm, 'don't be silly Clarence, I didn't realise that it was your duty to help me down, I had enjoyed the ride so much and was exhilarated and a regimental dinner will be wonderful.' She smiled sweetly at him.

'Really my dear, you seemed distant and uninterested at times, I was quite annoyed at your performance this morning.'

'No. no, I was concentrating on staying in the saddle. You forget I have hardly ever ridden a horse and staying on it took all my energy. And, do not be hard on those soldiers, they were only trying to help – simple souls, it would be an injustice to punish them. Let's forget about it.' She let the towel drop, moved towards him and kissed him on the cheek.

'Don't suppose we can do it tonight can we?' asked Clarence, his face reddening with embarrassment.

'We'll see, let's have dinner first and you can introduce me to your fellow officers.' Ellen was intrigued at the thought of a regimental dinner and looked forward to recreating a little of the fun they had experienced back home in England.

'I thought these were men only events Clarence?'

'Usually are, but some of the officer's wives travelled by sea and have been here waiting for them to drive up country. There will be one or two guests so I expect there will be plenty of ladies for dancing with.'

In the sergeant's mess, several of the non-commissioned officers were discussing the situation in Zululand.

'Looks like we will be on the move again tomorrow Patrick,' said Sergeant Jones, his plate of bully beef and potatoes rapidly diminishing as he spoke. 'I just got word from a Corporal who works in headquarters. He says he heard that the meetings have been concluded and we are to escort a Major back to Dundee.'

'So soon,' croaked Patrick, his face deadpan,

he, picking up his beer to lubricate his drying throat, 'so soon,' he repeated wondering if it would mean that he might not see Ellen again.

Ellen was having similar thoughts, she knew very well that the war with Cetshwayo was not going well, that the Lancers were part of the re-enforcement of the army for a second attempt at defeating the Zulus and chances were that Georgie and Patrick would be part of it. She looked at herself in the dressing table mirror, satisfied she had done her best at tying up her hair, she put her hands on her waist and twisted from side to side to see as much of herself as possible before picking up her lace gloves.

'My dear you look beautiful,' said Clarence fiddling with his bow tie. 'We will be the couple of the evening, might help with promotion, what.'

Ellen put on the sweetest smile she could, keeping him at his ease because the last thing she wanted was Clarence becoming agitated with a drink inside him. After meeting with his fellow officers he seemed over confident, she had seen him like this before and she knew that anything might happen.

She looked at her outfit in the mirror for the second time, turned sideways and held in her stomach. Clarence picked up his short mess jacket, blue with gold braiding and put it on. He looked just as impressive and his wish that they might be the couple of the evening looked possible. He gestured to his wife that it was time to leave and opened the door allowing her to sweep past, her dress rustling gently, her perfume lingering for a moment and leaving him feeling dizzy.

Within twenty minutes, they had arrived by pony and trap at the large tent that was to act as the Officers' mess for the duration of the Lancer's stay. Ellen held out her hand for Clarence to help her down, a lesson she had learned well after their altercation and as soon they entered the tent and she saw the smartly turned out officers strutting about excitement welled up inside her. For too long she had lived at the hotel, for too long she had been without a social life.

Since marrying Clarence she had developed a taste for champagne, introduced to her at social events back in England and once she felt accepted by this new social class she had ventured to try the fizzy drink and had loved it. She overstepped the mark only once and like one or two of the other wives, her husband had come to her rescue. She had begun to slur her words and when she stumbled, almost into the arms of a General, Clarence had ushered her away knowing that if he was going to climb the ranks of the regiment then his wife must be up to muster. The following day, in no uncertain terms, he had impressed that upon her and it was then she first realised how cold and calculating he could be.

'Champagne my dear?' enquired Clarence.

'Oh, yes please.'

Clarence raised his finger, gestured to one of the stewards to bring two glasses and turned back to Ellen to give her a knowing look and she responded with a slight nod of her head. The mess filled with officers and their ladies, it was a warm and pleasant evening, a last chance for the soldiers to enjoy themselves and to let their hair down before confronting the Zulus.

Clarence was acquainted to varying degrees with his fellow officers and during dinner reaffirmed some of those friendships and when the dancing started, he whirled Ellen around the floor nodding to all and sundry. Ellen was not particularly expert and clung on to her husband for fear of falling and he interpreted their closeness as just that.

As the evening wore on Ellen was in great demand by the unattached young officers and even though she was not a proficient dancer, they whirled her round the dance floor with gusto. Clarence spent the time chatting with some of the officers, reliving old times and discussing the war. His advice was in great demand for he had experience of the Zulus, but his knowledge had a price. Each soldier he spoke was required to produce a large whiskey, that would entitle the donor to some of his time, and by the end of the night, he was unable talk coherently nor to stand properly.

'Clarence it's time to go,' said Ellen. 'There are carriages outside to take those of us who are living in town.'

Clarence looked at her with bleary, uncomprehending eyes and Ellen had to help him out of the tent towards the waiting wagons where the night air had its effect. Twisting his head shakily towards her, his eyes looking in two different directions at once he mumbled incoherently. She had never seen him in such a drunken state and unsure of what to do, looked round for help.

'Madam' said an orderly, 'I will summon someone to assist you with your husband and to see you safely home.'

'Oi, Sergeant' the orderly called out to two soldiers passing by on their way from their mess tent. 'Give us a hand will you. I got a hofficer 'ere who can 'ardly stand an' e an' is lady 'ave to be taken back into town.'

Patrick stepped forwards his eyes suddenly aglow as he realised the lady in distress was Ellen. 'Here, let me help get him into the wagon. Georgie give me a hand.'

Georgie was too busy looking at Ellen to hear his request, it took a jab in the ribs to gain his attention and then, together, they managed to get Clarence into the back of the cart and lay him flat.

'Oh Sergeant would you be so kind as to accompany us into town,' said Ellen, 'I will not be able to get him up the stairs on my own.'

'What about me?' asked Georgie

'You get yourself off Corporal, myself and the driver will manage the gentleman.'

With that, he took Ellen's' arm and helped her into the wagon beside the prostrate Clarence and he climbed up beside the driver.

'Well, driver, get a move on will you.'

The driver clicked his tongue, shook the reigns and the wagon moved off, leaving behind a bewildered Georgie.

'Are you alright in the back there madam?' asked Patrick.

'Yes thank you Sergeant, I'll let you know if he is a problem.'

Clarence was not a problem; he was comatose, lost to the world and within a short time, the wagon was pulling up outside the Hotel where Patrick and the driver struggled with the unconscious Clarence. Slinging his arms over their shoulders, they frog marching him up to the room to lay him on the bed. Ellen undid his tie, and left him snoring peacefully before hastily chasing after Patrick and the driver who were walking back towards the carriage. The driver was a few paces in front of Patrick and did not notice Ellen tug at Patrick's sleeve nor him turning as she whispered in his ear. 'Stay with me Patrick, stay with me tonight.'

Patrick did not even break his step, simply called out in a soft voice, 'good night missus I hope you husband recovers.'

The driver climbed into his seat and asked whether Patrick wanted a lift back towards camp. He wasn't going all the way back but would happily give him a ride half way.

'No, I think I might have myself another drink. I know a little bar where there will still be a party going on.'

The driver nodded and kicked his tongue, coaxing his horse forward and with a wave set off along a deserted street and five minutes later the driver and his cart were out of sight. Patrick Quietly re-traced his steps towards the hotel, his heart thumping in his chest and peered down the alleyway alongside the hotel.

'Patrick,' a siren voice whispered from nearby, drawing him inexorably into the blackness and suddenly she was there, eyes glinting in the moonlight, the faint odour of perfume filling his nostrils and they embraced.

Chapter 9

Walking alone across the open country towards the small village, he called home, confused and upset he recalled the great battle and how the uVe and the other regiments had made their weary way to the capital at Ulundi and receive the King's praise. For their brave deeds and their triumph over the British, he had given them many bullocks to slaughter and feast upon and when they had gorged themselves on the meat and rested a while, he gave permission for the army to disperse and return to their homes.

Nkosinathi had joined in the celebrations but his heart was heavy, his friends Manelesi and Khulekani were dead and so too were many more of the comrades he had known as a Cadet. What of his favourite sister Nozipho, she was dead also and worst of all was the singling out and humiliation of Somopho as a coward. He remembered how Somopho had remained quiet when asked of his experiences in the battle, he had deflected questions and some had become suspicious. Was not Somopho as brave and fearless as any warrior in the uVe, had he not seen him charge the British line alongside the rest of them?

The whispers of a few had undone several warriors, their peers condemning them and once the InSangoma got to hear of individuals faltering, they hurried to the King with the news. As soon as the regiments had assembled before the King, the InSangoma had gone amongst them to smell out the cowards but the King was wise enough to realise that his army, though victorious, had suffered heavy casualties and did not order any executions. Instead, he had decided that it was better to spare them, humiliate them in front of their regiments and to spur them onto great deeds in their next battle, and so it was that Somopho's life was spared.

Looking straight ahead, his mind in turmoil he approached the entrance to the kraal, hardly noticing his father standing there.

'*Sawubona* my son, you have returned home safely,' boomed Mondli.

'*Sawubona* my father, it is good to see you again' replied Nkosinathi, snapping out of his thoughts.

'My son, you are a great warrior, you have brought honour to our family and I salute you.' Mondli reached to his ear and pulled the tiny horn from the lobe. 'Come, take snuff with me and tell me of your experiences, tell me how you killed the white men.'

For an hour father and son sat together cross-legged on the grass outside the Kraal and from inside inquisitive eyes watched them. News of Nkosinathi's approach had spread like wildfire throughout the village, he was the first warrior to return home, he had fought at the hill of the cow's stomach and everyone wanted to hear his story.

'Tell me how the White Man fights; were his guns useless against the medicine of the InSangoma, did you kill many of them?'

Nkosinathi remained silent, averting Mondli's eyes, a sign of respect in normal times, but these were not normal times and the confusion raging within Nkosinathi had made him circumspect.

'You are quiet my son, tell me of the battle,' commanded Mondli.

The young warrior shook his head slightly, clearing the daemons temporarily from his mind. 'We were resting in a donga on top of a hill overlooking the plain when a group of men on horseback stumbled upon us. The InSangoma had already performed the cleansing ceremonies and we knew that we were ready. We rose up, startling the riders and they withdrew. That was the start of it; we chased them down onto the plain of Isandhlwana and towards their camp at the foot of the great hill. They fired big guns at us.' He paused for a few moments as visions of the carnage filled his mind. He saw again those shots crashing into the massed ranks of the uVe, killing and maiming many of his comrades.

'Yes my son I have heard of this.'

Nkosinathi carried on. 'We chased them right into their camp and as it was foretold the sky became dark, the sun turned black and we felt the presence of our ancestors. The spirits were with us though, and it was not long before we had killed them all and their animals – nothing lived.'

Mondli leaned forwards, tipped some snuff onto the back of his hand, and passed the horn to Nkosinathi. 'A great day for the nation and now we can rid ourselves of the Europeans,' he said rising to his feet. 'Come brave warrior, come and eat for I have selected a fine animal to slaughter for the warriors homecoming.'

393

The camp at Khambula nestled near the crest of a hill, fortified with earthworks as a first line of defence with an inner laager of wagons as the main defensive position. The General had heeded lessons from the defeat and ordered that they chain or rope the wagons together to prevent the enemy from breaking through the lines, determined that there should be no repeat of the débâcle of Isandhlwana.

'Sir, there is a large body of horsemen approaching,' said the lookout, his field glasses tight to his eyes.

The lieutenant commanding the forward detachment lifted his own field glass and studied the ground. A hazy cloud of dust was rising slowly between some low-lying hills about six miles distant and beneath it, shapes of horses and riders began to appear. 'Hmm, they don't look like Zulus Private Cowper. What do you make of em?' asked the lieutenant.

'Don't rightly know just yet sir.'

'Sir,' called a voice from behind, 'look, natives approach.' The second lookout was higher up the side of the donga with a better view than the lieutenant.

'Thank you Corporal,' the lieutenant studied the base of the dust cloud and began to wonder if perhaps they were Zulu horsemen after all. 'Thomas, get ready to ride back to camp. As soon as I am sure who they are I want you to report to the Colonel's staff.'

He raised his glasses once more still unsure as to the nature of a force that was growing larger by the minute. Sure enough, the riders were natives and could be Zulus and perhaps they were making ready to attack the camp.

'Sir' said Private Cowper watching developments, 'Sir, they are wearing what looks like red bandannas tied around their heads and some have bush hats and they are wearing European clothes.'

After a short pause, the lieutenant whistled through his teeth with relief,

'I think it's the Natal Native Horse.'

He watched them for a further ten minutes until he could see clearly a European officer riding at their head. 'Thomas' he shouted to the man above him, 'take two privates and deliver this message to the Colonel's staff as soon as you can.' He said as he unfastened his breast pocket, took out his notebook and pencil as they watched the lead party of the oncoming column swung to the left to follow an almost invisible trail.

Standing high in his saddle surveying the landscape, the European officer commanding the force called a halt. With him the men of the Edendale troop, native scouts, tough, proud men who hated the Zulus and who still had past encounters high on their agenda.

'Gama,' said the officer to the man riding next to him, 'go and tell Lieutenant Browne I want to see him will you.'

'Yessah' said the trooper, wheeling his horse around to trot down the line and ten minutes later, he returned accompanied by the officer commanding the Mounted Infantry.

'Browne, the Colonels camp is about two miles over there and we are no doubt being watched by our forward sentries. I don't want any mishaps caused by a trigger happy lookout thinking we are Zulus, might I suggest that you and your men lead us into camp'

'Good idea, I'll move the men up straight away.'

Lieutenant Browne turned his horse, retraced his steps towards the troop of Mounted Infantry waiting at the rear of the column, and gave orders for the troopers to form up in twos. Waving his arm forward, he signalled them to follow him and to prepare for the final approach into camp.

'Well Georgie mi boy, looks like we're back in the thick of it,' said Patrick dismounting.

'Aye, and this looks a bit more like a proper camp than the one those other poor buggers were in.'

Sergeant Donovan' said Lieutenant Browne striding towards them. 'Get the horses watered and fed and then allocate the men their sleeping quarters, we have been given those tents over there by the field kitchen,' he said, pointing towards some smoke rising from the cooking stoves. 'There will be a liaison officer around somewhere to show you exactly which ones.'

At four 'o' clock the following morning a bugler sounded Reveille and it was a refreshed troop of Mounted Infantry that turned out ready for their first day at Khambula. Their orders were to scout the ground towards the approaches of the Hlobane plateau and it was then that Georgie learned between one and two thousand of the enemy were camped on the plateau and rumour had it that some amaSwazi warriors had joined the abaQulusi on the top of Hlobane. The tribesmen had been raiding farms and homesteads over a wide area, accumulating a large herd of cattle and it seemed that Colonel Wood was determined to put a stop to their marauding.

'Sergeant Donovan,' said Lieutenant Browne.

'Sir' Patrick replied, raising his open palm in a slow, early morning salute.

'Donovan, you and Sergeant Thomas will lead your sections to go and scout the base of the plateau. I want you to find us a trail that will take us up to the top. Spread the men out but do not stray too far from myself and number two platoon. We will keep our distance and provide covering fire should you encounter any opposition. Right, let's mount up and get on with it shall we?'

'Yes sir.' Patrick's tail was up, pleased at the chance to get back at the enemy. 'Corporal,' he shouted, 'come here my lad.'

Georgie walked the few yards towards Patrick pulling his horse along behind him.

'Sergeant.'

'Looks like we are on the move and it wouldn't surprise me if we're at 'em shortly. Tell the men to mount up and follow me.'

For each of the next three days, they left the camp immediately after breakfast and were well on their way to the stronghold of Hlobane when the sun came up and it was not long before they realised the difficulty of an assault on the plateau. Strewn with boulders and dislodged rocks, the only way to the top a narrow were a number of steep-sided valleys that cut through the main cliff at crazy angles, a hard climb for the horses and good cover for the abaQulusi.

Georgie was feeling hot and weary from the day's exertions as he lifted his grubby pith helmet to wipe his jacket sleeve across his forehead and soak up sweat running into his eyes. He let his helmet slip back, reached for his water bottle, and took a drink, throwing his head back to let the liquid flow and looked up along the Kloof. The vee shape of the small valley cut through an overhanging ledge and somewhere amongst the vegetation, he caught sight of a movement.

Forgetting his thirst, he let go of the water bottle and reached for his field glasses, lifting them to his eyes in search of the source. He saw nothing, he scanned again to either side, but still nothing then lowered the glasses and rubbed his eyes, the strong sunlight temporarily blinding him. He blinked hard several times and looked again and high above him he spotted two natives slowly climbing up a krantz. They were half way up, dressed in nothing more than loincloths and carrying spears and Georgie guessed that they were probably lookouts and seemed not to have noticed the Redcoats below.

Watching them closely, he became aware of the track they were taking and signalled furiously to the troopers to remain motionless. Little by little, the two natives climbed higher and higher and it became obvious to Georgie that they were following some sort of trail to the plateau above.

'Dickenson,' he called softly to a trooper not more than twenty yards away 'come here.'

The man pulled on his horses' reigns and gently nudged it with his knee, coaxing it towards Georgie.

'Ride to Lieutenant Browne and ask him to come and have a look.'

'What is it Corporal McNamara?' asked the lieutenant, riding up.

Georgie saluted and passed his field glasses across.

'Take a look up there sir, where that valley runs up to the plateau,' he said, pointing upwards.

Pickpockets and Zulus

After a few minutes the lieutenant lowered the glasses, 'I can't see anything, am I missing something Corporal?'

Georgie explained what he thought he had seen in more detail and with some coaxing, the lieutenant's eyes finally fixed upon the feature, revealing a clear though difficult route to the top.

'Well done Corporal, I'm sure Colonel Wood will be pleased. I have heard that several of these paths have been found, but one more will be helpful I am sure.'

The colonel had received intelligence from a variety of sources and was already formulating a plan to assault the Hlobane plateau. He was determined to eliminate the abaQulusi and their amaSwazi allies camped on the plateau with their stolen cattle but more disturbing, were reports that the main Impi was heading their way and he knew he would have to move quickly before the Zulu army arrived.

At two 'o' clock in the morning the troopers were roused from their sleep and after a hurried breakfast they silently saddled their horses ready for the attack on the stronghold at Hlobane. A thousand men and horses slowly winding their way out of camp in the dark, unobserved to put as much distance behind them as they could before sunrise and by noon the column was resting before making its way to the foot of the mountain and a deserted Kraal. To enemy spies they appeared to be making camp, settling down for an extended time and no threat. To add to the illusion the men made much of off saddling their horses, feeding and resting them and as the sun went down, they lit a large number of fires to complete the diversion. From their vantage points high on the sides of the plateau, the lookouts concluded that the Redcoats and their allies had indeed made camp for the night and would prove to be no danger that night.

The lead Induna gave orders to report the arrival of the enemy to their chief, Mbelini, and then he sent several runners out towards Ulundi to alert Ntshingwayo and the Impi still a good half days march from the Hlobane plateau. When Ntshingwayo received the first reports of the Mounted force and believing that they were no threat, called a halt to the march to allow the army settle down for the night. He called for runners and sent his instructions to the Indunas to ready the warriors for battle and then he turned to his advisors

'The British force has made camp, we leave at dawn to meet them in battle and defeat them. Tell the InSangoma to doctor the Impis and protect my warriors from the bullets of the enemy guns.'

Falling silent and steeped in thought, Ntshingwayo mulled over his tactics for the impending battle. He had pleased the King with his victory over the Redcoats at Isandhlwana and the King had entrusted him with the army a second time – he must not fail.

Not far away amongst the warriors of the uVe, Nkosinathi sat up when an Induna and a Sangoma came and passed amongst them. He had come to doctor the regiment, offering dagga leaves to chew on and sprinkling a fine powder on the bodies of the warriors to protect them from bullets and the Induna stood silent, watching the proceedings before finally addressing his soldiers.

'Brave warriors of the uVe, you will have the chance soon to show your courage and your skill as soldiers of the King. We leave at dawn for the mountain to destroy the invaders of our lands. *Bayete*'.

From the thousand warriors massed around him the reply "*Bayete*" boomed out across the plain

'So Nkosinathi, we fight the Redcoats tomorrow. I will kill many of them as I did on plain of the great hill. Their blood will mix with the earth,' said Lindani.

'And I will kill many Redcoats and make my father proud,' said Nkosinathi lifting his spear above his head and making a stabbing movement to show his determination.

He had grown up with only one thought in mind, to serve the King, fought well at Isandhlwana, seen his comrades die in battle and suffered a crisis of confidence. Now they were to fight the Redcoats again and as he looked around at his comrades, grinning, confident and chewing on the Dagga leaves, he exorcised all negative thoughts from his mind. Around him men were boasting of the great deeds they would perform, each one trying to outdo his neighbour with promises of bravery and slaughter. They had won a great battle against the invading army of Redcoats once and they would do the same again.

Cloaked in the of darkness of the night the mobile force of Mounted Infantry and Natal native horse saddled up, led their mounts out of the Kraal and made their way up the slope towards the base of the plateau. Once out of sight of prying eyes, they mounted the horses and the force divided into two.

'Sergeant Donovan, you and Corporal McNamara form your sections up and follow me. I have been ordered to take twenty men to join Colonel Buller's force for the assault on the plateau,' said Lieutenant Browne.

Within minutes, the two sections of Mounted Infantry were following the lieutenant to join a larger of the two forces. Georgie led his section close on the heels of Patricks' and together the whole force moved around the foot of the cliffs in search of the path to the plateau above. Scouts sent ahead guided them and soon they began their ascent, straightforward to begin with, but it was not long before loose rocks and boulders impeded their progress and at around three in the morning the column was forced to halt and dismount. The incline had become too much for the horses, the troopers had to struggle on foot, pulling their steeds along behind them, and steadily wind their way along the path up towards the plateau.

'Bloody raining again,' said a voice behind Georgie, as the first heavy spots began to splatter around them.

'Quiet that man,' retorted Georgie, well aware that abaQulusi lookouts might hear them. 'Whose side are you on?' he hissed.

The man fell silent just as a first finger of lightening flashed across the sky to illuminate the landscape, thunder rumbled in the distance and then a second flash. Georgie felt vulnerable, anyone could see them and then the rain became a torrent and thankfully they were once more enveloped in a cloak of invisibility.

The rain made the going tough, the ground became slippery and hanging tightly to the reigns, Georgie glanced over his shoulder to see how his horse was faring, almost invisible in the darkness with her black coat.

'Come on Blackie,' he coaxed.

He had ridden her many times during night hours but none had been as fraught with difficulty as the present. The horse halted, standing still for a moment and Georgie had to pull hard on her reigns, but still she would not move. He swivelled round and looked her straight in the eye.

'Come on girl, we have a job to do. We can't be holding up the rest can we? Come on, come on,' he said, gently tugging at the reigns.

It did the trick, Blackie snorted an indignant reply and put one foot forward, feeling for a purchase and then another and gradually she moved forwards. Georgie pulled a little harder, upping her pace until she was moving comfortably and for a further hour, the two of them negotiated the incline. Eventually the storm passed over, the rain began to ease giving some relief to the cold, wet soldiers.

They reached the crest of the plateau just as the blackness of the night morphed into the grey African dawn and they could make out the features of the land. For several minutes, they rested, checked their equipment and then, ahead of them, came the sound of gunfire.

Bullets whistled overhead and instinctively Georgie pulled Blackie towards the cover of some large boulders and from the direction of the shooting, he heard a man scream.

'Blast it,' he said out loud, 'you men get in here behind these rocks.'

The troopers took no second bidding, rapidly following Georgie's example and running for cover.

'Right, Barney, you and Dickinson hold the horses, the rest of you follow me.'

The well-drilled troopers were soon scrambling over rocks, through undergrowth and towards the sound of the gunshots. Away to his left Georgie caught sight of Patrick performing a similar manoeuvre, leading his men from cover to cover to close on the enemy. This was what they were here for, what the Army had trained them for and there was a burning desire in each man to avenge the death of the eight hundred comrades who had perished at the hands of the Zulus only a few months before.

Ducking low, keeping scrub and boulders between him and the ambushers Georgie caught up with a lead party busy firing at groups of abaQulusi holed up in a series of small openings in the rocky cliff face. On either side of the trail, men lay wounded and a few feet away a lieutenant was shouting orders then Georgie spotted a group of natives behind a large rock at the head of the narrow gully. He could see that just a few defenders holed up in those rocks could hold back a whole army if they so desired and he was determined break that desire.

'Thomas, Kilkenny, this way and keep low,' he shouted, waving the men towards him as he slithered across the muddy trail.

Unseen by defenders preoccupied with the column stranded on the narrow pathway, Georgie led his small party on an outflanking manoeuvre through the undergrowth and luckily the enemy were not looking in his direction. Carrying his Carbine in one hand Georgie gestured with the other for the men to lay flat, to work their way forward on their bellies and for a good twenty yards, they slid like snakes through the undergrowth. Eventually they reached a rocky outcrop, decent cover, within range of the defenders and one by one, the troopers took up their position.

'Let 'em have it lads', said Georgie and within seconds a hail of lead was screaming towards the native gunmen.

Two fell immediately, and then two more and then the others, stunned by the surprise attack, turned to run back over the crest of the escarpment but Georgie was determined to stop them.

'Quick lads, follow me,' he shouted, his tail up and ready for a fight.

Breaking cover, he ran towards the recently vacated positions of the abaQulusi and from there he was able to see a lot more of them and taking up new positions the troopers fired as fast and as accurately as they could, accounting for a good half dozen of the enemy. They were no match when it came to a shootout, their ancient weapons useless against the more modern weaponry of the troopers and overwhelmed, the attacking force hurriedly retreated, discarding weapons and leaving their dead and wounded as they went. Then it was the turn of the native horsemen whom the enemy had pinned down, they saw their chance and rose up to chase the retreating abaQulusi with blood curdling shouts, making short work of any they managed to catch.

'Good work Georgie,' shouted Patrick from across the pathway. He had taken similar action with his men but had been unable to secure good enough cover to have much effect able only to observe Georgie's progress.

Georgie nodded in reply, not taking his eyes off the path ahead for more of the enemy might be lying in wait for them. He scanned the terrain, the caves and boulders that might be hiding men and satisfied that they had cleared them out, called to his men.

'Anyone hurt?' and seeing that they were all intact said 'time to get back to the horses lads. The Colonel is already moving.'

Mounted on his Bay and followed by his men Colonel Buller, the officer in charge, came sweeping past. 'Come on, time to give 'em what for, get mounted and follow me,' he shouted.

By now, the sun had risen, the sky was clearing and Georgie joined the rest of the Mounted Infantry making their way towards the colonel who was gesticulating to his subordinates. The going was much less arduous on the plateau, mainly of a wide sweep of lush grassland and a stunning scene after such an arduous approach. However, Georgie had no time for sightseeing; in the middle distance, they spotted large groups of abaQulusi.

'Get the men into skirmishing order,' shouted Lieutenant Browne. 'We are to take the left flank as the colonel makes a sweep across to that hillock over there.' He pointed to a small brown mound surrounded by a few mimosa trees.

The troop cantered off to take up position, to spread out in an extended the line right across the plain and at a brisk pace, began to move forward watched by some abaQulusi who could see that they were outnumbered, out gunned, and were in no mood to take on the troopers. Melting into the grasslands, their threat to the colonel's force became non-existent and from his commanding view of the plateau, Colonel Buller issued his orders for the retrieval of the grazing cattle.

A few minutes later, an officer approached Lieutenant Browne who called a halt and exchanged words with him. Saluting the messenger wheeled his horse about and the lieutenant cantered across his line of his men telling them of his orders.

'We are to secure the flank whilst the Natal contingent round up the cattle, then we are to escort them to the lower plateau and on towards the camp at Khambula. It looks like we will not be meeting much resistance, but keep your eyes and ears open anyway. Carry on Sergeant,' he said to Patrick.

'You heard the lieutenant, let's get going.'

The sun was warming and Georgie felt his damp clothes beginning to dry off as he led his section across the grassland, fanning out to secure the ground they had already won. Each man had his Carbine at the ready and as the morning wore on, the troopers of the Natal Native horse rounded up several hundred head of cattle to begin moving them towards the edge of the upper plateau and flanking them Georgie was riding behind Lieutenant Browne when the lieutenant suddenly pulled up his horse.

'Hold it men, don't come any closer,' he shouted, frantically bringing his troopers to halt and jumping from his mount to crouch and peer over the edge of the precipice. They had stumbled upon a shear drop of over one hundred feet and could go no further.

'Sergeant Donovan, go and fetch the colonel will you.'

'Sir,' said, Patrick swinging his horse around to gallop the one hundred and fifty or so yards to where the colonel was observing progress.

'Sir, Lieutenant Browne asks that you join him immediately.'

Buller looked at him, returned his salute and without a word trotted across to the still dismounted Browne.

'What is it?' he asked dismounting.

'Looks bad sir,' said Browne, 'what do you suggest?'

'We will not be able to descend here, too steep and dangerous and it's a long way down,' said the colonel twisting his moustache between his fore finger and thumb. 'Might the men get down there if we leave the horses and cattle behind?'

'I suppose so sir, but it's still risky.'

'Hmm...' pondered the colonel. 'Tell you what, I will send Lieutenant Chatt on ahead with a detachment to bury our dead and we will just have to about turn and take the long route back down.' He spoke to one of his aides who had accompanied him and issued orders. 'Send Lieutenant Chatt and a detachment of thirty or so men to find and bury the dead whilst we re-organize this force. We'll about turn and head towards the more gentle slopes over there,' he said pointing to the far side of the plateau two or three miles away. 'Dashed bad luck, what' he said to no one in particular and gazed down the steep sided Krantz to see what might have been and suddenly froze. 'Gad, look at that lot.'

'What is it sir?'

'Look down there' said Buller feeling for his field glasses.

'Good heavens,' said Browne equally unable to contain his feelings, 'Is that what I think it is?'

408

'Certainly is lieutenant,' said the colonel concentrating hard on the view through his lens. 'It's the whole bloody Zulu Impi and they are heading our way.' For a few moments, he weighed the situation up, thinking through his limited options. 'Chatt is going to run straight into that lot, send one of your men after him to warn him and order him back.'

'Sergeant Donovan, despatch one of your men to go after Lieutenant Chatt and his platoon and tell them of the approaching Zulus and that the Colonel suggests...'

'Not suggests lieutenant, order him to head north and get himself and his men off this infernal mountain and that goes for us too,' snapped Buller.

Chapter 10

The first time Ntshingwayo had fought the British it was the middle of the southern summer and it was hot, but in early autumn sun was less fierce the regiments were more mobile, able to keep their loping run for longer periods and less need of water. He nudged his horse towards some higher ground to sit for a while and watch the magnificent sight of his army on the move. Arrayed across a vast area of undulating grassland, the air was thick with their regimental songs and war chants as the Impis streamed towards the high plateau in the distance.

Ntshingwayo felt proud and as the commander was not immune from the high spirits of the warriors even at seventy years old. He was still a fit and able warrior, determined to lead from the front and sliding to the ground from his horse, he beckoned one of his bodyguards, handed him the reigns and snapped his fingers in a terse order to the rest. The expressionless warriors, the best in the army formed up behind him and at a steady jog, Ntshingwayo led them towards the mountain, the regiments saluting him with their war songs leaving him happy to see his soldiers were eager for the fight.

As the warrior of warriors ran, he turned over in his mind the possibilities unfolding. His scouts had reported regularly with news of the Redcoats and he knew that they were not up against a large force. The column of horse soldiers could not hope to outrun them amongst the uneven ground of the steep and rocky trails where he would catch them and annihilate them.

The young warriors of the uVe felt excitement in their ranks as they trotted steadily towards the distant plateau. As he ran, Nkosinathi chewed on the dagga leaves, their effect to quell the hunger pangs and leaving feeling that he could run forever. Alongside him, the men of the uVe sang and chanted, chewed on their dagga leaves their bravado spilling over.

'I will kill ten of the enemy,' shouted a warrior next to him.

'Ten?' echoed others around him.

'I will kill twenty.'

'And I will rip their hearts out with my bare hands,' shouted yet another. 'I will show the white soldiers their own hearts as they stop beating.'

They cheered and chanted, the drugs having their effect, as a feeling of invincibility began to cloak reality and as the black horde swept along, a worried Colonel Buller watched them his field glasses.

'Looks a difficult situation, what d'you think Browne?'

'I think, sir, that our only chance is to abandon the cattle and head for the pass or find another route down to the lower plateau as quickly as we can before they start their outflanking manoeuvre. If they manage to surround us it will be extremely difficult to break through.'

'I know it man, deuce I know it. Tell the men to form up, take your troop to the vanguard and let us get off this God forsaken mountain before it's too late. The pass it is, we haven't time to look for another route; at least Russell's force is down there to give us some support.'

Hastily the Officers compiled a plan, briefed the N.C.O's and gave the order to abandon the prize cattle. Georgie and Patrick looked at each other with grim expressions on their faces and knowing that they were in for a fight they turned to wave their men forward.

'Guns at the ready men,' shouted Patrick, leading them at the gallop behind Lieutenant Browne followed by Georgie and his troopers and behind them came the native horsemen scattering the cattle as they ploughed through their midst. The herd would have made a good prize but the soldiers had their mind on other things, self-preservation was their top priority.

The abaQulusi, keeping out of range during most of the morning now sensed the tide was beginning to turn and started to attack, compounding the situation.

The natives on the plateau had heard of the approaching Zulu army and that knowledge had re-enforced any courage they had left. They had hidden themselves from view after the first assault by the British and Colonial soldiers, but now a new sense of confidence was driving them to make tentative forays against the passing column, and with increasing vigour, they pursued them towards the trail.

Reaching the edge of the steep incline under a hail of spears and gunshots, the native horsemen dismounted and began their tortuous descent. The main force of regular troops and white volunteers gave covering fire, pinning the abaQulusi down behind rocks and stout tree trunks. Their antiquated guns tending to miss their target for the most part, but as the retreat became more and more disorderly, they ventured out amongst the men and horses struggling to escape to use knives and spears.

The rains had made the ground treacherous for the horses and their steel shoes, leaving them incapable of acquiring a purchase on the slimy, wet stones and it soon became apparent that they were a liability. Some of the fleeing men abandoned them and ran pell-mell down the slope only to find more attackers waiting for them. It was a situation to the abaQulusi's liking, their stabbing spears and knives were much more effective against running men and they killed them with glee.

'Here, give those men some cover,' shouted Captain Browne, jumping from his horse, revolver at the ready.

First one, then another of the attacking abaQulusi fell to his accurate fire, the Mounted Infantry ran through the drills they had practised repeatedly during the preceding weeks. One man holding onto the horses' reigns whilst the rest took up firing positions to kill as many of the enemy as possible before retreating to another secure position to repeat the manoeuvre.

Georgie's main attribute was a clear head under fire, he soon despatched a number of the enemy, repeatedly finding a target, and then the order came to resume the descent. Seven hundred feet below native levies were proving that escape was possible but at a cost. Dead and dying men littered the path, horses staggered aimlessly, their bellies ripped open by the vicious, stabbing Assegais and captives screamed out as they were hurled to their deaths from the precipice.

413

'Get the horses and let's get out of here, those Zulus can't be far away by now and I for one don't want to be caught with my trousers down,' shouted Georgie as he grabbed Blackie's reigns to pull her after him towards the first of the slippery slopes. Georgie was certainly calm enough but what began to emerge from the undergrowth far below made even his blood run cold. The vanguard of the Zulu army had arrived and was moving through the trees, stabbing their spears into the panicking remnants of the native contingent and he could see that anyone on foot was as sure as dead.

'Follow me lads,' he shouted, mounting Blackie ready for the tortuous descent. It was now or never, the abaQulusi were becoming bolder by the minute, their numbers increasing and far below a far greater danger was asserting itself.

'Are you alright Georgie?' said Patrick as he and his troopers joined the general melee. Georgie did not look round, there was no need for he had soldiered with Patrick long enough to know what was behind him.

'I am,' he shouted, 'let's get out of here,' and after a short pause, 'Ellen will miss us if we don't make it.'

The remark galvanised Patrick. He had never been in love before and did not fully understand what the emotion could do to a man but on hearing her name he seemed to grow six inches taller and his eyes flashed with a steely determination. He was going to survive, he had to, he could not die out here amongst these heathens and never see Ellen again.

'I'm whit ye boy, let's get at em,' said Patrick coaxing his horse down through the mud and boulders.

There was a sort of loose coherence and discipline amongst the troopers, they were professional soldiers,

414

drilled incessantly for years, but there was also a feeling of every man for himself. Somehow, they managed to scramble down the treacherous ravine, shooting and slashing with their swords at the abaQulusi in their path and more than one soldier fell to an onslaught of spears, many a horse succumbed. Georgie and Patrick, fighting side by side, managed to mount their horses and attempted to force a way through. They rode as much as possible, dismounting and leading the horses on foot where the terrain became too difficult; several times Blackie stumbled and sank to her knees, before recovering to continue their descent.

'We will have to rush them or the Zulu horsemen ahead will cut us to pieces if we try to slip by one by one. Sergeant Donovan, Corporals McNamara and Jones form your men up as best you can and follow me at the charge,' said Captain Browne taking the lead.

Under normal circumstances, a charge would be in order but here it seemed almost impossible, the steeply sloping ground, lose boulders and slippery, muddy earth a hazard in itself, but it was their only hope. So, in a disorderly formation, Captain Brown led the Mounted Infantry down the sloping track and on towards the Zulu horsemen lying in wait.

The Zulus looked magnificent sat astride their ponies, great plumes of feathers sprouting from their headgear, their black and white shields held out in front of them and armed with some of the latest Martini-Henry repeating rifles plundered from Isandhlwana. The troopers could see the guns and wondered if they were about to breathe their last but the aim Zulu of the sharpshooters was as bad as ever, most shots passing ineffectually over their heads.

'Give 'em a volley men then we'll give them a taste of British steel. Charge,' shouted Captain Browne drawing his sword.

As one, the troop surged forward with their Carbines firing from the hip the rider's knees pressed tightly against their horse's ribs, knowing that fall meant certain death and two hundred yards away the sound of gunfire reached Nkosinathi's ears. The call of "*Usuthu*" rang out; the warriors of the uVe regiment surged forwards towards the fight, eager to prove their worth and from his vantage point Ntshingwayo watched the battle unfold. He lifted his eyes skywards, praying to his ancestors for a swift and successful outcome, control was out of his hands now, his Indunas were the ones in charge and they knew what they had to do. The soldiers of his Impis were strong and fearless and he believed that soon victory would be his for a second time.

'Come, we will follow the Impis to the mountain and watch the destruction of the white soldiers,' he said to his entourage of advisors and bodyguards.

Not far away the uVe had reached the foot of the pass, just as the first of the natives on horseback broke through followed by desperate men on foot. The blood curdling cry of "*Usuthu*" rang out again and again as the warriors fell upon the unfortunate men. Lightly armed and terrified they came crashing through the undergrowth in amongst the trees, scrambling over boulders and their eyes were wide in terror at the fate that awaited them if they could not break through the gathering ranks of Zulus.

A small group of native soldiers sporting ret headbands ran across Nkosinathi's path and immediately he gave chase, his war shield held high and his stabbing spear at the ready. Several more of the uVe ran alongside him, whooping and shouting obscenities to instil even more fear into the fugitives and ahead of them, a man stumbled, twisting his ankle, he was finished. Bravely he turned to face the approaching Zulus and still holding his gun he at least had the presence of mind to let fly several shots, wounding two of the warriors before the remaining pursuers overwhelmed him, driving their spears deep into his body.

Behind the fleeing native troops came British, Boer and colonial volunteers, the mounted men thundering through the Zulus ranks, the pure mass of the horses helping them to reach safety. Those on foot were less fortunate and having a difficult time of it and even as the horses passed the warriors drove their spears into their bellies, bringing down the riders. As they fell the Zulus closed in but these men were not as easy to kill, they were desperate, but they were tough and disciplined and each had a gun. The line of Zulus fell under the first volley but immediately a second wave took their place and soon it was hand to hand fighting. The Zulus were bigger and physically stronger that the Europeans but the troopers were fighting for their lives and it showed.

The Mounted Infantry reached the melee and Georgie drew his sword, slashing at the Zulus surrounding him and alongside him Patrick and the rest of the troop fought gallantly. Slowly they forced their way through the throng and reaching level ground the going became easier for the horses. Suddenly Georgie felt Blackie stumble as she took the full force of an Assegai in her chest and, stricken though she was, she carried him for a further hundred yards before sinking to her knees, blood gushing from the wound.

She was not yet dead, but Georgie knew instinctively that it would not be long as she rolled on her side her eyes wild, her tongue covered in a red froth. His sword fell from his grasp and he let go of the reigns, stepping away from her to pulling out his revolver and stand his ground. His coolness had not deserted him and he took aim, killing the first of two warriors bearing down on upon him, wounding the other. He fired again and then, from out of nowhere, a loose horse ran towards him offering salvation from the mayhem that was engulfing him. He reached towards the reigns dangling loosely from the horse's bridal and ran a few paces alongside the animal but he was unable to grasp them and his last chance seemed to have gone. Two more warriors came at him and he quickly shot the leading man, the other lifted his spear and Georgie pulled the trigger, but the chamber was empty and for once, his coolness deserted him. He felt desperation, a panic take hold as the Zulu approached, his stabbing spear at the ready, but it lasted only seconds, the Zulu's head whipped sideways and he collapsed to the ground.

'Hang on Georgie boy, I'm whit ye.'

It was Patrick; he had seen Georgie's predicament and his well-aimed shot had smashed into the Zulu's skull saving his friend. Quickly he rode his horse alongside Georgie emptying his revolver into some onrushing warriors as he came.

'Get yourself up here Georgie, come on lad hurry.'

Georgie took little persuading; with his heart beating madly he jumped onto the rump of Patrick's horse, gripping the saddle with both hands to steady himself as

Patrick kicked his horse into a gallop and easily broke through the remaining natives barring their path. On they went at a crazy gallop towards troopers who had already made it through the gauntlet and were regrouping under Captain Browne.

The troopers who were still armed let off a volley to dissuade any Zulus contemplating charging their position and on Captain Browne's order made their escape onto the relatively open spaces at the foot of the pass. After a while the panic subsided, the Zulu's were not pursuing them and Georgie was able to shift his position on the horse, sitting upright behind Patrick and for the rest of the day, the remnants of the force travelled back to Khambula in almost total silence. Once they realised that they were safe the men recovered their composure and keeping a watchful eye out for any Zulus made their way back to the camp at Khambula.

'Bejasus, that was a close one Georgie,' Patrick finally said tipping his helmet to the back of his head.

Georgie did not reply immediately, the cries of dying men were still ringing in his ears and the closeness of his own death had unnerved him. He had been in a few fights but this one had been the hardest and bloodiest and he thanked his maker that he had survived in one piece. Then he thought of Blackie, she was only a horse but she had saved his life and for that, he was grateful.

'It was..., bloody close, too close if you ask me. I think we lost a few good men today Patrick,' he said at last.

'Aye, we did, God rest their souls.'

Silence descended once more and as the weary troop reached the outer defences of the camp, a gap in the ring of laagered wagons opened up to allow them to pass through, the news of their defeat already common knowledge.

'Good on you lads,' said a voice as they passed. 'We'll give 'em what for next time' said another.

Even after the defeat moral was high, the men were confident their efforts to construct strong defences would pay dividends once the main body Zulus attacked. They had laboured long and hard in digging the trenches and throwing up earthworks and to a man, they were confident that they could withstand any frontal attack thrown at them. Everyone knew of the heroics at Rorke's Drift and even the lowliest of private soldiers understood the shortcomings of Isandhlwana.

'Jump down Corporal' ordered Patrick as they reached the picket line. 'Feed and water my horse corporal, and give her a rub down then we will see what to do about getting you a new mount.'

'Yes Sergeant' said Georgie, showing some respect in front of the watching Infantrymen.

'Sergeant Donovan,' called Lieutenant Browne. 'We've lost some good men today and the first thing I want to do is to have a roll call. After that, we can clean up and get some food; none of us has eaten since last night. Go and find the Colour Sergeant and get things moving.'

Patrick saluted and left to carry out his orders whilst Georgie led his horse to the picket line and took off its saddle and putting a bucket of feed under its nose. He looked at the animal's weary eyes, she looked blown and he found himself thinking of Blackie again. They had travelled the length and breadth of Natal together, been through a lot and now she was gone.

'Georgie,' called Barney snapping him out of his thoughts. 'Let's get some grub, come on.'

They made their way to the mess tents and along the way bumped into Patrick who told them that they had lost fifteen men from the troop, more than twenty horses and most had lost equipment in their haste to escape the clutches of the Zulus. Georgie was well aware of losses, he was left with no more than his uniform, his horse was dead, his Carbine and sword lost along the way.

Outside the mess tent, they lined up with other soldiers for their dinner and as usual it was bully beef but after their ordeal, it was very welcome. They soon had their plates wiped clean and lighting up their pipes the majority of them seemed unaffected by their experience.

'Do you think the Zulus will attack tomorrow Patrick?' asked Georgie.

'Nothing's so sure.'

The uVe, flushed with its recent success, resumed the march towards the British fortifications at Khambula. They were hungry too, they had not eaten for more than a day but spirits were high and the dagga helped stave off their hunger pangs. Once they had overrun the camp, they knew that they could gorge themselves on the spoils of war and it would not be long.

'We will win another great victory Nkosinathi and then we will return home to our Kraals in triumph. The King will give us many cattle to feast on,' said a warrior walking alongside him.

'Yes, tomorrow we will kill them just as we did today. Perhaps then the white army will leave our lands' said

Lindani. 'The King is pleased with us I know it. It is said that when we defeat the enemy he will give the uVe permission to marry. Yes boys that will be a just reward for us,'

The others grinned, their hunger forgotten for if there was one thing that took Zulu warriors mind off the hardships he endured in the service of the King; it was the thought of a woman. The King's permission to marry and the right to wear the head-ring was a prize indeed.

In the early morning, within a few miles of Khambula, Ntshingwayo stood with his generals scanning the countryside.

'The victory yesterday was easy oh great one, the King will be pleased, will he not?' said an Induna.

'He will and by now the messengers will have reached him with the news. Today we will destroy this invading army,' said Ntshingwayo, a hint of disdain in his voice. 'The white soldiers are brave and good fighters but they are no match for the Impi. We will ride to that hill over there,' he said, pointing with his spear and nudging his horse forward across open ground to meet the head of the advancing Impis.

Georgie was pleased with his new mount; she was strong and obedient, and trained and as he patted her neck, he looked around. They were six or seven miles from camp, on some high ground at the centre of the plain and the men of his section were alert and on the lookout for the enemy.

'Corporal, I think there is something under that hill,' said a trooper.

Pickpockets and Zulus

Georgie lifted his glasses and looked in the general direction, at first seeing nothing but then something did catch his eye, a shadow yet there was no feature of the land that could cast such a shadow. Suddenly his heart missed a beat and he involuntarily leaned forward as the realization dawning upon him that they had found the Impi. For several seconds more he examined the landscape until he was sure and then he tried to estimate the size of the approaching forces. He knew that their camp held around two thousand men but he was witnessing the approach of a far greater number. How many, he did not know but guessed at five thousand and this was only the van.

'That's them alright,' he said, lowering the glasses. 'How many do you think there are?' he asked the trooper next to him.

'Thousands, Corporal.'

'That is not very helpful you idiot. I have to report what we see and I don't want to give any false information.'

'Thousands Corporal,' the man said again, 'that will do for the General. There is a hell of a lot more of them than us, that's all he will need to know.'

Georgie could not argue with his logic. 'Come on then, let's be off I don't want to be here when that lot turn up.'

The troopers wheeled their horses round to head back to Khambula as fast as they could.

'Sir, I have to report the sighting of the Zulu army,' he said to the Adjutant standing outside the headquarters tent.

'Then you had better come inside,' said the officer, resplendent in a Lieutenant Colonel's uniform, a red sash hanging smartly across his chest, contrasting starkly with Georgie's scruffy tunic jacket.

The Commanding Officer was sitting at one of the tables engrossed in a map, when Georgie was ushered in. He had spent long weeks preparing his defences and now he was examining the various scenarios he considered possible when the attack came. He looked up as Georgie and the Adjutant approached.

'Yes man, what is it.'

'Sir, a report of the sighting of the Zulu army,' said the Adjutant.

Colonel Wood's head lifted immediately. 'Where are they?'

'Sir, the Corporal's patrol report seeing Zulu army several miles from camp and they are heading our way. Show the Colonel, Corporal' said the Adjutant.

'Heading our way? Well that's a surprise Gillard,' he said, no hint of sarcasm in his voice. 'Can you read a map Corporal? Show me where you think they are,' he said, beckoning Georgie towards the desk.

'Remove your hat in the presence of the Commanding Officer Corporal,' said the officious Gillard.

'Not now Gillard,' said the Colonel overruling him. 'Now where are they Corporal?'

Georgie peered over the map, he knew a little of basic map reading but out in the field the troopers tended to work with landmarks a compass and the passage of the sun. He recognised the hills surrounding the plain where he had sighted the Zulu army and from the compass point, he was sure that the location was correct.

'Here sir,' he said, pointing to a gap between the hills, 'this is where we saw them and they seemed to be heading straight towards camp.'

'How far do you think they are away Corporal?'

'I would say at least ten miles Sir.'

'Hmm...,that means we probably won't see them for another three or four hours, well after midday. Very good Corporal, do me one more thing and then you and your men can have your breakfast.'

'Sir.'

'Find Colonel Buller and ask him to come here at the double.'

'Sir,' said Georgie saluting and turning on his heel to march smartly out of the tent.

425

Chapter 11

'Donovan, get the men saddled up whilst I go and organize the other sections. We have our orders and will be leaving camp soon,' said Lieutenant Chatt.

'Sir' replied Patrick in his own inimitable way. 'You heard the man, saddle up and let's be off.'

The men mounted their horses and waited a few minutes until Colonel Buller appeared astride his horse to face his force of one hundred Mounted Infantry and native horsemen, a mixed bunch but good fighting men. Every one of them had seen action and none had been found wanting.

'Men, we've been keeping an eye on the Zulus ever since we discovered their path. The main Impi is three or four miles away and a patrol of Transvaal Rangers is keeping an eye on them. Colonel Wood has ordered me to engage part of that force and bring them onto the guns. You all know the colonel has prepared defensive positions and as he told me this morning there wouldn't be much point in all the hard work if he didn't put them to good use. So, you will follow me and we will engage the enemy, lure them onto the guns and towards the prepared defences. Once they begin to attack us we are to retire, d'you understand. Listen for my bugler sounding the retreat and fall back in an orderly manner.

We lost some good men yesterday and now it's our chance to avenge them so let's show these savages how a British Army can fight.'

There was a murmur of approval from the ranks but they knew that many lightly armed native allies had deserted during the night and more worrying still was the departure of a force of Boer Burgers, tough men who knew how to fight the Zulu but still, Colonel Wood was confident. He had spent much time and effort preparing his defences and felt the time was drawing closer when the British Army would have the chance to fight on their terms and reverse the failures of previous months.

Several miles away, Ntshingwayo ordered his army to rest and told the InSangoma to pass amongst the regiments to administer their protective medicines. His lookouts had reported the approach of a body of horsemen, and not far beyond them was the camp itself and in the ranks of the Zulu warriors excitement was building. The drugs had heightened their senses and as the commander ordered the Impis forward, they caught sight of the riders approaching.

'*Usuthu*' cried the voices of twenty thousand warriors slapping their spears against their shields, making a sound like thunder and then they lifted their shields high above their heads so that the watching Ntshingwayo could see where each regiment was before the battle started.

Ntshingwayo pursed his lips, keeping his own council and looked ahead towards the enemy camp. He knew from his scouts the strength of the British force, of the desertions during the night and the basic disposition of the camp's defences. His warriors outnumbered the enemy ten to one, they were brave – they would charge the guns and overwhelm the defenders. Yes, he would claim another great victory.

'Give the command to start the assault,' he said,

The great Zulu army began to manoeuvre into its classic Bull's Horns formation, the uVe took its place at the right horn, "*Usuthu*" they chanted again as they moved forward at a steady trot. Nkosinathi's heart thumped and he slapped the clenched fist of his spear hand against his chest

'Kill, Kill, Kill the Redcoats,' he shouted.

Suddenly, ahead of them, Buller's force appeared the horses and riders spread out across a wide front, a sight to fill any warrior with bellicosity. The uVe were no exception, young and over confident their war cries intensifying, they broke into a headlong charge and disengaged themselves from the main battle formation.

'We have them,' shouted a voice, 'kill them. "*Usuthu*" chanted others and the uVe surged forward, the young warriors eager for battle and with them came the iNgobamakhosi regiment and to Ntshingwayo's dismay he watched his carefully planned assault began to fragment.

Amongst the mounted soldiers, Georgie had his eyes on Colonel Buller, waiting for his command and as the Colonel reigned in his horse, he raised his arm. It was the signal for the riders to halt and for the bugler to sound the dismount.

'Dismount men,' shouted Georgie.

The trooper designated to look after the horses took his comrades reins, allowing the rest to take kneeling positions unhindered and ready for the approaching Zulus. They lifted their Carbines to their shoulders, took aim, the bugler sounded the order to fire and a hundred Carbines exploded into life. Most of the shots were accurate and many warriors fell as the troopers fired repeatedly, the lead bullets passing straight through the black and white shields. As warriors fell those still standing became enraged and were determined to kill the troopers but when they were less than fifty yards from the line of Redcoats the bugle sounded again. Hastily the troopers slung their rifles over their shoulders, remounted and turned their horses round to fall back three hundred yards before the bugle ordered them to repeat the drill.

Nkosinathi's blood was up, he and many like him were determined to reach the soldiers before they could remount their horses a second time but they could not cover the ground fast enough. Twice more they failed to catch the troopers and on the ground behind them over four hundred of their number lay dead or dying. The manoeuvre had worked, the young warriors, with no concept of tactics, had broken formation and had followed their tormentors into a trap.

'Fall back towards the laager men,' called Georgie as the bugle sound the retreat for the last time.

They had retreated in good order and were close to the laagered wagons and as he looked along the line to the west, he saw some native horsemen breaking out between the wagons and running away.

'Bastards,' he called after them then a spear narrowly missed him and reminded him of the attacking Zulus.

Kicking his horse forwards, he followed the rest of the troop through the gap between the wagons and once through Infantrymen quickly pulled the wagon back to close the gap. To both his left and his right riflemen were taking aim and when the order came to fire, the breech loading rifles poured twelve rounds a minute into the oncoming Zulus.

Nkosinathi was with the leading rank and running hard towards the defences, scarcely noticing the bullets, until on either side of him, he saw warriors falling to the ground. When he was within fifty yards of the defences, his courage finally failed him and he fell to the ground shaking. Desperately he searched for any cover that he could find as bullets whizzed over his head, around him, warriors were falling and he thought that this was not how it was supposed to be.

Amongst the defenders, Georgie unslung his Carbine from his shoulder, threw his bandolier to the ground, and crouched behind a wheel of one of the big ox wagons. He was not going to miss the chance of a pot shot or two at the Zulus. There were thousands of them and every shot had to count or they might all be lying dead by nightfall.

'Got you, you bastard,' he said as his first target fell twenty or more yards from the wagons.

'That's only one,' said a northern English accent. 'Thar'll need to put daan a few more that that lad.'

Georgie said nothing; he simply pressed his lips tightly together and squinted his eyes in search of another target. It was not long in coming. A huge Zulu sprang up from nowhere to leap over the wagon yoke, but even before he had landed, Georgie had put a bullet between his eyes and sent him flying back the way he had come.

'Good shootin' lad,' said the northern voice.

They defended their position vigorously until the assault was broken. The Zulus suddenly stopped their charge and retreated and Nkosinathi was amongst them, crawling across the grassy slope and slithering through depressions like a snake. Shots still whistled close to his ears and he felt alone, his comrades were dead or had disappeared from the battlefield and his only company were the wounded and the corpses. Most had died instantly, catapulted backwards by the powerful rounds of the Martini Henrys to lay spread-eagled, lifeless, their eyes staring into space, and he shuddered as he crawled past them.

It was not over yet; the uVe and the iNgobamakhosi were quite literally a sideshow, the main body, the centre of the horn formation, was moving forward on the attack, the older more experienced regiments and their superior weight of numbers beginning to tell. Overwhelmed, the forward positions of the defensive ring slowly fell back and behind the barricade of ox wagons, soldiers ran to new positions to counter the onslaught.

At first, the Impis came at the charge but as more and more fell, their advance slowed and unsure of the defenders positions, became unsettled. They were well versed in open country warfare where they had enough space to out manoeuvre the enemy. It had worked ever since the time of King Shaka, the father of the nation, but to attack a well-defended position such as this was a new experience.

Ntshingwayo watched the progress of the army, annoyed that the young warriors of the uVe and iNgobamakhosi had chased after the mounted force. Their ill-discipline in breaking ranks had disrupted the formation, leaving a wide gap in the line and so to try to retrieve the situation he sent Indunas to muster the retreating warriors and sent for his reserves. Looking again at the chest of the formation, he was horrified to see it falter and his intuition told him something was badly amiss. Then the Impis regrouped and the attack continued but to his dismay, white helmets appeared as if by magic from the ground as Infantry, concealed in trenches appeared to join the fight their guns finding easy targets. Warriors fell and the Impi faltered and from the barricades came fire that was even more devastating and his army began to crumble.

the sound of the increasing gunfire rang in Nkosinathi's ears as crawled the last few yards towards the shelter of some rocks and crouching low he managed to run the last few yards to safety and to his surprise, found that he was not alone. Many of the warriors were unable to withstand the concentrated fire of the Europeans and they too had broken ranks to escape the guns.

'Nkosinathi,' said a voice.

It was Somopho, sitting cross-legged and looking miserable and beside him, equally miserable, were more of the regiment.

'Somopho, my friend, what are you doing here?'

'The same as you I think, we have lost many friends today. The medicine they gave us does not work, the guns of the white men are killing us, and it is how it was at Isandhlwana. What are we to do Nkosinathi?'

'If we stay here and do not fight we will be found and clubbed to death as cowards by the King's executioners,' said Nkosinathi grimly, 'follow me.'

"*Usuthu*" they shouted, as Nkosinathi sprang to his feet, inspiring them and at the run, they renewed the attack.

''Ere they come again,' said the northern voice.

'Get ready men, take aim and fire on my command,' said the lieutenant in charge.

The soldiers had a good defensive position behind the ox wagons, the piled biscuit boxes and grain sacks making it difficult for the Zulu warriors even to see them and in front of the wagons was yet another obstacle to the onrushing warriors. The soldiers had filled in the uneven ground, sloping it up towards the line of laagered wagons and creating a killing ground without any cover whatsoever. Any Zulus exposed to the guns in this area would have nowhere to go and it was into this hell that Nkosinathi led his comrades.

'Fire at will,' a short, sharp order and the guns opened up their murderous barrage.

Bullets flew in all directions, buzzing like angry bees, striking home and killing most of the first wave of onrushing Zulus. Nkosinathi was lucky, the one with his name on it simply grazed his forehead but it was enough to send him sprawling to the ground, unconscious, and the attack failed. Surviving warriors began a disorderly retreat, finding cover wherever they could, crawling, and running, anything to escape certain death and within full view of the defenders lay Nkosinathi.

When he finally opened his eyes, the guns had stopped their cacophony and an eerie silence permeated the battlefield. Nkosinathi remained perfectly still, listening and then he heard the defenders cheering, a sure signal that the Zulus had been defeated. Lying still, awaiting his own death, for he was certain that the white soldiers would come and use their dreaded bayonets on him, he thought of Themba, his mother, Mondli and his brothers and sisters. Had he been a good warrior? All he

433

had ever wanted was to become a warrior and now it was over and only a matter of time before the white soldiers sent him home. But the spirits were kind to Nkosinathi.

Behind the barricades, the jubilant soldiers were catching their breath and thanking their lucky stars that they had won a victory over seemingly impossible odds but there was still work to do.

'Corporal McNamara, take your men and join up with the rest of the Mounted Infantry will you,' ordered Lieutenant Chatt.

He was under orders to round up the Mounted Infantry and make ready to chase the retreating Zulu army and very soon, the soldiers were eagerly urging their horses forward the gallop to pursue the fleeing Zulus. Their blood was up, they were eager to avenge Isandhlwana and more recently, the rout at Hlobane Mountain and any Zulu caught in their net could expect little in the way of mercy.

Georgie and Patrick led their sections across the open ground in front of the camp that had witnessed the greatest carnage. They galloped over dead and dying Zulus, hacking with their swords at any they found still alive, onwards into the bush. Deprived of proper rest and food for the past two days and many of them, traumatised by the events of the afternoon the Zulus struggled to outrun the horses and were easy targets for the mounted men.

Eventually a bugle ordering the recall, Georgie held up his hand to halt their charge and was about to turn back for the camp when, from behind a tree, a giant of a man stepped holding his assegai high above his shoulder ready to skewer him. Weariness showed in the man's eyes, he knew it was the end and he had decided that he would not die alone.

Georgie had already slung his Carbine back over his shoulder and was unarmed when the man hurled the spear, missing him by inches. Now the Zulu was unarmed and Georgie drew his sword, urged his horse forward to cover the few yards towards him. The tables were turned and for the warrior it seemed that throwing his spear was a last deliberate act before he died and as he faced Georgie, he bowed his head in submission, waiting for the inevitable and Georgie did not disappoint him.

Bare chested, resigned to his fate, the warrior stood and waited and with his sabre outstretched Georgie charged. His first lunge slashed the man across his chest, then he swung his horse round to find him still standing and charged at him a second time. With his sword outstretched, he found his mark, the blade passed straight through the soft tissue and muscle of his neck, severing the jugular and yet still he stood. Georgie reined in his horse and turned again to confront the warrior. Shocked at the sight of his piercing eyes boring straight through him, Georgie stayed his hand and the two warriors faced each other for one last moment. Blood spurted from the destructive wounds Georgie had inflicted and mesmerised by the sight of the indestructible Zulu, he found that he could not move. The Warrior took a pace towards him, making the hairs on the back of his neck stand up, a shot rang out and the Zulu crumpled to the ground.

'You seemed to be making a job of that Corp,' said Barney. 'Thought you needed a little help with that one.'

Georgie looked at Barney and then back at the Zulu. He was dead, he could see that, but what a brave man he had been, those eyes, Georgie could still feel the eyes of the dead man boring into his brain and he had to take a deep breath to clear the memory.

'Come on lads, let's get back to camp. I think we've killed enough of them for today.'

Finally, the darkness of the night closed in to conceal the death and destruction and Nkosinathi saw his chance of escape. Slowly, his head throbbing from his wound, he made the same harrowing journey crawling over the uneven ground past fallen comrades until he reached the undergrowth and relatively safety. In the distance, he heard the occasional shout or scream as the horse soldiers killed another of his fellow warriors and on one occasion, he heard soldiers ride close by on their return and then all was quiet. Remaining perfectly still for a few minutes he listened and satisfied he was safe enough, he got shakily to his feet and made his way as fast as he could away from the battlefield to walking all night.

By the time the sun was rising, he was many miles from Khambula and he looked to the distant hills for the way home. Exhausted and hungry he moved as fast as his legs would carry him and picking few edible berries as he went until he came upon a small group of warriors making their way back home.

'You are uVe?'

'Yes, my name is Nkosinathi, son of Mondli.'

'We are of the uMbonambi; we lost many comrades yesterday, and you, what of the uVe?' asked their leader.

Nkosinathi related all he could remember, his head throbbed as he recollected the horrors of the battle and he touched his forehead more than once, his audience nodding approval for he had demonstrated that he was a brave warrior who had not flinched in the face of the guns.

'Here, take this leaf and bind it to your wound,' said one. 'There is a stream nearby; you can wash the blood off.'

Water, oh how thirsty he was, he had not had a drink of water for more than a day and reaching the stream, he fell on his hands and knees to drink his fill. He bathed his wound, bound the healing leaf to his forehead, and sat against a tree to listen to the warriors relate their own stories. They were fortunate, amongst the older members of their regiment, at the rear of the attack and had seen men fall in droves as grape shot and concentrated rifle fire had scythed through the ranks. They had pushed forward with the rest but the front ranks finally broke, the panic was infectious and they too had escaped the battlefield.

The leader of the group stood and followed by his companions he began to walk in the direction of home and Nkosinathi decided to follow, in his mind re-living his experiences of the past twenty-four hours. He was weary and he was puzzled as to why they had been defeated so easily. Had not they attacked the camp in force, had not they been brave, resourceful and tireless in their assault? Why did the medicine administered to the warriors before the battle not protect them, why were so many of his friends lying dead on the battlefield? His simple mind was awash with questions for which he could find no answer.

In the military camp that same day, sitting at a table outside the mess tent, some of the Mounted Infantry were eating a hearty meal and recounting the previous day's victory. They had hardly lost a man and yet the bodies of fallen Zulu warriors lay everywhere on the ground surrounding the camp, a testimony to Colonel Wood's forethought. The charge after the Zulus had separated Patrick and Georgie had they not seen each other since their return but as Georgie put down his empty mug he saw Patrick striding towards them and grinning from ear to ear.

'Georgie my boy, Jasus it's good to see you. It was a fight an' a half to be sure,' said the big Irishman.

'It was,' said Georgie looking his friend over.

'I tell you lad, there was a time when I thought the buggers were goin' to overrun the camp. I was defending the horses in the corral when they came at us. To be sure I said one of my little prayers. There were a hundred or more came at the six of us and I taught this is it, but That luverly Captain of artillery saw our predicament an turned his guns on them. A few rounds of grape soon cleared them and here I am ready for my breakfast to be sure.'

Georgie grinned at Patrick speaking excitedly in his Irish brogue, becoming more confusing and obscure and he had to concentrate on what his friend was saying.

'We beat the buggers Georgie, we beat them. Perhaps it's some consolation for the boys who fell at Isandhlwana eh?'

'Yes Patrick, it's some consolation.'

Chapter 12

Ellen looked at herself in the mirror, twisted her bonnet a little on her head and picked up her parasol before leaving her room to descending the staircase to the lobby. The portly woman sitting behind the desk looked up and smiled.

'Good morning Mrs. Jameson, how are you today?'

'I am well thank you Mrs. Mortimer.'

'How is your husband, is there any news from the front? I hear that our boys have had another hard time of it up near Hlobane. Poor lads, don't suppose they realised what kind of people those savages are.'

Ellen blushed, she did not know whether the Lancers were, Khambula or not. Clarence had not written in over a month and for all she knew he might well be somewhere in that part of the country.

'I have heard nothing, will let you know if I do hear of anything.'

Ellen made her way onto the board-walk, the wooden floor extending only a few feet past the hotel and she was soon walking on the bare earthen roadway covered in half an inch of mud. It had rained during the night and the wagon wheels had churned it up but it would not prevent her walking the two miles to the military camp and as she walked, she began to wonder how

Georgie and Patrick were faring, aware that they were with Wood's column and were most probably at Khambula.

She had known she was in love for some weeks, in love for the first time in her life, but what could she do. She was married to an Officer and had little chance of escape but Clarence gave her a good life, far better than anything she could have imagined only three short years before. Clarence was her passport to a better future and it had seemed so simple when they married, to escape the poverty of her youth had been a wonderful thing but now she knew Clarence better and she was more than a little afraid of him and now Patrick had come into her life and she worried for his safety.

Reaching the Military camp, she walked past the sentries and towards the women's quarters threading her way past tents and stores until she came upon the one she was looking for and pulled the flap open.

'Good morning Ellen,' said a voice, 'the rain hasn't done those shoes of yours any good.

It was Mrs Kramer, the wife of Surgeon Major Kramer away amongst the fighting and she saw it as her job to muster together volunteer nurses to help staff the field hospital her husband would open in the coming weeks. Already rumours were spreading of a major battle and that the Army had suffered many casualties. The impossible had seemed to be happening; the native army of King Cetshwayo was beating the British Army of Queen Victoria but the news was of victory.

Ellen found a chair to sit and clean the mud from her shoes when several army wives appeared through the tent's entrance.

'Good morning Mrs. Jameson,' they trilled.

Pickpockets and Zulus

'Good morning Mrs. Bell, good morning Mrs. Scott.'

Greetings over, the women gathered round their teacher, donning pinafores, ready for the morning's instruction.

'Today ladies, I want to show you how stitch a wound and dress it. Ellen, will you fetch me the tray from the table over there please?'

'Thank you Ellen' said Mrs. Kramer, as Ellen placed the tray of surgical instruments and rolls of bandages on the table.

'Right, stitching a wound is not a particularly pleasant business, but is often necessary. Let us start by threading our needles.'

For the rest of the morning the women learned a little of stitching and dressing a wound, the kind an Assegai might make. Mrs. Kramer had seen soldiers with wounds of this type before; she had stitched and dressed many of them. Her husband had been with the Army in the Crimea and told of how the nurses there had pioneered the care of the wounded, saving many lives by the simple act of segregating the infected men and the constant dressing of wounds. She had learned the lesson well and felt it her duty to help train these volunteers in at least the fundamentals of caring for the wounded.

'Where is your husband at the moment Mrs. Bell?' asked Mrs. Kramer when they took a break.

'He is with Woods column up at Khambula,' she replied, sipping her tea.

'They have been fighting the Zulus, did you know that?'

'Yes I've heard and I just hope that William is safe but after Isandhlwana you can never be sure,' she said.

441

'Major Kramer is with Wood as well and I expect he has his hands full,' said Mrs. Kramer.

Ellen listened to the conversation, the women were naturally worried about their men folk and were determined that they should try to help in some way. She envied them; they obviously loved their husbands whilst she did not love hers, a hollow feeling was all she could summon when it came to Clarence but Patrick was another matter altogether.

Still thinking of Patrick, Ellen did not notice the medical orderly peer through the tent flap and speak to Mrs Kramer and when she finally looked for her, she was gone.

'Where is Mrs Kramer?'

'She has gone to see Major Kramer,' said one of the women.

'Something is brewing,' said another.

Ellen pursed her lips wondering what it might be, returned to her work, and as the women finished their endeavours for the day, they sat down to chat to await the return of Mrs. Kramer. Her husband had returned from Khambula only the day before and had summoned her to discuss impending orders and now she returned to the tent to tell them the news.

'Ladies, we are to pack up and leave,' she said, her face flush with excitement. 'As you are aware, I'm sure, the ladies who arrived so recently from England are nurses, sent out to look after the wounded and we have been asked to assist them. Major Kramer has just informed me of the plan and he is, at this very moment, organising wagons and an escort for us to go to the town of Dundee. Isn't it wonderful? We will be able to put into practice all the lessons we have learned and help those poor souls who are in need of nursing back to health.'

A buzz of conversation erupted in the room. They were to go to the front, well somewhere near to the front, and help with the wounded. Ellen listened as the women discussed the situation; some were thrilled at the thought of helping, some not so thrilled. For her part, she felt that it was a chance for her to escape the monotony of King William's Town, a chance to see that Patrick and Georgie were safe as well as contributing to the war effort. She was not too sure about Clarence though, she was his wife and could not ignore the fact that she had still not told him of her endeavour to become an auxiliary nurse. She thought about it for a moment, deciding that perhaps she would write him a letter, explain all that she had done and tell him how she was going to help care for the wounded, surely that would please him.

'So, ladies, I have explained what is to happen but Major Randall has stressed to me that he will only take volunteers. Which of you ladies will come with me?' asked Mrs. Kramer.

She had trained the dozen women who listened to her but in their eyes she could detect mixed feelings. One by one, they gave their answer and to her disappointment, only four were willing to accompany her.

'And what about you Ellen, will you come with us and help the wounded?'

Ellen nodded slowly, her agreement, 'Yes, Mrs. Kramer, I...I will come to help, I will come.'

Suddenly she felt quite proud and dignified; a product of the East End of London, a minor thief now thrust into the cauldron of war as a volunteer nurse. For most of her young life it had always been a case of survival, some days not knowing if she would eat, dressed in rags and without a future, but now she felt, perhaps, that she was somebody.

Edith Kramer beamed with delight, she knew little of Ellen's background but from her use of words and the occasional slip of the tongue, she guessed that she was from humble beginnings. Few officers thought they would be of any real use, but with willing volunteers like Ellen, she would realize their potential, prove that although it might be a man's world, it needed a woman's touch.

The volunteers, aided by those staying behind began work immediately, gathering together supplies of medicines and bandages and helping to load the wagons Edith had already obtained requisition notes and handed these to Ellen with instructions to visit the quartermaster's store.

'Ellen, you are my star pupil. I didn't tell you that did I?' Ellen said nothing. 'The others agree with me I know, you learn quickly and you are efficient and I want you to be my assistant, to take over whenever I cannot carry on. There will be hard at times and I am sure if there are many casualties and I cannot be everywhere at once then you must take my place. Will you agree?'

Ellen's cheeks flushed red with embarrassment, Edith had put her on the spot yet with newfound confidence, she rose to the challenge and nodded. 'Oh, yes would be pleased to be your assistant Mrs. Kramer.'

'Good, and call me Edith.'

'Yes...Edith. What would you have me do...?'

Pickpockets and Zulus

It took them two days to gather all they needed, to load the medical supplies and on the morning of the third day, the ox drawn wagons lumbered through the main street of King William's Town. Escorted by several platoons of Infantrymen and a squadron of cavalry on their way to join the main element of the army, the small convoy made its way out of the military encampment.

'Have you been so far up country before Edith?' asked Ellen.

'I have been to Newcastle, but not for over a year and what with the war with the Zulus I expect things will have changed a little. The Army changes things wherever it goes my dear. The Army will swamp small towns like Newcastle and Dundee. Look at Williams; it's grown to four times its previous size.'

'I have never been so far from civilization. Will we have proper accommodation or will we be living in tents?'

'You have been fortunate my dear, living in a hotel. You are lucky your husband has a private income to pay for such luxury. No, it will be tents for us, and sleeping on the ground. You will need to be careful of insects and other creepy crawlies in the night.'

Ellen's head spun round, horror in her eyes.

'What kind of creepy crawlies?'

'Oh spiders and ants, that sort of thing, don't worry' she laughed, 'we will make sure they can't get at us.'

'How?'

'Well, there are lots of things we can do. One simple trick is to dig a shallow trench around the tent and fill it with water. That normally keeps them at bay. Anyway we have our insect netting.'

Pickpockets and Zulus

Ellen's eyes fixed on a tree in the middle distance not liking at all the idea of creepy crawlies clambering all over her whilst she slept. She thought about her clothes, what she might wear on a night to keep her from the clutches of these annoyances and was still thinking about it when the Captain in charge called halt.

The wagons had covered fifteen miles and it was four 'o' clock in the afternoon, time to rest the oxen and make camp alongside a convenient water hole. Immediately barked orders set the infantrymen in motion to laager the wagons and positioned lookouts whilst the women unpacked food and filled cooking pots.

'Where do we sleep tonight?' asked Ellen.

'Why, under the wagon,' said the driver in a matter of fact voice. He was a Boer, stocky with broad shoulders, red faced from the sun and used to women who could cope with tough conditions. 'You'll be safe under there; anyway we are a long way from Zulu land so we don't expect trouble tonight. It might be different when we get up to the Buffalo.'

Ellen woke to the clank of spurs as the cavalrymen prepared their mounts ready to leave the overnight camp and patrol ahead of the wagons. The rain had managed to hold off and she had slept remarkably well but then large drops of rain began spattering on the woodwork and she could think of nothing else except keeping dry. She found shelter in the back of the wagon and sat on a box alongside two of her companions she watched the cavalry don their oiled cotton capes and trot away.

The Infantry struck camp, the drovers yoked their oxen to the wagons and by the time they were ready to move, the rain was coming down in sheets. Ellen's coat was no match for an African downpour and along with the other women, she sheltered in one of the wagons and at six o clock, the order came to move. For two hours they made slowly progress across country, the ground became thick with mud and the oxen began to struggle. The lead wagon had become stuck; the oxen could not move it no matter how much the drover cracked his long bullwhip forcing him to call for assistance.

'Get those men up here,' shouted an Infantry officer.

Troopers rushed forward to gather round each wheel, gripping the spokes and heaving, turning the wheels with brute force until gradually they inched the wagon forward and the oxen could take the strain and from her seat in the back, Ellen watched the gallant soldiers. She had not mixed much with this class of soldier, only Georgie and Patrick and felt heartened by then making light of such a miserable situation, laughing and joking as they struggled.

The second day proved just as difficult, progress was slow and they covered not much more than eight miles, but on the third day the rains stopped, the sun dried the ground and for several days they managed over twenty miles and finally the Buffalo River came into sight and they had reached the border with Zululand.

In Khambula, the situation had eased dramatically, the threat of attack gone, re-enforcements, fresh supplies were arriving almost daily, and the army had time to consolidate the victory.

'Sergeant Donovan,' said Lieutenant Chatt.'

'Sir,' said Patrick, raising his hand in a lazy salute.

447

'We have been ordered to form an escort detail for the wounded and to accompany them to Dundee. Captain Kramer has established a hospital there and sent word that he is ready to receive patients. I want you to find Sergeant Mills and the Corporals and pass on the orders to move out at daybreak. We will have a detachment of Infantry with us and we are taking the supply wagons back with us. Carry on Sergeant.'

Patrick had been checking over his tack when the Lieutenant had found him, he had expecting to be heading the other way, into Zululand not back to the Drift, but the wounded needed looking after and if those were the orders then so be it. He spotted Sergeants Jones and Mills chatting at the far end of the corral and walked towards them.

'Afternoon lads,' he said strolling up, 'seems like we are on the move again.'

'Oh and where might we be go-ing Sergeant Donovan?' asked Corporal Jones.

He already knew the answer. The bush telegraph was working well and only minutes before he had heard the news from sergeant Mills.

Jonesy and Patrick loved trying to outwit and outmanoeuvre each other and before Patrick could say anything, Jonesy butted in.

'I would have thought we would be cha-sing after Cetshwayo, but I bet they're sending us Dundee with the woun-ded. What do you reck-on Sergeant Donovan?'

Jonesy caught Patrick off his stroke, he had looked forward to dishing out the orders to move, it made him feel important but Jonsey had stolen his thunder and Patrick's eyes narrowed,

'Jonesy you bastard, how did you know?'

Sergeant Jones grinned at Patrick and tapped the side of his nose with his forefinger. 'Ah... Ser-geant Donovan that is for me to know and for you... to find out,' he said in his sing song Welsh twang.

They were of equal rank; Patrick could do little except grin and bear it. He looked at Sergeant Mills who was trying very hard not to laugh, then back at Jonesy who had mirth written all over his face. There was really nothing he could do except promise himself that he owed Jonesy one.

'To be sure we are escorting the wounded to Dundee at four in the mornin' so get you men organised whilst I find the others and spread the word. That is of course, unless they already know,' he said with some sarcasm.

Jonesy knew he had won the exchange and together with Sergeant Mills grinned as Patrick stormed off across the open space of the corral, past the rows of tethered horses towards the mess tent.

'What's up Sarge?' asked Georgie as Patrick approached him, face like thunder.

'Nottin.'

'Oh, right.' Georgie knew very well that something had happened.

'Bloody Jonesy,' Patrick muttered.

'Ha Ha,' laughed Georgie, now he understood and knew it was best not to antagonise Patrick in front of the men.

'We have orders to move in the morning, see to it that the men are ready. We are to escort the wounded to the hospital at Dundee. Captain Kramer has sent word that he is ready for them.'

'Hmm...Interesting,' said Georgie.

'What's interesting?'

Pickpockets and Zulus

'Well I heard only a few minutes ago that Captain Kramer's wife is heading there with some women from Williams. She has trained them up to be nurses. Wonder if Ellen is still there in Williams or might she be in Dundee?'

How was it that everyone else seemed to know what was happening before he did, thought Patrick. Ellen, he had not thought much about her for a while, not with all the excitement fighting the Zulus and now he did, puffing out his cheeks until his beard tickled his nose. He rubbed it with the palm of his hand as her face came to the forefront of his mind, Ellen, oh what a lovely name he thought as its syllables rang out like church bells in his head.

For the rest of the day he could not get her out of his mind and at four 'o' clock the next morning when the order was given to move off he could still see her face. Her bright blue eyes, her dark hair hanging down to her shoulders, even her laugh seemed fresh in his mind. He exhaled, shook his head and tried to push the memories to one side and concentrate on the job. It had been more than a week since the battle, he felt rested and his horse was in excellent condition when Lieutenant Chatt led the small column out of the confines of the fortified camp and they were soon alone out on the veldt.

Ever vigilant, Georgie leaned back in his saddle stretching his back muscles as his new mount carried him south towards Dundee. He was leading his section two miles ahead of the wagons and although he did not expect trouble he still he kept a wary eye out for Zulus.

Nkosinathi sat on the small hillock, a long stalk of straw protruding from his mouth as he kept a watchful eye on his father's cattle,. He had returned with the army to Ulundi, suffering the wrath of the King as his army assembled before him. The smellers of evil had passed amongst them to seek out those accused of cowardice and this time the King decided he needed to stiffen the armies resolve. He signalled the slayers to go in amongst the regiments, to follow the witch doctor's lead and several warriors were dragged away to be clubbed to death.

The cleansing of the cowards over, the regiments dispersed to complete the washing of the spears, sing their regimental songs and to recover their morale. An air of dejection pervaded the warriors and it seemed to emanate from the King. He had lost several battles during the past few months; the victory at Isandhlwana a distant memory and many of his warriors were dead or badly wounded. It had become apparent to all of them that the White Man's guns were proving more powerful than any medicine the InSangoma could produce.

'My son' said a voice, 'my son, you are well?'

Nkosinathi turned his head to see his father approaching and jumped to his feet.

'You are a brave warrior Nkosinathi; I have heard it said, you bring honour to the village and to me.'

'Thank you father, my only wish is to serve the King and to make you proud.'

'Come, let us sit a while and take snuff, tell me about the war against the invaders, tell me of the bravery of our warriors.'

Mondli gestured to Nkosinathi to sit with him and as they settled on the grass, he pulled the small horn from the slit in his ear.

'The war with the invaders does not go well I think.' Nkosinathi remained silent. 'The war with the invaders does not go well I think,' said Mondli again, demanding a reply.

'Yes father, we have lost many warriors to the Redcoats' guns. We have guns, we took many from the battlefield but we cannot make them shoot like the White Man. I think they have some kind of magic in their guns, something that only makes them work properly in the hands of the whites.'

'I have heard this. Here take some snuff,' he said after inhaling a little himself.

They sat in silence for a long time, each deep in thought. Mondli, the old warrior, had lived through the glory days of the Zulu kingdom; he had seen little change during his lifetime, but now the kingdom was in grave danger and he feared for the future. They were simple people, fierce warriors, but still simple people, farmers for all that and the White Man was slowly encroaching upon their land, changing a century's old way of life.

Mondli sighed, looked at Nkosinathi and wondered what he was thinking?

'What is it my son, what troubles you?'

After a brief silence Nkosinathi began to describe the events leading up to the battle at Khambula, of the fight at Hlobane Mountain, of the rout of the mounted men and then of the subsequent attack on the British camp. He described the bravery of the warriors, he told how he rallied them for a second assault on the defences, and Mondli's eyes lit up, fading as Nkosinathi told of the carnage, of the bodies of warriors strewn across the ground.

'But I am a warrior and I must fight until the death for my King must I not father?'

'It is true Nkosinathi that is what being a Zulu warrior is, to fight fiercely and defeat our enemies or die trying. It has been the way of our people for generations. My father and his father are with you on the battlefield, always remember that and should you fall they will pick you up.'

'Thank you father, I know my destiny, I will drive the invaders from our land.'

He felt happier, he had exorcised his daemons somewhat and his courage was returning.

Nozipho carried the tray of tea and cakes out to the table in front of the house where Paludan was sitting reading his newspaper. Concentration contorted his features as he read news of the war's progress, the victories at Khambula and Gingindlovu, he learned of the heavy casualties inflicted on the Zulus with little loss of life to the British and their colonial allies. It seemed that the tide had turned and the next battle could well be decisive he thought as the girl placed the tray on the table.

'Thank you Nozipho, and Manelesi, is he coping with the work in the fields?'

'He manages well enough with one arm but he is sad that he can no longer be a warrior.'

Paludan managed a half smile, she was bright and breezy, her burned flesh had healed as well as it could and with her scars covered by the brightly coloured headscarf, she was presentable. She remained disfigured but not nearly as badly as everyone had feared and what she had lost in her looks, she more than made up with in personality.

'He will be all right I am sure. With someone like you to help him he will make a full recovery and find a way to make a living just as you have done.'

Paludan was about to say more when a voice drifted from the house and across the garden.

'Ahh, there you are, I should have known you were out here Paludan. I have been re-arranging your books and lost track of time. I hope you have a cup for me Nozipho?' Inga joked, knowing that Nozipho would never forget her. 'Thank you, I can manage, off you go and attend to your chores.'

Nozipho skipped away towards the church, she had decided that she would put fresh flowers in the vases today and knew that would have to go to the fields for them and there she would find Manelesi.

'What does the paper say about the war?' asked Inga

'Our fear of invasion by the Zulus has abated and the population of Natal are a little more relaxed. It seems that they finally have the measure of the Zulus. Says here that the disaster at Isandhlwana was the fault of Chelmsford, splitting his force into two and leaving the camp badly defended. The colonists, especially the Dutch, warned them to laager wagons and chain them together, but he did not heed that warning. They do now though, it says here that the actions at both Khambula and Gingindlovu were successful because they took the trouble to construct solid defences, chained the laagered wagons together. The Zulus prefer to fight in open country; everyone in the colonies knows that, if they catch you in the open you do not stand much of a chance. Proper fortifications are the answer – look at

Rorke's Drift, doesn't that tell us something? There is a list of the dead and wounded from Khambula, about thirty dead, and nearly three thousand Zulu warriors they think. Isn't that amazing? They are heathens I know but I cannot help saying a prayer for them,' said Paludan reading further in silence.

'Paludan, what do you think will happen?'

'Mmm...oh it seems plain to me that with the new tactics and their superior fire power there will be only one out come, but at what cost, at what cost,' he repeated shaking his head.

Behind the house, Nozipho ran towards the field for her flowers amongst natives tending to the maize plants. In return for the sanctuary afforded them by Paludan and his mission, he asked that they labour in the fields, cultivate the crops that sustained the small community and there, amongst them, toiled Manelesi. He had not fully come to terms with his disability for it was only three months since he had lost his arm. Any normal person would still be convalescing but Zulus are stalwart people who wear hardship easily and Manelesi's swift recovery was astounding.

He was still unable to accomplish much, simply to carry baskets and light implements for the others and frequently had to sit and rest but each day, he grew stronger. For her part, Nozipho was full of joy and began to take more pride in her own appearance, covering up her afflictions, both physical and mental. The kindness and help she had received from the two missionaries had helped her to begin with and now, with the appearance of Manelesi, the transformation was profound.

'Manelesi,' she called out.

Pickpockets and Zulus

He was across the field pulling up weeds from between the rows of maize plants and hearing her calling him he paused from his work. She looked lovely in the morning sun and he knew he loved her but now he was the one that felt inadequate. He let go of his implement and stood motionless, all too aware of his missing arm and his pose did not going unnoticed by Nozipho.

'I have some mealie and some beer for you my man.'

'You still call me your man yet I am not complete, I cannot hunt, I dare not go home again having lived with the White Man. I cannot be your man.'

'Oh Manelesi, do not scold yourself so, you will become strong again. Are you not helping to provide our food? Is not life good here on the mission and have you not touched their God yet?' She said, her eyes radiating a kind and gentle love. 'Are we not both afflicted and would we not be outcasts amongst our own people?'

He looked at her, amazed at her resilience, her tenacity. He had saved her from death and helped her to escape the clutches of the Sangoma, never imagining that she would make such a recovery and now she was in the midst of this small, thriving community, respected and loved and together with these kind people, she had saved his life.

'Manelesi, it is Sunday tomorrow, will you come with me to church, learn the songs they sing? It will make you feel happy I know it will. There is nothing you can do for King Cetshwayo anymore, so do not think about the war, it is for others, not us.'

'These are strange words Nozipho, what ideas have these white people put into your head?'

Manelesi had little experience of white people his experience only that of listening to the stories of others returning from hunting trips or trading with them. His sole experience had been killing them.

Clarence looked over his horse, ran his hand across her back and noticed a cavalry officer's blue uniform approaching.

'Sir, compliments of the Major General, could you please join him in his headquarters tent,' said the lieutenant.

'Thank you lieutenant,' said Clarence returning his salute.

He patted his horses flank and ran his hand over her shiny black coat again and wondering what the Major General wanted with him. He had been the advance eyes and ears of the Regiment for many months and could only think that he wanted to ask his advice. He pulled on his jacket adjusting the white leather shoulder strap and belt and puffed out his chest. He needed to look smart in front of his commanding officer for after all the Seventeenth were the crack cavalry regiment of the British Army with very high standards and he didn't want this young lieutenant upstaging him.

'Captain Jameson sir,' announced the Adjutant.

'Send him in.'

'Sir, you sent for me?' said Clarence, bringing his heels smartly together and saluting.

'Yes, Captain Jameson, I believe I did,' said his commanding officer in a slightly dismissive way.

Behind his seemingly lazy façade, the Major General had the mind of a first class soldier, an officer who had seen action at Sevastopol as part of that fateful charge and a few Zulus were never going to bother him.

'We are to return to the battlefield of Isandhlwana to escort a burial detail. It will not be pleasant but it has to be done. We cannot leave those men any longer and have the Jackals eat them, though no doubt they will be in a sorry state by now. You Captain, I want you to take twenty handpicked men and cover our flank just in case any of those blighters decide to have another go at us. You have been out here a while Captain and I have read your reports. Good man, you seem to know your stuff. Anything to say?'

'Er, if I may be so bold sir,' added Clarence a little arrogantly, an arrogance not lost on the Major General.

'Carry on man, what is it?'

'Sir isn't it about time we applied the Coup de Grace to these savages, shouldn't we be pressing on to this Ulundi place.'

'Hmm, all in good time captain, all in good time. I can tell you confidentially that once the burials have taken place and morale boosted somewhat we will be going after the blighters, have no fear. Thank you Captain Jameson, dismissed.'

There was nothing more to say, burying the fallen of Isandhlwana was necessary, they had lain there for five months and their comrades still mourned them. Until they laid their bodies to rest, not one British soldier would feel comfortable but Clarence did not quite see it that way. He wanted to fight the Zulus and cover himself in glory.

Chapter 13

The volunteer nurse had only been in the military hospital for a few hours before they were ready to begin work and Edith Kramer enthusiastically organized them to prepare for the expected casualties.

'Victoria, will you and Mary clear the bed clothes from those two beds,' she said, pointing to two empty camp beds.

'Edith, your husband is asking for you,' said a nurse carrying a large jug of water into the tent. 'He asks, could you attend him at your earliest convenience.'

'Of course Catherine, thank you for informing me. Have you seen Ellen, she was supposed to be here but I haven't seen her.'

'She's outside, over by the doctor's tent. A wagon has just arrived with the first of the wounded men.'

'Thank you Catherine.'

She felt she must see to the casualties first, her husband would have to wait, but she felt sure that he would understand. She finished writing her log, closed the book and laid her pen in the groove at the front of the desk before getting off the high stool to reach behind her back to unfasten her apron.

'Looks like a nice day again ladies, the washing should dry nicely.'

'Yes Mrs. Kramer,' two women said in unison as they busied themselves making beds ready for the patients.

She turned towards the tent flap and emerged into the sunlight to find Ellen and another of the nurses helping a wounded man from the wagon.

'Good morning Ellen, what have we here?'

'Good morning Edith, some wounded just brought in from the camp at Rorke's drift. There are five of them, only the trooper on the stretcher is really badly wounded, the others have gunshot wounds and one has a broken arm.'

'Right, well there are two beds ready in number one tent and I think you might find some more in number two tent. Take their names and regiments and put them in the book will you, I have to go and see Colonel Kramer.'

Felling confident in their abilities she left her assistants busily carrying out their duties and crossed the compound to the small tent from where her husband worked.

'Edith my dear,' said Colonel Kramer holding out his hands to greet his wife.

She fondly grasped them and looked into his eyes with some concern, he looked tired from months of hard work and at sixty years old, he was not getting any younger.

'You wanted to see me George?'

'Yes, come and sit down. I have to tell you that I can already see how useful you and your nurses are, I don't know how we would expect to manage without you.'

Edith blushed, she had organised the women and taught them some rudiments of nursing, skills but it was due mainly to her husband. He was the one who had established the field hospital; he was the one who had worked tirelessly to provide the best medical facilities possible.

'Why thank you good sir,' she said, sitting down to face him across his desk.

Colonel Kramer leant his elbows on the table, clasped his fingers together and rested his chin on them.

'There will be many more casualties soon Edith, and I will need you and your nurses. I can tell you confidentially, though it is as plain as the noses on our faces, what is about to happen. Chelmsford had a shock with Isandhlwana. Frightened him I believe, frightened him into believing that his reputation was irreparably damaged.'

He paused for a few moments and Edith leaned forward in anticipation.

'The General has not wasted his time though. True we have had one or two setbacks, but all the while re-enforcements have been arriving from England and the Empire and since Khambula, old Cetshwayo has been on the run. Let me get to the point. The Army will be crossing the Buffalo in force very soon and this war will be heading to a final showdown. My guess is that we will move on Ulundi, the King's Zulu capital, what with all the fresh troops and equipment he must be a worried man.'

'And why are you telling me this George?' she asked.

'Ah, yes, remiss of me to leave you hanging there. Well Edith, there will be a lot of wounded men to take care of if past battles are anything to go by and I will need your nurses to help in a more forward position. The sappers have been constructing forts along the way and it is my intention to set up a field hospital in one of them, somewhere between here and Ulundi. Could be dangerous my dear so I will only ask for volunteers until we know better the outcome of the campaign. What d'you say?'

Edith beamed at him from across the table, pleased he thought so highly of her, pleased that she was able to help the wounded and pleased to be with him.

'Of course I will come with you, apart from anything else you are my husband. Should I ask the other women yet?'

'Oh good heavens no, not yet, not until the Army is on its way and we can see developments. No, leave it a week or two; I will let you know when we plan to move the hospital.'

Outside in the compound Ellen had a slate and chalk recording the new arrivals.

'What's your name rank and regiment soldier?' Ellen asked the first of the wounded.

'Johnston, Private, Seventeenth Lancers ma'am.'

Ellen stopped writing as the news sank in, perhaps Clarence was not so far away after all and she wondered if she might see him. She resumed taking down the man's details and moved on to the next patient, a colonial but a third man was Cavalryman, a Corporal Smith with a nasty flesh wound and obviously in some pain, but for all that, he was a talkative soul.

'Where are you from Miss?' he asked.

Ellen looked at him. 'I'm not a Miss I'm a Missus, soldier.'

'Oh sorry ma'am, I thought you were one of those colonial girls,' he said sheepishly.

Ellen grinned, the thought of being mistaken for a colonial girl intriguing her.

462

'My husband is an Officer in your regiment Mister Smith.'

'Oh...sorry ma'am' he groaned, sucking in breath as his wound shot pain through his body.

'It's alright; I haven't seen him for months. I did not know where the regiment was stationed until you and the Private came in today.'

'What's your husband's name?' he asked.

'Captain Clarence Jameson.'

'Oh, Captain Jameson, well he's a lucky man.'

'You know him soldier?'

'Yes ma'am, he was in command of the patrol I was with when I was wounded. Good horseman Captain Jameson, yes he knows his horses alright.'

'And where is the regiment stationed?' Ellen enquired.

'Mainly the camp at Rorke's Drift but I hear some are coming here to Dundee ready for the push into Zululand. Damn, I will not be going with them will I ma'am?'

'No, I don't think you will soldier,' she said, mopping his brow.

So Clarence was not far away, and what about Patrick, where was he right now?

Chapter 14

The night was dark, very dark and visibility was nil as the patrol cautiously made its way through the gauze bushes. Georgie rode slowly on ahead of his troopers, peering into the impenetrable blackness. He looked up into the sky and was puzzled why there were no stars; perhaps the African night was playing tricks. His horse pulled up without any command from him and he felt its ears prick up. Still he could see nothing, he listened and then he heard it, faint at first, the sound of a crowd in the distance, he could hear children shouting.

He slid silently from the saddle, slipped his Carbine from his shoulder and was about to take a step forward and then the clouds parted, moonlight illuminated everything and he stood still. His horse stood still and he looked around, turning to his left, and then to his right, he made to move forward and straight in front of him and to his great surprise, a Zulu warrior blocked his path.

The man was broad shouldered and muscular, a fine specimen of a man, and he seemed to tower over him. Quickly he dropped to his knee and raised the gun pointing it straight at the man's heart, his finger round the trigger ready for the shot. The man carried no weapon and his eyes seemed to have a faraway look in them, a look of resignation. Georgie looked into those eyes, squeezed the trigger and to his dismay found the gun would not fire. The mechanism had jammed and warrior, sensing that there was a problem, became more alive, taking a step forward. Georgie sensed his hostility and attempted to pull the trigger, but again the gun would not fire. The man came on, one-step at a time, holding Georgie's gaze as he approached, his large brown eyes peering straight into Georgie's and a panic seized him. The noise of the crowd increased, children's voices, grew loud and he recognised some of them. Suddenly a familiar voice called out his name. "Ellen is that you?" he tried to say but the words seemed to unable to escape his mouth. Again, the girl called his name, the warrior reached him and he felt weak, unable to defend himself, and then the warrior took hold of his shoulders and he screamed in terror.

'Georgie, what's the matter man?' asked Patrick leaning over him, one hand on his shoulder the other holding an oil lamp above his head. 'Jasus, you've woken us all up. Do we not get little enough sleep as it is, at all?

Georgie was sweating, his breathing short and shallow, gradually his eyes cleared as he became accustomed to the light and he looked around the tent to see his fellow soldiers staring at him with bewildered eyes.

'Sorry lads, I must have been dreaming. Crickey, that big black man I killed the other day was back again giving me a fright,' he said with some embarrassment.

'Get yourself back to sleep, we'er out on patrol in another two hours.'

Patrick turned down the lamp one or two of the troopers muttered obscenities, silence returned and

Pickpockets and Zulus

Georgie lay on his back looking up at the roof of the tent for what seemed an interminable amount of time. Those eyes haunted him, the eyes of a man he had tried to kill in cold blood and they made him shudder as he relived the confrontation. Ellen, why was she in his dream, was she reminding him of his childhood, calling to him as she had so many times before when they been heading for trouble. She was sharp, never missed anything, was she trying to warn him perhaps. He did not know, but he could see that she was still Ellen and he wondered where she was.

When dawn finally broke, the camp became alive with activity, the night patrol returned from picket duty and Lieutenant Chatt led the Mounted Infantry out into Zulu country. Twenty riders from the Natal Native contingent accompanied them, sixty horsemen altogether with orders to patrol up to twelve miles to the north, across the river and to harass any Zulus they found, burn villages and crops in their path.

'How are you lad?' asked Patrick as he came alongside his friend. 'It was a scary nightmare you were having to be sure.'

'Ha, only a nightmare Patrick, but I tell you what I wouldn't like to meet another like him on a dark night. Not on my own.'

Two hours into the patrol and the force, spread out across a mile of country, came upon a group of isolated Zulu huts. Appearing abandoned, the lieutenant signalled some of the native horsemen to take a closer look. Several dismounted and crept forwards and, satisfied that there was no immediate danger, disappeared inside. There were shouts and sounds of a scuffle and one by one the hut's inhabitants were brought out a few women and children and one old man.

'You want we kill dem?' asked one of the Native Horse.

'No, I do not want you to kill them,' answered the lieutenant. 'We do not kill women and children.' The man looked crestfallen. 'We're only after the warriors. Let them go and burn the huts.'

He looked towards the group of women and children, waved his arm in gesture and shouted.

'Go on, clear off, go on.'

The women said nothing, leading the small children by the hand towards the bush and relative safety. Alongside the lieutenant the Native Horsemen were leering, glad that at least they had a chance of retribution against the Zulus and it wasn't long before the thatched, tinder dry roofs of the huts were ablaze, black smoke rising into the sky.

Georgie watched from a distance, hearing the crackle of the timber frames as they began to burn and wondering where the men folk were, when from the corner of his eye, he saw a trooper lean over and slide from his horse. It was obvious someone had shot the man, the rifle's retort muffled by the sound of the burning huts. Then Lieutenant Chatt heard the sound of the gun firing a second shot and his head jerked up trying to locate its source.

'Dismount, take cover, someone is shooting at us.'

The troopers were already taking evasive action, several with their feet on the ground before the lieutenant's order and all of them were busy pointing their carbines in the general direction of the source of the gunshots.

Pickpockets and Zulus

A hundred yards away an enormous Baobab tree stood alone, its mighty girth of twenty or more feet had a dark opening, one large enough to hide a man. The native horsemen noticed the aperture and were the first to react, charging across the open ground to surrounded the tree and from their positions, the troopers watched their native allies with some wonder. Working together first one and then another took turns in reaching round the tree trunk, stabbing their spears into the dark void. As they stabbed their spears into the black interior a scream was heard and then a scuffle took place, a Zulu was dragged out feet first and this time the native horsemen did not wait for permission from the lieutenant. Each took a sharp knife from his belt and thrust the blade into Zulu's body and making short work of him.

'Bollocks!' exclaimed Lieutenant Chatt when he finally arrived on the scene, 'We could have taken him prisoner, and might have had some useful information. Right, too late now, Donovan go and see to our wounded man.'

Patrick dashed back to the small group that had surrounded the casualty and Lieutenant Chatt, satisfied that there was no longer a threat, ordered his men to re-mount and search the surrounding area for any more snipers.

'Sergeant Donovan,'

'Sir' replied Patrick.

'How is he?'

'He has lost some blood and I don't think his wound is so serious, but I do think we should get him back to camp as soon as we can sir.'

468

'We still have a lot to do today sergeant and I cannot spare many men for an escort so I want you and your section to get him back on your own. Carry on.'

'Sir,' Patrick saluted and walked towards his horse, waving at his men to follow him.

'You look in a sorry state Private Cape, how are you feeling?' said Patrick, black humour balanced by a concerned look in his eyes.

'I...'m not so bad Sarge,' said the man, his face ashen from shock.

'Alright, Cape, looks like your bandage is holding, do you want some water?'

The man nodded, Patrick reached up to his saddle for his water bottle and then helped Private Cape gulp down several mouthfuls. He was weak that was for sure and Patrick did not think he could ride his horse all the way back to camp. By his reckoning, it was more than twelve miles to the camp, it would take at least three hours, maybe four and would be nightfall before they could get there and then someone would have to take Private Cape to Dundee. No, he thought, better to cross the river and take him straight to Dundee.

'Soldier, ride over to the Captain and ask his permission for us to take Private Cape straight to the military hospital at Dundee will you.'

'Yes Sergeant.'

The Captain was busy organising his men as the trooper rode up with the request. The day was hot and Lieutenant Chatt was a little flustered, worrying that there could be more danger up ahead of them and he thought for a few seconds, deciding that it was a decent enough plan. However, he would attach some of the

Natal Native Horse to act as scouts and beef up the patrol.

'Sarge, the Captain says it's alright for you to head straight for Dundee, but thinks you will need these men,' said the private returning with four native horsemen in tow. 'He says they know the way and they could be useful if we get into a fight.'

'Did he say anything else?'

The private looked a little sheepish and said, 'he expects to be back in camp by tomorrow nightfall or soon after. He says don't get too drunk if you find a pub or he will make a stew out of your balls Sergeant.'

'Right, a pub did he say, to be sure it never entered my head that there might be a pub.' Patrick grinned; it was obvious to anyone who knew him it was a lie. 'I'm not happy with Private Cape here. Pearson, you are the smallest one amongst us so let's get trooper Cape back on his horse and you jump up behind him. Keep him upright and we'll swap horses every hour, that way we should be able to get to the pub before it closes.'

The rest of the troop grinned, there could well be a pub in Dundee and a few beers would be very welcome. They formed up alongside Patrick, the native riders moving out ahead and to the flanks and the patrol separated from the main force, small group heading North West. After a discussion with the lieutenant, they had calculated that it was around twenty miles to Dundee. The terrain was easy enough for the horses but they would need to find a ford across the river. The trackers would find it, said the lieutenant and Patrick realised that they would be a useful addition to his force.

'What's your name?' he asked the man leading the African horsemen.

'My name is Henry Dalmini, I am of the AmaNgwane.'

'Well Henry, we are heading for Dundee and will have to cross the Buffalo somewhere.'

'Do not worry, I know the country well. We will find an easy crossing for the wounded man. We will ride ahead of you, maybe a mile, and keep a look out for Zulus but I think they are gone from round here. You take this track,' he said, pointing to a barely discernible pathway of flattened grass.

For the rest of the day the troopers had an easy enough ride, the wounded man bore up well enough and as darkness began to set in, they reached the river. Patrick decided not to light a fire, he did not want them attracting any attention, telling his men that biscuits and water was all they could have. The troopers tied their horses to bushes, leaving them to graze before settling down for a few hours rest and the native scouts disappeared into the bush.

'Where are they off to sarge?' asked one of the men.

'Your guess is as good as mine, but from what I know of them, they won't be far away. I don't know when they sleep but I bet they will be out there all night keeping watch. Good men to have with us.'

Well before dawn, the men broke camp and Henry re-appeared with his natives to lead the patrol a few hundred yards along the riverbank to a shallow part of the river.

'You cross hear white soldier,' said Henry sweeping his arm in a gesture to indicate the shallows. 'You cross now and turn between the sun and the river. Go straight and you will find the kraal of Dundee.'

471

Henry did not waste any more time, cupping his hands and making a strange animal sound to gather his men and together they rode off into the bush and an hour later Patrick's troop were well away from the river and he pulled lifted his field glasses to his eyes. He took his helmet off, wiped his sleeve across his forehead and lifted his water bottle to his lips.

'How's he doing Pearson?' he asked the trooper sat behind the wounded man.

'I think he's alright Sergeant. He moans now and then and I think he's drifted off to sleep a few times but he's bearing up.'

'How do ye feel Cape?'

The man wounded squinted and turned his head on an angle, looking at Patrick, unable to say much and slowly nodded his head.

'I think we are safe enough now and there is only about half a dozen miles to go. I reckon we'll be there in a couple of hours, hang on lad.'

Private Cape's head slumped forwards; he was becoming weaker and a worry for Patrick. From the rear of the horse, Private Pearson gave a knowing look and then they saw Henry riding towards them.

'There is a stream over there,' said the native, 'a good place to water the horses. I think it will not be, long before we see some buildings.'

They reached the small stream, dismounted to stretch their legs and Patrick detailed two of his men to keep a lookout. They lifted Private Cape from the horse and lay him down on the grass and after drinking some of the cool water, he seemed to revive.

'Not long now Private Cape, hang in there,' said Patrick encouragingly.

Before mid-day, they sighted the tents of the military camp and rode up to the hospital tents. The troopers gathered round Private Cape, gently lowered him from his horse and carried him into one of the tents. He was white, ghost like and Patrick looked down at him wondering if he would make it, oblivious to the tent flap opening behind him.

'Get me some hot water will you, I will need to clean the wound and change his dressing, nurse get some fresh bandages and pass me those clamps,' said a doctor.

He gently pushed Patrick to one side, rolled up his sleeves and began gently to remove the field dressing. The nurse with him moved to the table to bring the clamps ready to stem the bleeding, almost bumping into Patrick as she passed.

'Oh...' she exclaimed, 'I didn't see you there' I...m sor....'

She did not finish the sentence, she looked up at the soldier and her heart skipped a beat.

'Ellen! er missus Jameson,' exclaimed Patrick, just as surprised.

'Look Sergeant, I cannot work with you hanging over me,' said the doctor, 'If you want to help go and fetch some hot water from a stove in the mess kitchen. Nurse Jameson start to strip these soiled bandages off whilst I clean the wound ready for the clamps.'

Patrick saw no more of Ellen that night, when he returned with the hot water, she was gone, sent to perform other duties by the doctor. He was tired from their journey, the horses needed feeding, a rub down and he needed billets for his men, and reluctantly he left the hospital tent.

On the trail from Rorke's Drift, a squadron of Cavalry struck camp for the final part of their journey escorting the sappers and infantrymen hauling the few serviceable wagons from the battlefield to Dundee. At the head of the column was squadron of the Seventeenth Lancers, resplendent in their blue and white uniforms.

'Lieutenant Bell, ride over to the native horsemen and order them out on scouting duties. I can't see any problems today; we're too far away from the enemy but it doesn't do to become lax, what,' said Clarence.

'Yes sir,' said Lieutenant Bell, his white gloved hand coming to the salute as he turned his horse towards a group of natives a hundred yards away and trotted towards them

Captain Clarence Jameson stood up in his saddle to look back at his charges and thought that the sooner he got rid of this lot the better, he was here to fighting the Zulus not to escort a namby pamby bunch of sappers.

During that same morning, Patrick had decided to give his men part of the day off to rest and under the pretext of checking the condition of Private Cape, he planned to visit the hospital and look for Ellen.

'Cape my lad, how are you today?' said Patrick standing beside the patient's bed.

'All right Sarge,' murmured the private.

'Looks like we'll be staying here for today so I'll get the lads to visit you before we leave, so I will.'

'Sergeant,' said a female voice, 'please don't disturb the patient, he needs all the rest he can get and these

474

other men, they too do not need disturbing. Can you please leave now?'

He turned slowly towards the speaker, the stern gaze of Edith Kramer having more effect on him than a whole Impi of Zulus.

'Sorry ma'am', 'I'll see ye later lad,' he said in a low voice.

Patrick knew when he was beaten and walked sheepishly past Edith to find another shock awaiting him. Ellen was approaching the tent carrying a bucket of acidic smelling liquid and as they met, he could not help turning on the charm.

'Ellen, to be sure it's good to see you. What are you up to; can I help you with that bucket?'

'No Patrick, I'm working.' She paused for a few moments, her heart beating faster than normal. This soldier did something to her, his mere presence made her feel weak at the knees and she could not pass up the chance to see him for a few minutes at least.

'Meet me over by the roadway in ten minutes, I have to go back into town on an errand and you can walk with me – an escort like.'

Patrick grinned, Ellen's escort, now that was a job he did not mind doing.

Ten minutes later, having delivered her bucked of disinfectant, she reappeared dressed in a hat and light coat and carrying a wicker basket. The rain had kept off during the night the road was dry and dusty, easy walking and soon after she had left the confines of the hospital, Patrick caught her up.

'Ellen it's good to see you, I have been thinking about you a lot and wonderin' if I would ever see you again.'

'Me too, but don't forget I am married to an officer Patrick,' she said biting her tongue.

If she reminded him too much, it might frighten him off and she did not want that. She need not have worried because Patrick was made of sterner stuff and the mere fact that she was married to an officer was unlikely to deter him.

As they walked along they chattered, Patrick told her of the fighting at Hlobane and when she heard of Georgie's narrow escape, she drew in her breath. He described the Zulus attack, subsequent rout and of their victory at Khambula, omitting to tell her details of the pursuit and slaughter of the fleeing warriors. For her part, she told of the boredom of life in King Williams Town and of how Mrs. Kramer had helped her with her reading and writing and her classes on nursing. She talked a lot about nursing, how she was doing something useful and how much happier it made her feel and as they came to a bend in the trail, hidden from the view of prying eyes and Patrick took his chance.

Facing her, he looked into her eyes, she returned his gaze, her eyes shining brightly, and he knew then that she was his. Pulling her to him, he felt her body go limp as her resistance dissipated and he kissed her, tasting her lips, taking in her perfume.

How long they held their embrace Patrick did not know, only a sharp blow to the back of his head bringing him back to reality. His eyes swam and he felt himself slip towards the black void of unconsciousness but it lasted only seconds and he recovered enough to stagger a few steps and distance himself from his assailant.

'I will have you shot for vis,' said an angry, upper class voice. 'Vat is my wife you are molesting; I shall have you court marshalled and shot. What is your name sergeant?' said an angry Clarence glowering down from his horse.

Patrick had seen perhaps too much action during the past few years. The Mounted Infantry were an unruly lot, disciplined to a point but most had minds of their own and all were survivors. He reached under Clarence's horse, squeezing its testicles just hard enough for the startled animal to rise up on its hind legs and unsteady its rider. Clarence reached out with his free hand in an attempt to hold his balance. That was all that Patrick needed, reaching up he grabbed the hand and pull hard, completely unbalancing the proud Captain and toppling him to the ground. Patrick's senses returned, he stood over Clarence with his foot on his chest and knew he had shot his bolt, but the embrace had been worth it and the look Ellen gave him was worth ten years hard labour.

'Don't you ever hit a man from behind like that again; especially not me or you might not be so lucky next time.'

Clarence lay in the dust helpless, his face red and his eyes bulging with rage.

'You'll pay for vis and you Ellen you'll pay dearly.'

'Now now captain, the girl is innocent, twas me that made the move and if she is your wife you should be takin' better care of such a delicate creature so you should.'

The horse recovered and walked slowly towards its master but Patrick was first, reaching out to grab hold of the reins and with one slick movement, leapt into the saddle. Sitting astride the animal, he pulled on its reigns, swung it round and after giving a swift glance towards Clarence, he kicked the animal's flanks.

Prodding it into action, he galloped passed a smirking Ellen who knew for sure that she had found the man she really wanted. It seemed though that Patrick had managed to get both him and her into big trouble and as she watched the hapless figure of Clarence getting to his feet the thought that perhaps she should be kind to him. She could handle Clarence and although it would not be pleasant for her, she knew she could get him back under her spell.

Chapter 15

The Zulu King sat astride his leopard skin covered stool, surrounded by trusted advisers and leaned forwards to rest his elbow on one knee, morose, unhappy at the recent turn of events. The council of war was to decide on tactics for the inevitable battle to come, the final battle for after the initial success of his Zulu Impis the invaders had gained the upper hand and dealt him one mortal blow after another. He had never wanted to enter into conflict with the British, knowing in his heart of hearts that ultimately they would prevail. His warriors, brave as they were, could not stem the tide against superior weapons and greater numbers. He was losing too many of them and realised that it would only be a matter of time before he was defeated.

Several young women appeared, walking towards the royal throne and bearing large earthen dishes on their heads. Averting his eyes, they came as close as they dare with food and drink for the royal party. The chief Induna clapped his hands and ordered them to place the dishes at the King's feet, and after they withdrew the King reached forward to take few morsels, but his appetite had deserted him.

He sat back on his throne, silent, and around him, none of his entourage dare voice an opinion until he himself spoke. The advisers and Indunas of the regiments were each acutely aware of the situation and they waiting with apprehension until Cetshwayo was ready to speak. Triumph had turned into defeat and the Zulu nation had witnessed failure for only the second time since the reign of great King Shaka.

'I am disappointed that my overtures of peace have gone unheeded, the terms of the peace agreement is unfair – they want everything and give us nothing in return. The word from our spies is that the British are leaving their camp by the river and heading into our lands. We have seen triumph and now we have seen reverses; we have lost many warriors. What is your advice now?' said the King to each advisor in turn.

Ntshingwayo, the supreme commander of the army, the Kings most trusted servant, spoke first.

'Oh King, it is true that we have suffered defeat at the hands of the White Men, it is true that the bull's horns did not crush their army but that is because they changed tactics.

'How so Ntshingwayo, explain to me.'

'At the great victory of Isandhlwana we caught them out in the open, our stage, our chosen battlefield, a place where they cannot beat us. It is only when they fight like cowards from behind barricades that we have been defeated. I know, as you do oh Great One that they are leaving the safety of their camp by the river and will come to Ulundi and it is here, on the Mahlabathini plain we will destroy them.'

'How come?'

'By drawing them on into the open countryside, by challenging them many miles from the forts they are building. Out in the open we can deploy the bulls' horns to great effect and finally destroy them. The army is still strong, there are more than twenty thousand willing to die for you and we *can* drive the White Man from our lands.'

'You have spoken wise words my general, we have more days yet to prepare and this time my brother Ziwedu kaMpande will lead the army. You my friend have done well but now another should shoulder the responsibility.'

Ntshingwayo looked down at the ground; he had won a major victory at Isandhlwana and Hlobane, had he not marched the fifty miles to Isandhlwana with his regiments, had he not led them, as a Zulu commander should? Nevertheless, the defeat at Khambula had left the King in no doubt that he wanted a change of command and the King's word was final. Ntshingwayo determined there and then that if he could not command then he would fight amongst the warriors and die gloriously.

The King clapped his hands, his decision made and he spoke to his indunas.

'Assemble the army, send the messengers to the villages to recall my regiments and prepare many cattle for the warriors. They will feast well before battle. Go now,' he commanded.

Mondli looked up to see the King's messenger approaching from the kraal entrance and, rising to his feet, he waited to hear his words.

'The King commands the regiments to assemble within two days. Call your sons and the sons of your elders; instruct them to sharpen their spears, tighten the skins on their shields and to come to Ulundi. The King has promised them his finest animals to feast on after the doctoring of the army,' recited the messenger.

'I hear the words of the King, it shall be done,' said Mondli.

Stamping his spear shaft twice on the ground the messenger bowed his head once to signify delivery of the king's message.

Lord Chelmsford's column stretched almost twelve miles across open country, eight hundred oxen drawn wagons, two cavalry regiments, artillery and twelve infantry battalions; an army of almost seventeen thousand men. They had field guns, a new rapid firing gun never before used in battle and the infantry had the proven firepower of the Martini Henrys.

As usual, progress was painfully slow, the great lumbering oxen drawn wagons bumping and twisting as they dragged their loads across the uneven ground, the infantry marching alongside and out on the flanks the Mounted Infantry.

'Looks like we are at it again Georgie boy,' said Patrick, shivering in the early morning mist. 'The bloody weather is more like home, is it not?'

Georgie nodded his reply, sat up in his saddle to look at the column spread out before him and after a few minutes spoke to Patrick.

'This is one heck of an army now, those Zulus are in for a pasting eh...' He swivelled round to take in the vastness of an army on the move, a procession of men and wagons stretching as far as he could see. They were riding the southern flank, half way along the column to keep a lookout for an enemy that might be lurking in the long grass. 'I've never seen so many wagons. He's not taking any chances is he?'

'No, I don't think he is; we'll finish the beggars this time to be sure.'

'I hear you were up to some mischief in Dundee Patrick. Are you going to tell me about it?'

Patrick looked a little sheepish. Who had been talking? 'How d'you know about that?'

'This is the British Army Patrick, nothing is sacred. What did you do? I heard that your section were expecting another night in Dundee until you came rushing up on someone else's horse, an officer of the Lancers no less, and ordered them back to camp straight away. Now I have known you for a long time Sergeant Donovan and for you to pull a stunt like that means you were up to no good. An officer's horse, where the hell did you get it from?'

Georgie looked straight at his friend and saw something in his eyes he had not seen before and an embarrassed Patrick took a deep breath.

'If you follow me out of earshot of the others, then I'll tell you, but not a word to anyone.'

Georgie nodded and called to his men.

'The sergeant and I are going to ride to that bluff and take a look up ahead. You men keep a good lookout here and we'll take a break for something to eat and give the horses a rest in an hour.'

That should keep them quiet for a while he thought as he kicked his horses sides to drive it forwards and catch up with Patrick. Together they rode the horses three hundred yards or so towards some high ground, and when they were well out of earshot Patrick turned towards Georgie.

483

'I met Ellen in Dundee...at the hospital, she's a nurse.'

That was a real shock to Georgie.

'Why didn't you tell me that before?'

'I woodda dun but I couldn't.'

'What do you mean you couldn't?'

'This is hard for me Georgie. If I survive this lot they will shoot me to be sure.'

'What...what for?'

'Flattenin' an officer and kissin' his wife.'

Georgie groaned, remembering their visit to Williams, the night Patrick had helped Ellen and her husband home and he had wondered then what he had done.

'Have you been chasing Ellen?'

'Aye, I have, she's a wonderful girl, makes my heart sing.'

Georgie groaned again. 'What happened, come on tell me. Bloody hell Patrick, what exactly did you do?'

Patrick sucked his breath through clenched teeth, embarrassment painted all over his face. 'I'm in love with the girl. I can't help myself.'

'What, Ellen, she's an officers wife. What did you do to him?'

'Me an Ellen was walking towards Dundee. I was escorting her like, an' we just started kissin.' Next thing I feels a smash at the back of my head an when I came round her husband was sat on his horse looking down at me, so I gets up an' pulled him of the horse and gave him a tump. Oh, and then I rode off on his horse.'

Georgie groaned for a third time believing that Patrick's predicament seemed worse for the telling.

Pickpockets and Zulus

'You silly bastard, he's Seventeenth Lancers and they are attached to this column. He's bound to see you one day, and yes Patrick, I can see you'll be court marshalled. Oh my, what are we going to do with you? First thing is shave your beard off and make sure you tuck your red hair into your helmet. At least that way you won't stand out so much and you might not be recognised.'

'That's a good idea. Look, if the worst comes to the worst will you tell your cousin that I love her. I know she's not happy with that struttin' Cavalry man.'

Georgie said nothing; just watched his friend for a few minutes and then he took out his field glasses. He knew nosey, eagle-eyed troopers were probably watching them and he reckoned that he should at least try to keep up appearances. His mind was in a whirl for if it was true, and he was sure that it was, then Patrick was for the high jump no question. In addition, what about Ellen, what would happen to her, Clarence obviously knew about her tryst. What a bloody mess and they had a Zulu army to fight into the bargain.

The fires burned long into the night, the warriors feasted on the King's animals, sang their regimental songs and regained some of their bravado. In the morning, they were to assemble on the great parade ground and wait for the Sangoma to pass amongst them for their final doctoring and then they would leave to fight the British. Obedient to their King, the warriors would die willingly for him, but there was doubt, doubt that the magic potions were not working. They had witnessed comrades falling under hails of bullets, seen too many die and it was beginning to unnerve them.

485

Pickpockets and Zulus

Nkosinathi rolled out his sleeping mat, his belly full of the King's meat and lay down to fall into a fitful sleep, his dreams so vivid. He saw the faces of fallen comrades, Khulekani, Manelesi and the rest, distinct and alive in his head and well before the appointed hour he awoke. For a time he lay wondering what the day would bring, and as light began to dawn and the warriors rose from their mats, gathering their few belongings, he joined them to assemble and await the King's address.

The ranks of warriors stood in utter silence until the King appeared to go and sit on his throne and survey his army. How anyone could doubt these men, dressed in their magnificent war plumage, their shields, their spears, a tribute to the tradition of Shaka. Raising his arms, he clapped his hands together three times to signify the start of the ceremony and the InSangoma moved between the ranks of warriors to distribute the dagga leaves.

'My soldiers, the time is drawing near for the final battle. The invaders are making their way here to Ulundi and we will stop them. You, my brave warriors will kill them and drive them back over the Tugela.'

He stamped his spear shaft on the ground, a signal that he had finished speaking, that the preparations for battle should begin and from the massed ranks came the sing-song orders of the regimental Indunas. In reply, twenty thousand feet thumped the ground, the cry "*Bayete*" rang out and in order of seniority, the regiments began to leave the Royal Kraal.

'We will drive them back this time Nkosinathi,' said a warrior of the uVe.

'We will avenge the fallen, we will kill them all,' replied Nkosinathi with some conviction, the

combination of drugs and the camaraderie of the
regiment lifting his spirits, instilling some lost
confidence back into him.

Far away, on the Mahlabathini plain, the invading force
reached the banks of the White Umfolozi River and
made camp. The wagons were laagered into a square
and chained together and the soldiers busied themselves
erecting tents for the night and within minutes the tent
was upright, the pegs driven in and the guys stretched
tight

'Private Williams will you join me at the horses for an
inspection.

The two soldiers walked the short distance to the
picket line and stood beside the private's horse.

'I noticed she seemed lame, what do you think, was
she walking awkwardly?'

'Not particularly corp, she seemed to stumble a bit
now and then but I put that down to the uneven
ground.'

'Look, here, she's got a thorn stuck in her leg,' he
grasped the tiny spear between his finger and thumb
and pulled it out.

'Ah, it's not much; she must have just felt
uncomfortable in certain positions. No harm done, I am
sure she's all right now. You can go and grab a bite to eat
if you want and tell the others that when they finish with
the tents they can fall out.'

'Yes Corporal.'

Alone, Georgie rubbed his hand down the animal's
leg, pleased that he had been right about its lameness
and had remedied the situation. He checked over the
other horses, finally coming to his own, running his

hand along her back, patted her affectionately and then he crouched on his haunches to inspect her underbelly. That was when he first spotted the soldier, just a pair of legs to begin with, walking slowly along the line of tethered horses and thinking nothing of it; he carried on with his inspection. Then he saw another set of legs converge with the first, the soldier's trousers blue with a white stripe and tucked into a pair of black polished riding boots and his inquisitiveness got the better of him.

'Hey you, sergeant of the Twenty Fourth,' he heard the man call out.

The first man spun round. 'Is it me that you're wanting Captain,' he said politely.

That was Patrick for sure, but who was the other man he thought ducking a little lower for a better view.

'Yes you, you blighter, you are the one who molested my wife and I will have satisfaction you know.'

Bloody hell it was Clarence, he had finally caught up with Patrick.

'You're not an officer so a duel is out of the question but I can have you court marshalled and that is exactly what I will do when this little lot is over. What is your name sergeant? If you refuse to tell me I will have you arrested now.'

'Donovan sir.'

'Right, Donovan if you don't fall in battle then be rest assured vat when we have finished with Cetshwayo and his army you will pay dearly for what you have done.'

'The lady sir, how is she?'

'Don't be impertinent — she is fine, our marriage is secure and no one shall come between us, least of all you.'

Pickpockets and Zulus

Clarence had vented his spleen and finally lost for words, he turned to walk away leaving Patrick standing still and Georgie dared to look over his horses back.

'Did you hear all that?' asked Patrick as he saw Georgie's head rise up.

'I did.'

'Looks like I'm finished in this man's Army Georgie. D'you think they'll shoot me?'

'Any witnesses?' asked Georgie.

'Only Ellen.'

'If she's in love with you I wouldn't worry too much. I know Ellen; well at least I think I do. She has changed a bit since our day's together back in the East End but I know she's strong and clever and if there were no other witnesses she'll come up with some cock and bull story that will get you off the hook – stop worrying.'

Operations began in earnest later that day when both the Mounted Infantry and the Seventeenth Lancers formed a large skirmishing party to cross the river and seek out the enemy. The sun was not as hot as it had been, the European soldiers found the conditions a bit more to their liking and the ford presented little in the way of an. On the far bank, after a relatively easy crossing, they climbed the shallow incline and watching them were Ziwedu's spies.

The horsemen picked their way across open country towards wooded a valley before spreading out over a wide area to search out the enemy and in amongst the trees the Zulu gunmen were invisible. The Zulu's kept out of sight long enough to let the enemy reach a killing ground before the first of their shots whistled through the bush.

'Close up men,' shouted Georgie, 'we'll ride into that gully over there for some cover and see what's going on.'

His men followed him as he galloped across thirty or so yards of open ground and into the depression where they made smaller targets for the enemy to shoot at. Dismounting, they slipped their Carbines from their backs to lay flat on the ground, trying to see where the enemy was and after a few minutes, it became clear that the Zulu shooting had not improved.

'There Corporal, look a bunch of em,' shouted Williams.

Sure enough, there were about forty or fifty Zulus behind some rocks several hundred yards away and on either side of Georgie's men other sections of Mounted Infantry were taking up similar positions. The Lancers had a different approach; they had a tradition to uphold, the regiment had been at Balaclava, charged the Russian guns, and now they were at it again.

Men of the Mounted Infantry and colonial irregulars watched in awe as the blue clad Cavalrymen and their magnificent black chargers rushed past and up the valley towards the enemy fire. Amongst them, eyes wild with excitement, rode Clarence with extended sword and as the Cavalry thundered past cheers of the soldiers on the ground rang out. The Lancer's charge was infectious and in their wake, the troopers re-mounted to follow but a fresh hail of shot from the flanks put a stop to that and eventually the Lancers charge petered out as the weight of numbers overwhelmed them. Zulu marksmen, combined with the changing terrain served to nullify the charge and the Lancers came rushing back hacking and slashing at any Zulus in their path and were lucky to sustain just a few light casualties.

490

The Zulus outnumbered them by a wide margin and on when the Lancers turned and ran they could do nothing else but chase after them and it became clear that there was a real danger they would engulf those still on foot. To Georgie's relief a bugler sounded the recall, the well-disciplined troopers of the Mounted Infantry fired as one, mounted and fell back fifty yards before repeating the exercise until they had put enough distance between themselves and the pursuing Zulus.

'That was a close one Corporal,' said Patrick when they met up on the ride back to the river. 'Didn't expect so many of the bastards.'

'Yes, there were a lot of them and it's a good job they are on foot. If they had been on horseback, we might be in a bit of trouble. Did you see those Lancers charging, bloody mad if you ask me,' said Georgie.

'Aye, bloody mad and I bet Captain Jameson is bloody mad too. Any of our lads hit?'

'No I don't think so. Good job the buggers haven't learned how to shoot properly yet. Look, there's the river, let's get across it and get some grub, I am half starved.'

The riders trotted into the shallow water and then, suddenly, from the screen of long grass, thousands of Zulus rose up to begin a second attack and caught the whole force off guard.

'Bloody hell, look, there's more of them. Come on men, at the gallop, quick,' shouted Georgie spurring his horse on.

From the cover of the long grass warriors emerged running to try to cut them off before they could reach the ford and as the two groups converged, the warriors came close enough to throw their spears to add to the already dangerous mass of bullets flying everywhere.

'Use your guns boys, shoot from the saddle,' shouted Georgie, slipping the Carbine from his shoulder. The others followed suit and before long, the whole force was riding as fast as they could into the ford, shooting with one hand and hanging on for dear life with the other.

Zulus jumped out of nowhere to aim their spears at the galloping troopers, one throwing his straight at Georgie whose quick thinking saved him as he deflected the spear with his rifle barrel and in the same movement shot his assailant. The man stumbled and still a threat produced a long knife but before he could bring it to bear Georgie ran his horse straight at him, knocking him flat.

Their position was perilous and Georgie knew it and then, from the far bank came the sound of gunfire, regular controlled shooting. The Transvaal Rangers, part of the original force, had already crossed safely back over the river and were providing covering fire to the retreating troopers.

'Good boys,' exclaimed Georgie as withering fire cut the Zulus down and extinguished their charge.

Waving his men on, Georgie led them through the ford and still in constant danger, the horses stumbled and splashed through the shallow water towards the far bank.

'Jesus that was close,' said a trooper. 'I didn't think we would make it that time.'

'Well we did, and look, the entire Platoon is across,' said Georgie with relief.

Bloodied and shaken by the ferocity of the Zulu attack the force made their way back to camp. Casualties were light but it had been a chastening experience and as The Mounted Infantry led their horses to the picket line and unsaddled, they swapped stories of their encounter, relieved they were still in one piece.

'I am looking forward to my dinner, what about you Georgie?' said Patrick slipping his horse's nosebag straps over its ears.

'I surely am sergeant, let's get some supper.'

He called out to the men of his section to dismiss them and send them to the mess tent for a well-deserved hot meal and after eating the soldiers retired to their tent to fill their pipes. Patrick sat with his back against a guy rope silhouetted by the light of an oil lamp and pricked up his ears.

'Hear that, they've come to sing to us.'

A slow deep moan, not unlike bagpipes, drifted over the camp and in the darkness, concealed by the bush, Zulus began to wind themselves up into full-blooded renditions of their regimental songs.

'It's their way of intimidating us,' said Georgie. 'Take no notice, it's only singing. I have never yet heard of them trying to overrun a camp during darkness. I hear they are frightened of the spirits.'

'Is that true Corporal?' asked one of the new men.

'I hear so.'

'Will they keep it up all night?' asked another.

'I reckon, but don't let it put you off your sleep. That is what they are trying to do, crafty so an' so's.'

The troopers sat smoking or playing cards for a short while, listening to the singing from the bush - melodic, rhythmic and disturbing.

Chapter 16

Well before the dawn, the Zulus stopped their singing and withdrew, resting for a while before the battle. In their midst a hungry and tired Nkosinathi tramped the few miles to the main army's camp and rolled out his sleeping mat. For months he had endured hardships, the march, the fighting leaving so many of his friends dead and the experience had taken its toll. No longer the bright, confident warrior he once was, no more boasting of the number of the enemy he would kill, his thoughts today were more about the afterlife. He was sure that his death was imminent, but for all that, it would be a glorious death, a warrior's death.

In their camp, most of the soldiers of Queen Victoria had managed to get some sleep two or three hours at most and it was still and the the sun would not rise for a further hour when the bugler sounded reveille. Georgie opened his eyes, shook off the last vestiges of sleep and rolled up his ground sheet. After collecting his bandolier, Carbine and water bottle, he followed the other soldiers into the dim greyness of the pre-dawn to the shouts of a Colour Sergeants organising the infantry.

As the dawn broke, Georgie's section joined a strong force of mounted and colonial irregular troops heading for the river crossing at the upper drift. The Zulus were waiting for them but their numbers were not great enough to pose much of a threat and after an hour or so of isolated skirmishes, they forced the Zulus to retreat far enough to be of no immediate danger.

Once the mounted men had secured the ground it was the turn of the Infantry Battalions to cross. The first of them had reached the riverbank just as the Zulus were driven off and on crossing into hostile territory they were ordered to form a square, three ranks to each side, the tactics of Waterloo.

The lead elements of the Mounted Infantry together with the cavalry pushed on ahead of the main body and as expected, came increasingly under attack from the Zulus. A bugle sounded the retreat the body of mounted men turned and retired in good order towards the advancing square of Infantry. The plan was working; the Zulus had begun to scent blood and were starting to throw caution to the wind, chasing the retreating Cavalry.

Georgie and his section approached the square at a steady trot and heard from within commands shouted, suddenly the ranks parted and the horses threaded their way through to the open centre. Further commands rang out, the ranks of infantry closed up to form a human fort, strong and well defended.

The square crept slowly forward towards the enemy, holding formation and within the cavalry moved forward with them and on a small hill not far away Ziwedu watched with increasing concern. He knew that he must do something and so, with a sweep of his spear, he ordered in his Impis forward into their final battle.

'Be brave my warriors,' shouted the Induna of the uVe. 'Today we drive them back, defeat them once and for all. *"Bayete"* he shouted and a chorus of a thousand voices answered him. The warriors stamped their feet, emphasising their aggression and sending a shock wave towards the enemy.

'Hear That Georgie,' said Patrick, 'they are coming, better get to our positions.'

'I hear them Patrick, good luck,' said Georgie saluting his friend.

Neither man knew what the outcome might be but they were ready when the chanting horde of Zulu warriors finally appeared from out of the bush and long grasses. Slowly at first, they came on and then the indunas sang out the order to charge. Nkosinathi felt good, the drugs were holding his tiredness and hunger at bay, his throat was full of song as the uVe, the iNgobamakhosi, and the uMbonambi charged across the Mahlabathini plain, their deep-throated war cries echoing towards the waiting British square.

Inside the slowly advancing square, the mounted men advanced quietly, awaiting their orders and Georgie had to steady his mount as she tried to pull away.

'Listen to 'em Corp, just like last time, singin' and dancin' as if they haven't a care in the world,' said a private holding straining his neck to look over the ranks of red coated infantry. 'I can see em', bloody hell, look at that. I reckon there's more than at Khambula.'

'Shut up, will you,' said Georgie, 'the last thing we need to hear is a running commentary.'

He managed to peer through a gap in the ranks of infantry and spied the black wall of warriors, stark against the light brown and greens of the tall grass. They were still a long way off but already their flanks were moving towards the square at a rapid pace as they initiated their encircling manoeuvre.

'Steady men of the Eightieth,' boomed the voice of a burly Sergeant Major. 'Hold your fire soldiers, wait for my command.'

The sergeant Major was a man of experience who marched backwards and forwards along the ranks of infantry, encouraging, cajoling and stiffening their resolve.

'Have no fear men, these darkies are in for a good 'iding. The discipline of the British Army will win the day. Hold steady now, wait for the hofficer's command to fire and make sure you have your sights set properly.'

At last the mass of warriors broke into a frenzied run and came within range of the field guns. The square halted its relentless forward march, a bugler sounded the order to fire and the guns opened up, blowing great holes in the advancing ranks, then the Martini Henrys began firing, and then from the far side of the square the methodical rat a tat tat of the Gatling gun.

They were in for a fight and they knew it and then, from the band in the middle of the square came the strains of 'The British Grenadiers', drowning out the sound of Zulu's war chants and the clattering of Assegais against shields and from the massed ranks of British Infantry, the Company commanders gave their orders.

'First rank - fire...Second rank -fire...Third rank - fire..' the crack of rifles, the roar of the field guns became incessant and men fell like rag dolls as the lead cut through them and above it all came the sound of the Gatling guns. Bang bang bang, they went at an almost impossible rate, spitting fire and mayhem amongst the Zulus and amazed at the results, Georgie watched the first wave of warriors falter.

Under the full force of the British guns men were dropping like flies the dead, dying littering the ground, the survivors searching for cover. Nkosinathi was one of them, the heat of bullets whizzing past his head had overcome his will to fight and his basic survival instinct had forced him to lie flat on the ground. Dismayed at his own cowardice, he tried to summon up enough courage to carry on the attack but he could not. He was not the only one, the attack had broken down all along the Zulu line and their spirit was broken.

All around Nkosinathi lay dead warriors of the uVe, bullets still whined over his head, forcing him to crawl on hands and knees to escape and finally he reached the relative safety of some bushes. He dared to take a backward glance as he concealed himself and was dismayed to see that the lines of red-coated soldiers were intact but not all the Zulus had given up the fight. Away to his left disciplined warriors still pressed home their attack, but it was obvious to him that they were making no impression on the massed ranks and he knew then it was the end. What had once seemed a glorious attack had turned into a rout and as the sound of the enemy guns diminished, the cheers of the Infantrymen replaced it.

It was a signal for the Cavalry to join the fray and from the middle of the square, the shrill tone of a bugle rang out and immediately gaps opened up between the platoons of infantry. Riders nudged their horses forward through the gaps and poured onto the Mahlabathini plain in pursuit of the fleeing enemy and set on revenge for Isandhlwana.

'Follow me men,' Georgie called to his section. 'This is for those lads of the Twenty Fourth that won't be going home.'

A roar of approval came from the troopers galloping after the hapless Zulus and at another side of the square Captain Clarence Jameson deployed his squadron of Seventeenth Lancers before leading the charge.

'You chaps get a move on, Lieutenant Beavers take your squadron out to the north and I will look after the southern flank. Keep a sharp lookout for the beggars; they know how to conceal themselves in this long grass. Don't want too many surprises, what.'

After the events of the past half hour, morale was high and he wanted to keep it that way as he led his squadron past the last of the Infantry.

'After me the glorious Seventeenth, remember Balaclava, remember Isandlwana, spare no one.'

Looking splendid in their blue and white uniforms the squadron spread out in a "Vee" formation, urging their magnificent black horses forward at a fast trot, then the canter and the slow gallop and their lances began to arc down as they began the charge.

In those few minutes before they caught the first of the stragglers, Clarence thought of Patrick and the score he needed to settle. He thought about the confrontation with Ellen when he had accused her of having an affair but her story had rung true and since then she had taken to her wifely duties, convincing him of her innocence.

He knew very well that the sergeant of the Twenty Fourth was the real villain and he would make him pay one way or another. The positive side of the quarrel was that at least he felt close to his wife and he had begun to confide in her. She did not know a great deal of his family for he had told her only briefly of his father and brothers. He had always felt afraid his father would disinherit him for marrying well below his station and in their moments of intimacy, he had told her about hm. He was a wealthy banker in the city of London and his financial support had done wonders for Clarence, purchasing one of the last commissions in the Guards and providing him with enough money to live life as a Guard's Officer.

'This, my dear, will all be yours should I fall in battle,' he had said.

He did not intend to fall in battle but he felt that the knowledge of the possibility that one day his money might be hers would make Ellen a little more pliable and it had. Then, suddenly his mind snapped out of his daydream as the squadron began to overtake the stragglers, stabbing with their lance and killing anyone in their path.

Half a mile away, the mounted infantry were also within range of the fleeing enemy. Georgie pulled out his Carbine ready for a quick shot as he saw a lone Zulu running through the bush. A trooper appeared bearing down on the same man, sabre drawn and he stayed his hand, watching. Then, from the undergrowth, a warrior unexpectedly appeared to thrust his assegai at the rider. The trooper screamed out in pain and shock as the blade entered his leg, his horse reared up in alarm and toppled him onto the ground. The warrior drew a knife and sprang at him as he struggled to his feet and Georgie could see the trooper was in mortal danger and quickly he took aim, shooting the Zulu squarely in the chest.

Pickpockets and Zulus

The trooper clutched at his wounded leg and looked towards Georgie and the rest of the troopers for help because he could not alone deal with any other Zulus concealed in the long grass. Georgie nudged his horse forward towards the man, gun at the ready and when he was within twenty yards of him, a warrior broke cover to run for his life. He did not get far; Patrick saw him, lifted his rifle to his shoulder and put a bullet in him, pitching the warrior forwards into a death dive.

'Corporal, detail one of your men to help that wounded trooper and then you and your men fall in with us and we'll take a look over by those bushes,' he said pointing to a small clump of stunted trees and bushes five or six hundred yards away.

Georgie waved the remainder of his men towards him, instructing one to help the wounded trooper back to the square following on after Patrick's section and not far away an excited and red-faced Clarence was enjoying himself. All his life he had dreamed of such a moment, drilling for years with lances and sabres, charging across the training grounds in England and now he was doing it for real. Parading before the Queen, providing escorts had been his lot, routine, mundane, not since Balaclava had the regiment seen active service and so it was with some pride he led his squadron across open country in pursuit of the fleeing Zulus.

With parade ground precision, the cavalry spread out across the plain in a wide 'Vee' formation, lances ready and at the apex sat Clarence. The Cavalrymen gave no quarter, perhaps fifty Zulu warriors lay dead or dying in their wake and now they were catching up with the bulk of the fugitives. Clarence spotted a group of warriors racing for their lives through the long grass and leaving trails as if they were small boats on the ocean.

He had tasted blood and wanted more, it was easy but although the Zulu army was defeated, an Induna in the midst of the fleeing warriors rallied them and they turned to face the Lancer's onslaught. Assegai met lance, knobkerrie met sabre and the two forces locked horns. English voices mixed with Zulu, the horses adding their own to the growing cacophony as their riders forced them onto the mass of black and white shields. Clarence's wild eyes betrayed his enjoyment of the killing spree and each time he stabbed at a Zulu body a sinister inner part of his psyche rose closer to the surface.

The mounted infantry reached some sloping ground, the small hill in front of them covered in thick vegetation and affording good cover to the fleeing Zulus.

'Sarge, I can see movement amongst those bushes,' said a trooper, pointing with the barrel of his gun.

'I see them, spread out lads and let's get at em.'

The troopers began their manoeuvre and from their flank, other Mounted Infantry sections converged to assist them. Altogether the force consisted of around twenty corporals and privates, and Patrick being the senior N.C.O., he ordered the troopers into a pincer movement of sorts to cut off any retreat the enemy might attempt.

Some of the Zulus still had fight left in them and those possessing guns fired wildly as the rest threw spears. It was enough to force the troopers to dismount and fight on foot and for twenty or so minutes, the two sides let fly at one another until eventually the Zulus, managed to melt away into the bush and Patrick called a halt.

'Phew, that was a good job done Patrick, eh...' said Georgie.

'It was that, I think they are on the run now.'

'What do you want us to do?' asked Georgie lifting his helmet and wiping the sweat from his brow. Patrick stood in his stirrups to survey the scene and looked ahead. The ground was uneven, full of ravines and covered in vegetation, ambush country. He took out his field glasses for a better look, saw black dots spread out across the hills and away to his right caught a glimpse of the Lancers.

'Up ahead looks like ambush country lads so keep a watchful eye,' said Patrick. 'The Cavalry seem to have the same idea as us, so let's show em' what we can do.'

Ahead of their pursuers the remnants of the uVe regrouped and although exhausted, their moral in tatters they were making good progress back towards Ulundi,

'We have fought badly today Nkosinathi,' said a warrior.

Nkosinathi said nothing, his head hanging with fatigue and disillusionment, his comrades had fallen like stalks of corn at harvest time, the magic potions of the Witch Doctors did not work, and he was at a loss.

'My heart is heavy with shame Bongani,' he said as they trotted together over the uneven ground then, suddenly shouting from behind warned him of approaching horsemen.

Those of the uVe who were able to run faster did, but many could not keep up and began to lag behind and Nkosinathi felt he could not go on much longer; the end of his life was near. He heard gunshots, the screams of wounded men and looked for somewhere to hide, diving in amongst some thorn bushes, his chest heaving.

The Lancers still two or three hundred yards away as the Mounted Infantry engaged the laggards but the thunder of their horse's hooves announced their imminent arrival and the two forces converged on the exhausted Zulus.

Some warriors turned for one last stand, magnificent and brave, men who would not die easily. For others the fight had gone out of them and these poor individuals simply stood facing the troopers and awaited their fate.

'Look over there Sarge, looks like the Cavalry are having a busy time of it,' said Corporal Mills.

Patrick let out a whistle; the Lancers were close enough for them to see what they were doing and it made his skin crawl. They were ripping into men incapable of putting up any resistance, just standing and waiting to die and the Lancers were obliging with glee. In the van Captain Clarence Jameson, wild eyed and red faced was sweating from his exertions.

'By George this is fun,' he shouted 'the blighter's have no right to their fearsome reputation. At them men and no quarter, d'you hear, no quarter.'

It seemed easy, but the Zulus were dead on their feet before the Lancers ever caught up with them and before long most were dead, a few lucky ones slinking away into the undergrowth.

'The Zulus are making for the broken ground Patrick,' said Georgie, dispensing with formality.

'I see them, come on lads, we'll try to cut them off if we can, over there by the slope.'

Pickpockets and Zulus

Georgie followed feeling a little sickened by the sights he had witnessed, the Lancers seemed to have no qualms about getting in close, drawing swords and ripping the Zulus apart.

Patrick kicked his horse into action, leading the men down into the valley where most of the Zulus seemed to be. Forcing the horses through the bush they looked for targets and despatched the enemy at every opportunity. The ground became uneven and treacherous for the animals, slowing their progress considerably and some had to dismount.

The Lancers too were slowing their advance and their formation was breaking up but still they chased the Zulus. Out in front, the intoxicated Clarence became detached and isolated, but he kept moving. Unaware he was out on his own, he came across a Zulu cowering in his path and with great delight spurred his horse on and reaching well out of his saddle, slashed with his sword to leave the unfortunate man headless.

'That's another one less to worry us' he said to no one in particular.

Further along the valley, the Mounted Infantry had cleared the bush and were picking their way carefully through boulders and across loose earth. They dare not risk pushing the horses too hard, a broken leg could spell disaster for both horse and rider. Georgie was high up the side of the hill when he came across some short, leafy trees, an ideal hiding place and pulled up his mount. Dismounting he nervously held his gun at the ready and holding onto the reigns with his free hand, pulled his horse along behind him.

Pickpockets and Zulus

Unexpectedly, from behind a tree, out stepped a warrior, naked except for his kilt of cow tails. Tall, well-built and defiant Nkosinathi looked straight at Georgie.

Georgie whipped his carbine to his shoulder and took aim, his finger closing around the trigger ready for the kill. Nkosinathi puffed out his chest ready to meet his death as a proud Zulu warrior should and as his finger tightened on the trigger, Georgie could not help thinking what brave men these Zulus were. He was about to send Nkosinathi to oblivion when somehow his finger froze on the trigger and the face that had haunted his darkest nightmares superimposed itself on this man, pleading, no charging him not to kill.

He had had his fill of killing, the war was over, the vaunted Zulu army was on the run, and in a split second, he made a decision. Looking straight into the Zulu's eyes, he swivelled his rifle barrel to point skywards and touched his helmet in silent salute. Nkosinathi slowly shook his head up and down, understanding, grateful and without a word, disappeared into the undergrowth and Georgie watched him go.

Further down the valley, progress had become painfully slow as the remaining Zulus made their escape over rocks too treacherous for the horses and Clarence had decided to halt. There was no sign of his men and as he tried to get his bearings, a warrior rose up from behind a boulder to confront him. He spurred his horse into action, covering the ground towards the warrior in quick time and raised his sword for the kill, but before he could apply the coup de grâce, a shot rang out and the man fell dead. Who had fired that shot, who had cheated him of his kill?

'Top of the mornin' sir,' said a familiar voice.

Patrick's sudden appearance acted as a red rag to a bull and with an animal roar, Clarence dug his spurs cruelly into his horses' sides and with his sabre pointing straight out in front, he charged.

Patrick could not believe that a Cavalry Officer would try to kill him and was slow to react; his horse was sideways on to Clarence, putting him at a severe disadvantage. He was defenceless with his back exposed to the onrushing Clarence and not for the first time feared for his life. Frantically he attempted to spur his horse away, but the Lancer was at full charge and would be upon him within seconds, he had no time to escape.

Then a startling development took place as two warriors witnesses to Clarence's murder of their comrade and hidden in the bush struck back. One speared the under belly of Clarence's horse whilst the other forced his assegai up through its rider's ribs and bringing him down to earth with a shriek.

Patrick witnessed the attack and managed to recover his composure, pulled his horse up short and with a clear view, lifted his Carbine to his shoulder. Bang, Bang and the two assailants were dead.

'Over here, over here,' Patrick shouted, 'Captain Jameson is hurt.'

Two troopers appeared, alerted by his cries and between the three of them, they attempted to staunch the bleeding, propping Clarence against a tree and cutting away his tunic to use his shirt for a bandage. It was too late, Clarence's eyes rolled, he began to cough up blood and then his head slumped lifelessly to his chest.

'Come on let us get the officers body out of here. Where's Corporal McNamara?'

'Over there sarge,' said one of the troopers pointing up the slope to Georgie sitting alone and staring into space.

'What the hell is he doing?' said Patrick, puzzled at his friend's behaviour as he remounted his horse to ride towards Georgie.

'Are ye all right lad, you seem a bit lost.'

Georgie turned his head towards Patrick, his face bewildered, a faraway look in his eye.

'Aren't we all a bit lost?' he said, pausing for a while. He had a look in his eye Patrick had never seen before and to his surprise Georgie added, 'I think I've had enough of soldiering.'

'What, the war is over now and there will be no more fighting, the Zulu's are finished after today. Hell Georgie you have another three years to serve before you can pack in soldiering.'

Georgie looked at Patrick, his mouth creasing into a smile as the old sparkle returned and he tipped his helmet to the back of his head.

'Patrick.'

'What.'

'Remember Dickie Henderson?'

'Dickie...wha...,' Patrick paused for a few seconds, confused, and then the penny dropped. He looked into Georgie's mischievous eyes, understanding, and they both burst out laughing, the echos bouncing across the valley.

Pickpockets and Zulus

Other Books by
Kelvin Robertson

iGoli City of Gold

Set in the goldfields of post union South Africa the story charts the trials and tribulations of an immigrant family searching for a better life. Greed and deception become the twin drivers of the head of the family when he becomes embroiled in a scheme to take money from unwitting American investors. Solomon exists in a different world, one in which he is forced to work in the harsh conditions of a goldmine to satisfy the Whiteman's greed. But Solomon has a talent and learns to use it to begin to free his fellow natives.

Amsterdam Traffik

In Ukraine, corruption and criminal activity are rife and the people have little say in the running of the country. FEMEN is one voice of opposition, young women prepared to bare all to publicize their cause at great risk to themselves. Katja is one such protester, the daughter of an officer of the Ukraine Secret Service. Her mother is negotiating an agreement with her opposite number from the British Secret Service, when she learns of her daughter's arrest, only then becoming aware of Katja's involvement. After rescuing her from the clutches of the President's men, a fateful telephone call sets in motion a chain of events that spread far beyond Ukraine.

510

Pickpockets and Zulus

Pickpockets and Zulus

Made in the USA
Columbia, SC
06 September 2018